Welcome to the Absolutely Astounding Life of Whistle Evel Fonzarelli Starr

by Shane Joseph Hopkins

I proudly dedicate this book to my absolutely astounding wife,

Lisa Marie Hopkins.

How she puts up with me, I will truly never understand.

"When I come home cold and tired,
it's good to warm my bones beside the fire."
~Pink Floyd

"Breathe out, so I can breathe you in."
~Foo Fighters

Introduction

Actually, there is no introduction necessary. You will see soon enough. So grab a drink, a snack, and buckle up. Because the journey's about to begin... Let's go!

CHAPTER ONE
A Starr Is Born

On September 11, 1970 at 9:11 p.m., an incredible boy named Whistle Evel Fonzarelli Starr was born in upstate New Hampshire.

As a very young boy, Whistle could remember some stuff, but like most kids, true memories started around kindergarten. The time when kids start forming new relationships other than the ones they have with their parents and siblings.

Actually, his first vivid real memory that stuck with him for life occurred on the very first day of kindergarten. When Whistle woke up that morning he was literally bubbling over with excitement. He was about to embark on an incredible journey with his mom.

When he went downstairs that morning, he could barely eat any of his breakfast due to the fact that his head was filled with endless thoughts of this great place called "school," whatever that might be. Little did he know he was about to find out the hard way.

The car ride in the early 70s flat blue Chevy Nova started out great. The cigarette smoke from Whistle's mom's third of the morning hung familiar in the car. Vented only by the two-inch strip of open driver's window. The 8-track filled the space with Olivia Newton John, and sitting on the front seat, even the thought of wearing a seatbelt didn't exist.

With the Nova parked, they walked toward the front of the biggest brick building Whistle had ever seen. The glint of the morning sun off the windows added to his nervousness and excitement. Mostly excitement, because he knew his mom would always take care of him.

"Ready Whistle?" his mom asked.

"Ready Mommy," he said.

As the front doors opened, Whistle was struck by so many new sights, smells, and sounds. It was overwhelming. Voices and the sound of footsteps on the tile floor filled his ears. Endless colors filled his field of vision, and all the smells of a school that are familiar to you were brand new to Whistle. He felt dizzy.

"Mommy, is everything going to be okay?" Whistle asked, slightly shaking.

"Everything is going to be just fine," she responded in a reassuring voice.

For such a young boy, he actually had the presence of mind to consciously calm himself as they walked hand in hand down, what was to Whistle, a gigantic hallway. After a while, they paused in front of an open doorway with so much activity inside that it was overwhelming. *Everything will be alright*, he thought to himself, *Mommy's with me*. After a slight pause, they stepped inside and were met by a pleasant enough woman.

"Hello, my name is Ms. Fisher, welcome."

"Thank you, I am Ms. Starr and this is Whistle. Say hello, Whistle."

"Hello," he responded in a very timid voice.

"Thank you Ms. Starr, I'll take it from here," pleasant Ms. Fisher said. Instantly Whistle felt the release of his mom's hand from his left hand, and the grasp of Ms. Fisher's hand in his right.

"Wait! What?" Instantly Whistle realized that this was not right.

"Mommy?" He looked up with panic.

"It's alright. Go with Ms. Fisher and meet the kids." There was slight guilt in her eyes.

"No, I want to stay with you," he replied.

"Ms. Starr, we deal with this a lot, you have to just go," Ms. Fisher said matter-of-factly. Whistle saw tears welling up in his mom's eyes as she turned and was simply gone. He felt the pain in his left hand and arm growing rapidly, his grip starting to slip as Ms. Fisher increased her pressure.

"What is going on? Why is this happening? What did I do wrong?" So many questions shooting through his mind. Grip slip…slip…gone. In an instant, Whistle was flung into a brand new world, one he didn't know, one he didn't like. Worst of all, he was completely abandoned by his mom with no idea why….

Life as he knew it was over for Whistle because he would never see his mother again. He was of course wrong about that. But what was true, his life would definitely never be the same again.

CHAPTER TWO
Pros and Cons of Early School Years

O f course, like most kids, Whistle settled into the routine of school. His mom did come back after that first day of hell and he knew in his heart she would never leave him again. That first year of school did go by rather uneventfully. In kindergarten he started learning the very basics of meeting others, but found that year extremely boring. School to him was little more than having a babysitter that really didn't care.

Whistle didn't realize it, but he was already starting to notice details about daily life that others never would. By the end of that school year, young Whistle just thought this was life from here on out.

Then one day summer showed up. Routine gone. What the…?

"Mommy, we have to go," Whistle said, puzzled.

"Whistle, it's the first day of summer," she replied sweetly.

The next couple of months came and went. Days full of sun, cartoons, Matchbox cars on the den rug and everything else that goes with summer. Still, no true friends except Mom, but he 1) didn't know better, and 2) didn't care. His imagination kept him more than busy enough.

Summer ended and first grade came. *Okay, I get it,* Whistle thought to himself. Routine, no routine, so on and so on. Whistle definitely preferred no routine much better. This left him more freedom, more time to enter his own mind and explore it. Routine just brought long days of boredom and trouble.

When you can't help but go into your own world while you're supposed to be learning, sometimes it doesn't work out well.

The next couple of years went by in similar fashion. The boredom of school grew increasingly worse and the imagination of summer grew increasingly great.

The fourth grade came and Whistle's world started to bust wide open. In one year he got a stepfather, his first friend for life, and a small group of other friends. When a kid of Whistle's age gets moved from one small town to an even smaller town in New Hampshire, he really has no idea what's going on. Throw in moving into a huge Victorian house with a slate roof, white clapboards, stained glass windows, and a massive attached barn.

This happened because Whistle's new stepdad was a lawyer and had some money. His name was Jack Peters, so Whistle's mom's name went from Ms. Starr to Mrs. Peters in an instant. Whistle had very mixed emotions about this and felt extremely protective of his mom. This changed after not too long a period because Whistle grew fond of Jack. He was a good man and treated Whistle's mom well. Also, he spent good times with Whistle. Finally, a father figure in his life.

With his awesome mother, and now a very good father in his life, Whistle felt solid and loved like never before. Two people that he was sure would never leave him. He always considered Jack his dad. He loved his new house and new town. Everything was perfect except for one thing…

Here comes a new school. The first day of school came super-fast.

"Mom, no one's going to like me." Spoken by a child who felt he was too old to call her "Mommy," anymore.

"You will be just fine, Whistle," Jack chimed in. Eggs, bacon, toast, black coffee and a cigarette in front of him.

"Eat up Whistle, we have to get going," from Mom. As on another long-ago morning, Whistle didn't eat that much breakfast. That was due to the same nervousness and excitement he felt on his first day of kindergarten, new school and all. So Whistle and his mom climbed into the new/used Volkswagen Jetta that Jack had bought her. A newer, smaller silver car, but some things remained the same. Still third cigarette haze with the two-inch driver's ventilation. Olivia was now on the cassette player as opposed to 8-track. Seatbelt was still not even a thought.

"Are you excited?" his mom questioned.

"No." Simply put. They pulled up to the entrance of his new school. He got out, watched his mom drive away, and had pangs of memories from back when his mom abandoned him the first time. Whistle put all that behind him, squared his little shoulders determined to walk into that school by himself…so off he went. The familiar brick and window glint, the tile and footsteps, voices, colors and smells. All familiar to Whistle now, new school or not. Walking into his new school he got his first true idea that he might see the world different than most. See everything far more detailed than most. It mostly made sense but he didn't fully understand it. One thing he did know was that this could not be a bad ability to have.

So Whistle walked down a hallway that didn't look quite as big as his first school hallway. Ironically he did take a left into his first classroom at his new school. Whistle chose the middle back row seat, which would become a lifelong habit of his. Remember that because it will become a common thread in more ways than one. There he sat waiting for home room to start, not knowing that by the end of the day he would meet someone that would crack open the door to his life that much more....

CHAPTER THREE
First Lifelong Friend

Whistle Starr, as he would be called that day for attendance, watched the classroom fill up with the other students. Well aware of all the other kids and where they sat. One kid stood out to him. A boy who sat to the front left of the room. This gave Whistle a look at the side of his face.

Once again, without him knowing, this was enough to tell Whistle if it was worth it to him.

He waited for his chance. Finally ten o'clock recess came. The shrill bell rang and they were released to the playground.

The crisp fall air was prominent. Leaves showed off their vibrant golds, yellows, oranges and reds. Whistle was definitely disoriented in this new environment. So many places to look. Back parking lot for kickball? Lower field for soccer and whatnot? Slides, swings, and monkey bars? Who *knows* where to look! Whistle could not find this boy that he knew he had to meet.

If you can say curiosity killed the cat, then you could also say curiosity also blessed the cat (maybe that's why they have nine lives). Whistle's "cat" curiosity led him down past the end of the lower field into the back woods beyond the school property. Already skipping school at such a young age, but definitely not realizing it.

There was a pronounced line between sun and dark, right where the large pines met the end of the lower field. Pine needles met green grass just as pronounced. Whistle's heart rate rose slightly as he took in all the contrasts of the colors and smells. What affected him the most was the difference he could feel and sense in the temperature between the shady pines and sunny field.

Whistle was aware that recess would end soon. He was about to start back to the building when he saw what his curiosity brought him down for.

There this boy stood, literally half in the dark and half in the light, staring at a tree for no apparent reason at all. Frozen like a statue. Whistle could not comprehend this so he ducked behind the nearest tree. As he watched, his desire to not get in trouble kicked in. He knew recess was about to end, but his personality would not allow him to let this boy get in trouble either.

"Hello," from Whistle, quietly. A flick of his eyes from this boy then back to the tree.

"Shhhh."

Whistle didn't know what to think as the shrill bell rang, signifying that recess was over. Trouble was once again sure to come for Whistle. This boy would not move. Whistle slowly walked down the pine bed until he was one tree away.

"Hello?" he questioned. This time the boy turned and looked at him with a judging eye.

"What are you doing here?" he whispered.

"You seem like a good kid, recess is over and I don't want to see you get in trouble," Whistle said.

After a bit of a pause, "Come here, but be quiet," said the boy, calmly. Whistle walked slowly up to the boy.

"What's your name?" the boy asked.

"I'm Whistle, Whistle Starr."

"Hi Whistle, I'm Mikey, Mikey Light," the boy answered in a way where Whistle wasn't sure if he was being made fun of or not.

Looking into Mikey's eyes, Whistle already knew they would be friends. Then Mikey told him to turn and look. Whistle turned to his left and there on the trunk of one massive pine were hundreds of monarch butterflies.

The two boys stood in silence for a long time. Both taking in the oranges and blacks. Watching all those butterflies slowly ascending into the treetops above.

"No one knows about this but me. Well, now you too. They come every year at this time for only a few days," Mikey spoke, looking up at the line between shade and sun.

The boys continued to watch this most impressive display of nature for some time. Then, without a word spoken, they walked out of the darkness of the pines into the sun of the lower field. The walk up to the school was met by the principal standing outside, waiting. Sitting on the bench outside the principal's office, they both knew they were in trouble... but they also knew they were already best friends.

CHAPTER FOUR
First Day of Summer

B y the end of the school year, the boys were indeed best friends. In fact it turned out they lived in the same neighborhood. Routine gone again, the summer gloriously began for Whistle. His first summer in his new house and with his new best friend. Whistle's life was about to change drastically and open up in ways that would affect him forever.

That first morning of summer, Whistle's eyes opened. Not due to the excitement of summer but because his internal clock told him it was time to go to school. Then, *Holy cow*, he thought to himself, *no school today!* He paused for just a bit. Just long enough to think for a moment and collect himself. No school, no routine, here we go….Freedom!

"Whistle you have a phone call!" His mom's voice traveled up the stairs.

What? Why on earth would Whistle Evel Fonzarelli Starr have a phone call? His bare feet hitting the cold hardwood floor, Whistle walked out of his bedroom and down the stairs. Suddenly Whistle's brain froze….

Then exploded like he had never experienced before. His body jolted and made him sit down on the fourth step from the top. The colors were unbelievable. Golds, greens, yellows, everything was in such focus that Whistle couldn't comprehend it. Slowly he started to look around and realized he could see everything. The railing on his right was made of oak, comfortably worn, and held up by four simple brackets. Third one from the top needs a new screw in the lower part. The green carpet running down the stairs has worn spots, seams, and even a cigarette burn at the bottom. The wallpaper exploded into Whistle's eyes. Left, right, it didn't matter where he looked, he was locked into this. The flower pattern was clear, then the next thing Whistle knew the wallpaper was figured out and the plaster ceiling caught his eye. Every crack, every stain jumped out at him. Even the little black spider sitting in his web on the right side caught Whistle's eye.

Whistle snapped back and had no recollection of how he had gotten from the top of the stairs to the bottom. He walked down to the smell of bacon, coffee, and cigarettes.

"Here's the phone," Whistle's mom said with pride because her boy was starting to grow up. For the first time in his life, Whistle answered the phone. It was a pea green dial phone hanging on the wall and the cord actually slapped him in the leg when he answered.

"Hello," Whistle timidly answered.

"Hello Whistle, I was just wondering if you wanted to play today," Mikey said.

"I don't think so." Panic raced through Whistle's veins. He hung up the phone and felt horrible about himself. He was thrown off by the phone call.

The phone rang again and Whistle answered.

"Hello?" Very guarded.

"Whistle, meet me at the top of Osborne hill." Whistle was very scared but his curiosity could not be held back.

Once again, curiosity can either kill the cat or bless the cat.

"Mom, Mikey wants me to go outside and play," he told his mom, thinking the answer was not going to be yes.

Next thing he knew, Whistle was standing outside and on his way to God knows what. As he stood there, early summer sun shining down, Whistle couldn't believe he was actually on his own. This was a huge moment in Whistle Evel Fonzarelli Starr's life.

He was truly on his own for the first time. That sunk deep into the boy's mind as he started to weave his way through the neighborhood toward the top of Osborne Hill.

While he walked he took in all the sights, smells, and sounds of the neighborhood. Every dog bark, the sun splayed out on the street, the smell of the early summer pollen just coming up filled his senses deeply. As he walked up the steep hill he saw Mikey standing there waiting. The unknown woods behind him. The street ended at the woods.

"Ready?" Mikey asked.

"I guess so," Whistle responded with a large amount of doubt. Mikey turned and walked up into the dark woods. The memory of the monarch butterflies and pines shot through Whistle's head. This made him pause for a moment, but then he followed. Once again in Whistle's life he walked from the sun to the shade. He also realized that life was going to be filled with sun, shade, sun, shade, etcetera…

He followed Mikey because he could not help himself. The pull of the unknown was far too strong for Whistle to resist.

As he entered the woods the temperature dropped and goosebumps rose on his arms. Then, his eyes started to adjust to his surroundings. He started picking up small details. Earth tones surrounded Whistle everywhere he looked. Two squirrels flitted and chirped in the tree branches above. Small rays of sun stabbed down and died out in the leaves, moss, and rocks that made up the forest floor. The biggest sensation that struck Whistle was the smell of the earth. Dirt, water, bark, tree roots, insects, every smell of nature filling his brain. This would remain Whistle's favorite smell for the rest of his life.

Whistle and Mikey started up the path deeper into the woods, the asphalt of the road disappearing behind them. *Wow*, Whistle thought to himself with great awe.

As if Mikey could read his mind, "Wow," quietly escaped his friend's lips. "What do you think?" Mikey looked over.

"Holy Moly," Whistle responded.

As the day passed, adventure after adventure rolled out before them. It was probably the fastest day of Whistle's life so far. Imaginations soared with every step.

The day shot by and as the boys walked out of the woods, the sun was settling in the west, blood red. The hue across the neighborhood was indeed magical. Their feet back on the blacktop, they started back down Osborne Hill. When they reached the bottom where they would split off and go to their own houses the boys paused.

"See you tomorrow." Whistle.

"Not if I see you first." Mikey.

They both started off in their own directions and Whistle's mind was lost in thought.

Just then the sun set completely and darkness flooded into the landscape. Panic jumped up into Whistle's chest, instantly knowing he was in deep trouble for being out so late. Making his way home in the dark, navigating by house lights and moonlight, Whistle's panic continued to grow.

The feeling Whistle had standing on the porch with his hand on the doorknob was indescribable. It was over. Life was over. Sign it, seal it, deliver it because Whistle knew he was dead. *Click*, the door opened and he walked in as quietly as possible. Through the laundry room into the kitchen with no one around. Okay, moving on, Whistle could hear the television coming from the den. As he passed the bottom of the stairs the blue light filled the doorway. Stepping in, Whistle saw his mom sitting on the couch.

"Hey Whistle," she said, eyes not leaving *The Lawrence Welk Show*.

"Hey Mom," he responded, glancing over at Jack, who was asleep in the recliner with his scotch half full and his Winston smoldering in the ashtray. Pausing, Whistle looked around the den not knowing what to do. Sheer confusion flooding through him.

"Good night," he said timidly.

"Good night, Whistle." Lawrence Welk bubbles filled the television screen. Whistle was out of the room, up the stairs, and in his room as fast as possible. Heart racing, he couldn't believe he wasn't in trouble. In his head, he thought about how they had no idea where he was all day, and that they didn't care to find out.

Whistle climbed into bed that night trying to comprehend his day with no success. All he knew was this was easily the best day of his life. Also, he wasn't in trouble with his mom and Jack. He thought about every detail of the day and knew that there was so much more to see. If that was one part of the neighborhood, what lay beyond to explore? As Whistle Evel Fonzarelli Starr drifted off, one thought kept returning: Freedom, freedom, freedom. The best sleep of his life deeply set in for the boy.

CHAPTER FIVE
First Town Fair

Whistle's summer continued and he met more people. His world grew from the path between his house and Mikey's to the whole neighborhood. The boys in the neighborhood became his friends, but Whistle and Mikey would always remain connected. So many exciting experiences filled their days. A fort was built of materials from who knows where. Many garage windows were broken by playing street hockey. The tallest willow tree Whistle could ever imagine was climbed to the very peak several times. Every part of a dairy farm was explored extensively. Whistle noticed every detail with great clarity.

Summer passed by quickly and the trees started to turn to their auburn colors again. Mornings started to crisp up. Whistle already knew that freedom was fading and routine was setting in again. He was beginning to feel it, but one more experience awaited him. One that would absolutely change his young life and stick with him forever.

The Champion Town Fair.

"Whistle, let's go." Jack's voice rose up the stairs. Feet on the floor, toughskins on, Whistle was ready to go. Breakfast was grits, toast, strawberry rhubarb, and of course, the familiar smell of the light haze of cigarettes. His anticipation kept growing as he tried to eat. Whistle already knew he had an amazing adventure ahead of him and could not wait to find out what it was. After breakfast his mom and Jack took him outside and both said, "Let's go."

They walked down the hill toward the center of town and Whistle's excitement continued to grow. He loved that because he was already realizing adventure was absolutely the name of the game. Center of town came and went. Walking forever, Whistle finally stood in front of a gate.

The whole experience enveloped him completely. They walked through the gate and Jack turned to Whistle.

"Here's five dollars, son. Don't spend it all in one place. We'll see you at home."

Then Whistle watched the two of them disappear into the crowd of people. He could not believe his eyes. Five dollar bill in his hand, Whistle stood stunned. As he started to collect himself, Whistle's mind clicked back over to acute awareness. Colors jumped out at him, smells were more pungent, Noises swirled around in an extremely substantial way. Five dollar bill securely tucked into his left front pocket, Whistle stepped forward into a world he knew nothing about, but his confidence propelled him. Cotton candy from far away registered in Whistle's nose. The smell of dirt and diesel filled his lungs. He was excited and scared all at once but he plodded on. The sound of the fair washed over him in such an extreme way that he had no control over it. Everything was absolutely perfect.

Then Whistle's mind snapped back to reality and he found himself standing at the railing of an oxen pull ring. *How did this happen and how did I get here?* Whistle thought to himself. Oxen pull ring? What the heck is that? It took less than a minute for Whistle to realize the whole oxen pull game. Two huge animals pull the weighted sled, the one that goes the farthest wins. Whistle understood and moved on through the fair.

His next stop was the first time Whistle ever spent money in his life. It was a hot day and he thought something cold to drink would be perfect. As he walked, he noticed a booth to his left. He had to stop, he was hot and thirsty.

"Can I help you?" the girl asked.

"Yes, please. Can I get a lemonade?" he asked as polite as he could be.

Next thing Whistle knew he was holding the best thing he had ever tasted and was walking down a road of mystery that his mind screamed to learn about. The lemonade cost fifty cents. Fifty cents meant everything. Whistle Starr walked down the dirt path toward the midway with four dollars and fifty cents in his pocket and he was ready. Next stop was the dreaded ticket booth. That's where the money left you and Whistle knew this.

"Three rides, two dollars." Weariness filled the worker's eyes.

"Yes, please," Whistle answered as he turned the bills over. Two fifty left as he approached his first ride. That turned out to be The Octopus, which he found exhilarating. The spinning and whirling lights were amazing. Beyond amazing, actually. The height of the ride gave Whistle a bird's eye view of the fairgrounds. He took everything in.

Stepping off the ride a bit wobbly, Whistle walked deeper into the midway, absolutely astonished that life could be like this. What caught Whistle's attention next was the barker's voice taunting him to pop the balloon with the dart and win a prize. Fifty cents later three darts were thrown and he had nothing to show for it. Now with just two dollars left, he could absolutely not resist the massive wand of blue cotton candy. You know, that first treat every one of us loves to hate...another seventy-five cents out the door.

As he finished his melting wand of sugar, the day waned on, the sights and sounds became at least a little familiar to Whistle. After he passed through the 4-H barns and all the arts and crafts he turned right, back onto the midway. The very end of the midway. Coming around the corner, against the sun, now almost completely set, there it stood, looming high into the evening sky, lights blazing, Lynyrd Skynyrd lovingly pouring out from within. Every ounce of good and bad was right in front of him. Newly achieved comfort level diminishing, Whistle walked up to his third ride of the day:

"The Rock and Roll"

As he got buckled in he had no idea what was about to happen. Then just like that, the ride operator's voice rang out.

"Rock and Roll!!!" Holy shit, rock and roll was right because Whistle Evel Fonzarelli Starr's life opened and exploded like never before for the next three and a half minutes. His mind clicked deep as he was shot high into the sky, spun around left and right, dropped back to earth and flung in every direction he thought possible. His mind couldn't help but soak in every detail. Every second of those few minutes burned itself deep into his memory. The minutes passed in what seemed to be seconds and suddenly the ride stopped. Snapping back into real time, he couldn't remember what just happened, but every detail was ingrained in him forever. He stepped off the ride and started working his way back up to the front gate.

Night had fallen as Whistle left the fair and started his long walk home. It occurred to him that he was by himself at night, quite far from home and he was in absolutely no trouble at all. Whistle not in trouble? Holy cow, he could not comprehend this. Stomach slightly shaken by the cotton candy and Rock and

Roll ride, Whistle passed through the center of town and up the hill toward home.

Walking into the house, his mom and Jack were already in bed. Whistle made his way up the stairs, knowing every creak. In bed, Whistle thought about the day. A few thoughts struck him profoundly. The lemonade was incredible, the rides were even better. Especially the Rock and Roll. The fact that he was left to himself and completed the day without one single problem was amazing. Best of all, Whistle still had a dollar and twenty-five cents tucked deeply into the front left pocket of his toughskins. He fell asleep that night feeling that life was great. The innocence of youth enveloped him like a warm blanket.

CHAPTER SIX
Jack Takes Flight

Elementary school passed by and life was perfect for Whistle. Except for the extreme boredom of school, literally watching the minute hand of the clock slowly tick the minutes of the day away.

Trouble and Whistle did have a knack for finding each other at school. Never anything too serious. Mostly just things that involved him always having his head in the clouds. He was described by his teachers as a boy who was very smart, very clever, and highly imaginative. His problem clearly was that he grew bored very quickly and very easily. If a class interested him there was no problem at all. If there was no interest, it just wasn't going to happen and he would find himself in a pickle yet again. As a matter of fact, Whistle had barely any recollection of ever bringing a book home, let alone doing homework. The only books he really remembered bringing home were books from the library. Books he could find himself, that would jumpstart his mind and send him away to new worlds. Where there were new people to meet, new lands to see, and new adventures to experience. Often, these books would find themselves back to the library late.

Whistle's favorite part of school, besides the library books and recess in general, were the few short days he and Mikey would spend at the beginning of each year just inside those pines with the monarch butterflies. Standing there just past the end of the lower field in silence. Just admiring everything that surrounded them. They did usually make it back up to school before recess ended, but still spent their fair share of time on the bench outside the principal's office.

The years of elementary school and summer passed by. Whistle and Mikey were sure life would remain as close to perfect as possible forever. Even when he was in trouble, Whistle was never overly bothered. He took it in stride and mostly everything would roll right off his back, always searching for the next new experience.

Then, one certain Christmas came and Whistle got his very first bike. Of course, Mikey got his first bike too because their dads always went Christmas shopping together. Plenty of scotch and beer throughout the trip. His first bike was a black, shiny Huffy. It sported a white banana seat with a chrome sissy bar and white handle grips. Oh, it was the most beautiful thing he had ever laid his eyes on, and the wait for spring to come so he could ride it was excruciating. It sat out in the barn neatly parked, just waiting for him. Whistle must have walked out to admire it at least a thousand times that winter. Conversations about the boys' new bikes revved their anticipation levels to new heights.

Then it finally came. The first Saturday of early spring, the snow and ice had receded back just enough to somewhat make riding a bike a "semi safe" endeavor. Winter sand still on the street diminished the level of safety from "semi" to "barely."

Nevertheless, the boys set out that first time, excitement tingling through them like electricity.

This was another day that ranked among the best in Whistle's young life. Needless to say, the day shot by like a rocket, and that night in bed, Whistle settled into a deep sleep. Dreams of the new level of freedom his new bike provided filled his head.

That school year finally passed and summer showed up again. Another perfect summer and life was great. The boys' new bikes absolutely expanded their worlds yet again.

"You know how much faster we'll be able to get to the Champion Fair?" Mikey asked.

"Oh yeah, it's gonna be great," Whistle responded. Without another word spoken, their first ride to those fairgrounds began. It was uncanny how much these two boys could read each other's minds. Once there, most of their time was spent flat tracking their bikes around the deserted demolition derby ring. Crashing in the corners, dirt flying everywhere and laughing with sheer bliss.

Back in the neighborhood, after dark again, they split off to their own homes.

"See ya."

"See ya." Both bikes looked mean with all their mud and dirt. Even with how dirty Whistle was, still no trouble from his mother and Jack when he walked into the den. Life was just grand. Sleep was great again that night, especially knowing what was going to happen the next morning.

Breakfast done, good mornings exchanged, Whistle was out the door with the wind in his hair as he tore through the neighborhood. On his beautifully dirty new Huffy with its white handle grips, white banana seat, and beyond cool chrome sissy bar, he made his way. Within minutes he arrived at Mikey's house. He was standing in the driveway with his equally dirty, equally beautiful new bike waiting.

"Good morning," Mikey said with cheer.

"Goood morning." Cheer was returned.

Then the boys proceeded to wash their bikes with the garden hose, early sun warming up the day. They washed every inch of those bikes back to pristine and their pride was obvious. Without knowing it, they both realized that taking pride in things sure was important. By the way, at the end of the day those boys and those bikes were filthy again because a second ride to the fairgrounds was bound to happen.

Summer fun worked its way through the calendar and the fair that year had arrived much faster because of the bikes. Everything that year was somehow a little more magical. Whistle's mind kept exploding with detail. The lemonade, the oxen, derby and fireworks fully filled him with warmth and comfort. The Rock and Roll at the end of the midway still shook him up a little in the best way. Bed that night, and just like that, the next morning sixth grade started.

The year started out just fine except for the boredom of class. The visit with the monarchs in the pines was once again awe inspiring. The library continued to feed Whistle's imagination, though he considered school in general to be a nuisance. The holidays came and went, leaving winter to work toward spring. Life could not be any better for him even with school. Mom, Jack, Mikey, bike, books, everything. Always life would be this way for Whistle Evel Fonzarelli Starr. Always and forever, surely.

Then one afternoon Whistle came home from school and found his mom sitting at the kitchen table, head down in hands quietly sobbing. Cigarette smoke hung in the air heavier than usual. As he noticed this he also noticed there was a glass of scotch next to her. Instantly his love and protectiveness for his mother shot up in him.

"Mom, what's wrong?" as he went to her. She couldn't answer as the sobs continued. A sip of scotch was taken. Whistle moved in next to her, hugged her deeply and true, not knowing what was wrong but understanding her pain was real and hurt her badly.

"Mommy?" he whispered, reverting back to a younger age because he loved her so much, his worry rising rapidly. She still couldn't answer him and they sat there holding each other in silence for some time. The only sounds in the room were her low quiet sobs and the tick tock of the grandfather clock against the wall. Whistle noticed this profoundly. After some time, a cigarette, and a couple more sips of scotch, she finally squared her bloodshot and hurt beautiful eyes to him.

"Whistle, your dad is gone," she finally said in a slightly slurred voice.

"What do you mean, Mom?" he asked as the afternoon sun diminished from the windows.

"I don't know how to tell you this so I'll just say it. He said he wasn't happy anymore and had to go. He walked out the door, got in his car and drove away. We're never going to see him again."

"I don't understand," he said. After a pause, his mom got up and grabbed her drink.

"I love you Whistle." She slightly stumbled across the kitchen and turned right, up the stairs to find her way to bed. Obviously a long, horrible day for her, and Whistle fully understood this. He sat at that table for a while and suddenly understood everything. The feeling of being abandoned again was sharp and it slapped him hard. Very little sleep came to the poor boy that night. He knew in one instant he would never care for Jack again.

CHAPTER SEVEN
A Major Transition

The next morning, Whistle got up and walked downstairs into the empty kitchen. His mom was still upstairs asleep. He made himself a bowl of cornflakes and sat at the table. He took a few small bites but mostly stirred and stared. Shortly he realized breakfast was not going to happen. Bowl in the sink, Whistle reached for the pea green wall phone.

"Hello?" Mikey's voice came through.

"Mikey, Jack's gone," Whistle said.

"Wait, what? Wait a minute, what do you mean he's gone? When will he be back?" Confusion in his voice.

"Mom says he'll never be back. Something about him wasn't happy anymore and he had to go." Slight hitch in his voice.

"I don't get it," Mikey said, truly not understanding at all. Why would Whistle's dad leave?

"I don't get it either but that's what Mom told me." Also thinking, *Why would my dad leave? What did I do wrong this time!?* The feeling of confusion starting to get a bit of anger mixed in with it.

"Mikey, I'm scared," Whistle said.

"Meet me at the fort," replied Mikey.

"Okay," Whistle answered.

As he was walking out the door, he heard his mom's footsteps coming down the stairs. Instead of going back in to see his mom, he continued out because he had to talk to Mikey. After the worst bike ride through the neighborhood of his life, they were both in the fort. They sat down and started to talk.

The boys talked and talked for hours, and for the first time since they had known each other, they didn't let their imaginations deviate from reality. Somehow they both understood the magnitude of the situation. After a very long, emotional several hours, the boys stepped out of the fort, not any closer to any answers about what was going on. The only thing they truly knew was that they would always be together. After all, that's what best friends were for, right?

As Whistle hopped on his Huffy to make his way home, he couldn't make out details like usual. Everything was dulled because his mind was completely cluttered with confusion. With no memory of the ride, Whistle was home, his Huffy lying on its side in the grass instead of being parked safely in its usual spot in the barn. As he walked across the porch and through the door, the sun was ready to go to bed, leaving only about ten minutes of light left.

Entering the kitchen, the windows were deep orange, rectangles casting a stunted hue throughout the room. This would have been magical under most any other circumstance. Tonight, it was not. One lamp was on in the corner. Sixty watt bulb, dimly lighting a small area.

There Whistle's mom sat again, exactly in the same spot at the table. Same heavier than usual cigarette haze and glass of scotch in the same spot. The biggest difference was the bottle now stood at attention next to the glass, ready to not let it end up empty.

"Mom?" implored Whistle timidly.

Nothing...she just stared down at the table with no reaction. The sun, now blood red, deepened down and made it clear the light in the room was about to go out. Whistle just stood there watching his mom as the light did blink out to darkness. This left only the sixty watt to stretch light out as far as it could. Not far, as Whistle looked at his mom with great sadness. In that moment he realized that he wasn't the only one that got abandoned. What did I do wrong became what did we do wrong.

After a while, Whistle kissed her on the top of her head, told her he loved her and started up to bed knowing they would not speak that night. Going to bed that night, he was sure little to no sleep was likely due to the gaping, gnawing pit in his stomach. After a while, the emotional exhaustion allowed him to pass out and get some much needed rest.

The next morning, Whistle woke up ready to go for about three seconds before he remembered what was going on. Getting out of bed that morning, dread refilled his whole body instantly. With the pit in his stomach slowly returning, he started downstairs. Walking into the kitchen, he noticed the ashtray, scotch glass, and bottle were in the same place. Also, the same sixty watt bulb was still burning. His mom was not downstairs again and he knew she wouldn't be for a long time. Breakfast was a feeble attempt with no result. Whistle walked into the den, turned on the TV and wasted the day. Not like him at all. That night, still no Mom as he went to bed with no sleep or dinner.

A couple of weeks went by and life remained grey and listless. Whistle and his mom were talking again but it wasn't the same. Even his time with Mikey felt a little bit different. Like seasons change, Whistle knew something was coming.

Sure enough, Whistle was told that he was leaving his great house, his great neighborhood, and most importantly, his best friend. Apparently his mom could not afford to stay, and she had to move them to a bigger town so she could find a job and a cheaper living situation. Fortunately, she did receive a bit of money from the sale of the house and it helped carry the two of them through a little while.

The band aid was abruptly ripped off, and in an instant, Whistle lost his connection to his best friend, and to the whole world he knew and loved. Talk about abandonment. The only person he had left was his mom. Come to think of it, she had left him before. Also, this new place might as well be New York City to Whistle. *How am I going to deal with this?* he thought to himself.

His mom pulled up to their new two-bedroom apartment in the small U-Haul truck they'd rented for the move.

"Here we go Whistle," she said.

"Okay," he replied. It did not take long to unpack everything and get it into the apartment. Whistle brought his minimal belongings to his room and just felt grey in his heart. That night his mom returned the U-Haul and showed up with McDonald's for dinner. He ate quietly and promptly went to bed.

Laying in his bed that first night he felt lost. Instead of dreams, this boy in his brand new environment had horrible nightmares with a common theme of being out of control. These type of dreams would haunt him for the rest of his life. This sucks, everything sucks.

Today's gonna suck, he thought as he woke up, disoriented, to his new surroundings. Worst of all, he knew he had to start at a new school yet again, in just a couple of days. He also knew he would be lost and he was terrified. He would be alone and nothing about this would be fun.

The next couple of days just slowly marched by. Nothing was exciting at all to Whistle. His mom did get a job bartending at one of the local watering holes. At least some money would be coming in. Still, no comfort came to Whistle.

Chapter Eight
Welcome to
a New School

Sure enough, the day Whistle was dreading had arrived. It arrived fast and he didn't feel ready for it. The size of that first kindergarten hallway was instantly dwarfed by what his mind was telling him was about to come. This new school was going to be gigantic, filled with all new kids that already knew each other. Not good at all. In the silver Volkswagen filled with the familiar smell of smoke, Whistle's mom drove him to school. This time Johnny Cash was on the radio, singing about a ring of fire. Oh Boy, did Whistle ever feel like he was entering a burning ring of fire, about to be swallowed whole. Still no thought of wearing a seatbelt at all.

Mom pulled the car up to the curb and as Whistle got out, "Good luck," was all he got.

"Thanks," he mumbled back. He closed the door and watched his mom drive away, Johnny's cavernous baritone voice instantly muffled by the sound of a new reality.

As he stood facing the pavement, he was instantly aware of the din of noise behind him. Kids talking, going back and forth, waiting to start the school day. Whistle froze, sensing that this was a time his mind would allow him to absorb great detail. However, the details were blotted out by fear and melancholy. So once again, little ol' Whistle squared his shoulders and turned to face a brand new world.

Holy Cow! The level of activity was overwhelming to him. With confusion as his partner, he walked up to the very fringe of the crowd and waited for the doors to open. Waiting for school to start, finding his first classroom and staking out a back row seat where he could feel relatively safe. *How long will this take?* he thought to himself.

As he stood there, he took in some things, but without much detail. Time passed and his desire to just walk away from the whole thing grew. He actually almost did leave, but then he noticed two kids toward the middle of the crowd. He couldn't hear what they were saying but it was clear to him that the bigger boy was pushing the smaller boy around. Whistle tried to ignore it but the boy kept going. As hard as he tried, he could not let it go because the boy kept pushing.

Before he knew it, Whistle Evel Fonzarelli Starr was in the first fight of his life. His mind, for the first time in a long time, clicked over to detail mode. He pushed through the crowd and punched the much larger boy square in the face. This kid turned toward Whistle and came at him. It was on and he hadn't even set foot into the building yet. As all this happened he thought to himself, *At least that other boy isn't getting harassed anymore.*

So they fought, and the circle of kids that formed around them was the most prominent detail Whistle took in. Everything else was a blur as he swung and took punches to the face, head, and torso. It seemed like it lasted forever, but it was probably only four or five minutes. Whistle did, in fact, get the better of the bully before they were pulled apart, and he had a great feeling even as the first stop at his new school was the principal's office. He knew that the other boy wasn't being bothered anymore.

In the principal's office that first day, Whistle got suspended for the first time. Suspended? What was that?

"Leave school and don't come back until tomorrow," the principal explained. Whistle walked out of the office and out the front door without seeing ninety-eight percent of his new school. *Now what? I'm in soooo much trouble!* he thought. He started making his way home without really knowing where he was going. After a couple of hours, using only his sense of direction, he finally found the apartment.

Now what? he thought again as he realized it was only eleven thirty in the morning. He couldn't get himself into the apartment and knew his mom was going to kill him when she found out that he'd gotten suspended. Trouble was certain but he had a whole afternoon to kill now. So… what to do… what to do?

Well, Whistle started to explore the meager yard and everything else around. He walked around the building, checking everything out. Then, there it was. In the back of the building there was a tree that stretched up to the roof.

Unable to resist, Whistle started to climb. Up and up he went. When he finally got to the roofline, he realized the tree was thin and further away from the roof than he thought. With a lot of nervousness, Whistle finally made his way onto the roof.

Now on the roof, he started to take in his surroundings. He was on a flat roof that went up to a peak. Of course, he had to get to that peak. Once he was there, he saw that the peak traveled the entire length of the building, all the way to the front. Of course, he followed the peak the whole way. After working his way all the way forward, he straddled the very edge of the front of the building. The sight of the ground, more than thirty feet below, made him feel dizzy and alive for the second time in just a few hours. Thank God because life had been dull and depressing for what seemed like a real long time. The fact that he was in a lot of trouble for being suspended on the first day at his new school that he'd barely set foot in faded away. Everything drifted away and his mind clicked over. It was truly awesome.

The afternoon sun washed over him. The heat was amplified by the roof shingles. His view of the surrounding neighborhood was incredible. The dry autumn wind brushed over him, blowing his hair back a bit. The colors, scents, and sounds of this new setting were overwhelming. He saw a traditional white New England church steeple off in the distance. Closer, everything was still beautiful but not quite as much. White and all colors turned gradually into dark grey asphalt, buildings and telephone poles. Power lines spiderwebbed through his field of vision. Whistle took everything in deeply, his mind lost in thought.

After a while, the sun started to set. By the way, the sunset from the rooftop was absolutely breathtaking. Whistle finally made his way back along the peak and down to the flat corner of the roof. Sun setting deeper, he had to navigate himself into the tree top. A couple of skipped heartbeats later, he swayed in the top of the tree. Then he worked his way down through the branches and finally he felt the ground. Almost dark now, Whistle opened the door to the new apartment knowing he was going to have a problem.

"How was your first day of school?" his mom asked.

"Fine," Whistle answered.

"That's great! See I told you everything was going to be fine." Whistle noticed the weariness in her voice. He couldn't believe his mom had no idea he'd been suspended that day. The fact that he spent the afternoon on the roof waiting for her to come home was also unbelievable to him.

After a quiet dinner of Salisbury steak, boxed mashed potatoes, and canned green beans, Whistle made his way to his room. He laid in bed that night still in shock that he was not in trouble.

Whistle started to drift off with the thoughts of the day in his head. School, fight, suspension, the walk back home, the afternoon on the rooftop. Finally in his bed, he drifted off, uncomfortable because he didn't quite feel at home. His dreams were fitful, full of nightmares. What was going on with poor Whistle? He was truly lost in a world he didn't understand. He wondered if it was possible that he might actually be the only junior high student who'd ever been suspended before actually making it beyond the doors on his first day. He was protecting a boy he didn't know and he would do it again if he had to. After all, right is right and that is that.

As sleep finally came to him that night, there was one thing Whistle didn't realize. There was a boy watching him closely that day when he beat up that big kid. Little did Whistle know this boy had a good eye, watching everything that first day. He was going to meet him soon, as long as he didn't get suspended again.

CHAPTER NINE
Second Lifelong Friend

A couple of days went by and Whistle wasn't getting a ride to school anymore. A two mile walk to school, and two miles back. Classes blended, people blended, and poor Whistle was completely lost. He simply didn't know what to do. Then it happened.

In class one day the boy that watched Whistle on the first morning spoke up.

"Hey," he said quietly. Whistle, not realizing it was directed toward him, didn't respond.

"Hey," again, waiting...

Finally Whistle turned to his left, and sitting next to him was one Eric Flow. Dark hair and dark eyes, just waiting for a response.

"Hey?" Questioning.

"My name's Eric. What's your name?"

"Whistle."

"I saw you the other morning and I wanted to ask you a question," Eric said.

"What?" Whistle responded, no idea what was coming next.

"Why did you fight Billy Hudson the other day?"

"I don't know, I just felt it was the right thing to do."

"Well I think you're crazy because I thought he was going to kick your ass," Eric said.

"Me too," was the answer.

"Why, then?"

"I don't know. The boy looked like he was having a hard time and needed some help," Whistle said.

"Georgie does get picked on a lot," Eric said.

"Well, I didn't want to see that, so I did something about it."

"You've got balls, my friend!" Not realizing they would be truly best friends for the entire rest of their lives.

"What are you doing after school?" Eric asked.

"I don't know," Whistle whispered.

"I'll see you after school." Just like that, the bell rang and Eric walked out of the room. Truly not knowing what to expect, Whistle continued his day, clueless as to whether he would even see Eric that afternoon. Sure enough, as he trudged out the front door, there Eric stood at the curb.

"Ready?" Eric asked.

"I guess so," replied Whistle.

After a long walk the two boys found themselves sitting on a bench along Main Street. Another overload of details enveloped Whistle's senses. Everything was completely surreal. Cars passed by with great clarity. People passed and all the buildings were crystal clear.

Cracks in the sidewalk jumped out at him and even the disregarded piece of gum on the curb stood out to Whistle.

Then he snapped back into reality and continued his conversation with Eric.

"Hey, you alright?" to Whistle.

"Yeah, sorry. I've just never been down Main Street before," back at Eric.

"It's pretty cool, and the best part is you just never know what's gonna happen next." So true.

The boys sat on that bench and started to get to know each other. The day ticked by and everyone went about their lives. No one paid any attention to them as they delved deeper into the conversation. Whistle finally started to feel alive again and he loved it. He needed it badly.

So they sat that afternoon, talking, watching the sun slowly wash gold over the landscape. Both already knew now that they'd be connected to each other the rest of their lives. They continued to talk deep into the afternoon, forgetting all reality. Stories and imaginations soared that day. Then when the sun started to give way to the moon, they realized they had better get home.

Getting up off the bench, they walked down Main Street, turned left and started up the hill. A couple of blocks later they paused and looked at each other.

"I'll see you tomorrow?"

"See you tomorrow." And just like that, they walked their separate ways. Whistle continued up the hill and finally hung a right onto his street. Darkness swallowing everything as the apartment finally came into view. Using his house key, he walked in and everything was quiet. His mom wasn't home and Whistle felt very alone. A couple of Oreos later, Whistle was on his way upstairs. In his still uncomfortable room he got ready for bed. Lying there, he couldn't stop thinking about his new friend. The afternoon's conversations ran through his head over and over again. Excitement did well up in his chest a little bit as he started to nod off. He couldn't wait to see Eric again.

Something great awaited, and Whistle was going to find out what it was no matter what. That night he passed in and out of sleep, and when he woke up he was ready to go. "Hi Mom," breakfast, and two miles later, he stood in front of the school, waiting to be let in.

"What's up?"

"What's up?" Both trying to be cool.

They were already connected and they knew it. Doors opened, the boys walked in and they separated to their classes without a word. They both knew they would see each other later that day.

The boredom of school plodded by in a miserable manner. Finally the two met at the curb again, not knowing what was going to happen.

The afternoon was their oyster. Unchecked by any authority, the day proceeded. Experiences filled the afternoon and Whistle couldn't have been happier. The two walked new streets, stopped into the local record store with not a penny in a pocket. Steve Miller, Pink Floyd, Aerosmith and Kiss begging to be bought. Not today, not yet. When the day finally ended, Whistle was alone in his room again. He went to bed and a stronger twinge of excitement filled his chest. Maybe moving wasn't so bad, and just maybe Whistle Evel Fonzarelli Starr could figure it all out. Maybe, we'll see. Confidence took a slight move in the right direction as he drifted off into a very vibrant dream world.

His dreams were elaborate that night. Whistle's mind popped into an imaginary world that he didn't even know existed. Knights slayed knights, and the winning shot was scored with just three seconds left, Muhammed Ali and Howard Cosell went back and forth. That night, the Olympics took place and new planets were discovered. Whistle could not slow his mind.

How the hell am I supposed to go to sleep tonight? he thought to himself. Not knowing that his hyper electric imagination would be a burden he would carry with him all his days.

That night, sleep came very slowly to Whistle. What he did know was that his mom was still there and he had a great new friend. As he drifted deeper into the night, Whistle's memories drifted back to his early childhood. Fisher Price, Legos and sidewalk chalk, the unmistakable scent of Play-Doh, all making a nostalgic appearance as he blissfully enjoyed the kind of lively yet peaceful sleep only the young can truly experience. Donny and Marie, Evel Knievel jumping those buses, the Fonz and Evel shaking hands in that moment. Within the fantastic dreams of a child of the seventies, all was right with the world.

Finally, the dazzling, colorful slideshow in his mind slowed down and a purple Matchbox car was the last image his mind's eye saw before he finally sailed off to slumberland.

CHAPTER TEN
Seventh Grade
Settles In

The next day came and there was plenty to find out about. The more Whistle became comfortable at his new school, the more small details he noticed. The layout started to fall into place. Different teachers' personalities started to reveal themselves. The style of each classroom became more defined. Whistle, as always, somehow always seemed to stake out the back row middle seat. The only place in any classroom that felt right to him. A good vantage point to discern which kids were cool and which were best to steer clear of.

Actually, figuring out other kids was the easiest part of the program. A short conversation let him know what was up right away. Observing an interaction between two of his classmates had them both decided. Just watching how they acted sitting alone at their desk told Whistle everything he needed to know. Did they hunch? Were they reading? Were they looking off into space, lost in thought? Carving their initials into the desk? Eyes up? Down? Confident? Shy? Facial expressions, dress, where they chose to sit in class, all invaluable clues to a seventh grader in a new town, or anyone for that matter, and they were plain as day to Whistle.

The bell rang and it was lunchtime. Whistle exited the classroom, took a right, and headed toward the unmistakable smell of the cafeteria. After gathering his mystery chicken cubes, cheap fries, some unidentifiable green stuff, mixed fruit, and a ten-ounce carton of skim milk, he found a seat off to the side. The brown foldout table with kids he didn't know waiting. Green plastic tray hitting the brown table top, he sat down with all the confidence of the day pouring right back out of him.

Realizing that his part of the school had started to feel safe and familiar, it also dawned on him that the school as a whole was massive and the cafeteria was the Grand Central Station where all the little pockets, cliques, and mini-neighborhoods came together. A bubbling, buzzing stew of adolescent energy, insecurity, innocence, judgment, secret crushes and pressure all storming through the bustle. Eyeballs were everywhere and thankfully Whistle found an out of the way seat at the far side of the room. With his head down, no appetite for the "lunch" on his tray, the feeling of being lost once again overcame him. All he could think about was Mikey, Jack, his Huffy, the old neighborhood, the old house, the Champion Fair with the Rock and Roll, the woods, and how much he missed it all. Blocking out this new world, he just sat there. No one cared, no one even noticed him, nothing seemed to matter much anymore. Lost Boy…

"Whistle?" someone said. No response.

"Whistle?" again. Whistle still a thousand miles away.

"Whistle?!" This time with a poke to the left shoulder. Not knowing who was poking him, he started to come around. However, before he did, a profound thought came to him:

It feels like yesterday I was a young boy, and my life was filled with comfort and love. I had a mom, dad, and a best friend. Now I truly have now idea what's going on.

"Whistle!" the voice persisted, accompanied by a more aggressive push to the shoulder.

"What?" Just then, the bell rang, and the lunch period was over. He looked up, cleared his eyes and saw Eric looking at him.

"You alright?"

"Yeah, sorry," Whistle responded, still a bit blurry.

"Okay, I'll see you after school?" Eric asked.

"Okay, I'll see ya."

As they went down different hallways, Whistle took comfort in the fact that he'd see Eric later that day. That afternoon, sitting in history class, Whistle stole a moment.

He thought to himself, *Whistle, you are no longer a boy. You are starting to become a man, so get your shit together and forget about small town life. Just suck it up and forget it. Be open to everything and work toward becoming a man. You can do it.*

Whistle snapped back and sat through history until the bell released him. With school over he stood at his locker, which struck him as funny because he had almost nothing in it. So many of the other kids had books, clothes, pictures and anything else a junior high student could possibly own. Whistle had basically nothing but didn't want to look stupid. After a fair amount of time standing at his locker feeling awkward, he closed his locker and headed for the front doors. The late afternoon sun pouring through the doors and dancing off the tiles seemed to taunt him. He was starting to feel claustrophobic and walked faster.

All of a sudden, panic set in deep. The hallway narrowed and kept getting longer, not letting him reach the door. All the sounds of school letting out blended into a deafening white noise and the strong scent of lead overwhelmed him as he struggled not to pass out right there in the hallway.

Without memory, Whistle pushed open the doors, escaped into the sunlight and fresh air. With no understanding of what was going on with him, Whistle ducked around the corner and found a nook where he could sit and regroup. Finally finding some privacy, his breathing and pulse started to regulate. The afternoon sun felt good on his face. The sound of kids and buses became background noises and Whistle actually started to doze off. He was almost asleep and entering a dream state…

"What the fuck?"…No reply.

"You gotta be kidding me." A familiar voice cut through the void.

"Huh?"

"What are you doing? Get up!" Eric demanded.

"I'm okay, I gotta get home," Whistle responded, still clearing his head. As he focused he was very happy to see that it was Eric he was talking to because his instincts were telling him to just get away.

"Let's go."

As they walked, Whistle felt better and better. He made a mental note of this and for the rest of his life, he knew he could rely on a good, brisk walk to clear his head.

The two boys spent the afternoon talking in the park. School out of the way for the day, they sat.

"Sorry about that, I don't know what happened," Whistle apologized.

"No worries," Eric replied. So that day the two boys sat and once again talked deep into the dusk as the golden sky turned purple, eventually cradling the stars and moonlight.

"Why don't you just stay at my house tonight?" Whistle asked.

"Okay."

The boys left the park and walked into Whistle's unwelcoming apartment. They walked quietly through the door, so as not to wake Whistle's mom up. Making it safely to his room, they looked at each other and couldn't help but laugh. Without Whistle's mom knowing that Eric slept over, the boys settled down to get some sleep.

"Eric?"

"Yes?"

"You're from here and everybody knows and loves you. It's easy for you. I don't know anyone, and they all look at me like I'm just a misfit freak."

"No Whistle, there's a lot of kids who like you. Don't sweat it."

"Fuck that, but I'll go along with you Eric."

"Whistle, more people are interested in you than you think."

"Okay, I'm gonna let it go, I just want to get to know the school. Just be a normal kid."

Sure enough, Whistle eventually settled into seventh grade.

As the school year rolled on and his friendship solidified, Whistle was starting to feel more stable. He didn't see his mom much, but that was okay because he knew she had to work.

Whistle and Eric occupied themselves in a manner perfectly suited for junior high boys and before they knew it, summer was well within sight... Let the good times roll.

CHAPTER ELEVEN
First Summer in the Capital City

The final bell of seventh grade rang, closing out the year. Whistle went to his locker and noticed everybody else cleaning theirs out. Pictures coming down, papers thrown in the trash and also on the hallway floor. Kids laughing and yelling back and forth. Excitement filled the air and Whistle took it all in. The clang of the locker doors all around him. The sound of crumpling papers multiplied into a kind of white noise punctuated by the occasional "Have a good summer," and "See you next year."

Standing there, Whistle realized he didn't have much to clean out of his locker. No pictures, no books, barely any papers. The few scraps kicking around the bottom, he had the common courtesy to throw in the trash.

As time passed and things continued to quiet down, Whistle slowly made his way to the main school entrance. As bad as he wanted to be free for the summer, he couldn't help but steal a moment.

Pausing, he looked around, taking in the trophy case, the principal's office and bench that he was already familiar with. Posters on the walls advertising events that had already happened. Standing there, Whistle exhaled and knew he was ready to go. He turned and walked straight toward the front doors.

Walking outside, the early summer sun cascaded down on him. He looked around and saw there weren't many people around. The ones that were could care less about what Whistle Starr was up to. No Eric, no friends, no mom, no teachers, no nothing. So he just started walking the two miles back to the apartment. A long walk, but when your mind takes off it goes by before you know it.

That walk was an interesting start to his summer because excitement didn't roar through him for the first time ever. He walked and walked, one street became another, one dog's bark blended into the next and the next. Usually this would be the time that Whistle's imagination would run absolutely wild. Things would be shot, mountains would be climbed, cars would win races, and fires would rage and heroic firemen would put them out. But not today.

A long, boring, lonely walk ended with the sound of a key sliding into a lock. The tumblers falling into place as the key turned clockwise. The door opened and Whistle walked into an even lonelier "home." A couple of light switches later, he stood in the kitchen alone. Feeling very desolate, he heated up some leftover kielbasa. After it was done, he squirted some yellow mustard on his plate and headed for the living room. Sitting on the couch with his plate on the coffee table, the television turned on. Don't mind the line at the bottom of the television. That's just the way it is. After a while, you won't even notice it. Just watch the show by yourself. The blue light from the television washed over the living room as Whistle ate his dinner.

Happy Days rolled into *Laverne and Shirley*, followed by *Different Strokes*. Finished with his kielbasa as he took his plate to the kitchen. After washing it and putting it away, he returned to the living room just in time for *All in the Family*. And you knew after that *The Facts of Life* would never let you down. After *Mork and Mindy* capped the night's entertainment, Whistle went to bed. Door locked and all the lights off, he remembered his mom was still out. "She still loves me?"

Click, his table lamp came on. He put his Kiss "Destroyer" album on his cardboard Bee Gees record player as he got ready for bed. He felt supremely alone at that moment and he loved and hated it all at once. He got in bed, shut off the light, and his mind began to wander.

He thought about his last moments at school earlier in the day, every detail filling his head. Lockers, trophies, teachers, and of course the principal's bench filled his mind. But summer was here and it was time to rock and roll all the way to the opening bell of eighth grade. A whole new city was waiting to be explored. Eric, Whistle, and the rest of the guys were gonna see everything. Believe me, they didn't see everything but they sure did see a lot.

But before we talk about that let's talk about Whistle, who drifted off and had a wonderful dream. This dream was truly magical and stayed with Whistle forever. It went like this:

Standing on the beach looking at the Atlantic Ocean, sand covered the toes of the boys' Converse All-Stars. The sound of the waves crashed heavily in his ears as the sun beat down on him. People frolicked everywhere, and as usual no one paid any attention to him. That was fine with him. He was more than happy to be invisible. Suddenly he decided it was time to go, so he turned west.

He walked out of Hampton Beach and everything started to speed up. West came fast. New Hampshire went by with one stop at Baker's Farm for a quick snack of rhubarb. Vermont was a blur and New York flew by. He was now in a full run and it was so effortless. Every step seemed to equal a mile. Every state to the Mississippi was a breeze. The flow of the river seemed as gentle as a brook.

Now standing at the eastern edge of the muddy Mississippi, he paused briefly and then ran at the water as hard as he could. He swam hard and actually felt that he was going to drown. The current pulled him downstream and he struggled. Breath escaped him as the muddy water filled his mouth. Barely making it, he lay on a boat ramp catching his breath. Easily the most horrifying experience of his life, dream or not. After he collected himself, he continued. A Big Mac in Colorado with those awesome fries, Whistle peeked over the Rockies and ran towards California.

In a matter of strides, Whistle went from the peaks of the Rockies to the beautiful redwood forest. The massive trees humbled him. After admiring these West Coast mammoths, Whistle took two steps to the west and was standing facing the Pacific Ocean. *How the fuck did this happen?* he thought. The ocean stood before him. People didn't register to him because he couldn't believe he traversed the entire continent in a matter of minutes. After a long pause of appreciation, he turned east and began to run. States flew by and the Mississippi was behind him. New England hit and Whistle came home.

Before he knew it, he was back in his apartment and he couldn't help but think it didn't feel much like the first night of summer. Loneliness pinned him down as he slowly drifted back off to sleep.

This sucks, he thought to himself. *I'm all by myself; I guess I have to deal with that. You really can't count on anyone so you just have to take care of yourself.*

Self-preservation, what a miserable thought. Whistle just wanted to share his life with other people and enjoy everything. He finally drifted back to sleep all alone in an apartment that he hated. He truly felt like all was lost and then…

"Come on, fucker! Let's go!"

"What?"

"Get up, it's summer, let's go!"

Whistle didn't understand what was going on as he opened his eyes. There, Eric's face filled his field of vision, and—

"You have ten seconds to get up before I throat punch you," as he cocked his right fist back.

"Okay! Okay! Just give me a minute," Whistle said as he started to get up. Ten minutes later he was dressed and they were headed out the door. Before he went out he checked his mom's room and unfortunately she still wasn't home. Where the fuck was she? Worry found its way to the pit of his stomach. For now he would let it go because the excitement of exploring a new city was too overwhelming.

Whistle's Huffy now replaced by a sleek grey Mongoose with white mag tires, they headed out. The day was easy and Whistle's spirit soared. He felt so much better than he did the night before. It was so good to be with his best friend and have no rules and no boundaries. Their new bikes expanded their world beyond what they'd ever imagined. They rode all the way out to the quarries that day, a place Whistle had only heard of. Epic to see as they sat high on the cliff.

The water called out to them from forty feet down. Small wind driven ripples worked their way from right to left. The sun glinted off the water not in the shade of the cliffs. Birds chirping in the pines above filled his soul with peace. Robins plucked worms from the ground and cardinals darted back and forth through the treetops. Goldfinches and Baltimore orioles came and went as they pleased. Life was good.

Then it struck Whistle, and he stood up at the edge of the cliff. He started to undress and told Eric to do the same. Now both boys in their underwear stood at the edge of the cliff. Midday sun shining on them as they stood and hesitated. Without speaking a word, they both had the same thought.

"What the fuck are we doing? For real! What the fuck are we doing?" Then, after a quick glance at each other, they turned to the water and just jumped.

Shit! This is too much! Whistle thought to himself as his feet left the security of the solid granite ledge. As he was free falling through the air, Whistle never felt more alive. Crashing through the deep emerald water, an immense rush shot through him and it took his breath away. He found himself deeper underwater than he was ready for and he panicked. Looking up, the glint of the sun above the surface seemed impossibly far away. His breath already diminishing, he tried to swim to the surface but it felt like he was making no headway and was sure to pass out.

After furiously propelling himself toward the light, he broke the surface and took the biggest breath of his life. After collecting himself, he looked over at

Eric and saw him in a similar state of confusion. What an experience. Something they would both keep forever. Freedom, terror, friendship and nature blended together. The cold water and warmth of the sun blended as well.

"Holy fucking shit!" Eric yelled, as exhilarated as anyone could be. Whistle shared that sentiment as he regained his breath and looked up at the tall granite surrounding them. This was unbelievable, no one knew where he was besides Eric and that brought freedom to a whole new level. New bike, new world to see, the whole summer ahead of him, it was clearly time for Whistle to take life by the balls and experience everything he could.

The boys laid on a huge flat granite slab drying off in the afternoon sun, as happy as any two kids could be.

"Man, that was crazy!" Eric said.

"Yup." Enough said. With no other words spoken, they stayed there for another hour. Bright sun once again started to slide into the gorgeous colors of dusk. They hopped on their bikes and headed down the mountain back to town. Bikes in full tilt till they finally split ways to head home.

What a difference a day makes. As Whistle opened the apartment door, he had to laugh at how much better he felt than yesterday. Life was good even though he barely saw his mom due to her working so much. The upside was he got a real taste of freedom and he was going to enjoy it. The summer passed by and Whistle had all kinds of new adventures in the Capital City. Becoming a teenager seemed to hold endless promise throughout the long, hazy days and Whistle was going to soak it all in.

CHAPTER TWELVE
Summer Continues

Whistle did see his mom from time to time and they still had fun together, then a realization came to him. His mom was enjoying her new freedom just like he was. This actually made him feel a whole lot better because now he knew she still loved him. She was simply living a life of her own and that was a good thing.

With the worry of abandonment behind him, the adventures continued, like the whole gang crossing the train trestle, hoping not to hear the rumble of an oncoming locomotive in the distance until they were within spitting distance of the edge. The graveyard at the foothills of the quarry was massive to the boys. He discovered an island way out in the middle of the Merrimack River and walked a good ways upstream until he was sure not to get carried past once he jumped in the river and swam out to it. Happy to be spot on, Whistle pulled himself out of the water by a gigantic tree root and promptly laid on the wet, hard packed mud of the shore and took a moment to catch his breath. A light but cool breeze blew across the island. Slowly the warmth settled in and his mind started to think about this great new land he was about to explore. His mind put together a plan. He knew he would work counterclockwise along the shore. He got up, collected himself for a moment, and began to walk. Looking to his right, he filed away a slight thought about how far away the shore was and that he'd have to swim back at some point. Putting that thought out of his mind, he continued to explore.

So much to see and he devoured it all. Every rock along the shore was so clear to him. The way every step settled down was sent up through him and registered. River air entered his lungs, the rapids thundering in his ears. It was truly awesome to him. The walk continued on and the shade of the branches passed over his head. In his mind he was truly an explorer and he absolutely loved it. The boy was so lost in himself it took over an hour to walk all the way around the shoreline. Not so much because of how big the island was, but more due to how much detail he couldn't help but take in. Recognizing he was at the spot he started from, Whistle came back to reality a little. He glanced right again and saw the day getting older. He absolutely knew that the swim should be made right now. Looking up the middle part of the island with its trees and brush, concealing its mystery, the desire for exploration gripped him hard.

One more glance to his right, Whistle turned back, forward, and knew he was walking. He rationalized this with the thought of, *I still have some time. Just a little more.* So off he went and very soon the sun was quite blocked out by the foliage above. As his eyes adjusted, he started to take things in. The first thing he noticed were the smells. River smells blended with the scent of the woods. He was astounded at how different ecosystems could exist so close to each other. Smooth round river rocks were replaced by jagged granite fieldstones that provided homes for different kinds of moss to live.

A thing that really struck Whistle was how many chipmunks wove between the rocks, up and down the trees, calling to each other warnings of this new intruder they had never seen before. The boy felt bad about disturbing them, so he sat quietly and waited for them to settle. After a period of time things were quiet again, so he continued walking. With much less objection, the chipmunks watched.

He did a lot more exploring until he finally noticed he now could see almost nothing. *Oh no, this is not good.* He knew he needed to walk to the shoreline. Not remembering which way was which, he had a decision to make. After some thought, he decided to pick a line and go. He did an excellent job of keeping his line straight and eventually found the shore. Coming out of the trees by late dusk, he quickly realized he was on the wrong side of the island.

"Fuck," escaped his lips. Turning around to face the island again, he knew he had another decision to make. Should he try to pick a line straight through the deep heart of the island, facing darkness but saving a lot of precious time; or follow the shore, the safer route, but time consuming? Caution not really being his style, straight back into the woods he went. Into the trees, small spots of dusk from above afforded him some light. Once again, he did a rather good job of keeping his line straight. After a chunk of time with a lot of stumbling over roots and rocks, and two falls later, Whistle emerged on the right shore. Standing there, looking across at the riverbank that he couldn't make out, even Whistle knew a swim right now would be stupid.

Now he knew he was spending the night in this brand new land. It was exciting but terror was crawling in quickly. Vision almost completely vanished as night firmly took hold. Whistle hurried to find the best nook he could. After finding it, he hunkered down and hoped sleep would come.

Guess what?

No sleep came. His fear took him over. Bugs walked over him and sounds were amplified. The stars were the one thing he did notice about that night that was beautiful. As the night moved in it got colder, and Whistle knew a fire would bring heat, light, and most importantly a sense of security. There would be no fire that night and it was easily the longest, scariest night of his life. Curled up wide awake in his nook, his imagination continued to race with panic. The night passed as slowly as one could imagine. As the sun was just about to rise, Whistle relaxed just enough to finally fall asleep.

In what felt like the blink of an eye, Whistle woke up with the merciful morning sun blinding his eyes and the much friendlier songs of birds announcing a new day. Shielding his eyes, Whistle got up and stretched his stiff body, scratched at several bug bites acquired overnight, and gathered his wits to take on the long hard swim across the Merrimack River.

Ha sat on a rock, looked across the river, and knew time was of the essence. If his mom was home, what was she gonna say?

After a bit of psyching himself up for the task, he stood up, walked forward, and entered the ice cold water. His calves went numb as he went up to his knees, then his thighs, and of course, his business, which needless to say sent a jolt through his system. That's when he decided to just dive in head first. Just like that his breath left him and he was already drifting downstream rapidly. Swimming hard once again, things got scary fast. Swim, swim, swim, on and on. Limbs feeling so heavy, breathing extremely difficult, the feeling of getting nowhere all encompassing.

A thought struck him just then. *I must be a shitty swimmer because every time I go swimming, I almost drown.* Little did he realize at the time that he was actually an excellent swimmer, just too reckless in his risk assessment.

As minutes ticked by, he went downstream and tried to plug forward. With no memory of the rest of the swim, he finally reached the shore. Lying there, out of water from the waist up, he passed out. When he came to, he had no idea what time it was or where he was. Dragging himself out of the river, an ominous feeling set in. Somehow he found a gas station and got the key to the men's room around the side of the building.

Unlocking the door and entering, the heat felt wonderful and the acrid smell was horrific. He vomited a small amount of bile into the sink that left his throat burning. He washed his hands and face, rinsed his mouth out as best he could, and got ready to move on. Leaving the bathroom, he returned the key and started walking up the streets that ran parallel and upstream to the river he just barely survived. This was all done by instinct and feel because he was in completely unfamiliar territory. As he kept going, it was already past noon and hunger, thirst, and fatigue all but drained him.

Then something happened that Whistle would certainly never forget. He came around a corner in a still unfamiliar area and there was a Burger King. The rear of the building abutted a vacant lot that led back down to the river. Feeling much despair about his situation, he started to notice certain details. First off was the garden hose at the back of the Burger King. Walking up to it, noticing the greasy feel of his steps on the concrete, he turned it on and instantly drank the water. The lukewarm water turned colder and Whistle could instantly feel the benefit of it inside his body. Things became clearer just like that.

After his thirst was quenched, he was instantly reminded how hungry he was. Dumpster? Let's check it out. Sure enough, it was easy to pluck so much wasted food out. A couple of cups of hose water, plenty of food later, head and hands as clean as possible, Whistle found himself in the back of that deserted lot safe from any trouble.

This good boy ate and drank until sleep took him over. This time, nestled down in the brush, sleep gripped him hard. When he finally woke up, dusk was coming around again.

"Fuck," he whispered for the second day in a row. Still not knowing where he was, he got up and continued on his way. The boy was actually more than six miles from the apartment. Walking kept up and dark came quick. At least he felt good after sleeping, eating, and drinking, so he walked on. But still, what was his mom gonna say? After walking for a long time, he finally recognized his surroundings, which was a huge relief. Now in familiar territory, he finally made it home. He opened the door and there was his mom.

"Where have you been, Whistle? I was scared out of my wits!" she exclaimed. This boy who did nothing wrong had to now try to explain to his mom that honest adventure simply couldn't hold him back.

"Mom, I'm tired. Can we talk about this later?" he said, obviously exhausted.

"Okay, but we're talking about this tomorrow." Fair enough, as they went to their bedrooms and shut off the apartment lights. Whistle slept deeper than he had in a few days and it was well needed. He couldn't believe everything he just went through. What an unbelievable experience he just had. Truly, most kids his age had no clue about stuff like this. Certainly none of the gang, and even Eric had no clue. An absolute adventure that he would keep to himself. His own treasure, a jewel just for him. *I guess I'll deal with Mom tomorrow, but I wouldn't trade any of it for the world.*

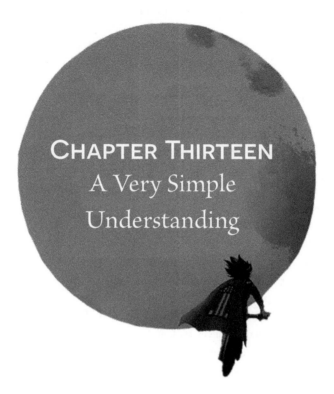

CHAPTER THIRTEEN
A Very Simple Understanding

In late morning, Whistle woke up to the sounds of kitchen noises. Pots, pans, plates, silverware cling clanging busily. The smell of butter, bacon, coffee, the faint smell of cigarette smoke. His hunger activated, Whistle's mom placed a tasty plate in front of him. He started to devour it as she sat before him with her own plate. Silently, they ate for a while. After they both were edging toward full, and just picking, they began to talk.

"Whistle?" Mom asked.

"Yes?" as he took a bite of delicious bacon.

"I want us to talk because I haven't seen you in a couple of days, and I'm a little worried," she hedged, trying to sound as motherly as possible. Suddenly, a tinge of anger flooded through him. He was not a small boy anymore and definitely didn't like being treated like one.

"Yes, we should talk because I haven't seen you in days." Heels digging in. This struck his mom, and he saw weakness flit across her eyes. At that moment, his heart filled with understanding. He understood that his mom was imperfect, good and bad all at once.

"Mom, I'm sorry I didn't come home last night, but you have to understand that adventure captured me and I had to go."

"What do you mean adventure captured you?" she asked, confused.

"I have to see everything."

Whistle's mom had no idea what to say to this, so she just looked at him silently. They looked at each other awkwardly, but still knew they loved each other. Whistle grew up a lot that day.

"What do you mean you have to see everything?" his mom asked.

"Mom, no one understands me but I have to go everywhere and see everything." With that they both knew their worlds were splitting apart. Whistle was craving exploration and his mom leaned toward a single, comfortable life.

"I love you," his mom said.

"I love you too," Whistle responded. "I'm growing up and I absolutely have to go where I have to go."

"I know, and I want to explore my new life as well."

At that moment, a simple understanding came to both of them.

"Well, go have fun today," his mom said.

"You too," Whistle answered.

From that point on, their relationship was less mother and child and more like roommates. It was sad to Whistle, but he understood. He would always love his mom, but he would never look at her as a protector again. So the understanding between the two of them was reached. "I love you, you love me, but let's go see what there is to see out there."

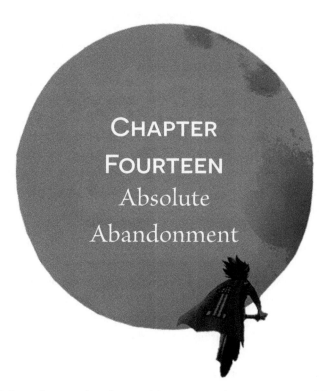

CHAPTER
FOURTEEN
Absolute
Abandonment

Eighth grade started and everything was starting to even out. Mom working, Eric by his side, and his imagination working overtime. He even began to accept his new apartment as a home. The school year marched on. Halloween, Thanksgiving, Christmas, New Year's, all were fun and enjoyable. The boredom of school didn't even bother him anymore. He knew how to get around that. Simply get up, walk out of class, not a word to the teacher and not a word back. Go down to the lower wing and check out all the shop classes and chat with whoever was around. Those teachers were really easy going down there and couldn't care less about a skipped class here and there. Walk back up to the front office and tell them he had a dentist appointment.

"Okay, see you tomorrow," the secretary said without looking up.

So easy, he thought to himself. "Alright, let's see what the afternoon has in store!"

School ended and he met Eric at the park. The boys had fun defending the compound from Indians, slaying the three-headed dragon that towered over them. They even found time to destroy the asteroid headed for earth, threatening all of mankind. As night rolled in, they headed home.

"See ya."

"See ya."

Walking home, Whistle had a bit of an uncomfortable feeling in his stomach. He didn't know why because this was just like any other day. He walked up onto the porch and slid his key in. Quarter turn of the lock and he opened the door. No lights and silence welcomed him. Whistle instantly knew his mom wasn't home again. Microwave dinner and some mindless television later, the boy went to bed. As he lay there he was well aware he was all alone. His mom was not there and something felt very wrong. He tried to ignore this and sent his mind to adventure. After all, his mom rarely came home at night since they moved there. So why should tonight be any different? But it was and Whistle could feel it. Something was just not right. Around one in the morning, Whistle drifted off, finally forgetting everything that was bothering him. Dreams worked their way in and off to slumber he went.

The next morning came and the boy got up, used the bathroom, got dressed and headed downstairs. Still his mom was not home. He heated up a couple of strawberry pop tarts and washed them down with a big glass of grapefruit juice. He grabbed his backpack and headed off to school for another day. That afternoon, his mom still wasn't home.

The weekend came and went with absolutely no fun because Whistle could not let go of the fact that his mom hadn't been home and didn't even call. He knew his mom was making a lot of mistakes, for instance dating a real dirt bag that she met at the bar where she worked. This guy, who seemingly had a natural dislike for the boy, but disguised it in "good-natured" ribbing, seemed to be setting up a "him or me" situation without saying as much. Whistle could feel it nonetheless. Plus the boy noticed the smell of weed on his mom when he did see her, and her eyes now had a frantic, there-but-not-there look about them. She seemed to always have her mind on something other than her son at all times now and it hurt the boy deeply.

Whistle and his mom always respected each other's privacy, but after she hadn't come home for multiple nights, he decided to go in her room and see if there were any clues as to what was going on. The first thing he noticed was the smell of something that had been burnt, but not weed or cigarettes, something else, almost a chemical smell. The mix of perfume and her boyfriend's body odor made it tough to decipher. The room was a mess and the bed was unmade as well. The boy had a sick, nervous feeling that started to grow in his stomach.

The closet door was slightly open and he went in and was shocked by what he saw. Empty hangers, suitcases gone, and a handful of spoons in the corner of the floor that had been burnt in the middle.

"Oh fuck no," Whistle moaned to himself. He turned around and went to the bureau. Opening drawers, he saw no socks, no underwear, no T-shirts and no jeans. Refusing to believe what his brain already knew, Whistle walked around the entire house like a zombie. He started to notice various knickknacks missing.

That's when it truly hit him. Whistle's mom had skipped town without even so much as a note. When was she coming back? WAS she planning to come back? He had no way of knowing as she clearly hadn't been acting like herself lately. The boy went to bed and cried for hours until exhaustion finally allowed him to sleep.

The next morning came and he woke up happy for all of two seconds before reality reasserted itself in his waking mind. Whistle curled up in a ball and tried in vain to go back to sleep. After about fifteen minutes, he realized it was no use and got up to make himself breakfast. As he ate, he came to the conclusion that his school days were over as far as he was concerned. He had bigger problems to tend to, like figuring out what he was going to do. Days went by, the phone would ring from time to time, but he would never answer. If it was important enough, they'd leave a message. He could barely muster up the will to even take a shower or change his clothes. At the door more and more mail piled up, as well as newspapers.

One morning there was a knock at the door. It was a familiar knock, followed by a familiar voice.

"Hey! Whistle! Open up," Eric shouted in his good-natured haranguing tone.

"Whistle! Open up, dickhead!" Again, trying his best to sound upbeat.

Whistle was in no mood or condition to deal with anyone, so he just sat still, hoping Eric would give up and go away sooner rather than later. He had just poured himself a bowl of milk and cereal, which was sitting there getting soggy as Whistle sat like a statue.

"Oh, what the fuck!" Whistle muttered to himself as Eric stood at the front door, alternately knocking, yelling, and trying to peer through the windows. Finally, the concerned pal's silhouette seemed to disappear as Whistle watched, hoping to see him hop on his bike and head home, so he could eat breakfast in peace...not a chance.

"I see you fuckhead! Let me in," Eric shouted through the kitchen window, standing on some milk crates.

Whistle didn't respond, he just exhaled and seemed to deflate after sitting perfectly still, holding his breath for who knows how long. Gathering his strength of will, he eventually got up to go let Eric in.

"What do you want?" Whistle asked in a resigned tone.

"Where have you been?" Eric asked.

"Here."

"Well, no shit. I mean, why haven't you been at school?"

"Dude, my mom took off. I have no idea where she is."

"I do," Eric said, getting Whistle's attention in a hurry.

"Wait, what?"

"Yeah. She got arrested. My mom's friend's husband is on the force, Detective Brenner. I guess they caught her shoplifting, and she had coke on her too."

"What...the...FUCK?!" Whistle was so shocked he forgot to chew his Cheerios.

"Yeah, she was with that guy from the bar, I guess."

"Of course...Fucking piece of shit."

"Well look, I guess they want you to go down to the station. They need to figure out what happens with you while she's serving her sentence."

"What do you mean?" Whistle asked.

"I don't know. I imagine they need to figure out who you're going to stay with and how you're going to get to school and whatever."

"I'm not going back to school and I'll stay right here, I can take care of myself."

"You don't have to convince me, man. Just go down there and figure it out. Brenner's cool. He's been over the house for cookouts and stuff."

"Ok," Whistle responded. With that, Eric took off to leave Whistle to ponder his future.

CHAPTER

FIFTEEN

Transition

Leads to Change

Whistle rode his bike into town that afternoon and caught about a foot of air off the curb at the edge of the entrance to the police station. He set his bike in the rack out front. Realizing he forgot his lock at home, he figured if someone had the audacity to steal a bike directly in front of a police station, they deserved it.

"Hello. I'm here to see Detective Brenner," Whistle said to the woman at the window.

"Do you have an appointment?" the woman asked.

"Uh...no. I...uhhhh didn't know I—"

"One moment, please." The woman cut him off, sliding the window closed just shy of a slam.

"Come on in," Whistle heard as he looked up from the "Just Say No" brochure he picked up to avoid staring into space like a zombie while he was waiting.

"I'm Detective Brenner. Have a seat."

"I'm..." the boy started to reply.

"I know who y'are, pal." Detective Brenner smiled. "You need a drink? Soda machine down the hall, I'm buyin'."

"Sure," Whistle said, starting to relax a little.

"Great...Let's take a walk."

The two walked down the all-business tile hallway and it didn't take long for the detective to break the silence.

"I'm assuming you know what happened?" he asked the boy matter-of-factly.

"Yeah," Whistle answered, assuming the veteran cop was a "just the facts" man.

"Ok well, legally we can't let you stay alone while all this gets worked out."

"I'm fine, I know how to feed and clean myself. I'm not going to go play in traffic."

"I've met thirty year olds that don't have those kind of credentials. But, you're a minor and the law is the law. We have a place you can stay for a few days and a nice lady that's gonna help you out with anything you need. Next week we're going to have a place set up for you with a really nice couple about an hour south of here until everything gets worked out."

"How long is that?" Whistle demanded.

"I don't know. Hopefully not that long, just have to take it one day at a time. We're here to help, buddy. Let's go downstairs and we'll get you all set up in your room."

Whistle got settled in what seemed to be an empty office with a TV and cot. He was brought by the apartment to get his things. He got the feeling the staff at the station weren't set up for this kind of thing, and were kind of forced into babysitting. The weekend passed and Sunday night came. Like it or not, he was getting sent south the next morning. He lay on the cot that night sleepless, and despair completely engulfed him.

He whispered in the night, "God, it's Whistle. I know I don't talk to you a lot, but I really need your help right now. I'm lost, please help me." He finally fell asleep for a short while.

"Whistle," someone said quietly.

"Huh?" he responded, barely awake.

"It's time to get up."

"What?" As he came to that morning, a feeling of abandonment overcame him. Nothing and no one left to turn to, and he was being sent away. As he opened his eyes he saw a pleasant looking woman who reminded him of Ms. Fisher, his kindergarten teacher.

"What's going on?" he said, trying to collect himself.

"Whistle, I'm Allie West, and you have a big day ahead of you." Her soft brown eyes looked at him with compassion.

"Yeah, I got it. I'm getting put in the van and sent down south. I'll meet some people who I can't stand but will be expected to live with them. Don't worry about it. I realize you're just doing your job, but this sucks."

"Whistle, you're not going to be sent south," Allie replied.

"What?" More confusion.

"You have a friend, Eric? Well his parents have asked that you come live with them." Her comforting, honest eyes gave him the slightest start of trust. He was so damaged that his guard was automatically up.

"Yes. They are all waiting for you at their house. All your stuff from the apartment has been brought over, so all you have to do is pack your bag here and I will drive you over," Allie said.

Whistle packed his belongings and got in the car and took the ride to Eric's house. When they got there, he got out and thanked Allie. Once again, Whistle looked at a new situation and took in as much as he could in the moment. He once again squared his shoulders, walked up to the house, and across the porch to the front door. With no hesitation he knocked and waited.

One bag over his shoulder, the door opened and Eric's mom welcomed him.

"Come on in," Mrs. Flow said. "I'll show you to your room." As they entered the room to the back right corner of the house, Whistle noticed that all his belongings from the apartment were there. He was touched by the kind gesture and thankful that he didn't have to set foot in that apartment. Tears instantly flowed down his face and he was embarrassed.

"I'm sorry Mrs. Flow and thank you so much." She hugged him very hard without a word said, and Whistle felt loved for the first time in a long time.

Closing the door with his small bag over his shoulder, he looked around the room. The afternoon sun poured in, covering a four by eight block on the carpet. The bed was a simple New England single. Knitted quilt. French bureaus, crisp, clean pillows and sheets. Bright, white, and laid out evenly. He shut the light off and went to bed.

The next morning he woke up and looked at all his neatly stacked belongings. Five boxes contained his whole life. Oh, and one over the shoulder bag. He unpacked in no time and when was almost done there was a knock at the door.

He opened the door and was relieved to see Eric. He hugged him and was thankful to have at least one person in the world to turn to.

"Let's go," Eric said.

"Where are we going?" asked Whistle.

"Don't worry about it," Eric shot back over his shoulder as he walked out of the room. Sitting up, the boy had no idea what was coming. All he really knew was he loved it, whatever "it" was.

"Now what?" Whistle asked with anticipation. Quickly Eric was gone and Whistle followed. Before he knew it, he was standing in a clearing in the middle of the woods. Sun poured down into the clearing, heating up the bed of pine needles.

"What are we doing?" asked Whistle. Then just like that, Eric turned and sprinted toward the far end of the clearing. Whistle ran as hard as he could to catch him. He finally came to the edge where the woods began and the sun was blocked by the tall pines. Flashbacks of monarchs at recess in grade school stirred in his memory as he looked for Eric. After a while, with no luck, he decided to head back.

"Whistle," Eric called.

"Whistle!" again.

"Where are you?" Whistle replied.

"Come here!"

Whistle followed the sound of Eric's voice deeper into the woods. As he continued, he realized he was standing at the opening of a cave.

"Eric?"

"Yes, come here!"

Whistle stepped down as his eyes adjusted.

"Where are you?" he asked again, confused.

"Keep walking," Eric replied from the dark.

Continuing on, Whistle walked down into the damp, musty tunnel. Taking a left, feeling his way along the walls, he eventually found Eric in a tiny lighted room, down a deep tunnel.

He was surprised to see him sitting there in the middle of the room with a huge joint hanging out of his mouth.

"Dude?!" Whistle exclaimed, confused. "What are you doing?"

"Step in," Eric said as he gestured for him to sit down. Whistle could barely move in the tiny room.

"How you doin'?" Eric's voice echoed through the cave.

"What?"

"Are you okay?"

"Yeah, give me that," Whistle answered as he took the joint and hit it. As he held in the smoke, his whole life flashed before him and everything became clear.

Mom, Jack, Ms. Fisher, Mikey, Dale Brenner and even Allie West. *Holy Moly! I guess it's time to grow up.* Passing the joint, Whistle waited while Eric took a hit and held it in. One more drag for Whistle and he was off to dreamland.

Chapter Sixteen
Whistle's Dream

The pot in Whistle, sleep did not come hard. Drifting off, the boy was finally comfortable. Three, two, one, blast off……

"What? What's going on? Fuck no, I'm the boy that is supposed to catch trout out of the river. The river in New Hampshire where I feel comfortable. Please leave me alone."

There was no leaving Whistle alone that night. He was strapped into the shuttle and headed for space. Blast off!

He remembered hearing the roar of the engines and feeling the power of the whole experience. Overwhelming is not the word. Who would have thought Whistle could be an astronaut? His dream went like this…..

"Hello, my name is Whistle Evel Fonzarelli Starr, and I'm in space. I remember coming up here and I was so lost. Listen to me. If your space suit has a leak, you're screwed. Let's do this." The door opened and Whistle walked out. His steps were gigantic, slow and effortless compared to back on earth. To Whistle's credit he moved forward with an aggressive attitude. Rock and roll!

He stood on the moon, looking back toward the earth, and breath escaped him. Looking up toward blackness and stars, he continued forward. Once again, squared shoulders with him, every step he took was like four steps. Comfortable confidence grew within as he worked his way over grey hill after grey hill. He even started to think he had earned the experience. Well, that was until Whistle crested the next grey hill.

Looking down, he saw something that had to be man or alien made.

"What the hell?!" resonated through his helmet. Bounce stepping down the hill, things made sense.

"Holy shit!" Whistle yelled and tried to run toward the object. He quickly learned that running on the moon actually gets you nowhere fast. He had to calm himself so he could continue his slow bounce step down. The lesson learned was lack of gravity and running just aren't compatible.

Finally making it to the bottom of the hill, Whistle stood in front of something he couldn't believe. He was very aware of the lack of noise coming from his respirator due to the fact that his breath was simply taken away. Space is a silent void, but when you're not even breathing silence is truly at its fullest.

There before Whistle stood the American flag from the first moon endeavor. Standing straight out, crisp and new as it was since the day it was planted. Talk about one small step for man and one giant leap for mankind! He fully understood this, and all confidence drained away. Humility quickly took over. Trying to breathe again, his breath came short and labored.

Whistle turned to his left and put his hand on the iconic Red, White and Blue. Taking in every stripe, every star, and yet again every stitch. Even the way the lack of gravity easily slid it back into its original position.

"Amazing," Whistle said, aware that he was now out of air. He had been out too long.

"What a greedy adventurer," he said to himself. Turning back to his right, the view of the earth filled his field of vision. So there between the American flag and the view of the earth, Whistle almost passed away and he knew his body would stay there perfectly preserved for eternity, never to return back to earth again.

CHAPTER
SEVENTEEN
Wake and Walk

*I*f I'm dead, why am I shaking so hard? Whistle's first thought threaded through his brain. With a good amount of effort, he finally opened his left eye. His right was still sealed with gunk. His eye opening didn't help him at all because pitch black was there. Closing his eyes, he uncomfortably fell back to sleep.

Three hours later, a similar thing happened. He opened his left eye with no success on the right. Now his freezing shaking made him realize that he had to do something or he could easily be in trouble. Pitch black still encased him. This boy did realize that he had to prioritize his needs so he stopped. Listening, he heard water dripping off the ceiling just to his right. Putting his hand out, he felt where it was dripping from. Laying down, Whistle opened his mouth and tasted the beauty of fresh cave water dripping. Still in blackness, he slowly rehydrated his body. He felt his thirst quenched. He also felt freezing cold. Small amount of drifting to sleep, but not really. Finally the cave water dripping on his face unsealed his right eye. Both eyes now opened, but still blackness. Lying in a dangerously cold situation, Whistle felt beyond desperate.

"Eric!" he yelled as loud as he could.

Echo coming off the cave walls, Whistle stood up. With no answer, Whistle listened and felt his way. He remembered that he was in a cave that ran right to left. Or was it left to right?

"Eric!" Waiting.......Nothing. Still no daylight, Whistle was feeling that he was done. Just then, Whistle noticed a slight wind coming from his right. "My way out?" he asked himself. "Maybe, but go up toward the cold, or down to the heat. Usually heat rises and cold sinks. So why, in this case, is heat pouring down and cold ripping up to the top of this cave?"

As a boy, Whistle did not have the best skills, but his instinct took over. *I am freezing, so why wouldn't I follow the heat? That is a resource I can utilize.* So he began to walk toward the warmth.

"Eric!" Whistle yelled just as his sneaker struck something soft.

"Umph." This from the ground below.

"Eric?" he asked quietly. Click, click, click, a lighter lit.

"Shit, the flashlight's dead. Well, let's go. Do you know what time it is?" Eric asked.

"No idea," Whistle responded. Good thing Whistle ran into Eric because he got up, stretched with a yawn, and walked toward the direction of the cold, knowing exactly where he was going. The only reason he went slow was because it was pitch black. Whistle followed, thinking to himself, *What if I continued toward the warmth all by myself? How far would I go, and where would I end up? At the end of wherever I was going, would I have made it or would I have died? Imagine that, die in your dream only to wake up and die in real life.* As these thoughts stole his attention, Whistle lagged behind a little.

"Whistle," Eric called.

"Huh?" Whistle responded.

"Let's go!" Eric again.

The two boys walked slowly forward. After walking for what seemed like an eternity, and taking endless turns in the dark, the two boys finally stepped out of the mouth of the cave. This was great, but what wasn't great was that their surroundings were barely visible as it was now night time, and the stars were the only light source on this moonless night.

"Aw fuck, Whistle. It's after dark and we're in trouble."

What else's new? Whistle thought to himself. They made their way back through the clearing and back to Eric's house. Sneaking up, they looked through the window at the clock on the kitchen stove, which read 2:38 a.m.

"Man! Okay, follow me," Eric whispered. He followed as they made their way to the back door. It was unlocked and with minimal noise, they entered the house. A short tiptoe later, the boys took a left and entered Eric's room. A quiet click and the door was closed. Looking at each other, they couldn't believe they had gotten away with it. Giggling, neither boy was the slightest bit tired. One, they had just spent hours passed out, dreaming deep in a dark cave. Two, the adrenaline of the whole adventure coursed through their veins.

They spent the next few hours lost in whispered conversation, talking about everything that had just happened.

"Eric, that was the first time I've ever smoked weed. I remember seeing you sitting on the floor with that joint in your mouth. I remember you telling me to sit and handing me the joint. I also remember taking a drag off of it and feeling the burn in my throat. I waited a second and took another, still felt nothing and took another."

"I know, I didn't think you were ever going to hand it back," Eric interrupted, laughing. "That's where the saying 'Puff, puff, pass' comes from!" Both now were laughing a little too loud.

"Shhh…" Eric was still chuckling with his right index finger to his lips.

"I remember watching you do your thing, then you handed it back to me. I took another drag and that was it. Eric, it was like my mind shot to a different level! I remember we went back and forth for a while then it happened," Whistle whispered.

"What happened?" Eric asked.

"My friend, I was on the moon! I walked in zero gravity. I looked back at the earth and touched the moon mission American flag. Eric, I even died on the moon." Whistle was now getting emotional.

"Wow!" True awe in Eric's voice.

"Fuck yeah, wow!" Whistle agreed.

"Whistle, I was standing on the very top of the Empire State Building needle. I had absolutely no fear up there. It was night and a firm wind blew by. If I looked east, all I could see was blackness where the Atlantic Ocean stretched out toward Europe. If I looked west, city and town lights sprawled on forever. I could even see the black line of the Mississippi River separating east from west. Then when I was done, I just walked down the side of the building with no effort until I was standing on the sidewalk."

Eric finished his story and they both sat in silence for a while. With nothing else to say, they finally dozed off. When they awoke later that morning, they were starving. They walked out to the kitchen to see Mr. and Mrs. Flow sitting at the kitchen table with their coffee and newspaper.

"Good morning," Eric said, and guess what? They surely were in trouble yet again. They both felt it was worth it anyway.

That summer passed with some good times, but mostly bad times. Thoughts of his mother filled his head. Warm days turned cooler and ninth grade approached. Considering what he had been through, going to a new school was not nearly as worrisome as it used to be. Whistle was determined to walk in with his head held high and shoulders squared. He was a man now.

CHAPTER EIGHTEEN
High School!

Finally the day came. Whistle woke up as optimistic as any boy could be. Wait, as any MAN could be. After all, Whistle Evel Fonzarelli Starr was going to start high school on top come hell or high water. There he stood, looking at yet another new school. It was so huge and he knew almost no one. He wasn't all that bothered by this and he walked in and looked for his first class. The bricks, tile floors, and gleaming windows were more numerous than he ever thought. Every other school Whistle had been to, waned in comparison to this. Talk about feeling lost. Truly lost.

Walking through the front doors, Whistle noticed the massive trophy case to his right. So many heroes looking at him. A most daunting situation indeed. Walking a bit further, he saw the principal's office on the left.

"I'm sure you'll get to know me," the boy said under his breath. No, it was going to be different this time. He was a new person and he was going to make good.

Walking down the tiled hallway, his mother's memory flooded his emotions. Her laughter and love, abandonment, and selfishness as well. What a double edged sword. What a beautifully cruel world we live in. He finally took a right and walked up the stairs. Walking into that hallway, all sensations hit him at once. The color of the lockers, the odd smells coming from the biology lab, and the sound of students and teachers coming and going, tending to high school matters large and small. All hustle and bustle on the first day of school.

Everything in high school was tightly structured and more grown up. This was ideal for Whistle as he longed to keep his mind occupied and staying busy was a good way to avoid feeling awkward and alone. High school might be alright after all.

Just as he was about to head to his first class, Whistle had a flashback to the monarch days. Mikey, oranges, blacks, sun, shade, school bells, trouble, life and death swirled in his mind at a dizzying pace. Snapping out of it, he continued on. Passing room after room of teachers giving instructions and telling the students what to do. Whistle already knew he didn't want any part of it.

Walking forward, he finally found his room. Taking a right, he entered and noticed a girl in a jean jacket. Her dark curls fell flowing around her face. She smiled and Whistle blushed with no idea why.

"Hello," she said, flashing a wholesome smile.

"Hey," was all he could sputter. Walking away slightly embarrassed, he made his way to the back of the room. He got his back row seat, smack dab in the middle, but he still felt slightly uneasy. Sitting down, he was surrounded by the din of pre class conversations. Nervousness welled up inside him as he looked around. A paper plane flew over his head and some girl laughed loudly from across the room. He began to feel claustrophobic as he tried to slow his breathing but the buzzing of the fluorescent lights was adding to his anxiety. He was about to get up and leave when the teacher walked in.

"Sit down! Quiet! Sit," she demanded. The din died down and everybody sat. At this point Whistle evaluated the whole room. Teacher up front with her white blouse, grey skirt, and practical black shoes. Hair in a tight ponytail and not a trace of makeup. Boys and girls sitting in a uniformed grid, waiting to do whatever the teacher tells them to.

Whistle was starting to feel squirrely. Not comfortable with any of this. Just like that, it occurred to him. *I've got to go! I got to go spread through life fully.* He stood up and started to make his way to the door.

"Mr. Starr, where are you going?" This coming from the one and only high school teacher he would ever know.

"I don't know, but as long as it's not here, I figure I might be on the right track." Turning his back, he walked out of the room. His walk continued down the hallway, down the stairs, through the lobby with its trophy case, and outside through the main doors. As he walked down the hill, he felt the warm sun on his face. It felt good. With the first step off the school property, he knew he was free and there was no turning back. Most definitely the shortest high school career ever. Fourteen and a dropout without even sitting through one class. Oh well, here we go....

Whistle spent the rest of the day walking back to Eric's house. When he finally got there, no one was home. Sliding through the back door, Whistle made his way to the basement. Digging around down there, he came across an old olive army backpack. Stenciled on it was "E. Flow." Obviously, Eric's dad's backpack from Vietnam. Whistle felt ashamed and proud all at once because he knew stealing was wrong, but the backpack would be put to good use as he was about to go on a great adventure, at least that was the plan.

Continuing upstairs and into his room, Whistle started to stuff things into the pack. Not paying attention to what he was packing, the boy just kept going until there was no more room. When he was done, the pack went on his back. It was heavy but felt good, and he squared his shoulders. Whistle walked out of his room, leaving behind most of his belongings. Feeling thankful for the Flows' generosity, he stood in the front yard. Suddenly Eric entered his mind.

"Eric, I'm sorry but I have to go. I love you, but this place is not for me. I have to see what else is out there. I know I'll see you again someday."

Wiping tears from his eyes, stepping off the lawn, he started south. Ironic because that's precisely what he didn't want to do just a few months ago. Regardless, as it stood that day, that's the direction his gut took him.

He spent the rest of the day weaving his way through neighborhoods, over fences, through side yards with an occasional stop for a drink out of a garden hose. Time passed and the sun started setting. With a golden hue sitting heavy in the autumn sky, Whistle finally made it to Interstate 93. Looking around, he took it all in. Glaring sun setting in the west, cars and trucks roaring by, he made his way to a thicket of pines. Exhausted, he made a bed out of the rust colored dry needles and used his recently acquired backpack as a pillow. He laid down and before long was lulled to sleep by the sound of the evening traffic. Life felt really good and freedom was finally in his grasp. Wow!

CHAPTER NINETEEN
Down Day

The next morning, Whistle woke up very peacefully. Stretching, he looked to his right and saw a beautiful deer looking at him. Not moving, he held his breath. The deer slowly moved towards him. Whistle was absolutely stunned by this. Frozen, he lay there as the deer moved closer. Whistle could hear its hooves tapping lightly on the leaves and pine needles. Closer it came, and Whistle kept still. He had seen many deer in his life but never like this.

The whole experience washed over him and goose bumps appeared everywhere they could. The deer moved closer and Whistle stayed silent. Motionless, he watched as the deer cautiously walked up to his feet. The deer proceeded to take everything in, smelling and looking everywhere. Whistle lay motionless as the animal sniffed him over.

Finally, the deer came up to his face. Whistle could hear it breathing in and out. His exhale went into her inhale. He cautiously opened his eyes. Looking back at him were gorgeous black eyes. No judgment, no ridicule, just understanding. Whistle felt peace as he lay there looking at her. Absolutely expecting the deer to run, the oddest thing happened. Something that could only happen to Whistle. She pressed her forehead firmly against Whistle's to let him know she was in charge and didn't sense a threat from him.

Whistle was blown away by this as he remained as still as possible, and then something even more amazing happened. The beautiful creature bedded down next to a very vulnerable Whistle. After some time, he slowly put his hand on her forehead. She breathed deeply and Whistle knew she was asleep. He drifted off with the heat of the gentle, trusting animal next to him. This was absolutely magical until the deer woke up.

Whistle awoke to a cluckin' and buckin' deer. Before he knew it, his ass was fully kicked. That loving deer worked Whistle every angle to Sunday and walked away without a care in the world. Unfortunately, this lesson was driven instantly into the boy's mind. I only say unfortunately because a little more of Whistle's trust in the world eroded. Lying there, black and blue in the pine needles, the boy started to collect himself.

"Let's see," he said. "How can I be so nice to a deer and she fucks me over like this?" was his next thought. His jaw was sore and his right shoulder was on fire. He actually wound up with a very clear hoof bruise directly in the middle of his forehead. Pulling up the needles around him, Whistle decided he was going nowhere. Beat up, hungry and thirsty, Whistle lay there, a mass of bruises and confusion.

Beautiful sun poured down and warmed him. He knew cold was coming, so instead of trying to make his way south, for the time being he would hunker down and just be. That exit where 93 and 89 met would be his home for the night. Amazingly, sleep came easy to Whistle. He felt very comfortable sleeping in the pine needles. Spider bites and bee stings equaled freedom as far as Whistle was concerned. The boy spent the rest of the day lost in thought. Sore but comfortable, he took everything in. So lost but so found poured through him. *I win, I lose, all at once. What's a fourteen-year-old boy supposed to do?*

Whistle decided he would take the rest of the day off. Pulling pine needles up with him, Whistle got up and took a look at the freeway. Lights ripping by, he felt secure in his little spot in the upper pines. He felt a benevolent force watching over him and somehow knew he was on the right path. Whistle spent the rest of the day relaxing and eventually sleeping soundly through the night. He would need to get as much rest as he could because traveling was most certainly on the agenda as the next move.

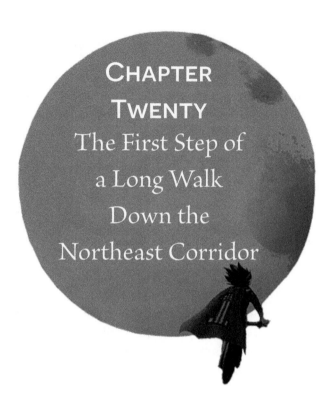

CHAPTER
TWENTY
The First Step of
a Long Walk
Down the
Northeast Corridor

Whistle woke up with a dry throat and the sun in his eyes. Disoriented and groggy, he started to look around. The traffic below continued to chug on by. Standing up, the boy shook his hands through his hair. Needles floated down around him as he gathered his wits. The memory of the deer from the day before appeared with a sharp jolt of pain in his ribs as he stretched. Suddenly it occurred to him that he had a choice to make.

Turn back and head to the Flows' house where stability resided. Go to school, get your diploma, and move on. Get a good job, find a nice wife and have a couple of kids. March steadily forward through life. Maybe even have a grandkid or two and ride into the sunset right in line with the manual.

Or square up, rock and roll, put New Hampshire to your back and go.

Guess what, Whistle Evel Fonzarelli Starr started walking south. He spent the day walking through the woods and backyards. Almost no distance gained before the sun already started setting again. Whistle walked for a while longer until he arrived at a backyard that caught his eye.

The first thing he did was wash his face and hands in the below ground pool. After that, he made his way to the pool house. Fortunately, it was unlocked and Whistle let himself in. The smell of chlorine and cedar was a welcome reminder of more carefree times. He looked around to familiarize himself with the layout and contents of the pool house, taking advantage of the last faint rays of daylight.

There in the middle of the room was a hot tub. Behind it was a kitchenette with a refrigerator; to the right, a day bed that appeared beyond comfortable. He chugged an entire bottle of water, taking a few moments to catch his breath and relax. Grabbing another bottle and a can of Pringles, he walked over to the hot tub, stripped, and got in.

After sitting for a while, letting the hot tub work its wonders on his tired, bruised body and finishing the can of Pringles, he got out and dried off with a towel he found hanging on the wall.

Feeling horrible about using whoever's pool house this was, he looked around for a pencil and paper. Finally, he found a box of crayons and a box of Kleenex. Ripping the back off, the boy started to write.

> To whom it may concern,
> Thank you for your shelter. I know you don't know me, but I fully appreciate your help. Thank you so much for the water and Pringles. Someday I hope to be able to pay you back.
> Your unknown friend,
> Whistle Starr

He put the green crayon back in the container and set the note on the counter. He looked over at the burnt orange comforter draped over the day bed. It looked so comfortable he just fell back on it, and curled up into a ball and fell into a deep sleep.

"Hello?" came a voice from right outside the window.

"Huh?" was all Whistle could muster.

"Motherfucker, you're in my pool house and I will shoot you!"

"What?! I'm just passing through! I was tired and thirsty. I ate some Pringles and drank some water; I swear I will pay you back!"

Trying to avoid trouble, Whistle stayed still. Before he knew it a massive left knee pinned him to the bed. A right hand clamped around his throat. Dealing with a Glock nine-mil pinned against his forehead, Whistle tried to think.

"Sir?" was all he could think of. The grip around his throat tightened substantially and his vision started to go dark.

"Sir?" Again, pleading. Feeling the knee and hand ease up a bit, Whistle took in a tremendous breath of fresh night air and was staring at a man who clearly knew what he was doing.

"What the fuck are you doing here, boy?" Nine millimeter pointed straight at his face.

"Sir, I'm just trying to walk south, I don't want any trouble. I am sorry if I insulted you in any way!" With virtually no effort, Whistle was yanked up, jerked right, and thrown against the back wall. With the wind knocked out of him, he stood breathless.

Trying to inhale a breath that wouldn't come, his vision faded in and out. His ears rang, and vulnerability showed its face entirely. While he was trying to keep his knees from buckling, he saw the huge man step forward. *Oh no!* he thought. *This is it!* As a giant silhouette approached rapidly, he felt two massive hands grab him by the front of his shirt.

"Sit down, boy," came to him from a great distance away. He felt himself being manually seated. The next thing he knew, he felt mercifully cool water against his lips. Opening his mouth, the coolness came in and he started to swallow greedily.

"Whoa boy, slow down or you'll make yourself sick," the man said. Pause, drink, silence, repeat. This continued for some time and Whistle regained his bearings as his breathing began to regulate. Slowly, some clarity returned to the boy. In the orange glow of a couple of floor lamps, the crisper light from the pool coming through the front window, and a few lit candles glowing on the center coffee table, Whistle looked around.

"Who are you?" the man rightfully asked. His face glowed in the candlelight as he leaned across the table. Whistle, still dazed, was lost in the contrast of the orange and blue light.

"I asked you a question," the man persisted, though in a much less threatening way this time.

"I'm sorry sir, what was your question?"

"Who are you?"

"My name is Whistle Evel Fonzarelli Starr," he said, now looking down.

"Walk south, what does that mean?" The man's brow furrowed, and Whistle noticed the gun was now sitting on the table, albeit not at all out of the man's immediate reach.

"I don't know sir. I guess I just have to go see what I can see."

"Why?"

"Don't know, but if I get out of here alive, I intend to find out," he answered as he stole a quick glance at the gun.

"Whoa buddy, I'm not gonna hurt you." And just like that, the man clicked the magazine out onto the table, turned the nine onto its side, and racked the round in the chamber out. Whistle watched as the bullet spun rapidly up into the air. As the bullet found its arc, everything went into slow motion.

The man's left arm reached out in front of the blue pool window and the bullet landed squarely in the man's hand. Confidently, the nine was put down, undressed, magazine laid out next to it and the chamber bullet standing up with its primer kissing the table harmlessly. These items were lined up in an unmistakably military fashion.

"Who are you?" Whistle asked, meekly.

The man leaned in toward Whistle across the table once again. Closer this time, the deep lines in his face cut sharp and black against the glow of the candles. For a moment, Whistle was reminded of the monarch butterflies from grade school, another lifetime ago as it seemed now.

"Who are you?" Whistle asked again, quietly waiting for an answer.

The man got up and opened the door to a small fridge tucked away under the kitchenette counter and pulled out an Italian grinder and a bag of Lays from Cumberland Farms and tossed them to Whistle, along with another bottle of water.

"Just call me Hellcat," the man finally replied.

"Sorry?"

"Hellcat.…..Wilson." He offered his hand to shake. Whistle shifted his dinner into the crook of his left arm to respond in kind. After devouring the gas station delicacies, he began to regain his faculties a bit as he closed his eyes, enjoying the feeling of a semi full stomach for the first time in days.

"You alright?" Hellcat asked.

"I think so, sir."

"Not sir.…Hellcat."

"Sorry.…uh, I'm ok."

They sat in awkward silence for approximately forty-five seconds and then it was on.

"Hey Whistle, I bet you could use a drink."

"Sure," the boy replied, not sure what he was getting into.

Before he knew it, a snifter of good whiskey with just the right amount of ice was set down in front of him.

"Cheers," Hellcat said as they clinked their glasses together. A small sip and Whistle's throat was on fire. He almost threw up right there. Fortunately, Hellcat went outside to relieve himself, so Whistle had a moment to finish gagging from the shot. Soon after, he walked back in the door.

"Sir, I appreciate what you've done for me. I'll never be able to repay you. Thank you!!!"

"Don't sweat it, and you never know, someday you just may.…And call me Hellcat, I'm not a cop," he said with a chuckle.

"Okay, Hellcat," he tried the feel of the word in his mouth. Another sip of whiskey and Whistle's stomach felt less knotted and more heated, and his brain was fizzing while still finding a place to land. He eventually relaxed and listened to Hellcat make small talk as they put a respectable dent in the whiskey.

The night rolled on. A proper bourbon buzz rolled over Whistle and the orange and blue light swirled around Hellcat's face as he sat there, telling stories and laughing to himself as he realized Whistle was hammered already and probably needed to be shut off.

"Hellcat, tell me another story." The boy slurred as he fought to sit upright and keep his eyes open. He finished his shot and crawled under the comforter he'd planned to sleep in earlier. Fighting to keep one of his eyes open and focus on Hellcat as he recalled his time serving in Vietnam. So many friends left there, for no good reason. Blood, sweat, mud, tears, bullets and all the rest that make up the daily reality of war. Whistle tried to contribute to the conversation, but by this point, his faculties were on vacation and he wasn't far behind as he drifted off to a drunken dreamland.

CHAPTER
TWENTY-ONE
A Helpful Morning

Whistle woke up and was sure a cat had taken a shit in his mouth. Laying there with his head pounding, he tried to collect himself. Just then a ray of sunlight came through the window and pierced Whistle's retinas. He pulled the covers over his head and hoped he would be able to fall back asleep, but with an immediately pounding headache, sun coming up and glaring brighter by the minute, and irritatingly cheerful birds singing and chirping right outside, he knew it would be a lost cause for the moment anyway. As he gave it another try, the door opened and he heard heavy footsteps. Still fully under the covers, the boy waited.

"Whistle?" Hellcat piped up. Whistle pretended to be asleep, hoping to be left alone to ride out his monstrous hangover for a few more hours.

"Hey! Wake UP!"

"I'm up, I'm up!" the boy replied as he sat up, astonished at how hard his head was pounding.

"Listen, I have to go to work but I want to talk to you," Hellcat said as he handed Whistle a bottle of water which he couldn't drink quickly enough. When he finished, Hellcat spoke.

"Listen, sleep as long as you like, there's food in the fridge as well. Pack a lunch and some water, go find all the adventures you want, but be super careful. The world is a fucked up place, it'll chew you up, spit you out, step on you and grind you into powder......Here's a hundred bucks to help you on your way.

"No thanks. You've already done more than enough for me," Whistle said as he was starting to get dizzy from the pounding in his head.

"HEY! It's not a request. Take the money, get some sleep, grab some food for the road and go kick ass." Hellcat slapped down five twenty-dollar bills, turned, and opened the door. Before stepping out he turned around and said, "Whistle, go experience everything you can. Good luck to ya, boy."

And just like that, he was out the door and off to work. Feeling guilty for not thanking him, Whistle reluctantly fell back asleep. After a few fitful hours he dragged himself up. Looking around, he tried to collect himself. Another water and two strawberry pop tarts later, Whistle began to feel somewhat normal again. After he packed his bag, he looked around. This was definitely an experience never to be forgotten. He pocketed the money on the table and started toward the door.

The bills snug in his front pocket reminded him of walking home alone from the Champion Fair. Now he actually had $107.29. A pack with essentials, a good amount of water and some food. Pausing at the door, he looked around.

"Thanks, Hellcat," he said to the empty room as he closed the door behind him. Eyes welling up, he headed south toward whatever was to come.

Chapter
Twenty-Two
Tollbooth Reality

Walking aside Interstate 93 South as the morning moved along, cars rushed by and three hawks circled above. Starting to find his stride, the boy found a comfortable pace. Pavement to the left, woods to the right, Whistle marched on. Figuring he'd make better time, he walked close to the road on the dirt and recently mowed grass. Cars and trucks blasted by him, almost knocking him over till he got used to the timing of bracing himself as he heard the vehicles coming up fast on his left side.

Late morning turned to noon as the sun hung lazy in the sky. A couple of small cotton clouds later, the boy was fully on the move and feeling great. He continued along, step by step, as the hours and miles stretched out behind him, as the day turned to early dusk and the sun turned the sky an urgent red, soon to be followed by purple and eventually nighttime. Knowing this full well, Whistle picked up his pace.

Eventually, nighttime came as he saw a cluster of bright lights about a half mile up the freeway. As he approached, he realized he had reached the Manchester Toll. Walking behind the main building, Whistle looked for a semi-comfortable place to rest.

No such luck tonight. The best he could do was a cardboard box to lay on, and another for a blanket. Freezing and shivering, Whistle looked through his pack. Meagerly, he drank a third of the water and ate one bar of a Kit Kat before putting the rest back in his bag. Knowing to conserve and stretch his resources, the brave boy made do.

He thought to himself, *I'm fourteen years old, on my own. I'm supposed to go to school this fall. Fuck it.* Rummaging through his bag, he found a small blanket and tried to get some sleep.

As the night dragged on, it was a pattern of shiver, eventually doze off, hear a noise, wake up, repeat. *C'mon, go to sleep,* he thought to himself. A fisher cat's shrill call filled the would be quiet night before Whistle finally drifted off from sheer exhaustion. Nothing to worry about anymore. All would be well. He knew it was true. So many people in his life had told him so. If that many people told you something, it had to be more true than not. As far as Whistle was concerned, he was ready for the good life.

The good life for the boy started with a very peaceful warmth on his face. Turning onto his back, the warmth continued. Without opening his eyes, he could tell the beautiful sun was shining down. This was sure to be a great day for traveling south. For this particular moment in time, Whistle Evel Fonzarelli Starr felt invincible. A feeling of perfection poured through his veins. The waterfall he heard nearby was peaceful and inviting.

The sound began to wake him up, intrigued to see the amazing sight of cascading water. Adjusting his eyes to the morning sun took a few moments. Once he regained clarity of sight, he turned on his side, anticipating a beautiful sight...not quite.

Whistle stared in disbelief as a man was just finishing relieving himself against the back wall of the building. Zipping up his fly, he turned on his heel and walked around the corner, leaving Whistle and his belongings speckled with urine. What a way to start the day.

Back to reality for the young Whistle. He got up with his mood very much knocked down and packed his few things. Headed south again, at least walking through the day did improve his mood to some degree. Unfortunately, the thought of the morning's disappointment never quite left him. Maybe a good night's sleep in the woods alone would tamp down his agitation by morning.

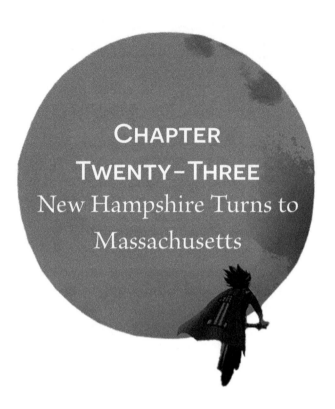

CHAPTER
TWENTY-THREE
New Hampshire Turns to Massachusetts

Whistle was well aware that most of the day was already behind him, along with the crazy experience. He started walking south again, now walking along I-95, and tried to make up as much distance as he could.

The sun was already golden below the treetops to his west. The boy just kept walking while the world zipped by to his left. After sunset he traveled by the sound and lights of the traffic. He walked deep into the night until he was completely exhausted. When his mind wouldn't work anymore, he turned right, up the bank and into the woods.

Just inside the tree line, he dropped his pack and used it as a pillow again. He was even too tired to pull his blanket out. Whistle passed out and slept like a rock. A completely blank, visionless sleep. When you're too tired to dream.......you're tired.

As he slept, bugs crawled all over him. A tick that he would never know about found a home under his right armpit. A porcupine smelled his face before walking away and climbing a tree to sleep in.

Morning came and Whistle awoke with an unstoppable urge to take a shit. He jumped up and walked about ten feet with clenched cheeks. Barely dropping his drawers in time, the boy squatted down and exploded vile waste all over the ground. The cool morning breeze relieved his sweating body. He took a couple of minutes to gather himself. After feeling a little better, he realized he had to wipe.

Looking around, he saw nothing but pine needles. Not good. Not good at all. After doing the best he could with some bark, Whistle stood and pulled his pants up. He now stumbled weakly about fifty feet from his mess and collapsed onto a refreshingly cool patch of moss. Sleep grabbed him again.

A while later he woke up, brushing a centipede off of his face. The boy's throat was on fire, and his stomach was gnawing at him for food. Taking a bottle of water out of his pack, he slugged it down along with two blueberry pop tarts and immediately felt the goodness of calories and hydration setting in. He fell asleep for another half hour and woke up feeling much better.

Judging by the sun, Whistle estimated it was early afternoon. Time to make some tracks to wherever he was going. Where was he going? Good question. While we're at it, what day is it? Is it really early afternoon? With all these confusing questions swimming around in his head, he figured either way, the time was now to get a move on.

As he walked along, his mind was lost in thought. All the people in his life flashed before him. He missed his mom terribly. What was Eric up to? Had Ms. Fisher greeted a new kindergarten class yet? The Rock and Roll ride at the end of the midway at the Champion Fair, the monarchs ascending into the trees for another year.

Continuing on, he walked the day away. Night came again and, with no idea where he was, he settled down for another sleep. More prepared this time, he made a crude bed out of fir boughs. Under his little blanket he slept quite well. His dreams were rather pleasant and comforting.

Morning came and he got up. A water and some Ritz crackers later, the boy stood alone. His mind talked to him. *Whistle my friend, your pack is quite light. Walk back north and find comfort. School, Eric, Mr. and Mrs. Flow, all waiting to help you. C'mon, don't be an idiot. Turn it around and head back home. Everything you know is north, nothing you know is south.*

Once again, that boy squared up and continued south. Safety north and adventure south. His path was an absolute no-brainer for him.

He walked for a couple more miles then decided to duck into the woods. Setting up his camp, he thought a fire might be in order tonight. That would bring light, heat, security, and a way to cook food. As he finished a Slim Jim, he thought to himself how awesome it would be to have an actual meal that required cooking. Cow, deer, chicken, pig, fish, anything that would provide some protein.

The next morning came fast and everything went the same. A lot of walking, very little food and even less water took over his life. With a deep feeling of being lost, he marched south. He was surely on a fool's errand.

Just when all seemed lost, Whistle spotted a sign ahead. As he got closer he could make out the glorious words on the royal blue sign:

"WELCOME TO MASSACHUSETTS"

"Holy shit!" The boy couldn't believe it. He had never been out of New Hampshire in his entire life. Adrenaline pumped through his veins and he felt invincible. Stopping for a moment, he stared at the sign. Whoever put it there probably couldn't care less. Another day's work, another paycheck, but to Whistle, this moment was truly monumental. Pausing, he found himself having a hard time stepping forward. A new, undiscovered world awaited the curious boy. He took a step and placed his left hand on the word "Massachusetts." Then ducking under the sign, he realized that life would never be the same.

The boy took a major step toward becoming a man that day. Three miles later, Whistle stopped. He climbed into the woods and started his nightly routine. Take a piss, lay out the blanket, eat his last granola bar and water. Falling asleep, he was excited and terrified all at the same time.

CHAPTER
TWENTY-FOUR
Whistle Travels

The next day started with pouring rain. Soaked, the boy grabbed his pack and headed deeper into the woods. Up the hill, he found a small cave that would be his home for the day. Darkness, spiders, and snakes filled his world. Even worse were the ticks, bobcats, coyotes, and poison ivy. He settled down and found sleep. After a very good nap, Whistle woke up in northern Massachusetts.

Morning routine started with a piss and was followed by quite simple steps. One, pack your few belongings. Two, walk because you have nothing to eat or drink. He left the cave, walked down the hill, and dropped out of the tree line. Then, making his way back to the highway, he hung a right and continued his journey south. It was already late afternoon and Whistle knew that he had no food or water. Four miles marched on by easily because Whistle felt at home on the move. Thirst and hunger took him over eventually and Whistle was starting to fade. Listening to the dizzy voices in his head, trying to figure out a plan. Just keep walking.....

Two more miles down the road another sign appeared. "Food, Gas, Lodging." It might as well have said "Paradise" to a boy in Whistle's current state. He walked another half mile and made his way down the exit. At the end, he followed the right hand arrow toward what he was looking for. Cresting a small hill, there they were. The Golden Arches. Beckoning him. McDonald's, here we come!

"Can I help you?" came from a girl that had more pimples than Whistle had ever seen in his life.

"A number three, please," he answered. Handing the girl a crumpled ball of ones and a few coins, he got his tray of sustenance and walked outside. He sat down at one of the thick, round cement tables and devoured two cheeseburgers, an order of fries, and a vanilla milkshake. After a decent pause, letting the calories do their work rejuvenating his body, he got up and headed back up toward the highway. Pack on his back, he made another nine miles before he decided to bed down for the night.

A couple more days went the same way for the boy; Walk, be hungry, be thirsty, eventually tap out sometime late into the night and find a spot in the woods to sleep. Every day the same car noises, the same smell of b/o from not showering, the same nagging question: Did I really think this through?

Walking along the freeway, lost in thought, the path veered left and there it was. Golden afternoon sun poured down as he came to a sign that said, "Boston, 11 Miles." Picking up his pace, eventually he cleared a hill and saw the majestic city skyline rise up before him. Whistle felt humble in that moment. Without knowing what treasures or hardships the city might hold for him, he steadied himself and kept on. Excitement carried him well into the evening, but before he reached the North End, he decided to rest in the now familiar woodland and take on Boston first thing in the morning.

A short walk into the brush and pine with almost no light on this cloudy night, he lucked out and found a granite crag. He sat, legs dangling over an almost perfectly angled cliff. He swung them in rhythm with a tune that had been stuck in his head for several days. Looking at the twinkling city lights, he wondered what Beantown had in store for a boy, barely a teenager, on foot with virtually no belongings, no money, dirty clothes, a crazy man's dried urine on his face, and a serious case of funk from walking a marathon and going almost a week without showering.

He put reality out of his mind for a moment as he pulled out his blanket, tried to fluff up his pack, and laid his head down for the night. As he drifted off, gazing at the twinkling lights and angular structures off in the distance, he had a thought.

"I'm Whistle Evel Fonzarelli Starr, and I will kick ass. I have about ten miles before I hit Boston and then the world is my oyster. I will walk into that city and do whatever I want. Rock and Roll!"

CHAPTER
TWENTY-FIVE
Clover's Barbershop

B irds began to chirp, oranges and deep reds scraped the horizon to his left as Whistle sat wide awake, gazing at the skyline to the south. Mysterious lights of the city still dancing in the distance stole his imagination. He knew what lay ahead would be nothing short of incredible. He could wait no longer, so he quickly pulled up and packed away his blanket and started up towards the freeway. A decent slice of the day flew by as Whistle walked and became incredibly thirsty. After a while, he realized he couldn't follow I-95 South any longer or he'd be on the upper deck of the bridge leading into Boston. Veering off down a steep hill, his excitement was great, but before anything else, Whistle had a pressing matter to take care of.

As luck would have it, he literally walked down the hill right into what he needed at that moment. Whistle crossed a small parking lot and entered a Store 24. Fluorescent lights and every color in the world appeared before him.

"Do you have a bathroom?" he asked the long-faced cashier.

"Yeah, back to your right."

Not looking up, Whistle walked back, tried the door and found it was locked, so he waited.

A short time later, the door opened and an incredibly large woman somewhere in her fifties walked out.

"Be careful in there, but just know it wasn't me," the woman said.

"What?" Whistle asked with no idea what she was talking about.

"Just walk away," the woman said as she turned and left.

Still not putting two and two together, Whistle just knew he really had to use the bathroom and was really looking forward to getting a drink and a quick wash in the sink.

Opening the door, the most horrific smell imaginable almost knocked him over. His urge to evacuate his bladder was stronger, so onward he pressed. Looking to his right, he knew he would not be drinking from that sink.

Glancing up, he looked into the cracked mirror on the wall. He realized he was dirty and getting thinner by the day. Not wanting to deal with it, he turned to his left and looked for a toilet. When he found it, he knew instantly where the brutal smell was coming from. The smell and the visual, which I will not subject you to, was truly awe inspiring in the worst way. So Whistle got out as quick as he could. Walking back into the store, he bought a hot dog off the roller machine, an eighty-nine cent roll of toilet paper, two twelve ounce waters and a pack of peanut M & Ms. With no money left, the boy walked out. The hot dog was in his belly before he could even turn the corner. Getting out back, twelve ounces of water were already guzzled down as he squatted in the weeds. After using a wad of that eighty-nine cent toilet paper, Whistle packed up and continued.

It only took him about three or four blocks before he realized he had no idea what he was doing or where he was going, so he stopped. Looking for help, the boy found a barbershop. All he wanted was information. Classic barber pole turning outside, Whistle opened the door and walked in.

"Hello," he said, being friendly. The whole shop stopped and stared at him. That's when Whistle realized everyone in the shop was black.

"I'm sorry," he said, turning to leave.

"Sorry for what?" came from behind him.

"I'm just looking to move my life on and avoid trouble," Whistle replied, honestly.

"Trouble?" asked the barber.

Whistle was so scared he didn't know what to do. A young white kid from New Hampshire was totally lost in this situation.

"What's your name, son?"

"Whistle, Whistle Starr, sir," he replied.

"Well now, look at what we have here," the gravelly voice said with a world weary chuckle.

Whistle turned around to see a kind old black man holding scissors and a comb, wearing a white barber's coat. Stifled laughs echoed off the tile floor and plaster on the walls.

"Whistle, I'm Clover Green. Have a seat, son."

Before Whistle knew what was going on, Clover was cutting and clipping with the speed and precision of a true master. Just a few minutes later and Whistle looked like a new man. Staring at himself in the mirror and thinking his haircut would look even better if he could wash the grease out of it, Clover spoke up.

"That'll be a hundred dollars."

"What!?" he replied, scared and confused.

"One hundred dollars, boy," Clover said again, in a stern voice.

"Mister, I...uh... I don't have any money!" Whistle stammered.

"Looks like we got a problem." Clover was holding the straight razor up. Whistle tried to get up and bolt out of the barbershop. He was firmly reseated. Clover walked out around the chair and faced him. Razor in one hand and scissors in the other. He broke out laughing, "I'm just playin' son!"

All Whistle could think was, *Holy shit!* After a few moments, he caught his breath and regained his composure.

"What do I owe you?" he asked, with exactly zero dollars to his name.

"Sweep the floor, we cool," came as Clover tossed him a long handled broom.

He spent the rest of the afternoon sweeping and keeping his mouth shut. He listened to the banter, stories, and good old fashioned ball-busting that bounced around the shop between the men. The fresh new smell of shaving cream and aftershave put him in an optimistic mood. The snipping, clipping, hair dryers and brushes swishing and smacking the trimmed hair off the shoulders of the customers provided a hypnotic rhythm to his first afternoon in Boston.

Before he knew it, outside it was getting dark. Pausing, he looked around and realized he was all alone. All of a sudden, a deliciously tantalizing aroma filled the shop.

"Hello?" he called out.

"Uh....Hello?" Again, no reply. Walking to the back of the shop, Whistle opened the curtain and there Clover sat at a small table, minding a hot plate going with a pot of who knows what.

"Sir, I'm done, I'll let myself out. Thanks again for the haircut....looks great."

"You hungry?" Clover asked.

"Smells great but I'm good. You've done more than enough for me."

"Sit down, here," the kind barber said as he fixed an extra bowl of the mysterious gumbo. A bottle of water and some white bread, Whistle felt like he hit the lottery.

They sat and ate in silence. When they were done it was well past dark.

"That hit the spot, sir. I can't thank you enough....Well, it's getting late and I gotta get rolling," Whistle said as he put out his hand to shake Clover's.

"Hang on, this ain't the greatest neighborhood at night. I have a cot if you want it," he replied, pointing to the corner of the room. He looked and saw a simple green fold up cot, sleeping bag, and Spiderman pillow. A king-size feather bed at the Ritz-Carlton to a boy who's been sleeping on the hard ground for about a week now. He promptly laid down and fell asleep in the middle of saying thank you to Clover Green.

After seven hours of glorious sleep, Whistle woke to the even more glorious smell of bacon and eggs sizzling away on the hot plate. Clover again at the helm, spatula scraping the eggs off the hot surface and stirring the bacon around.

"Mornin' boy." World weary eyes glanced over.

"Morning," Whistle replied, yawning and stretching.

"Get up, breakfast's ready." Clover gestured to grab a plate, which Whistle promptly did. Once again they sat together, eating in silence. When they were done, Clover cleared the table.

"Look now, I gotta go cut hair. Take your bag upstairs and do a load of laundry, take a shower, get dressed, and come back down when you're done," Clover said as he headed out through the curtain to the shop floor. Turning back briefly, he added, "Whistle Starr, don't steal anything or screw me in any way."

"Absolutely not, Mr. Green!" Whistle gathered his things and headed upstairs. He took a well needed hot shower, got all his clothes washed and dried and repacked, folded neatly and everything. Feeling a million times better when he was done, he walked down the stairs to the back room. Noticing one last piece of bacon in the hot plate, he couldn't help but eat it. No point in letting it go to waste. Before heading out to the main room, he took a good look around the room, wanting to remember his first night in Boston.

He pushed through the curtain out to the real world. The shop seemed even busier today, with all the hustle and bustle, sights, sounds, and smells of yesterday turned up a few notches on this bright, fresh summer morning.

"Whistle," Clover called. "Come here, son."

He walked over and Clover put his huge arm around Whistle's shoulders.

"Listen, I could use some help around here if you're interested."

Whistle could tell he wasn't just being charitable; he actually could use the help. Feeling somewhat guilty, he answered.

"I'm sorry Mr. Green, but I have to go and find out what this life is all about."

Their eyes met in that moment and innocence and wisdom met perfectly in the middle.

"Are you sure you don't want to stick around for a few days?" Clover asked in a fatherly manner.

"I would love to, but the world is calling," Whistle replied, already eyeing the front door.

At that moment, Clover led Whistle to the corner of the shop, reached into his pocket, and pulled out an exceptionally crinkled twenty-dollar bill.

"Take this," he said, as he pushed the bill into Whistle's hand.

"Take this too." He pulled out a comb with the barbershop's name and phone number on it and offered it. "Call that number or just come by if you ever change your mind."

"I will, Mr. Green. Thank you."

With the twenty in his front pocket and comb in the back, he hugged Clover Green and just like that, they parted ways. With the door's bell ringing above his head, he was out the door and back on the streets. Glancing over his right shoulder at the barbershop pole one more time, he was on his way.

CHAPTER
TWENTY-SIX
Digging into Boston

Clean, full, and happy, the boy headed south. A twenty firmly in his pocket with a brand new comb from Mr. Green, he couldn't lose. The day was spent navigating the streets. Every now and then he would get a glimpse of the Boston skyline, but it just didn't seem to get any closer. Whistle marched forward well into the late afternoon as dusk settled on the city. Finding shelter in a playground jungle gym, he bedded down for the night. It seemed to be the perfect spot until...

The first kid's foot stepped on his hand.

"Shit!" he yelled, pulling his hand away.

"Mom!" the boy also yelled. Frozen for a moment, Whistle thought.

"Mom!" This time even louder. Bag grabbed, Whistle jumped out of the jungle gym and darted across the playground. The last thing he heard was, "Someone call the police!" All he wanted was a place to sleep, and now people were trying to get him in trouble. Whistle ran out of the park and down a couple of streets. Out of breath, he ducked down an alley. Finding the steps of a back loading dock, he sat down. As he gathered his breath, he looked around. He saw nothing but brick walls, dumpsters, and grime smashed into the ground. Realizing this wasn't a place to relax, he moved on.

Street after street went by and the Boston skyline finally grew a little. Night set in and Whistle slept. A couple more days went by, exactly the same.

After meeting some interesting characters, Whistle walked proudly into Boston. A small boy was actually in the big city. Walking through the streets, everything looked extremely intriguing. Life was fantastic.

Whistle Evel Fonzarelli Starr stood at the edge of Boston and looked toward the future.

"Fuck it, let's go." Stepping forward, he walked on. The sights, smells, and sounds were like nothing he'd ever experienced. The boy kept traveling in what he thought was a southerly direction. Sometime later, he came to a river. With no idea, he stood on the banks of the River Charles, like the Standells sang about. The water was indeed dirty, compared to the pristine, rushing rapids of the White Mountains that he was used to.

He decided to turn right and continue. After all, left or right, it was a fifty-fifty gamble. He moved on, taking in as much as he could. The sun flashing off the river to his left, he saw these weird skinny boats with young men rowing and cutting through the water. One voice from each boat yelling some kind of order to the rest. Strangeness surely was everywhere around him.

A while later he came across a granite stone bridge that crossed the river, so he hung a left and took it. After crossing, he walked straight down the street. About five blocks later, he came to what seemed like a main road traveling perpendicular to him. At this intersection, the activity all around him was extraordinary. To his right across the street was a liquor store. To his left another Store 24. There was a midget, the first the boy had ever seen, in front of the store playing a violin with his case on the sidewalk. Whistle walked past and entered the store.

Looking around, he found the bathroom. This one was a lot cleaner than the last one. After doing his business, he utilized their paper instead of his own. He even found another roll in a small cabinet and it made its way into his backpack. Hands and face washed and a belly full of Boston sink water, Whistle walked back out. Back in the main store, he decided to buy a Hostess apple pie and a Mountain Dew, then walked out.

Finding as quiet a corner off to the side as he could, he sat down on a curb. Eating the apple pie and sipping the soda, he took everything in. Left, right, or straight, what now, Whistle? He dismissed straight ahead right off the bat, because it seemed like a smaller street that led into what looked more like a neighborhood type situation.

So….Left?…..Right? Absolutely life changing. He looked both ways and they looked equally promising. *Damn it!* he thought to himself. He was hoping it would be a more obvious choice. He actually would have flipped a coin, but he only had an even eighteen dollars left, all in bills. He certainly didn't have the balls to take a coin out of the violin player's case, so he paused.

Just then, a huge green and white train entered his field of vision from his right. The sun glared directly into his eyes momentarily, reminding him of walking into some of his first schools for the first time. It pulled up and stopped directly in front of him out in the middle of the huge street. The doors opened, people got off, people got on, the doors closed, and the train continued down the road, exiting Whistle's vision to his left.

His answer was instantly clear. Standing up, he looked right for a moment and for some reason his eyes met the violin player. It was like the small man knew he was on some real life adventure and gave him a nod. Whistle felt somehow touched by this, so he took out his eighteen dollars and dropped it into the case on the sidewalk. Imagine that, for a moment, a young boy on the road, giving his last eighteen dollars to a complete stranger. Somehow he was sure it was the right thing to do. No dollars left, they glanced at each other one more time. Whistle saw understanding and appreciation in the man's eyes. Then, that was it, he turned away and headed left down the sidewalk toward whatever adventure lay ahead.

Walking for a while, he came to a point where the road had a right hand bend. Rounding it, there was the Boston skyline closer than ever. Excitement instantly surged through his body and his pace picked up. The only thing was, the road before him seemed extremely straight and impossibly long. Once again, with no clue at all as to where he was, Whistle was walking to a place made famous in song, down Kenmore Avenue directly toward Kenmore Square. The sun quickly slid behind the buildings and he knew he had to figure something out for the night.

A bit further down the road, he found a brick wall in front of a brownstone building. Looking behind it, he saw a mulched garden with some bushes. It seemed perfect, so he ducked behind and made himself at home. Pack as his pillow again, he laid down and listened to the traffic. Dim lighting filtered down through the bushes, leaving a spotted pattern all around. The voices and footsteps of people passing by were merely feet away. Oddly enough, it actually put the boy at ease and his eyelids grew heavy. Sleep grabbed him for a while.

Then he awoke to sounds that he didn't recognize at first. As he became more aware, he realized he was hearing the sound of two people having sex coming through an open window somewhere close by. Before he dozed off for the night, the last thing he heard was someone saying to someone else, "I love you so much." He chuckled to himself, wondering how true that might be as he drifted into a deep sleep after a long day.

CHAPTER
TWENTY-SEVEN
Shortstop Nipples

The next morning arrived in a blink. Morning sun poured through the bushes, heating up Whistle's space. He took a moment to gather himself as people walked by, waiting for the right moment to slide out from around the wall. Obviously, not the right time; he was met with plenty of looks of disgust or indifference. Not one smile or any gesture of empathy.

Like he's been known to do, Whistle squared his shoulders, held his head high, and marched forward. Feeling super self-conscious, like everyone was judging him as they glared at him and hurried by. Needing some kind of energy, he stopped and drank the rest of his warm Mountain Dew. Discarding the bottle in a trash can, he moved on. Feeling a little better, he found his stride again.

By noon, Whistle entered Kenmore Square. Just when he thought he could not be overwhelmed anymore by the city, his awe instantly multiplied ten-fold. Everything he saw was dazzling. New sounds everywhere. There was no rhyme or reason in any direction. Cars zoomed by every which way. People filled the sidewalk. Smells were too complicated and the confused boy started to have a panic attack.

Eyes darting around, his breath increased rapidly along with his pulse. He was very dizzy and had no idea what to do. Barely composing himself, he went around a corner and found some privacy just in time and proceeded to vomit. After he finished, he tried to spit the vile taste out of his mouth. Unfortunately, he had no saliva left, so he walked around another corner and found even more privacy. In some strange back alley walkway, the chills hit him and beads of sweat rose up on his forehead. He tried to collect himself, but an uncomfortable loud buzzing filled his ears, brain, and body as his vision went black. Then he passed out and dropped to the dirty ground, striking the side of his head. Whistle's blood dripped down, contributing to the grime. As the day turned to night once more, Whistle was sprawled out completely helpless in the back alleyway.

"Hey," he heard as he felt a hand gently push on his shoulder blade.

"Hey," the voice said again, this time pushing a little harder. All Whistle could respond with was a weak, primitive groan.

"C'mon now," the voice said with a bit more urgency.

"Wha…?" was all Whistle could manage.

"Hello there." Another shoulder push.

"What? Stop pushing me." Whistle's confusion cleared up a bit. He felt his head being lifted and something being wrapped around it. This instantly sent Whistle into another round of panic, so he snapped to and opened his eyes to still see nothing.

"Stay still, you've lost a lot of blood. Do you know where you are?" the voice asked, matter-of-factly.

"No, who are you?" Whistle answered back.

"You're in the north side of Kenmore Square. Where are you from?" came the reply, ignoring the question.

"I'm from New Hampshire," Whistle answered, still in darkness.

"No wonder." This, followed by the snap of a lighter and its small flame in Whistle's face. Instantly blinded, he winced and immediately shut his eyes.

"Open your eyes."

Slowly, he complied. His blurry vision came into focus. The orange lighter illuminated a very curious sight before him.

The impossibly deep creases of the face before him filled his field of vision. The soft glow of the light made his dark eyes twinkle as they explored Whistle's face as well. Then the goofiest grin he had ever seen in his life spread across the small black man's face, deepening the creases even more. Putting his right hand up to his completely bald head, he let out a small, deep chuckle.

"Well aren't you just a sight for sore eyes, boy," the small man said in a surprisingly deep voice. That's when Whistle noticed the man had no shirt on, and he suddenly had a brief thought that something bad was about to go down. Equally as sudden, he could see that the man had a kind face, void of contempt or malice.

By the way, the thing wrapped around Whistle's head was the man's shirt. Talk about giving the shirt off your back.

"Wow!"

"What's yo name?" the man asked as a still dizzy Whistle slowly sat up.

"I'm Whistle." He reached up and felt the shirt wrapped around his head.

"Whistle what?" An intent stare.

"Whistle Starr, Whistle Evel Fonzarelli Starr."

"Whistle wha? DeFonzi who?....What.....kinda FUCKED up name izzat?"

"Evel Knievel and the Fonz were my mom's idols. Who are you, anyway?" Whistle responded as he tried to focus on the man's face.

"I'm Shortstop."

"Shortstop what?"

"Shortstop Nipples," came the answer, right hand extending out toward the boy.

"Wow! Who was YOUR mom a fan of?" Whistle joked as he shook the man's hand.

"Ok, ok! We're both fucked up." The man chuckled. "Let's stand you up and see how you feel."

Shortstop stood up and took Whistle's other hand as his eyes started to adjust to the dark. Standing up, wobbly, he unwrapped Shortstop's Samuel Adams now bloody T-shirt, thanked him, and attempted to stagger off.

"Where are you goin'?" Shortstop asked.

"Don't know," Whistle replied.

"Well, what's your plan?"

"I figure I'll just keep walking."

"Keep walking?" Shortstop was now concerned. "Walking where?"

"I guess I'll know when I get there."

"Do you have any money?"

"Nope, I gave my last eighteen dollars to some midget playing a violin in front of Store 24."

"Holy shit! That's Vinny. He's a cool cat but he does way too much coke. Don't worry, I'll get your money back," he said, matter-of-factly.

"I don't want it back," the boy said.

"Yes you DO. It's one thing to help somebody out, but it's another to be taken advantage of."

"I guess," Whistle said, woozily.

"I have a place near here that you can crash for the night."

"That would be great," a thankful Whistle replied.

He followed Shortstop out of the alley and back into the hustle and bustle of Kenmore Square. They walked down the sidewalk and before young Whistle knew it, Shortstop had acquired two Granny Smith apples, a block of sharp cheddar cheese, a small loaf of Italian bread, and two ice cold waters. He handed Whistle an apple, which he promptly chomped away at, leaving only seeds and a stem in a matter of seconds.

"Daiimmmn, son!" Shortstop cackled.

After a while, they took a right on to a smaller street. Walking about four blocks, a ten-foot chain link fence stood in front of them. Just by that, cars screamed by below.

"That's the Mass Pike," Shortstop said, extending his arm in a grand gesture. After a moment, they turned around and went back the way they came. A quick half block later, Shortstop announced that they were there. They took a right and headed down a dark, dirty alley. Feeling very uncomfortable, Whistle reminded himself that if Shortstop was going to jack him, he could have already done it. Shit, he was pretty much fully jacked when Shortstop found him.

Waiting for Shortstop to bring him through a door into an apartment, he was surprised when they stopped in front of what looked like a huge garbage pile. Almost to put a fine point on the situation, a rat the size of a Chihuahua scurried across his foot.

"C'mon," Shortstop said, ducking in between a shopping cart full of tin cans and an old moldy mattress. Whistle followed, both intrigued and scared. Once inside, Shortstop lit an oil lantern and the boy looked around.

"Holy shit!" quietly escaped his lips.

"Welcome to Newbury Street Extension. It's not paradise, but it's MY paradise," Shortstop said with a hint of pride in his voice. Every manner of junk made up the walls of the shelter. Old plates, used windows, bicycle wheels and everything imaginable created Shortstop's paradise. Throwing the boy a Red Sox blanket, Shortstop said, "You can sleep here." Grateful, he took it and laid his pack down for his pillow. He was quite comfortable as they shared the cheddar cheese, bread, and water. Dry, warm, and full, he felt a sense of security, at least for the night.

"Thank you," was all he could say as his eyes grew heavy.

"Hey, it's nice to have company for a change." Shortstop proceeded to tell Whistle his life story. The better part of it would fall on Whistle's deaf, sleeping ears. He'd never know that Shortstop was a Vietnam vet, that he killed someone in self-defense in his own home. He had been married twice with four kids that he hadn't seen in years. He confessed to Whistle that none of his kids would want to visit him in his dirty garbage den. Was he a grandfather? He had no idea.

All talked out, he looked at the boy, noticing the innocence of his face, and ruefully chuckled to himself, "Sleep good, Whistle Fonzi Whatdafuk."

Chapter Twenty-Eight
A Hell of a Day

When morning came, Whistle was completely disoriented. Right before he opened his eyes, he had a huge flash of the monarchs taking flight. Oranges and blacks completely filled his mind's eye. When he opened his actual eyes, a couple of butterflies seemed to flit away, leaving trails of light. It did not escape him that this was the time of year they would be in the pines at the end of the field behind his elementary school.

Eyes focusing, the first thing he saw was a huge stop sign staring back at him. Looking around, there was trinket on top of relic on top of artifact on top of who knows what else. A Chewbacca action figure caught his attention. To his left, a traffic light. To his right was, of all things, a Rubik's Cube. Matchbox cars, old shirts, Lego pieces, coat hangers and endless tin cans. The colors, shapes, and textures formed a kaleidoscopic 3D mural to the still out of sorts Whistle.

"Mornin' Whistle. How's the old bean?"

"Pardon?"

"Your head. How's your head feelin'? I figured I could show you around a bit if you're up to it."

"Oh, it's fine," Whistle replied, dismissing any need for concern.

He reached up and felt some dried blood and, truth be told, he did still feel a bit of a headache but he'd had worse. A short time later, they both exited the fort and stood in the alley. Walking out, a day of complete exploration began for Whistle. As they walked, Shortstop explained that he was not a bum, but a "can man," how the five cent refund for every can worked and all the other ins and outs of the can business.

Whistle didn't say much. He just listened, spellbound. He observed everything he could focus on and made mental notes, as he figured the information would serve him well.

One thing he noticed and found curious was that Shortstop was like two different people at times. In the smaller back streets and alleyways he was outgoing, chatting with everybody and introducing Whistle to his friends. Out in the main drags in "normal" society, he was timid. With his head slightly down, he walked off to the side as much as possible, telling the boy to follow. It was very clear to him that Shortstop was trying to keep as low a profile as possible.

The day went by and questions piled up in Whistle's mind, but he was fed and had a friend who seemed to know the territory so he didn't sweat it. As twilight set in, he found himself on an anonymous fire escape at the back of a third-floor apartment. He was smoking some herb with Shortstop and a couple of other people, presumably friends of Shortstop. Looking out, the famous Citgo sign glowed bright in the distance, just like it did during the Red Sox games on TV38. The Hancock and Prudential buildings were also on full display from this most excellent vantage point. The herb made the sparkling skyline almost too overwhelming as he reflected on his current reality.

"Shortstop?" Whistle said, barely audible. With no answer, he continued to grab the fire escape rail and look out over the city, now afraid to move all of a sudden as the inevitable paranoia seeped in. Just then, he felt an arm gently wrap around him with a hand landing on his left shoulder.

"What's your name, sexy boy?" Another joint was placed between his lips.

Holy shit! Whistle thought to himself as he inhaled and held it for about twenty seconds before he exploded into a coughing fit, smoke billowing out of his nose, mouth, and probably ears. He felt a bit unsteady, but high and happy just the same. He gripped the railing tighter and tighter and tried to focus on the lights of the skyline in between glancing around for Shortstop, who seemed to have stepped away from the proceedings.

"What's your name, sexy boy?" His left arm and hand were grabbed a little tighter this time. That's when this slightly weathered but still innocent boy felt a hand grab his crotch.

"Oh, oh, OH!?" was all the stoned, confused Whistle could muster.

"I'm Candi, baby," the woman purred as she slid her hand slightly up and down.

Nervousness and complete confusion flooded through him. He looked to his right and couldn't believe his eyes…Candi was actually gorgeous. He leaned back toward her arm and moved his hips forward. There, this beautiful girl proceeded to unzip Whistle's jeans and started going to work on him. Whistle was certain he had found his soul mate.

The lights of Boston sparkled as Whistle's physical feelings, thoughts, and emotions were completely entangled and whipped around intensely, like a tornado of confusion and bliss.

"I love you!" Whistle reflexively spat out.

"Me too," Candi replied, completely indifferent. Her hand quickened and Whistle released in his pants. He clucked and bucked, threw out a weird face along with a weird noise. Whistle was lost in a completely new world. All he knew in that moment was that he was in love.

"That'll be twenty bucks my sexy boy," she declared, holding out her right hand as she wiped her left hand on Whistle's dirty jeans.

"But I love you!" he replied, naively.

"Yeah, me too honey. Twenty bucks."

Whistle felt cornered on that fire escape. Trying to gather his wits, he stammered, "Candi, I...uh...I don't have any money."

"Then we got a fuckin' problem!" Candi snorted. She shoved Whistle so hard that he fell backwards and felt his shoulders dig deep into the metal rail of the fire escape. Candi stood him up and dusted him off. He felt blood trickling down his back. He tried to reason with Candi but she wasn't having any of it. She proceeded to bang Whistle up all over that third floor fire escape.

He tried to defend himself but Candi was too strong. Any other people that were out there were nowhere to be found. Whistle threw an inexperienced punch that only made Candi angrier. She threw a throat punch that left Whistle completely vulnerable. Candi pushed the boy back till he was arched over the fire escape. Thirty feet and gravity were breathing down his neck. Whistle had a thought at that moment.

I've been through a lot for someone my age, but I feel I'm just getting started and I don't want to go out like this.

With that, he grabbed at Candi's eyes and she pushed back hard. Whistle's feet went in the air and he was sure he was done for. They continued to scrap and tussle as Whistle lost ground. The railing dug deeper into his lower back. Candi grabbed Whistle's throat with both hands and was ready to push him over the edge. She pushed harder and the boy knew he was in trouble.

"Bitch! What the fuck you doin'?" Shortstop exclaimed as he simultaneously got between them, grabbed Whistle with his right hand, and clocked Candi square in the noggin with the other. She staggered back, dazed. Shortstop quickly lunged forward and grabbed Candi and easily pinned her down.

"What the fuck Candi!? What are you doing?" Shortstop demanded.

"You spray, you pay!" Candi wailed.

"He's just a lost boy from New Hampshire, on the road with no money!! Get the fuck out of here right now!" Shortstop shouted an inch from her twisted, scowling face.

With that, Candi angrily slinked away and Shortstop started laughing with Whistle at the absurdity of the situation. They started laughing so hard that neither one could make a sound.

"Ahhh mannnn, that was something else!" Shortstop said as he wiped his eyes. "Okay boy, I think that's enough excitement for one day. Let's head on back."

"I'm with you on that," Whistle replied.

The two of them climbed down, hung from the bottom rung, and dropped the last seven feet to the street below. When Whistle landed, some blood from his back finally made it down his pant leg and onto the ground. This was the second day in a row Whistle left blood on the streets of Boston. Oh well, nobody said city life was easy.

They both walked in comfortable silence down the alley to Shortstop's hideout. Once there, they ducked inside and Shortstop lit the lantern as Whistle climbed under his Red Sox blanket, exhausted from the day's "festivities."

"'Night, Whistle Evel Fonzarelli Starr, you crazy boy."

"Goodnight Shortstop Nipples." Whistle giggled as his eyelids grew heavier and heavier.

As Whistle slept, his dreams replayed the events of his adventure through a funhouse mirror, but it was a restful sleep regardless.

Shortstop blew out the lantern, knowing that there was something special about Whistle. Closing his eyes, he was fast asleep in minutes as well. Like Whistle, vivid dreams filled his night as well.

CHAPTER
TWENTY-NINE
Love to Stay, Gotta Go

Over the next couple of months, Whistle got to know the area and learned as much as he could. His fondness for Shortstop grew. The boy figured out that this nice little black man was the closest he'd had to a dad since Jack up and left him and his mom. This in turn made him think about how much he loved her and how much he completely missed her.

After a while, the days began to shorten and a slight crispness filled the air at night. The two continued their routine, until one night when they were eating fruit cocktails and peanut butter crackers. Suddenly, they heard someone pissing on Shortstop's heap. Jumping up, Shortstop shot out and Whistle followed.

There he was. Vinny, the midget violinist, pissing away, obviously drunk.

"Asshole!" Shortstop yelled. Vinny shook himself, zipped up, and looked at Shortstop bleary eyed.

"What's your fucking problem?" the midget said, looking up.

"You dipshit!" Shortstop shot back at him.

Then Vinny looked over at Whistle. After a pause, his eyes focused on Whistle's.

"Hey…..I know you!" he slurred as Whistle remained silent.

"Yeah! You're the boy who gave me eighteen dollars. Thanks! That really helped me out."

Whistle remained silent, and just as the silence was about to get awkward....Shortstop to the rescue again.

"Actually, you need to give that money back."

Whistle was relieved as Vinny turned his attention back to Shortstop.

"What do you mean?" Vinny asked.

"You heard me. Pay the boy back before I beat your ass and throw you down onto the Mass Pike."

Vinny knew he was overpowered and Shortstop was serious, so he took all the money out of his pockets and gave it to Whistle....$9.17 in total. With nothing more to be said, he went tromping off with his violin over his shoulder. Shortstop and Whistle looked at each other and burst out laughing uncontrollably. For several minutes, they just could not stop. They simply couldn't. When they finally got a hold of themselves, they looked at each other. "Let's go in."

Inside the heap, Shortstop lit the lantern. The soft glow filled the space and made them both feel safe.

"Here!" Shortstop said as he handed the money to Whistle. "At least you got half back."

"Thanks! I appreciate you taking care of that for me," the young boy replied.

"Don't give it away again."

"I won't, I promise."

Whistle was slightly embarrassed at his own naivety, but he knew he was learning how to survive on the streets and get by on his wits. With the nine dollars and seventeen cents now securely tucked deep in his pocket, he once again crawled under his now favorite Sox blanket and started to doze, but just before he did....

"Shortstop?"

"Yes, suh?"

"Am I supposed to be here?"

"Boy, I truly don't know. I'm glad you are here. But when the time comes for you to move on down the road, you better go. I certainly will remember our time together fondly and wish you the best on your adventure."

"Thanks Shortstop," Whistle said as he fell asleep. Less than a week later, Whistle's travelin' jones started stirring as the weather grew colder. Shortstop, the streets of Boston, and sleeping more or less outside made sense in the summer, but it didn't take a meteorologist to figure out that the birds flying overhead in a V formation had the right idea, and if you were "outdoors," so to speak, it would be wise to follow their lead.

As Whistle's birthday, September 11, rolled around, he figured it was as good a time as any to keep on keeping on, as the saying goes. That morning he woke up, packed his things, and debated whether to wake up a still sleeping Shortstop. Looking around, he took everything in. There was a Jack Daniel's bottle and a Steve Miller Band album propped up right next to each other. For some odd reason, there was a *Christmas Carol* leg lamp from Italy and a magnet from the Eiffel Tower stuck to the ceiling. After some time, he knew he had to wake Shortstop.

"Hey," the boy said with a timid shoulder push.

"Shortstop."......Again, this time with an extra push.

"Hey Nipples?" Still nothing.

Whistle was a bit distraught because he didn't want to leave his friend, but the boy knew he had to move on. He looked at the sleeping homeless man who became his de facto guardian angel during his stay in Boston, and for that, he would be eternally grateful. Shortstop was still out like a light, so Whistle bent down, kissed his forehead, told him he loved him and headed out.

The very first snowflakes of the year were wonderfully cold and crisp against the warm sun still peeking here and there through the clouds producing the flurries. Whistle was back on the move. He weaved his way out of Kenmore Square and walked to the top of Boylston Street. Stopping for a moment, he looked out over everything. The street before him was amazing with all its colors, smells, shops and characters. A step forward and squared shoulders, it was time for Whistle to rock and roll.

That's exactly what he did as he made his way south and eventually out of the city. As night fell, Whistle knew he had to find a place to stay for the night, especially since it was getting colder. Walking into a parking lot, he was ready to settle for anything he could find. He eventually found an abandoned minivan to sleep in and a dumpster behind a strip mall that contained a king's ransom of discarded Pizza Hut leftovers.

Figuring he had food and shelter handled for the night, he struggled with the door of the banged up minivan, eventually getting it to open. He slinked inside and made his bed in the way back. He realized as he fell asleep, slightly shivering, how he had gotten comfortable and maybe a little soft staying with Shortstop. If he was going to make it, he'd need to be resourceful. He'd need to think fast, move fast, and stay a step ahead of winter as he made his way down the Eastern Seaboard and into the great unknown.

CHAPTER
THIRTY
A Period of Good Travels

The next morning, Whistle woke up, climbed out of the minivan, and found a McDonald's down the block. A bathroom break, the best clean up in the sink he could manage, and a good look at himself in the mirror. His skin was spotty and his hair was greasy and getting long and stringy. His clothes were dingy, full of stains, and were really starting to smell ripe. He realized that the disapproving looks he was now getting on a regular basis were somewhat understandable.

Walking out, he stood in line and ordered a Sausage McMuffin along with a free cup of water, which he promptly devoured. Grabbing a handful of napkins and a cupful of ice from the machine, he was out the door.

Gathering his stride, Whistle worked toward travel routes that would lead him down the Northeast Corridor. The walk through Southie proved to be a maze of small streets, parking lots, and deserted tenement yards with way too many backtracks. That night he slept underneath a small building overhang with a light rain falling just feet away from the concrete Whistle lay on.

The next day, Whistle woke up cold and sore from the damp, cold pavement bed. Nevertheless he stood up, gathered his meager belongings, stretched the knots out of his neck, squared up his shoulders, and pressed on. Two more days went by in much the same manner until Whistle was well out of Quincy. He found Interstate 93 and was relieved, as travel was easier and more familiar through the woods along the highway. All the solitude you could ask for with society just a stone's throw away if you were in need of another human's assistance. Like an old friend, the highway was always there, always humming its song to you as the miles rolled by. Telling a million stories as the cars, trucks, vans, motorcycles, and semis roared down that concrete river like steel bellied multi-colored salmon racing downstream.

A fleet of school buses carried a football team, marching band, cheerleader squad, and color guard to a Friday night football game at a rival high school. They'd have hot coffee and donuts; the cheerleaders would be cute and wholesome, shaking their pom-poms, dancing and making pyramids. Proud moms and dads would cheer wildly as their boys pulled out a game winning drive in the fourth quarter. Announcements of 4-H Club raffles and bake sales coming from the press box would mingle lovingly with the marching band playing "We Got the Beat" by the Go-Gos, slightly out of tune on account of the crisp night air wreaking havoc on the horns as the drum line pounded out a primitive rhythm that was as old as Plymouth Rock itself.......the sound of New England in fall.

He watched the fleet turn onto I-95 South and took it as a sign to follow the warm, fuzzy feeling the buses left in their wake. It came in handy on a cold night sleeping outdoors. He kept walking a few more hours and began to notice his feet getting sore, so he found a seemingly secure spot and made his bed for the night. He looked at his shoes and realized they were fairly blown out. He was hungry, tired, sore, and winter was nipping at his heels. As he fell asleep, he realized he'd have to make better time heading south.

Waking up shivering in the predawn cold, something dawned on Whistle. It was getting around the time of year that a snow storm was a rare but real possibility. That's when he made his mind up, he'd have to hitchhike. Trying to make himself as presentable as possible, without a comb, mirror, soap, or water, in the same dirty clothes and shoes he'd been living in the whole journey, he made his way down to the freeway and started southbound, turning and sticking his right thumb out whenever a promising sounding engine came roaring down from the north.

Before too long, a silver sedan slowed down and pulled over. Whistle thought how LUCKY he was that someone was willing to give him a lift before a statie saw him. Dirty as he was, he was still young looking, even for his age, which was definitely young enough for DCYF to get involved in his life.

As the car waited, now with the passenger window down, Whistle jogged happily up to the car, tucking his gear underneath his arm.

"What the hell are you doing, kid!?" the driver asked before Whistle could bend down to look the driver in the eye.

"I'm just trying to catch a ride, sir."

"Get in, quick," the man said as he leaned over to unlock and push open the passenger door.

Whistle climbed aboard and immediately was hit with the strong aroma of peppermint and stale cigarette smoke, both of which brought back pleasant memories of early childhood. As he snapped back to the present, the car was already off the shoulder and they were well on their way down the road.

"You must be crazy, kid! You can't just hitchhike on the highway," the driver said.

"I didn't know that," Whistle responded.

"Well now you do. What's your name, kid?"

"Whistle. Whistle Evel Fonzarelli Starr, sir."

"Well Whistle, I'm Larry Clarke….So where you headed?"

Thinking for a moment, the boy replied, "I'm just headed south, sir."

"South, huh? Well I'm headed to Mystic if that helps you out."

"Mystic?"

"Yeah, small town in Connecticut."

"Sounds good to me!"

Whistle felt grateful for the ride as they zipped down I-95 south. *How long would it take to walk it?* he wondered. Plus Larry seemed like a nice guy. He worked for a small insurance company and was married with a son in college. As they continued to make small talk, the "Welcome to Rhode Island" sign appeared, stirring up some quiet excitement in Whistle. He was finally getting somewhere thanks to one Larry Clarke.

"Whistle, if you're going to hitchhike—which you shouldn't!—do it at the bottom of an on-ramp as opposed to on the highway. Be kind of low key about it and watch for cops, because they WILL take you in. Also, watch who you take a ride from; there's a lot of wackos out there." Larry semi-lectured Whistle in a fatherly fashion that made Whistle feel looked after in a general sense.

"Yes sir."

"Call me Larry."

"OK, Larry."

They drove through Rhode Island without saying much more, the radio tuned to a local classic rock station. A DJ named Carolyn Fox was giving away tickets, and the city of Providence, with its Superman building downtown, Federal Hill La Pigna, and Big Blue Bug, served as welcome distractions. Another solid stretch of not much more than pavement and greenery passed before they reached Connecticut.

"So, Whistle, whereabouts down south are you hoping to get to?" Larry asked, trying not to sound like a busybody.

"I don't have a specific plan, just hoping to stay one step ahead of winter," the boy replied, trying to sound as cheerful as possible about his current situation.

Larry nodded and gave Whistle a wry look. He knew by Whistle's appearance he could probably use a hot meal, shower, and bed for the night, so he made the boy an offer.

"Whistle, my boy is away at college. Why don't you stay at our house tonight? You can sleep in his room and my wife is a great......uh......decent cook," Larry joked.

"Thanks Larry, but I can't. You've already saved me a few days' walking and I don't want to be a bother to you or your wife."

"Bother? Our son is at school and we could use the company. He left behind a bunch of clothes that are like new, he just outgrew them. Please! We'd love to have you."

Whistle could tell that Larry was truly sincere about his offer, and it all sounded so good that there was no way he could resist.

"Okay, if it's really no trouble…"

"No trouble whatsoever."

With that, Whistle thanked Larry again as they took the off-ramp to Mystic. A short trip through the quaint little town, and they were at Larry's house. They got out of the car, Whistle grabbed his bag, and they headed in just as it started to get dark. Inside, Larry's wife came around the corner and her eyes gave away her shock and confusion as Larry quickly introduced her to Whistle, asked her with a peck on the cheek to start dinner, and brought the boy upstairs.

"Here's a towel, and I'll put some clothes on the bed for you," Larry said as he gestured to the last room at the end of the hall, adjacent to the bathroom."

"Thanks Larry!"

"Fuggetaboutit." Larry chuckled, making light of his generosity.

Larry jaunted back down the stairs as Whistle turned on the water in the shower. He took a quick look in the mirror and could understand the shocked look on Larry's wife's face. As quickly as he could, he got out of his dirty clothes and in the shower. It felt incredible to watch all that grime wash down the drain and to wash his hair with good shampoo and lather up with expensive soap, no doubt purchased by Larry's wife.

The hot water and steam felt so good that if it wasn't for the promise of a home cooked meal waiting for him downstairs, he wouldn't have turned it off. When he finally did, he stepped out of the shower and dried off with a towel that was so soft and dry, that he was actually curious what kind of detergent Mrs. Clarke used.

Returning to the bedroom, there was indeed a set of clean clothes on the bed and a slightly worn pair of sneakers on the floor. Putting everything on, he was amazed at how good it felt to wear clean clothes, as it had been a while. He finished tying the laces of his new/used Converse All-Stars and made his way downstairs. Before he even made it halfway down, the heavenly smell of that home cooked meal grabbed him by the nostrils and pulled him the rest of the way.

Walking into the dining room, Whistle was relieved to find Larry had successfully explained everything to Mrs. Clarke because she was very nice and almost motherly. It didn't escape Whistle that maybe she was missing her own son. The three of them sat down to a meal that the boy promptly devoured in the most polite way possible. He tried his hardest not to appear greedy and remember his table manners, but boy it was hard.

Perfectly cooked meatloaf, the smoothest mashed potatoes with salt, pepper, and plenty of butter, sweet green beans and soft, warm bread filled the boy's belly. Also, he could not remember the last time he drank cold milk. *Too long*, he thought to himself.

Feeling the wholesome nutrition do for his insides what the shower and change of clothes did for his outsides, Whistle couldn't help but let out an enthusiastic groan, trying not to talk with his mouth full.

"Must be good, nobody's talking," Mrs. Clarke joked.

"I'm sorry, but this is so delicious...."

"Eat up, glad you like it," Larry interrupted.

"There's plenty more if you have room for seconds," Mrs. Clarke chimed in.

Whistle had seconds and an extra glass of milk. Now he was so sleepy he could barely keep his eyes open. Mrs. Clarke gave Larry a knowing glance which he took as his cue.

"Come on, son," Larry piped up, leading Whistle upstairs. Before he knew it, Whistle was tucked happily into the most comfortable bed he'd ever slept in. Falling asleep, he couldn't help but feel lucky that Larry happened to pick him up, take him in, and completely hook him up with a great meal, change of clothes, shower, and shelter for the night. Today was a good day indeed.

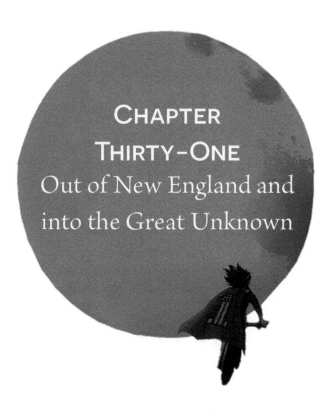

CHAPTER
THIRTY-ONE
Out of New England and into the Great Unknown

The next morning, Whistle woke up around eleven. He was once again confused for a moment before he remembered where he was. Whistle smiled, stretched, and took a few more minutes to enjoy the most comfortable bed he'd ever laid in. Eventually, he got up, got dressed and headed downstairs. He found a notepad and pen next to the fridge. He wrote a note thanking Larry and Mrs. Clarke for their hospitality and explained that he had to move on. He set the note down on the counter, using a coffee can for a paperweight. He picked up his backpack, locked the door behind him, and started down the road. He was just about to turn the corner when he heard a voice.

"Whistle!" Larry called as he drove up the street behind him.

"Whistle!" Again he called as he pulled up and rolled the passenger window down, almost like a rerun of the day before.

"Get in, I'll give you a ride to 95."

"Okay," Whistle replied sheepishly.

They drove in silence that was awkward and familiar at the same time. When they got to the on-ramp, Larry pulled over. With the car idling, Whistle opened the door. He was just opening his mouth to thank Larry when he was interrupted.

"Hang on, son," Larry said, putting a hand on the boy's shoulder.

"Listen, your pack has fresh socks and underwear. I know you gotta do what gotta do but just know, if you want to stay with us for a while, we would love it." He spoke out of true concern for the boy.

"Thanks Larry, I would love to stay but I need to keep moving south and the longer I stay, the harder it's going to be to go."

"Yeah………Yeah well, here, take this," Larry insisted as he stuffed three hundred-dollar bills in Whistle's palm under the pretense of a handshake, the way your uncle would on Christmas.

"I can't take this!" Whistle protested.

"You're takin' it or I'm callin' the cops to haul you in, I got some friends on the force," Larry half joked.

"Thank you Larry, I…..thank you." What could you say?

With that, Whistle stepped out of the car, shut the door, and waved as Larry drove away. As he stood there at the on-ramp, he took a moment to evaluate his current situation…

I'm fourteen years old, recently showered, belly full of food, pocket full of cash, and even a new set of clothes. Heck, even three bottles of water, he thought to himself as he promptly twisted the top off of one and took a nice, refreshing swig.

He walked uphill along the on-ramp and started down the side of the freeway, which was fairly busy at this particular day and time. Feeling a lot less self-conscious thumbing a ride than yesterday, he only had to walk about a mile and a half before a box truck pulled over. "Where you goin' bro?" the driver, a large Latino man, shouted over the noise of the truck.

"Just heading south, as far I can go," Whistle shouted back.

"Well, get in if you want," the man said as he unlocked the door. Whistle climbed up in the cab and stowed his pack between his feet.

"Thanks! Thanks a lot," Whistle said over the noisy engine.

"No worries, G. So what's your name?" the driver inquired as the truck bounced them around.

"Whistle, what's yours?"

"Juan….Hey, I'm getting off just outside of New York City, cool?" the driver said as he lit a joint.

"That'd be great, thanks."

"You smoke?" Juan asked, holding out the joint.

"No thanks," Whistle replied politely, waving his hand.

"Well hold it for me for a sec." This, as he shifted and cut over into the left lane.

"You ever smoke weed before?" Juan continued.

"Yeah, one or twice, makes me paranoid," Whistle responded.

"Well, do yourself a favor and hit that. It's mellow."

Figuring Juan was holding it together pretty well, he took a hit. Holding it in as long as he could, he exploded in a raspy coughing fit.

"Haha….Easy, homey," Juan chuckled as he took the joint back.

They drove down through New Jersey and shot the shit for a while.

"Your name's Whistle? Whistle what?" Juan asked, more or less to make conversation.

"Whistle Evel Fonzarelli Starr. What's yours?"

"Juan Martha Winkler."

"No way!" Whistle responded.

"Yeah, Martha's my great grandmother's name."

"No, I mean, that's a trip as well, but Winkler is Fonz's real last name. Henry Winkler? My middle name's Fonzarelli? It's destiny."

"Huh….Wow," Juan responded, trying to sound like he got the connection, though Whistle suspected he was just being polite.

As they trucked on, Juan produced a cooler full of eight-ounce Miller Lites. They both opened one and finished the roach. Speeding down I-95, Whistle felt good. Another Miller later, he was in the groove. The sun was shining. The wind came through the window and cooled the cab perfectly. A moment of perfect contentment.

"Okay buddy, this is where we get off," Juan said as he cut over to the right lane to make the exit in one half mile.

"Right on," Whistle said, snapping out of his blissful daze. "Nice to meet you. Thanks for the ride and the beers."

"You bet….Take care of yourself."

And with that, Whistle climbed down, slammed the door to the cab shut, and found himself once again next to an off-ramp at sunset thinking about his next move. His beer buzz just starting to wane, he climbed up into the woods just north of New York City. He found a high ledge that provided a stunning view of New York City—The Real Deal Big Apple. No better place to ponder his options until he faded out for the night.

"If I can make it there, I'll make it anywhere," he half sang to himself as he laid out his blanket, taking a moment to marvel at the Empire State Building, Twin Towers, and all the other landmarks he'd seen in movies, television, and pictures his whole life.

Whistle managed to build a small fire to dry his socks out and give himself a sense of security. Another bottle of water was cracked and gulped down as he was feeling a bit dehydrated. As he sprawled out on the blanket, he thought about the fact that tomorrow he'd be taking a bite out of the Big Apple. Don't mind the maggots…..

Chapter Thirty-Two
What a Ride it Would Be

Whistle woke up early, not exactly according to plan. He usually tried to get as much sleep as he could before it was time to hit the road but....not today, not with the Big Apple, home of the Yankees, Mets, Jets, Giants, Knicks, *Saturday Night Live*, KISS, and the Statue of Liberty within his sights....right there, beckoning to him from that ledge. Never in a million years did Whistle ever think he'd see New York City in the flesh, but there it was, sparkling and fantastical at night but in the cold mist of the early morning hours, it looked like it meant business....

Whistle walked out of the woods with clean socks and underwear, a pack on his back, a wad of cash and a belief that nothing was going to stop him. He got along the freeway and walked toward a skyline that seemed to stay out of reach as the miles stretched out behind him. He figured he'd be in Manhattan by nightfall, but it was looking like it would be another day or two.

That night, the sun set on a bewildered Whistle as he ate the crust of a Domino's Pizza he found in a trash can at the far corner of a strip mall. After a lousy night's sleep in the tangles of weeds in a nearby abandoned lot, he woke up to the sound of road construction so loud, the jackhammers rattled his teeth. "Ugh, time to get a move on."

After yet ANOTHER day of walking and no one willing to give him a ride, night fell and the skyline appeared close enough to feel like he was making at least some progress, so he hunkered down in a campsite for the night and promised himself, one way or another, he was going to make it to the city by tomorrow night.

The next morning came and Whistle barely found his stride when he caught a ride at the on-ramp just north of New York City. Oh boy, what a ride it would be! Walking with his thumb out, he was facing forward, focused more on walking than catching a more and more unlikely ride, if the past couple of days were any indication....But, you never know.

Way off in the distance behind him, he heard the unmistakable, guttural roar of a '67 Chevy Impala. As it approached, he heard a familiar guitar melody, cranked all the way, yet still barely audible over the Detroit steel fast approaching. Was it?......It was! Ace Frehley's guitar solo in "King of the Night Time World," from Destroyer, the best album KISS ever made. He had to turn around.

What he saw was indeed a sight to behold. A perfect, jet black Chevy Impala with white racing stripes, black leather interior, chrome rims, and fat Goodyear tires. The perfect combination of beauty and menace.

"Hello," Whistle said timidly as he bent down to meet the eyes of the driver.

"What's up, fucker?" he heard coming back at him.

"I'm Whistle."

"Well get in, asshole. We're about to kick ass!"

Not giving fear a chance to talk him out of it, Whistle got in.

"I'm Travis, who are you again?"

"Whistle," the boy replied as Travis gunned it and immediately pinned both of them to their leather seats.

"Could you slow down a bit?" Whistle couldn't help but plead as his fingernails dug into the arm rest.

"I suppose I COULD," Travis replied as he dug the gas pedal into the floorboard. This is when one of Whistle's worst nightmares took place.

"Hey man, let's just stop somewhere and smoke or something," the boy implored.

"No fuckin' way, brother. I'm on fire tonight!" Travis proclaimed.

"I'll just get out here," Whistle replied.

"The fuck you will. We're gonna ride this bitch all the way home!"

"Seriously, I think I'm going to throw up!" Whistle pleaded, not sure if he was being truthful or just grasping at straws.

"Quit being a bitch! HAHA!!"

"No, I'm serious! PLEASE let me out!"

"Just puke out the window! WHOOHOOO!"

"Dude! WHAT THE FUCK! STOP!" Whistle shouted, now beyond scared. Larry wasn't kidding about being careful who you get a ride from.

Just then, Travis downshifted and pulled over, thankfully.

"Thanks for the ride Travis, nice to meeEE……"

And before he could unbuckle his seat belt, Travis gunned it again and once again pinned Whistle to his seat, almost giving him whiplash.

"WHAT THE FUCK!" was all Whistle could manage.

"I'm huntin' heathens and chasing the dragon's tail, HEEEHEEEEE!"

Whistle didn't know what that meant other than he was in trouble as the speedometer crept past a buck ten. His mind raced as he quickly realized his life was currently in the hands of a complete psycho.

"Do you wanna slow down?!"

"Wellllll……NOPE!" Travis was now gunning it to a buck twenty.

Out of options, Whistle reflexively punched Travis in the side of the head as hard as he could, which, given the G-force, the angle, and the state of mind Travis was in, barely fazed him.

"C'mon! You can do better than that!" the maniacal driver yelled as he swerved over four lanes, barely missing a box truck much like the one Whistle was riding in two days prior.

Zipping down a tunnel of insanity like a bullet, Whistle searched his mind for some way—*any* way—to get out of the situation.

"Hold the wheel," Travis said, letting go of the wheel before Whistle even had a chance to respond. Whistle grabbed the wheel and Travis poured out a bump of coke and snorted it from the back of his wrist.

"Here, take a bump!" Travis said, not even looking at the road.

"No I'm good. PLEASE slow down!" At this point the boy's pleading was like a mantra.

"Focus on the road, I'll worry about the speed limit," Travis wisecracked as he did another bump, three or four times as big as the first. As Travis commandeered the wheel again, Whistle sat back and thought to himself, *If I ever get out of this, I'm gonna do like Larry said and be REAL careful about who I take a ride from.*

They kept driving with the radio and the car so loud that any kind of polite conversation was impossible, but they were way past that point anyway. The screaming Impala cut through the traffic as if it was standing still as Travis white-knuckled the wheel, grinding his teeth, talking to himself and staring wide-eyed at the road as Whistle mentally adapted to the situation just enough to at least try to formulate a plan…

That's when he noticed Travis now staring wide-eyed at the dash as the car bucked a bit. Turns out they were just about out of gas, mercifully. He got off at the next exit and pulled into a Sunoco at the bottom of the off-ramp. He pulled into the station and up to the pump, almost fishtailing. The maniac driver jumped out of the car and ran in to pay the cashier, seemingly forgetting all about Whistle. Just as the boy grabbed his bag and was about to make a run for it, Travis's fist was in Whistle's face, gripping a Slim Jim.

"Here, eat this," Travis said as he went around the front of the car to the pump. Whistle was so hungry that he couldn't refuse it and chomped it down. Figuring he'd already been through the craziest part of the ride and Travis seemed to be coming back to earth, the boy figured he might as well "ride this bitch all the way home." Wherever that might be.

"Alright, give me a bump," Whistle said.

"Ju got it, mang!" Travis said as he poured a tiny mound of coke on the back of Whistle's hand.

He put his other hand over it to keep it from spilling as Travis gunned it back up to the highway.

"What are you doin? Snort that shit!" Travis exclaimed as they burned along down the passing lane.

Whistle was having second thoughts when Travis was on him again.

"SNORT IT! Don't spill that shit!" So, just like that, up Whistle's nose it went.

A rush came over him like nothing he ever felt before. He'd never felt so simultaneously in and out of control at once. Suddenly, Travis seemed like a completely reasonable person. The boy had a strong urge to climb out the window and onto the hood—while going a hundred miles an hour—to stand there and tell the world to go fuck itself in no uncertain terms.

A split second later, he was freaking out about the speed again.

"HEY FUCKHEAD! SLOW DOWN!" Whistle said, now feeling more fight than flight.

Travis turned and looked at Whistle shocked, and promptly broke into a guffaw, mouth agape.

"HAW HAW HAW…..HEEEE HEEEE!" he brayed as he shifted and put all his weight down on the gas. Whistle punched him again; this time he connected square in the throat, which made Travis lose control of the car. Whistle jumped into the driver's seat, pushing Travis against the driver's side door as he managed to bring the car to a stop.

As the dust cleared, the boy collected himself. His anger grew, the coke was rushing through his system and his adrenaline would not subside. Travis was a little slower to gather his wits and looked at Whistle in a way that was impossible to read, so Whistle just punched him again, square in the chin, knocking him unconscious. The boy knew that the only option he had left was to open the driver's side door, roll this psycho out, and take this beautiful piece of machinery for a joy ride as far south as he could go.....so that's what he did.

Whistle drove the Impala as far as it would go until it eventually ran out of gas once more. He pulled into the breakdown lane and onto the shoulder of the road. Without a second thought, he grabbed his bag, left the car, and jogged down the road until he found a good patch of woods. He hooked right and found a decent spot to bed down and hopefully wind down enough to catch a few hours of shut eye. He tried to put everything out of his mind and slow his heart rate down. He kept thinking about the car back up the road in the breakdown lane. He finally gave up on sleeping for the meantime and ran back up to the car to do a sweep for any belongings he might have left behind. He reached in the driver's window, popped it in neutral, turned the wheel to the right, and pushed. The car rolled surprisingly easy and went down a ditch, landing deep enough into the brush to be fairly incognito to anyone driving through. Satisfied, Whistle headed back to his camp.

Coming down off the coke, he was definitely ready for sleep. Closing his eyes, the boy instantly realized it wasn't happening until he settled himself with a few things. First of all, he was sure he'd never do coke again. That stuff was absolute shit.

Next came the thought of Travis Fletcher. Whistle felt bad about pushing him out of the car and driving away. Despite committing numerous crimes over the past couple of weeks, each more extreme than the next, the boy had a good heart, so he was conflicted.

"The fucker was high as a kite and almost killed me numerous times, and the way he was driving, there's a good chance he could have got in an accident and hurt someone, most likely himself. As a matter of fact, I'd say I did him a favor," he rationalized. "I had to do what I had to do.....Fuckin' a'right I did." He laughed to himself as he made peace with his decisions.

Lastly, he didn't like pushing the car into the ditch, but he didn't need cops coming around, searching the area and finding him. That would be a major snag with endless questions. All in all, he knew everything wound up as it should be, so he shut his eyes and within minutes was sound asleep. Tomorrow would be a new day with the same objective: get further south than he was right now.

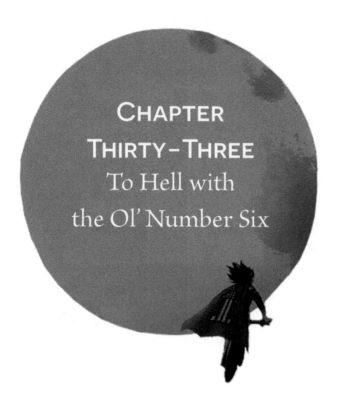

CHAPTER THIRTY-THREE
To Hell with the Ol' Number Six

The next afternoon came and Whistle could hear the traffic from down on I-95. He was very hot and his head was pounding. After a while, he slowly opened his eyes and saw by the sun in the sky that it was well past noon. He was dehydrated and his endorphins were depleted from the coke. He knew he'd need to feel more like himself before he could deal with New York City, so it would have to wait until tomorrow. The thought of no more coke ran through his mind as he took another bottle of water out of his pack and chugged it in seconds, giving his headache some relief. He laid back down and dozed off again for a spell.

He woke up in the late afternoon still feeling like crap. He knew he had to piss, so the boy forced himself to get up. Whistle took a short walk into the brush and relieved himself. He staggered back and dropped back down onto his blanket. Turning to lay on his back, he stretched his arms over his head and felt the chills set in. His body sweated out all the nasty chemicals and stress of the previous day.

The afternoon turned to evening and the boy's imagination started working overtime for some strange reason. He started thinking about his mom, Shortstop, leaving high school, Eric's family and all the security that staying with them provided. He wondered if Ms. Fisher was still teaching and if New York City would be everything it was cracked up to be. He thought about Mikey and the monarchs, dressed in their beautiful vibrant colors. He thought about the kind people he met like Hellcat Wilson, Larry and his wife, and also people who at the end of the day were only thinking about themselves. He figured he was pretty good at getting a read on people, but he'd have to sharpen that skill even more if he was going to continue on his journey.

His mind ping ponged, ran laps, and climbed the walls of his skull, carrying alternately positive and fearful thoughts, until he mentally wore himself out enough to fall back asleep. He was just about there when he heard a ruckus. He awoke, startled, but quickly breathed a sigh of relief to find three squirrels chasing each other around, either mating, fighting, or playing. Whistle didn't care, he was just happy it wasn't a creature of the human variety. Those had proved to be the most trouble so far on this wild journey. He laughed at the absurdity of this thought as he fell back asleep, and before long he was visiting a strange dreamland.

He found himself in a bowling alley. He was twenty-one years old and was on a bowling team, knocking down candlepins. He was wearing a black and red official league shirt with "Stardust" written across the back. His shoes were red, white, and blue. He slid around in them as they were just a bit too big for him.

"It's all up to you," a man said, with the unmistakable smell of Busch beer on his breath.

"What?" Whistle asked, confused.

"The championship is on the line and it's all in your hands. Stardust Music has never beaten Willy and Wally's Hardware and this is our chance. It's all in your hands," the man emphasized again. Whistle waved the man away as he focused on the perfectly waxed lane, candlepins at the far end, taunting him.

As he picked up the first of the three bowling balls he was allotted to knock down the pins, he noticed it looked like an oversized gumball, all blue and pink swirls with a satisfying weight that felt good in his hands. He peered down the lane with cheering from the Stardust team and jeers from Willy and Wally's creating a cacophony behind him. With a thunderous *crack!* the ball hit the maple boards as his shoes squeaked and echoed through the alley. The ball glided along and took out everything but the pins numbered five and six. With two pins and as many balls left, Whistle decided to aim for the outside pin first. He picked up another ball, this one blue with sparkles and gold swirls. He chucked it down the lane and barely nicked the number five pin, which juuuust missed spinning and taking the six with it.

"OOOHHH!" he heard from the crowd behind him, now growing in size.

Picking up the last ball, this one pink and gold, he squared himself and held it up to his face, peering over it at the last pin standing. Plenty of pins on the ground all around it, seemingly more than he started with, he was just about to take that last pin out when one of the guys from Stardust yelled "HO! Hold up!" Whistle barely caught himself before he released the ball.

"What?" Whistle replied, somewhat annoyed.

"You gotta make this, or you're fired," the man said.

"I don't even work for you, but if you want to win, you need to get off my back! The pressure isn't helping matters," Whistle replied, now annoyed.

"Okay, Okay…..Just win. Focus on the pin," the man said as he went back to join the crowd.

Whistle shook his head and turned back toward the lane. He took several steps and launched the ball perfectly down the maple wood towards that last pin, favoring the center of the lane. As the bowling ball glided towards the pins like velvet, it looked like a perfect shot. When it hit the first deadwood, Whistle knew he had won the tournament for his team. The only problem was the bowling ball hit the deadwood around the pin and exploded into a cloud of dust. And there stood the six pin. Willy and Wally's would take home the trophy. Whistle turned to his team.

"What the fuck just happened!?" Whistle exclaimed, confused.

"No problem at all! You get three more balls because it's the championship," came the strange reply from his teammates. Confused, the boy decided to take them because in this dream, he really wanted to win for his teammates. Three balls, one pin, and plenty of deadwood to use. Stardust once again had an opportunity to reclaim the trophy, thanks to Whistle.

The boy threw his first ball as hard as he could, confident that as long as he hit the deadwood, the six pin would fall. The ball hit the shellac glossing the maple boards with an all too familiar crack and proceeded to rumble down the alley. He turned to his teammates, hearing the pins cling-clanging around at the end of the lane, certain he had won. The look on his team's collective face said otherwise, however. Confused, he turned around to see twice as much deadwood around the one remaining standing pin….*Impossible,* Whistle thought to himself.

"Come on! Win this thing already!" the team captain with the beer breath shouted, now chiding him more aggressively than before. Whistle bent down and grabbed the next ball and thrust it down the alley with all his might and when it reached the pins, they all flew around in every direction….still somehow missing the last pin standing. Whistle rubbed his eyes in frustration and when he looked back down the alley, all the downed pins had disappeared, leaving just the number six, standing upright and defiant.

"MUTHAFUCKA!" Now it was personal. He took careful aim and released his third and final ball. It rolled so smooth and was bang on the line, headed straight for the last pin. Right as it was about to knock that thing into outer space, the ball somehow veered left, just grazing the pin, wobbling just enough to seem to mock Whistle.

"What the?" was all Whistle could manage to say. He had lost the game for Stardust. So instead of the hero, he'd surely be the heel. At this point, he was just happy to be done with the whole strange ordeal.

"That's ok, you get three more balls....on account of it being the championship and all!" a short, stocky, pleasant looking man with a round face exclaimed.

"Can someone else take my turn? I don't seem to be in the zone today," Whistle said.

"No can do....that's in violation of the rules. Don't worry, you can do it!"

Without another word, the boy picked up a green and silver sparkle ball and chucked it down the lane in frustration annnnnnnd.......gutter ball.

"Shit!" he spat under his breath.

"Alright, here we go." Ball gliding down the lane aaannnnnnd......a little too far to the left and down the back without even touching the pin.

"Come ON!" Whistle was losing it now. He tried to breathe deep and take it down a notch but was having no luck. Well, whatever. He fired the third ball down the lane. It came out of his hand a bit wild but started to settle. With every foot of lane that passed the ball looked truer and truer. This was it! Finally, Whistle was about to win the game for Stardust. Go home Willy and Wally. Twenty feet from victory and this time the ball burst into flames, leaving just a scorched puddle of resin just inches from old Number 6.

"Okay, what the fuck is going on here?" Whistle said, now fuming.

"No problem, son. Three more balls."

Three more tries, three more misses....this was getting ridiculous!

"It's alright, son. You get three more balls on account of it being the championship."

This would be his last three attempts. If that pin was still standing, he was gonna burn the whole joint down. Starting with that fucking pin!

The first ball hit the alley and bounced up vertically and put a hole in the ceiling and never came back down.

"Man!" Whistle growled.

The second ball released and looked real good. This was definitely gonna knock old six down to win the game, until the black marble ball turned into a bobcat before his eyes, stopped in front of the pin, and actually took a second to sniff the pin before it turned around and looked at Whistle.

"Fuck…" Whistle said under his breath. Just then the bobcat started sprinting back up the lane toward the boy with one thing on its mind: to sink its fangs into Whistle's throat and do as much damage as possible.

The boy had just enough time to brace himself for the inevitable. He closed his eyes and waited for it…

"C'mon boy! Get with it!" the Busch beer drinking captain yelled. Whistle slowly opened his eyes and saw that the rabid animal had vanished. Nothing in front of him but that lone, standing pin. With no understanding of what just happened, he picked up the third and final ball. Getting ready to throw it, he realized he was terrified to do so. Not so much because of the game, but because of what the ball might turn into this time. Maybe a grizzly bear that could take his face off with one swift swipe. OR, maybe a stack of hundred-dollar bills that he could just pick up and walk out with? Whistle highly doubted it as he took aim with great trepidation. *Well, here we go, all or nothing,* he thought to himself.

He took a look around the place and soaked in all the sights, sounds, and smells. Then, focusing once more on the remaining pin, he launched the ball….seemed right on the money….still rolling….still rollll…..wait a minute….why is it slowing down?

"Come onnnn." Whistle tried to urge the ball on with telepathy.

The ball was right on the money but ran out of steam just in time to roll up and kiss the pin, making it wobble just enough to give Whistle hope but ultimately remain upright. This finally sent the boy over the edge and sprinting down the lane at the pin in a fit of red hot rage, his slightly large shoes clip-clopping everywhere. He didn't care, all he knew was that pin was going down with or without a bowling ball. As he ran, he noticed the pin wasn't getting any closer. He looked down and saw the lane moving slowly backwards, like a treadmill. Looking behind him he saw the crowd watching him, nonplussed. As if this were an everyday occurrence.

He turned back towards the pin and launched himself at it with all the speed and force he could muster. He lowered his right shoulder and tackled the pin. As he made contact, he felt his right clavicle and scapula turn to powder. The pain was so intense that it woke him up from this strange, otherworldly dream. As he lay there on the cold forest ground, he reached up and felt his right shoulder to make sure it was still intact…Yep, all good, as he chuckled to himself at what a psychologist would say about such a bizarre dream.

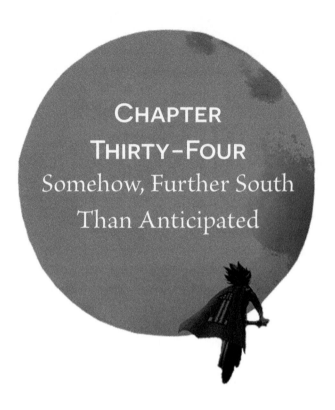

CHAPTER
THIRTY-FOUR
Somehow, Further South
Than Anticipated

The next morning, Whistle awoke with a start. He sat up and looked around. The level of confusion that washed over him was like nothing he'd ever experienced before. Finally, normality slowly began to come back. The sounds of traffic and the relative safety of his camp gave him a sense of reassurance. He shook his head, smacked his face a few times, wiped his eyes and grabbed his last bottle of water. As he sipped the water, he tried to piece together the past twenty-four hours in his mind. But, between the coke, Travis Fletcher, and the strange dream that took place in a bowling alley in a galaxy far, far away, the poor boy was completely lost. All he could think to do was to pack his stuff and head out to the highway. He stepped into the breakdown lane and took a right. A short walk later, he glanced at the ditched Impala in the brush and was reminded what an insane situation he narrowly escaped.

A lot of questions ran through his head as he walked along the highway. One: Where was he? Two: Where did the New York City skyline go? Three: Would there be any ramifications for stealing the Impala? Four: When he left Travis, he was unconscious. What if….well, can't do anything about it now.

Realizing he had no idea where he was going and therefore expending time and energy to potentially backtrack, he veered back into the woods to re-group and formulate a better plan.

It was already afternoon, so he decided to try and hide from the heat on this unusually hot, humid day for late fall. He crawled into a low mossy nook that was just perfect. Laying down, he fell asleep in what felt like an instant. The little bugs that crawled all over Whistle didn't bother him one bit. Damp moss met his face, shade cooled him down, and he was comfortable and able to rest easy. He would stay here the remainder of the day.

Night fell and he slept straight through until morning. His eyes opened to see the beams of gold and orange sunlight blaze through the branches and leaves of the same colors. He was once again thinking about Mikey and those monarch butterflies from way back when.

He believed this was where they must live. Of course, it wasn't, but his youth allowed him to suspend reality if just for a few moments.

A new day was upon him and Whistle was determined to find his way to New York City. Just the thought of it was intoxicating. More than ready to get a move on, he wasted no time packing his bag and getting back out to the highway. He figured the best bet was to head south and walk down the next exit with food, gas, and info. The next exit had a Wendy's at the bottom of the ramp, so Whistle ran down the grassy hill and straight into the restroom, got cleaned up real quick, came out, ordered a few things from the dollar menu, wolfed them down, put the wrappers in the trash, slid the tray up top, got a refill of coke, plenty of ice, and he was out the door. There was a large blond woman with three kids in tow coming in as Whistle was leaving.

"Excuse me, ma'am," Whistle said, shyly.

"Yes?" she replied.

"Could you tell me how to get to New York City?"

"Well, first you need to get on I-95 North."

"Pardon?" Whistle replied, confused.

"You need to get on I-95 North. The on-ramp is just on the other side of the underpass, right over there." She pointed across the parking lot to the red, white, and blue sign, barely visible through the traffic.

"No, I'm headed south….New York City," he repeated, assuming the woman didn't hear him correctly.

"If you want to get to New York, I-95 North is the only way I know, seeing as it's north of here," she said good-naturedly as she walked in behind her kids, obviously impatient to order food.

"OK. Thanks," Whistle said, not wanting to take up any more of her time.

Totally confused, he went outside and found a picnic table under a tree just behind the restaurant to sit and attempt to get his bearings. After a long time he was about to start crying due to sheer frustration. Just then, the back door opened and a boy that worked in the kitchen took a bag of trash to the dumpster then walked over to the table, sat down, and lit a Marlboro. After a big drag and a long exhale, he paused and looked at Whistle.

"You alright?" he asked.

"Yeah, I'm fine, thanks," Whistle responded as he got up to leave so the boy could enjoy his break in peace. Not to mention he didn't want to draw attention to himself.

"Wait a sec. You look like you're on the move. I'm gonna hook you up," the boy said as he jumped up, set his smoke down on the edge of the table, and galloped back to the kitchen.

"Hang tight!" This, as he ducked back into the kitchen.

Whistle thought the kid seemed legit, so he figured whatever he was going to hook him up with was going to be worth hanging around for. The kid was right back out with two big Wendy's bags. One full of burgers and the other full of waters.

"Thanks, but I can't. I don't want you to get in trouble."

"Trouble?" The kid laughed as he picked up his smoke and took another drag. "They just throw the extra burgers out and they tell us to take water home all the time. Trust me, dude."

"Well thanks, man!"

"Not a problem."

"Then here, lunch is on me," Whistle said as he took out two burgers and two waters. They sat a minute and ate together, not saying much until Whistle spoke up.

"How far is the city from here?"

"About twenty-five miles north," the kid replied.

"I've been traveling south for days and I haven't hit the city yet," Whistle said, half to himself.

"I don't know what to tell you, dude. Twenty-five miles north. Anyway, my break's over. Good luck to ya," the kid said as he got up.

"Thanks man, and thanks for the food too," Whistle said.

"Think nothing of it!" the kid said over his shoulder as he headed back to work.

"What the fuck?" Whistle said to himself as he tried to figure out how he missed the city. Then it hit him: between the coke and all the insanity with Travis, not to mention stealing the car and keeping an eye out for cops, it was possible that he'd already been through the city at some point and not even noticed.

He thought about going back because, if you're going to travel through the country to see what it's all about, New York holds a lotta sway. But the more he considered it, he figured he got a crash course on life in the city that never sleeps. He did enough coke to put him off it the rest of his life, got in a fight, stole a car, and was now on the run from the law for multiple offenses committed in a '67 Chevy Impala going north of a hundred miles an hour the whole time. Good enough reason to keep heading south one step at a time, and with winter on the way there was no time to waste.

CHAPTER
THIRTY-FIVE
A Major Grown Up
Experience

The sign read "Yardville: Three and a Half Miles," and seeing as Whistle had already hoofed it for a straight nine, his feet were screaming at him and he wanted nothing more than to be off of them for a good long spell. He kept going until he saw a "Motel 6" sign peeking up above the trees, and the temptation of living like a human for a night, complete with a shower, bed, privacy, and even TV! It was just too much for the boy to deny himself.

He walked down the exit and entered the lobby of the Motel 6. Right away, the smell of stale secondhand smoke hit him. It made him feel nostalgic and instantly put him at ease.

"Can I help you?" the man behind the desk muttered without even looking up.

"Do you have any rooms available?" Whistle asked.

"Yep." Still not looking up.

"Okay, I'll take one, please," the boy answered.

"Twenty-four dollars."

"Okay," Whistle responded as he dug into his pocket.

He paid up, grabbed the key, and found his room, #211. He slid the key into the lock, turned it, and opened the door to his room, a sparkling clean paradise with all the luxury and privacy he could imagine, especially considering the conditions of his journey up to this point. He dropped his stuff, walked around the room, turning every light on. He went into the bathroom, turned the light on in there as well, and looked at himself in the mirror. He looked dirty and disheveled, so a shower would be first on the agenda. He put the air conditioner on high, so the room would be cool and dry by the time he got out, went back in the bathroom and turned the shower on.

After a long, luxurious shower, he got out and dialed the front desk.

"Front desk," said the voice on the other end of the line.

"Hello, I'm in #211, do you happen to have a razor and shaving cream?" Whistle asked.

Within minutes, Whistle was provided with a full toiletry kit, complete with razors, shaving cream, toothbrush, toothpaste, deodorant, mouthwash and extra bar soap. Not to mention a menu from room service….*Hmmmm, pretty reasonable prices*, he thought to himself.

One half hour later, Whistle was propped up in a king size bed, air conditioner on full blast, keeping the cotton sheets cool as a cloud from heaven, a big plate of buffalo tenders with a side of celery and blue cheese, and a couple of ice cold Cokes to wash it down. He grabbed the remote to do a little channel surfing and landed on a rerun of *Happy Days*. At least for the time being, all was right with the world.

Whistle got sleepy after dinner, but tried to stay awake to experience as many hours of relative luxury as he could. He wanted to get his money's worth so he fought to keep his eyes open, but exhaustion finally won out as he fell asleep to the rumble of the air conditioner and the ramble of the local news.

The next morning he woke up to a freezing motel room. Almost feeling irresponsible for wasting so much energy, he had to remind himself that he was paying for it. He stayed under the covers and tried to fall back asleep for a while, but with the sound of families with kids running up and down the hall and the urge to empty his bladder growing stronger by the minute, he reluctantly got up and officially started his day.

He decided to take another shower and shaved again just because he could. After brushing his teeth and drying off, he walked back out to the room and shut off the air conditioning, got dressed, and packed up his belongings. He had a nagging urge to clean up after himself even though the maids were going to give the room a complete once over anyway. He straightened up the bed, picked up the towels in the bathroom, and felt satisfied enough to leave the room and turn in the key.

Whistle made his way down the hall to the elevator. There was a pause, then, with a *ding!* the doors opened. He stepped in, nodded to a young couple already in there. Someone had pressed the button for the main floor, so Whistle stood quietly until the doors opened again. When they did, he got out first and headed for the front lobby.

"Good morning!" An attractive young woman smiled from behind the desk.

"Good morning," Whistle smiled back.

"How was your stay?" she asked.

"Absolutely fantastic," he replied with a bit of a goofy grin as he slid the key across the desk.

She took the key and typed on a computer for a minute.

"Mr. Starr, here's your final bill for incidentals. How will you be paying?" she asked, with green eyes that stunned him. He would swear his heart skipped a beat or two.

"Mr. Starr?"

"No one's ever called me that before." He laughed awkwardly. "Uh, right. I'll pay cash."

As he tried to collect himself, an interesting thought came to him. If he wasn't on the go and lived in the area, he might just might be able to work up the courage to ask this beautiful girl out on a date. But...he was on the move, and had more than a few reasons not to take an extended pit stop here. All settled up, the boy asked, "Is the continental breakfast still open?"

"No, I'm sorry, Mr. Starr, it closed twenty minutes ago," she replied.

"Whistle," he said.

"Excuse me?"

"I'm Whistle, Whistle Evel Fonzarelli Starr. What's your name?" he asked.

"Sylvia. Sylvia Rose Delvecchio."

"Well Sylvia, I think that's a great name and I think you're a wonderful girl," he said, not believing what was coming out of his mouth.

"You are too kind, but I don't think so!" She giggled.

"I do," he said, making eye contact before they both looked away, shyness asserting itself.

"Anyway, I better get going, I have a long walk and I need to find some breakfast. Nice to meet you." He was trying to shrug off the obvious mutual attraction. He had places to go.

"Wait. Em, where are you going?" she asked.

"Oh, uh, south," he answered, simply.

"South to where?"

"I'm not exactly sure."

Getting the gist, Sylvia said, "Tracy, could you take the desk for a minute?"

Tracy came out of the office and took over at the main desk. Sylvia immediately walked around and stood right in front of Whistle.

"C'mon." She smiled; her perfume was like nectar from another universe.

Having no idea what to do with himself, he folded his hands down in front of him, fully aware that nature was doing things to him that he didn't want Sylvia to see. He was pretty sure she looked down briefly, then met eyes with him again. He was putty in her hands.

"You can't start walking on an empty stomach," she said, moving in a little closer. Whistle just stared into those eyes like a deer in the old headlights.

"Come with me," she almost whispered. Her lips looked so soft and kissable. Whistle was sure at that moment, he would have done anything she wanted.

"Follow me." She smiled at him as she turned away. Whistle followed as they walked across the lobby, a little slower than Sylvia, due to a sudden slight limp. She unlocked a door and led Whistle in. Once inside, the door was securely relocked. She led him into the pantry where all the continental breakfast supplies were kept, but Sylvia had other business in mind.

She turned around and pressed her lips against Whistle's before he even knew what was happening. Getting himself back a little, he couldn't believe he was now making out with this beautiful creature that he didn't even know ten minutes ago. Things escalated quickly as hormones and romantic chemistry swirled around that tiny room like a tornado of sexual force. With the two of them grinding and squirming on the stainless steel table and clothes all over the floor, there was a tremendous amount of cluckin' and buckin'. Enough to make anyone outside think there was a construction project taking place in the pantry.

With a release that left both of them completely depleted, they both collapsed. Breathing deep, slow and in rhythm with each other, their heartbeats slowed as that incredible moment came over both of them where, at least for the time being, they were one. As they looked into each other's eyes, Whistle felt complete happiness like he hadn't in a long time, if ever.

After a while, Whistle kissed Sylvia deeply and got up without a word. There was a mutual understanding between the two of them that this experience would never be forgotten by either one of them.

As they got dressed, Sylvia knew she wanted to help Whistle in any way that she could. It was clear to her that he was on some kind of great adventure.

"Hey!" she said out of the blue, "Let's go shopping." Giving him a small but firm kiss on the lips that said, "I know you're going, but we will always be connected."

"Shopping?" Whistle replied, confused. Before he knew it, Sylvia had a big bag full of non-perishable goodies tucked away in his pack. Small cereal boxes, granola bars, Welch's mixed fruit packets, a large Ziploc of salt, pepper, and sugar packets and who knows what else.

For example, only green-eyed, sexy Sylvia knew there was her tiny purple and black thong tucked away at the bottom of the bag. As she tucked it away, she wondered where Whistle would be when he found it. A sly smile came across her face.

"Thanks!" Whistle said, unaware of the underwear.

"You're welcome." She smiled coyly and gave him a wink.

"What?" Whistle asked.

"Nothing!" She giggled.

They sat at the stainless steel table across from each other, holding hands. Sylvia put together a quick breakfast for the two of them consisting of cold pancakes and syrup, cold sausage patties and bacon, cornflakes with two percent milk, orange juice and instant coffee to wash it all down with. They didn't say much, but nothing really needed to be said as they gazed into each other's eyes, lost in the afterglow. After a while Sylvia spoke up.

"Whistle, I gotta get back. You gonna be alright?"

"I'll be fine. You gonna be OK?"

"I'm serious!" she said, brow furrowing. "I don't know where you're going or what for, but be careful."

"I will, I'll be fine, don't worry."

"I hope so," she said as Whistle gave her another kiss.

"Listen, I don't want to stand out in the lobby and say goodbye to you, so can we just say goodbye right here?" Whistle said, second guessing his decision to leave what at the moment felt like the love of his life.

"Of course," Sylvia said, feeling the same.

"I'm so glad I met you, and if I was staying here, I would make you mine," Whistle said, meaning every word.

"I know, and you better believe I would too," Sylvia responded with another deep kiss.

Sylvia opened up a door that led to the side of the building to let Whistle out.

"If you're ever back in Yardville, make sure you come and find me!"

"I will," he responded as he grabbed her for one more kiss. Sylvia started getting frisky again with her mouth on his neck and her hand working its way south.

"Don't do this to me, I gotta get walking," Whistle said.

"Fuck that, come here!" Sylvia commanded. She pulled him behind a row of hedges as he pinned her against the wall. After their pants were around their ankles, Whistle turned Sylvia around and pressed her against the bricks as they satisfied each other once more. After they were both cleaned up, and got dressed, they looked at each other. Neither wanted it to end, but they both knew it had to.

"I don't want to sound stupid and say that I love you, but we get each other so well, I think I might," Whistle said, trying not to get choked up about this girl that he didn't even know an hour ago.

"Don't cry, honey. I know that we already love each other, but I also know that you have to go. So go, and like I said, if you're ever back this way, find me and we'll see what happens."

"Sylvia, you are beyond awesome," Whistle said.

"Whistle, you are beyond awesome," she replied with a kiss on the lips.

And with that, Sylvia slid back in the side door and after a quick trip to the powder room, headed back to her post at the front desk and Whistle walked across the empty parking lot and back up to the on-ramp....Southbound, lonesome, and no longer a virgin.

CHAPTER
THIRTY-SIX
Good Progress Is Made

Thumb out, he caught a ride after a short time. He barely talked and found himself lost in thought. *Am I fucking up? Should I be with Sylvia? Should I go back north? Should I keep forging ahead, southbound? Am I anywhere close to doing the right thing?* The boy simply had no answers to any questions, and let himself go get a ride from whoever the hell this was and get dropped off wherever the hell he would be. Amazingly, he fell asleep for a good long while. Whoever this guy was, eventually pulled over.

"I gotta get off here," the driver said to Whistle, gently shaking his shoulder to wake him up.

"What? Oh, Ok. Hey, thanks so much. I appreciate the ride, take care!" the boy replied, almost on autopilot, not quite awake yet. He grabbed his bag, got out, and waved to the guy as he drove away. He walked and followed down the same exit. After he got off Highway 13, Whistle looked around and his instincts told him to take a left, as he was fairly sure that would take him south. In a way, it took him south of the border, as he eventually found a Taco Bell. After a quick bathroom bath, and two tacos, Whistle headed back out to the street. He spotted a kindly looking elderly man sitting on a bus stop bench, eating a peach.

"Excuse me, sir?" Whistle called, respectful as could be.

"Huh?" the man replied, looking up. Whistle tried not to give away that he was a little thrown by the huge cataract in the man's eye.

"I'm sorry, could you tell me where I am?"

"You, young fella, are innnn...Accomack, Virginia," the elderly man said with the inflection of a world weary game show host.

"Thank you, sir. Have a good day!" Whistle was in a good mood since he got laid.

He continued down the street and, good mood or not, he was pretty wiped out. After a mile or so, his feet were so sore from the accumulated miles between Accomack, Virginia and New Hampshire, that he had to sit for a while on a comfortable patch of lawn that wasn't exactly out of the way, but whatever, he was just sitting down, minding his own business, not bothering anybody.....except the owner of said lawn, another elderly man who left his TV dinner and the nightly news to come outside and tell Whistle in no uncertain terms to, well, get off his lawn.

"I'm gettin," Whistle responded in a good-natured mockery of the man's deep fried southern accent. He got up, kept on down the road and finally settled for a culvert that would shelter him for the night. His camp that night was primitive, but very comforting at the same time. His sleep was spotty and sporadic, fitful and full of strange dreams. Regardless, the sun came up, Whistle woke up, and he was anxious to get moving. After completing his minimal morning routine, the boy emerged from out of the culvert, squared up and surveyed the landscape.

He decided to go left off of Route 13 and follow his instincts and see where they led him. Whistle figured the toughest winter weather was well north of him so he was afforded some leisure time to explore a little. After walking for a bit, the smell of sea salt hit him. He was obviously excited by this and sped up his pace a bit, weaving his way through side streets, noticing people in their front yards and driveways packing towels, floaties, coolers, fluorescent plastic pails, shovels and boogie boards. This was obviously a beach community and it seemed like a great place to spend the day.

Turning the corner off of Sand Dollar Street, Whistle noticed two things straight away. First, there was a huge sand dune in front of him. Second, he heard the sound of his first wave crashing ashore. He couldn't help but break into a sprint as he came across a weathered set of rickety wooden stairs that led him over the sand dune. Beach slat fencing ran down both sides of the stairs and the sound of the ocean grabbed him. A short time later, Whistle Evel Fonzarelli Starr crested the dune and looked out. He couldn't help but lose his breath a little as his heart skipped a beat.

The vastness of the Atlantic Ocean spread out before him, with the sun rays dancing off the water. He was at a loss for words, even in his own mind as tears started welling up within him. He stifled them as best he could as he looked out with true awe.

Whistle walked down the stairs that led to the beach. He took his first couple of steps in the sand and looked around. He noticed plenty of people around. The water looked beyond inviting, but he was hesitant to leave his belongings unattended as they amounted to the entirety of his earthly possessions.

He gave it some thought and figured he'd walk south along the beachfront. Being his first time, he quickly realized that barefoot was the only way to travel in this situation, so he took his shoes off, put them in his pack and kept going. Feeling the waves, sand, shells, and seaweed between his toes seemed to fill him with a life force from the soles of his feet on up through the top of his head. He knew immediately why people flock to the beach every summer and vacation in tropical places in the middle of winter.

As he noticed the crowd grow thinner the further south he went, he eventually came across a small grove of trees to his right that seemed somewhat secluded. He veered off and went to investigate. In short order, the boy found the perfect spot. It was up and tucked away from everyone but still provided an incredible view of the ocean. The breeze that came off the water was cool and helped keep the bugs away.

Whistle was quite content as he dropped his stuff. He decided it was time for a swim, so he stripped down to his pants and then walked across the beach and ran in eagerly. It felt incredible as the cold water enveloped him. Whistle swam out until the water was over his head. He realized there were no lifeguards around so he decided to head back in after a short while.

The swim back was total peace for the boy. Stepping back onto the beach, he felt absolutely fantastic. When he got back to his shady oasis in the trees, he plopped down in the shade and went to sleep with the salty breeze blowing across him and the sound of the waves rhythmically crashing along the shore.

When Whistle woke up, it was dark out and a level of disorientation swept over him again. After a few moments, things started to come back to him as moonlight streamed down through the trees. He pushed a crab off his right thigh, got up and emptied his bladder. After that, he stripped naked and went for another swim. After a while, he got tired and went back to his spot in the trees to hopefully get a good night's sleep.

The next morning came and Whistle didn't feel like going anywhere, so he spent the next week or so camping in the trees and scrounging for food and water wherever he could. Life was quite comfortable for him. Now, with his hair below his shoulders and a scraggly teenage beard starting to fill in, he could feel it was time to move on again. One swim later, he packed his things and began again to make his way south along the shoreline. He still had a fair amount of money in his pack, as well as Sylvia's wonderful care package. He did realize, however, that he hadn't spoken to anyone in quite a while and missed the social interaction. He figured he'd work his way down the shoreline and eventually duck back into town and try to find a cheap motel room. Maybe get a haircut, a shave, and do his laundry before pressing southbound any farther.

For the next few weeks, Whistle took his time. Walking when he felt like it and resting when he got tired. He felt no need to rush as winter was really no longer an imminent threat to someone basically living outdoors. Everything flowed perfectly and he was very much at peace. The days provided exciting adventures and the nights were easy and restful. He still didn't talk to many people, but that was okay with him. Somehow being a bit of a loner felt right for this part of the boy's journey, so he went with it. The days passed and he had experiences that would stay with him forever. Many kinds of birds flew overhead at different times. Amazing sunrises greeted him in the morning from the east. An occasional light refreshing rain provided relief from the heat, breaking up the heat and humidity the southeast is known for.

Heck, Whistle even watched a crab and a seagull fight over a dead fish that had washed ashore. The crab's pincer claw clipped the seagull's left leg clean off and with a horrendous screech, the bird flew away with no dinner and one less leg to stand on. Whistle figured the crab had won that round as it piled the leg on top of the fish and dragged the whole package down in the hole it called its home.

Food and water were relatively easy to come by for Whistle and regular swims kept him fairly clean. It also provided a tan and some good all-around exercise. He hadn't seen himself in a mirror for a while, but he imagined he either looked like a hippie at Woodstock or a homeless man sleeping in the street, which wasn't too far removed from reality.

Continuing south, he finally came to the small town of Kiptopeke and walked in. It was early afternoon and one of the first places he saw happened to be a barbershop. The familiar red and white pole swirled around and around as he opened the door. The bell hanging from the doorjamb jingled its familiar, friendly welcome. The atmosphere was pleasant, fresh, and familiar as he sat in one of the well-worn leather chairs in the waiting room. There were only two men before him so it wouldn't be a long wait, but long enough to pick up a *Time* magazine and read an article on the founder of Apple, who claimed that one day everyone would have a computer as powerful as the one that sent a man to the moon in their pocket.

"Alrighty there young fella, you're up!" a jovial, heavy set, white haired and mustachioed southern gentleman said to Whistle, snipping his scissors in one hand and clippers in the other in time with his greeting. "What're we doin'? Shavin' it all off? Hehe, just kiddin', don't be scared, nah," he said as he motioned for Whistle to come sit down.

"You know what, yeah, let's shave it," the boy shot back, realizing in the moment that it made all the sense in the world.

"I was just kiddin' around, sonny. I've been tellin' that one liner since Elvis's been popular, 'n young fellas come in here, they daddies draggin' 'em by the ear, tellin' me ta cut off dis greazah mop. Kinda put me in a tough spot."

"I can imagine," Whistle chuckled. "Well I walked in here on my own accord, and I'm tellin' you, I wanna cut off dis greazah mop. I claim full responsibility."

"Fair 'nuff young fella...3...2.........1." The clippers clicked on, buzzed a hearty buzz, and mowed his scalp like a baseball field in less than a minute. A couple of touch up zings and zangs to even it out, a straight razor for a clean shave up front and a straight line in back, a splash of some good smelling, Jaguar green cologne, and a few swipes and slaps across the back, neck, and shoulders with the sandalwood brush and Whistle looked like a new man.

He paid up, thanked and tipped the barber, but he could tell something was up. Before he could leave, the barber said what was on his mind.

"Son, no offense, you look like a million bucks now, but smell like an I.O.U."

"Yeah, I know. I'm traveling south and showers are tough to come by sometimes as I can't afford a motel room but every once in a great while."

"You drivin'?"

"No, walking."

"Well, in about twenty miles, you're gonna come up on the Chesapeake Bay Bridge Tunnel and there's no way they're gonna let you walk across," the barber replied.

"Thanks for the head's up. I guess I'll have to figure it out once I get there. I'd like to catch a shower on the way. Are there any reasonably cheap rooms between here and there?"

"About four miles down on your left, there's the Chesapeake Clipper. There's a young lass there by the name of Missy Cabral. She'll take care of you."

"Thank you so much! Was a real pleasure meeting you," Whistle said as he shook the man's hand. He walked out and down the street the four miles and sure enough, there was the Chesapeake Clipper and inside was, sure enough, Missy Cabral.

"Hello, my name is Whistle Starr and I was hoping to get a room for a night." Noticing that Missy Cabral was quite cute, he wondered if he was destined to be attracted to motel desk clerks. He didn't know, but for now, he didn't mind, so he enjoyed the conversation with Missy. There was definitely a rapport between the two as she checked him in.

"Mr. Starr, you are all set. Here's your room key."

"Call me Whistle, please," he responded. Whistle smiled at Missy then turned toward the elevator. He entered Room #319 and was surprisingly impressed. It was clean and neat. The bed looked crisp and comfy. Of course the air conditioning worked great and he made sure the toilet worked and the shower had decent hot water and pressure.

He got in, got cleaned up, and about an hour later, he headed for the hotel bar. Whistle was starving and was hoping the bartender might serve him a couple of cold delicious beers without asking for an I.D. No such luck; however, he was able to devour a French dip sandwich, salty fries, and a half dill pickle and wash it down with an ice cold Coke.

When he was done, he noticed that Missy walked in and sat at the other end of the bar. The boy sat and wondered what he should do. After all, he kind of knew what he was doing now and Missy was damn cute. He went to the bathroom to wash his greasy hands as she sat alone having her shift drink. He stayed in the bathroom for a minute or two, looking in the mirror, trying to think of a cool, funny line to approach her with, without coming off like a dipshit…….Nope…….nothing. He'd have to play it straight and see where it goes.

"Hey, Missy!" Whistle said somewhat awkwardly as he sauntered up to the bar.

"Hey Whistle, how's your Coke?" she replied, with a playful poke to the chest.

"Just as good as all the others I've had," he replied, somewhat surprised that she remembered his name.

"Hmmmm. Hey Stilts, give my new friend a shot of Jose and a Corona with lime."

"Ok Miss Missy, give me a sec to punch in for my shift," the new bartender replied.

"No, thanks anyway, I don't want that," Whistle replied, not sure if the previous bartender had mentioned to Stilts that he was underage. He didn't need that kind of embarrassment at this moment.

"Trust me, you do," Missy said with a slight wink.

"Trust me too, you actually do," Stilts chimed in.

"Well then, I guess I do," Whistle answered as he sat down next to Missy, confident he was in the clear with Ol' Stilts, a six foot eleven Ichabod Crane looking gentleman, who looked to have the same amount of pounds as years on him, Stilts was a great third wheel to have in this situation.

Whistle and Missy made small talk, had a few beers and a few shots with Stilts hanging around the other end of the bar, watching a baseball game and polishing glasses. He'd been a bartender long enough to know how to fade into the background and give people space when they're clumsily trying to get to know each other over drinks.

For at least a good hour or two, they asked each other the usual questions that people ask each other when they're trying to hook up: Where are you from? Any brothers or sisters? What do you have in mind for a career? etc... Every now and again, Ol' Stilts would seemingly float on over like a ghost with more drinks and maybe a quick joke or story about a guest if he could tell the conversation needed a little jumpstart, and then he went right back to being invisible….Man, he was good!

As the two young people got more of a buzz on, talking turned into touching and flirty eyes and before Whistle could even think about his next move, Missy made it for him.

"Do you want to go up to your room?" she purred.

"Do I….Do you? I mean, yeah I do!" he sputtered, drunk enough to laugh at his own lack of suave.

"Stilts, a bottle of Jack and a six pack of Coke, please. Could you put it in a big, paper grocery bag so I don't get any looks out in the lobby?" Missy called down the bar to Stilts.

"You got it, sweetheart," Stilts replied in a sing-song manner.

"Pay the bill and we'll get outta here," Missy whispered in Whistle's ear.

That's exactly what he did, even if it put a big dent in his travel funds. Well, he wanted adventure. If you're gonna ride the rides, you gotta buy a ticket.

CHAPTER
THIRTY-SEVEN
Room #319

The elevator door was no sooner closed than Missy's hands were all over Whistle. She grabbed parts of him that he didn't even know he owned. Then, the doors opened and they were on the third floor. They stepped out and took a left. Soon, they stood in front of Room #319. Missy was a big help, fishing the key out of Whistle's pocket as she playfully bit his neck. She opened the door, slipped the "Do Not Disturb" sign on the knob and shut the door behind them in one graceful move, almost as if she'd done this a time or…..well, who cares.

"Come here," she said as she sat down on the bed, seductively striking a pose like a Vargas Girl. Mmmmm, mmmm.

"Uh, I really have to use the bathroom. Don't go anywhere!" the boy pleaded, a quarter joking.

"Hurry up, Honey Bunch!" she lazily replied as she fell back on the bed, arms above her head, looking somehow even more delicious.

"I'll make us a couple of drinks," Missy called from the main room as Whistle searched the entire bathroom for condoms, hoping someone might have left a few in one of the drawers or they might be included with the toiletries kit. Long shot, but hey…

"Cheers!" Missy greeted Whistle with a Jack and Coke on ice in a glass from the minibar. Man, she knew her way around a motel room. They sat on the bed, tapped glasses and immediately started kissing. Whistle started moving down Missy's neck, but second guessed himself and started moving back up to her lips. She could sense his relative lack of experience and decided to really take charge.

"You're way too fuckin' sexy, so let's go!" she said, as she pushed him down onto the bed. Missy pulled off her top to reveal the most perky pair of breasts Whistle had ever seen. It's not like he'd seen a lot, but still. She leaned forward, arched her back, and brought her breasts to Whistle's mouth. He more than gladly obliged.

Another swig later, they lay in silence. It was beautiful as they softly touched each other.

"I gotta piss," Whistle said as he got up and went into the bathroom by the front door. When he was done, Missy followed suit, came back out, and jumped on the bed and straddled Whistle as she playfully tickled him. Whistle knew he was truly experiencing perfection. They drifted off into a deep sleep and the boy's dreams were vivid and lucid, in full color, including the dramatic oranges, blacks, and whites of the monarch butterflies.

He woke up and Missy was not in bed. He called out "Missy?" figuring she might be in the bathroom....Nope. Whistle chuckled to himself and stretched as he thought, *Life on the road definitely has its advantages.*

He packed his things and made his way down to the front desk. "Well look who's here!" Whistle said as he sauntered up to Missy, working behind the counter. She shot him a look that basically said, "We don't know each other...Shhh!" As she formally and somewhat sternly asked him how his stay was and presented him with his bill, Whistle caught on as he saw the manager just inside the office off to the side, occupied with paperwork, but still within earshot of any conversation between the two. He paid his bill, played along, and bid a polite, "Have a nice day," back to Missy before he was on his way.

Whistle headed out and made it down the road about three miles before he strolled by a very comfortable looking patch of woods. Since he didn't get a lot of sleep the night before, he was feeling groggy and sluggish, not to mention a little hung over. He went deep into the brush and found a decent spot to bed down for a while, so that's exactly what he did.

After what seemed like a few hours, Whistle was woke by the hot, blaring sun in his eyes as it traversed the sky and found a clear shot at Whistle through a space in the branches. He shielded his eyes as he opened them, so as not to burn his corneas, sat up and pulled a can of Coke and the bottle of rum out of his bag and threw back a couple of shots.

Leaving Kiptopeke, he walked eight miles and came to a small bridge. It was a classic two lane bridge, one lane north and one lane south, with endless marshes east and west. Both sides showed the ocean each way. The sun was setting to his right and showing crazy colors to his left. Whistle bedded down on Fisherman's Island for the night. The next morning, Whistle immediately realized he needed a ride to get across the Chesapeake Bay Bridge and Tunnel.

Thumb out, the boy waited at the north side of the bridge. The whole day went by and nobody picked him up. He understood because he didn't think he'd pick himself up, being as dirty as he was. The next morning, Whistle stripped naked and had a swim. After he got as clean as he was going to get, he dressed himself, got back up to the road, and resumed thumbing for a ride. Again, no luck.

The boy spent a long weekend on Fisherman's Island. Swimming, sleeping, and trying to get a ride until he became discouraged again. Finally, however, someone pulled over. Whistle ran as fast as he could up to the car.

"I'll give you a ride across for a hundred bucks," said the driver, not even making eye contact with Whistle.

"I'm sorry, too rich for my blood," Whistle replied, visibly deflated.

"Just kiddin', get in," the driver said, as Whistle climbed into the early seventies red Barracuda. That's when Whistle met Chief Petty Officer Jack Fast.

"You tryin' to get across the bridge?" Jack asked.

"Yes sir," Whistle replied, looking down.

"Look at me, boy," Jack said.

"Yes sir." The boy was sure to not piss off the only ride he might get for a long time to come.

Jack shifted left, then right, straightened out and shot toward the bridge. Whistle was pressed back into his seat and felt the acceleration take him over.

On the bridge, the ocean shot by on both sides. They entered the tunnel and Whistle went into a void. He looked left and Jack was pegging it. The speedometer read one-o-five.

"It's ten miles and I gotta get to work."

Whistle closed his eyes and didn't care where Jack would leave him. The red Barracuda tore the bridge up, they glided through the tunnel and screamed across the second section of the bridge. Ten miles of bridge came and went in a heartbeat. The tunnel was fantastic. Jack and Whistle cruised to the end of the bridge and eventually, Jack stopped and dropped Whistle off.

"Good luck, buddy!" Jack said, giving Whistle a salute as the boy quickly opened the door and got out, not wanting to hold Jack up, as he was in a hurry to get to work at the navy base.

"Thank you, sir!" Whistle saluted back as the Barracuda peeled off, tail lights fading in seconds flat. Standing there alone, Whistle assessed his situation. He was actually not in bad shape. He had money in his pocket, food in his pack, a little bit of rum, and he was across the bridge.

The beach was right there, empty aside from a few bonfires and couples walking along the breaking waves. He found a comfortable spot and plopped down. The wind was strong but warm, and Whistle settled in for the night. The boy spent the late afternoon watching the waves crash onto the shore. The sound was completely delicious. As the sun settled west, Whistle ate some granola from the lovely Sylvia, courtesy of Motel 6. He washed it down with a shot of rum and laid on his back, looking up at the stars. Full bellied and buzzed, he was feeling good and drifted off to sleep as the waves crashed on the beach and the breeze rushed in over the Atlantic.

CHAPTER
THIRTY-EIGHT
Terrifying

W hen a dream starts in the middle of a frozen lake, and the first thing you do is slip and fall on your ass, you hope it gets better. No, wait....It's night and you have no clue where you are. Whistle stood up and noticed his right ass cheek really hurt when he put weight on that leg. He rubbed it a bit and looked around. A three-sixty look-a-round later, Whistle realized all he could see was pitch black outside of a four foot circumference around him. Fortunately, he was properly dressed and had a headlamp. After a small pause to collect himself, Whistle picked a direction and went for it.

The shore looked very far away, but he could see some lights, so he kept moving forward. After a while, he realized the lights looked further away than they did before and the ice was changing its texture. His headlamp started to dim and he felt freezing water enter his boots.

He heard a massive crack to his right as the ice split. It was shortly followed by another crack to his left. The sounds were as loud as a shotgun and at least as disheartening. A loud pop in front of him and another behind him and he realized that he was essentially on an iceberg in the middle of a lake, in the middle of the night, in the middle of nowhere. He was beyond scared.

Ironically, his dream provided him a canoe paddle. The boy paddled toward the light on a shrinking chunk of ice. It seemed to Whistle that this was a race between getting to shore or being in the drink. Darkness covered him and he couldn't help but wonder what was below. Paddling forward, the feeling of futility overcame him as he clung to his ever decreasing chunk of ice.

Shortly after, the ice was gone and Whistle treaded water with a paddle under his arms. The lights were no closer and the water was freezing. His breath escaped him and his head dipped momentarily below the water. Fighting to stay above water, Whistle was truly terrified and knew he had to fight for his life.

Just then, a snapping turtle came up and bit off the two smallest toes from the boy's right foot. *This can't get any worse*, he thought to himself….until the whiteout started. Freezing with blood in the water, his head dipped under again. One more push and he felt the snow covering his face. He also felt as if it was his last breath. Body frozen, Whistle let go and sunk under the water. The snapping turtle circled back around and bit off his left ear.

Not noticing, the boy sunk deeper down into the abyss. His last conscious thought was that dying wasn't so bad. Coldness overtook him and he was fine with it. Just before he left this mortal plane, he woke up on the beach in Virginia.

"Wow!" he said to himself, looking and feeling around to make sure all his extremities were there and functioning to full capacity. Dreams were strange these days, as was waking life. No idea what tomorrow would bring and no time to try and make sense of yesterday.

CHAPTER THIRTY-NINE
Meat Cutter

Getting himself together, Whistle packed up and continued walking south again. It was a strange day for him as his dream stayed in his mind and hung over him like a storm cloud on an otherwise sunny day. *What did it mean?* he thought to himself as he walked along. He did recognize a pattern, however. Most of his dreams revolved around a common theme, trying to solve a problem. He gained a lot of ground that day and eventually stumbled across a small nondescript campground just off Route 1-90.

Exhausted, he paid for his permit and found his campsite. The blisters at the bottom of Whistle's feet were huge. He awoke the next morning crying in pain. Instantly knowing travel was not an option, he dozed back off. A couple of hours later, he got back up and headed for the camp office.

As he walked, he felt the left blister burst, filling his shoe with sticky puss. Not six steps later, the right one burst as well. Both shoes filled up, Whistle walked on and tried to grin about the whole situation. Grinning did not come easy on this day.

In the office, he decided to buy two more days. Limping back, his shoes came off and the relief was incredible. Whistle hung his wet socks over a branch and went to sleep feeling the last of the puss draining out of the bottoms of his feet.

Two days of sleep followed, interrupted only by bathroom breaks every now and again. Feeling well rested, he walked out on feet that were a little sore, but a lot better that they were when he got to the campground. He was energized and felt the calluses starting to form on his feet.

The next few days flew by easily. He made great time and his feet were healing and hardening up. Before he knew it, the boy camped in the great dismal swamp just west of Route 17. Several days later, Whistle crossed into North Carolina and finally spent the night in Morgan's Corner.

As he walked up on Morgan's Corner, he stood in front of a classic, old school general store. Opening the door, he heard that old familiar jingle of the bells hanging from the doorjamb, just like at the barbershop several days before. "Welcome to Read's Country Store," said the sign hanging over the door.

"Hello," he said, as he walked across the well-oiled oak floor. He picked up a pepperoni stick, a pack of Hubba Bubba, two waters and three oranges, and brought them to the counter.

"Hello," a wheat-haired, blue-eyed girl said from behind the counter. "That everything?"

"Jeez," Whistle said to himself, dazed by the girl's natural beauty.

"You okay?" she asked.

"Oh...yeah. This is everything," he replied, trying to snap out of his daydream.

"Thanks," he said as he walked out with his bag of fresh supplies.

He walked about another mile before he eventually found a good spot at the bottom of a dam. The sun set and the boy enjoyed half a pepperoni stick, drank a water, and chewed on some delicious Hubba Bubba, sending a shot of sugar through his body The continuous sound of water pouring over the dam was soothing to Whistle. Sleep came super easy. The next morning, Whistle took a quick swim, got dressed, and walked back to Read's.

"Can I help you?" the wheat-haired girl from yesterday said as he walked up to the counter.

"Yes, I noticed you have a help wanted sign out front," he replied.

"Yeah. They're looking for a deli worker," she answered, not really paying much attention to him. "Would you like an application?"

"Sure," he said, as he took the application and a pen and promptly filled it out down at the other end of the counter, giving the girl her space. When he was done, he handed it to the girl, who gave it to the old man who owned the store, who promptly gave Whistle a job as a meat cutter. Two weeks went by and Whistle's situation was improving dramatically. He had a job that paid a decent wage, free food pretty much whenever he felt like it, and a nice spot to camp out down by the dam, at least for the time being.

One day he was down there washing his socks in a bucket of water and some dish soap he "borrowed" from the store.

"Whistle!" he heard, from seemingly out of nowhere.

"Huh?" he somewhat nervously replied.

"Do you even know my name?" the wheat-haired girl from the store asked as she walked out from behind some tall brush.

"No," Whistle replied, as he turned his attention back to his laundry.

"I'm Heather Stride, and it's sure nice to finally meet you!"

"I'm Whistle Evel Fonzarelli Starr. Nice to meet you," he responded, somewhat sheepishly.

"Okay, well if we're doing formal introductions, my full name is Heather Silver Stride and I can probably help you."

"No thank you," he politely but sternly replied as he once again went back to his laundry, feeling somewhat embarrassed that this attractive girl that he had to see at work every day now knew that he was homeless. He tried his best to avoid her in the relatively small space in which they both worked, but after about three weeks, she finally confronted him and gave him a verbal smack down.

"Listen, I have a cozy little apartment with enough room for two and you're sleeping on a rock. Come stay at my place for a few nights. It's supposed to rain pretty hard for the next few days and you can sleep on the couch, do laundry, and have hot meals."

Well, that was most certainly an offer he couldn't refuse and Whistle moved in that night, planning on a few nights at most, and then most likely getting back on the road as he'd already spent more time in one place than he had planned on. But, as you may have guessed, a sweet girl turned into a sweetheart, a temporary job turned into a two year run at Read's, Whistle making his way all the way up to assistant manager, and a place to crash for a few nights turned into a home.

For this stretch of time, life was pretty solid and stable for Whistle. Days spent working at Read's with Heather, cutting meat, manning the counter, loading in deliveries out back and stocking shelves. Nights and weekends were spent in and around town. Going to the movies on Friday nights, bonfire parties on Saturdays, church and fishing on Sundays, hanging outside the Tasty-Freeze just like Jack and Diane. Life was good, but it was starting to look and feel like a bit of a rut. Heather was a great girl, and would make a great wife, and Whistle could tell that she was thinking the same thing. Dropping hints every once in a great while turned into once in a not-so-great while. He didn't need a weatherman to know which way the wind was blowing. Then, one day, he sat her down.

"I love you and care about you, but I gotta go," Whistle said as they sat on the couch that he slept on for the first time almost two years ago to the day, roughly speaking.

"I know, I haven't been happy in a while either," Heather replied. "We're obviously growing apart, and it's a good time to call it while we still have time to find our own paths," she finished, surprisingly philosophical about the situation. "Do you need a ride anywhere?" she asked, trying hard to appear not to be fazed.

"No, thanks, I'm just going to pick up where I left off and hoof it south," he said before he really thought about how handy a ride might come in. Then again, he had an easy time getting out the door and he didn't want to push his luck, or he might end up staying for another two years....It can happen.

And just like that, Whistle hugged and kissed Heather, and got while the getting was good. He couldn't believe he spent two years in one place. Just like that, he was twenty-one, back on the road and at a crossroads, both literally and figuratively. Going left would bring him to the ocean and going right would bring him to Windsor, down Route 17. He decided to head toward Windsor, walked a few hours and eventually found a campsite, settled in and went to sleep. Waking up the next morning, he ate and cleaned himself up the best he could and continued on down Route 17 and made great time. A two year rest will do that for you. The next several days went by in much the same manner. Walking all day and sometimes well into the night before he found a campsite, sometimes official and sometimes not so much, but far enough out of the way to not be stumbled upon by a hunter, police officer, park ranger, or worse. He'd seen *Deliverance* and he certainly didn't want to find out if it was real. His feet had gotten soft again and the blisters were starting to return. He'd have to focus on hitchhiking a little more or it was going to be a long, tough slog through the southeast.

He crossed the Chowan River Bridge and found a place to camp out another night. The next morning, he woke up early, took a swim in the river and walked up to the main road and started south with his thumb out. Before long, a young man around Whistle's age pulled up in a Ford F-150.

"Where are you goin?" the driver asked in a thick southern accent.

"As far south as you're goin," Whistle replied, a mild southern accent of his own starting to develop from years of living south of the Mason Dixon line.

"I live in Windsor."

"That'd be perfect. Thanks!" Whistle said as he climbed up into the cab.

"Listen friend, I'm dog tired. Didn't sleep real well last night and I wouldn't mind grabbing a quick nap if you don't think it'd be rude."

"Be my guest," the driver said as he turned on a sports radio station.

"Thank you kindly," Whistle said back, already starting to drift off.

Eighty-six miles and a quick nap later, the young man spoke up. "Ok pal, we're here."

"Oh....Ok. Hey, thanks for the ride!" Whistle replied as he woke up from his nap, a little out of sorts for a few moments. He shook the driver's hand, got out quick as he didn't want to hold the guy up, and waved to him as he drove away. Whistle felt bad as he realized he never got the young man's name. He checked his bag and his pockets reflexively, making sure he didn't forget anything in the truck. As if there was anything he could do about it at that point anyway— the F-150 was long down the road.

He made a mental note to try and stay awake while hitchhiking. Number one, he doesn't know who he's riding with. Number two, when waking up, you don't have a lot of time to get your wits about you and make sure you didn't leave your wallet or anything important behind. Number three, you never know what you might be missing along the way. Maybe there's a more interesting place to stop between here and wherever you were originally going to get dropped off. You'll never know if you're sleeping through the best part of the journey.

As he watched yet another set of tail lights fade in the distance, Whistle's stomach started rumbling. He walked another block to a Taco Bell and got himself three tacos and a Coke, which he promptly wolfed down, and after a quick trip to the men's room, he was back on the road. Walking most of the night, he eventually found a campsite alongside the Cashie River. Sleep was easy with the river rushing in his ears. Could it be that it reminded him of his childhood and the home he had back up in the White Mountains? He thought so as he drifted off into another night's peaceful slumber.

The next morning started with a quick swim/bath and drying on a huge flat rock. He didn't feel the need to go anywhere that day, so he just laid there getting even more of a tan than he already had, which made him look like a SoCal surfer. After about a week of swimming, sunning, and fifty cent tacos, Whistle felt the call of the road once again. It had begun to feel like Groundhog Day at the Cashie River and, as pleasant as it was, he knew it was time to keep moving.

CHAPTER
FORTY
Askin, Virgo, and
Burgundy Eyes

Walking hard for a week, straight down Route 17 South, Whistle ended up in Askin, North Carolina. There didn't seem to be anything particularly special about the place. Small town with a bank, a gas station, a general store, a tiny town hall, an even smaller rec hall, and a pizza parlor, complete with pinball machines, slightly outdated video games, and a jukebox at every table.

The boy found a place to sleep in a corn field. The stars were amazing, and he pictured endless animals in their patterns. The air was sweet and the owls hooted and the coyotes howled far enough in the distance to not make him uneasy. Whistle thought to himself that this was a place he could spend the rest of his life if things worked out that way.

He fell asleep with his stuff lying next to him. All was right in his world when he woke up the next morning to the early sunlight rays streaming in through the tall cornstalks. The boy smiled as the sun just started to dance across his face and a cricket landed on his chest. Lazily, Whistle looked down and asked the cricket how it was doing. With no response, the cricket hopped away. Whistle couldn't help but laugh at this.

A little later in the morning, he made his way to a huge barn. Finding a side door, he stepped in and was instantly hit with the strong odor of hay and horse manure. Everything was cool, dark, and comforting, so Whistle ate the rest of his food and curled up in a corner. He was fast asleep when he heard a new noise. Sitting up, Whistle tried to let his eyes adjust.

"Hello?" he asked, rather timidly. He was instantly answered by a huge stomping sound.

"Hello?" he asked again, and again, was answered by another loud stomp. His curiosity got the better of him as he got up and started to explore the barn. Walking down the center, he noticed horse stalls on each side. Almost all the way down, he heard another two very loud stomps. Whistle kept walking in the direction of the noise and turned to look to his right. There she was, with perfect moonlight shining through the barn window, landing on her body just right.

Stall Number 9 had a nameplate that read "Virgo." It instantly hit Whistle as a little ironic because he was a Virgo himself.

"Hello, girl!" he said with quiet surprise as he walked up to the stall. He was met with another loud stomp.

"You're alright, you're alright," Whistle whispered. With one more stomp, and a neigh, Virgo calmed down. Her dark beautiful eyes looked at him. The boy slowly put his left hand in and placed it flat on Virgo's pure white blaze, which ran down the front of her face. She was easily the largest horse Whistle had ever seen.

She towered over him and had gorgeous chocolate brown hair. Virgo's coat was solid except for her white blaze. Also, her mane and tail were different. Golden colors stretched down Virgo's neck. Her tail was gold as well. Chocolate, gold, and white, blended together beautifully.

The boy couldn't help but open stall nine, walk in, and close the door behind him. Virgo stepped left and briefly pinned Whistle against the wall.

"You're alright, you're alright," Whistle said, the breath knocked out of him. After a pause, Whistle asked the horse a simple question.

"Do you think you could get off of me?"

Virgo released him, seeming to sense that he wasn't there to mess with her. The boy kissed her blaze, gave her a quick pat on the neck and decided to not just hang around in her home uninvited. He found the ladder that led to the hayloft and climbed up. Sleep came relatively easy that night, considering he was on someone's property and in their barn to boot. The next morning, he found out who that was.

The new day started with the sound of a diesel tractor. *Wub,wub,* **wubwupwupwapwap**.

"Grab dem two bayles der 'n throw 'em down," Whistle heard an older man yell over the tractor.

"A'ight," a younger male voice responded.

Before Whistle had time to even process the fact that this was not a dream, he heard the young man open the barn door and immediately start to climb the ladder to the loft. Whistle dug into the hay as much as he could and held his breath. The boy almost tripped over him as he opened the loft door and threw down the two bales. The boy jumped back down the ladder in two or three steps and was back out in the field, loading the hay onto the tractor before jumping on himself, and he and his dad were headed down to the other end of the farm. Close call.

After taking a minute to simultaneously wake up and calm down, Whistle gathered his bag and the odd few items he had to take out so it could double as a pillow. He climbed down the ladder and, sure enough, the second his foot hit the floor, he heard a huge stomp.

Making his way to stall nine, Whistle and Virgo looked at each other. He felt a connection to the horse that made him stop for a second and think about staying awhile. He ended up spending a month sleeping in the loft with no one but Virgo knowing about it. His connection with the horse was deep, but he knew that hanging around, sleeping in the barn at night, and avoiding the farmer during the day had run its course.

"I love you," Whistle said to the horse, and one foot stomp later, he knew Virgo got the message. Leaving out the side door of the barn, he walked deep out into the cornfield and after a while, he heard the farmer driving the tractor back into the barn for the night. He was in the middle of nowhere, and at the moment, had no idea which way to proceed. Waiting for sundown to see which way was west seemed like the only reasonable option at this point.

Deciding he wasn't up for any travel by the time the sun set, he made a camp in the cornstalks for the night. It wasn't the most comfortable sleep, but his exhaustion finally won the night. As he drifted off, he wondered how far he'd have to walk to finally be able to see more than a few feet ahead of him with more than the sun for a guide forward.

He woke up the next morning with a few cuts and scratches from all the husks on the ground and a stiff hip from lying on the hard, lumpy dirt. It was midmorning, and the sun was in the east, as always, so the sooner he got moving, the sooner he'd be out of the cornfield.

He walked and walked and walked some more. It was disorientating walking through the maze of maize, so to speak, with no long view. Just endless rows of corn with no idea if he was ten steps, ten minutes, or ten hours away from freedom. He listened for cars, tractors, voices, farm animals, anything to give him some hope that he would make it out before he passed out, which was starting to worry him as he was starting to feel loopy. He sang to himself as loud as he could as someone might hear him and help him. No dice.

After sunset but before it had gotten dark enough to give up and resign himself to the cornfield for another night's less than luxurious sleep, Whistle noticed something different in the way the wind sounded and felt, almost as if it was stronger and more direct. A few more steps and Whistle finally came upon a dirt road. It was just a dirt road with more endless cornfields on the other side—as far as the eye could see—left and right, but at least it was a change of scenery, and it provided a sense of space and direction. He stood and looked at the road and tried to get a gut feeling on which way to go, but he was in no condition mentally or physically to make any decisions or follow through with them, so back into the corn he went for the night to get some sleep and start fresh the next morning.

When dawn came, Whistle woke up and drank a bottle of water that he had refilled at the barn. He could have sworn it had a hint of an aftertaste of horse manure....Oh well. Gathering his things, he made a mental note as he walked back out to the road that it appeared to be marked with what looked to be tire tracks washed over by a few heavy rains, but at least it was a sign of civilization.

He had a feeling he was headed in the most advantageous direction, and being that it was a particularly hot day and he only had one more bottle of manure water in his bag, he was most certainly hoping he was right. He walked for what seemed like days, but in all reality was probably close to seven or eight hours. As he followed the dirt road now curving slightly left, he thought he heard the faint sound of a motor. He was slightly lightheaded, so he wasn't sure if it was the blood rushing in his ears.

Continuing on several minutes later, he heard another. This time, unmistakable. Luckily, it wasn't long before the road curved again and led out to an actual blacktop road. Finally! The temperature of the tar made Whistle almost pass out. At this point, he was well on his way to being dehydrated. He stood, looked around, took a most unpleasant swig of his last bottle of water just to stay upright, and started on down the road, looking for something or someone in the heat distorted distance.

After a few admittedly slow miles, the sun began to ease up and the air began to feel cooler. He turned a corner along the road and came upon what he was sure had to be a mirage. There, in all its majestic teal and white glory, was none other than The Neuse River Motel. He couldn't believe his eyes as he ran, or rather limped, into the parking lot, looking around for a soda machine as he made his way to the main office. He walked up to the front desk and was greeted by a disapproving look from the teenage boy manning it.

"Can I help you?" the boy said in a voice that seemed only about a year or so removed from cracking.

"You got a room?" Whistle replied, knowing full well he didn't look or smell polite, and he was too tired to act it.

"Room 11 is available," the clerk replied, realizing Whistle had been traveling on foot and the terrain was pretty rough around here.

Whistle paid up in advance as was the policy here at this motel in the middle of who knows where, and made his way to Room 11. Opening the door, he realized this wasn't the best room he'd ever stayed in but it sure beat the cornfield. Shower worked, so that was good. Bed was free of bedbugs, another bonus. It even had a TV, hey, might even be able to catch up on the news.

The boy set his things down and worked with what he had. He stripped down and got in the shower. At least the water was hot, so he stayed in there a good long while, using up all the cheap, slightly expired soap and shampoo. Whistle had enough road time under his belt by this point to know to put the plug in the drain so he could do laundry in the soapy water after he was done showering. Saving his cleanest stuff to put on after his shower.

Clean shaven with somewhat long hair, Whistle got dressed with not the best looking mismatch of clothing. He walked toward the front desk, veered off down a hallway, and soon was at the entrance of the Bounty Bar. He sat away in the corner and ordered a cheeseburger and a water. Still hungry, he ordered another, this time with a soda, followed up with a whiskey on the rocks…Ahhhh, a pauper to a prince once again.

He looked around and noticed to his right a super sexy brunette with burgundy eyes looking back at him.

"Hello," he finally said, shyly.

"Hello," she answered, shy as well.

"What brings you here?" he asked, somewhat awkwardly.

"I actually don't know," the girl answered somewhat honestly. They talked a bit into the night and got to know each other.

"You are very pretty and I would be lying if I didn't say I was very attracted to you."

"I'm attracted to you as well," Burgundy Eyes said.

"What the fuck?!" Whistle was pushed back a little bit in his chair. He immediately got up and squared toward whoever thought they were going to push him around.

"She's my girl, so back the fuck off," a man said, surrounded by three friends, not a friendly face among them.

"I was just trying to talk to someone and have a normal conversation," Whistle replied, honestly, but in a way that sounded like someone who got caught with their hand in the cookie jar.

"I was just trying to bluh blah blah de blah blah blah," the man replied, mocking Whistle, much to his friends' amusement. "Listen, Mr. 'Normal Conversation,' you don't talk to her and you don't talk to me!"

"Alright, fine," Whistle replied, knowing to pick his battles. Burgundy Eyes and Whistle Evel Fonzarelli Starr looked at each other one more time and, just like that, she was out the door with her boyfriend and his posse. Whistle sat and finished his whiskey, feeling humiliated.

Lying in his room that night, the boy couldn't help but be pissed off. He thought the girl was cute and she was told not to talk to him. Whistle eventually cooled down enough to fall asleep until late afternoon the next day. He got up, took a shower, and got dressed in the driest clothes he had available. He spent the day checking everything out and eventually ended up back at the Bounty.

Sure enough, Burgundy Eyes was there, looking beautiful. Whistle sat by himself and couldn't help but look at her. He was just about to go talk to her when he felt a hard slap against the left side of his face. A numbing silence covered him and instinct took over. A quick right step and a right hand to the throat followed by a nose breaking punch took out the man that slapped him.

Instantly, Whistle saw stars floating before him. *What the hell?* he thought. Another punch later and the boy was dragged out the back door and into the alley.

"Can't we just talk about this?" Whistle asked whoever was launching this rollicking attack on him.

"Talk time's over!" the man said with another leveling haymaker.

Poor Whistle was beaten so badly that he was left for dead at the edge of the parking lot. Broken nose, busted lips, some cracked ribs and blood coming from more places than he could imagine, he passed out.

The next morning, he woke up in the weeds with ants all over him. He was beaten so bad the whites of his eyes were red and his whole body was purple with bruises. He just lay there trying to figure out what the fuck happened. Piecing together what he could remember, he tried to turn over.

Shocking pain sent him flat on his back again, ants and all. His whole body was on fire as he spit a mouthful of blood on the ground next to him. Whistle's throat was so dry, he thought he somehow swallowed a shard of glass. He passed out again and didn't wake up until after dark.

A reasonable thought came to him. *How can I be at the edge of the parking lot all day in this condition and nobody does anything?*

Trying to move again, the pain was overwhelming. His next thought was, *How the hell am I going to get back to my room?* Later that afternoon, the boy did manage to get himself sitting up against a spruce tree. He managed to get his fly down to relieve himself. Whistle noticed there was as much blood as there was urine on the ground. Whistle found this extremely unsettling. Panic started to settle in as he finally made his way to his feet, literally holding on to the tree to keep him upright. His head swam, and he fought hard not to fall back on the ground.

Sometime later, he had collected himself enough to try and make his way across the parking lot. Late afternoon sun shone down. Whistle didn't know if it was hot out or if his body was on fire from the beating he took. Sweat dripped from his head and blurred his vision. He staggered a bit before steadying himself again. Blood oozed from various cuts and abrasions as he took small steps that were manageable. Finally, he found the back door and let himself in. It seemed like hours before he finally reached the bed, but at least he didn't have to climb any stairs.

Whistle Evel Fonzarelli Starr was completely broken. This was definitely a low point in his short life. He slept hard and was abruptly woken up by the shrill ring of the phone along with the blinking light.

"Hello?" he answered, realizing that he was clearly dehydrated and starving.

"Mr. Starr, it's after checkout so I'm going to have to charge you for another night," the anonymous voice from the front desk explained.

"Alright, I'll be down tomorrow and figure it all out." Whistle groaned as he hung up the phone. After a few more hours of sleep, he woke up and coughed up a little blood.

Shit, he thought to himself as he went back to sleep. The next time he woke up, he knew he had to at least drink some water, so he started the painful process of getting out of bed. Finally off the dirty, sweaty, blood soaked sheet, he made his way to the bathroom. Bending over in great pain, he turned the shower on. He slowly stripped down, crying in pain the whole time and eventually making his way into the tub.

He actually put his face under the showerhead and drank deeply. The water going into his body felt beyond priceless and the shower washed away the grime, dirt, and dried blood, making visible the seemingly endless cuts and bruises, but he felt better. Whistle put his heel over the drain and let the tub fill up some, but the water was so dirty, he let it drain.

The water continued to rain down on the boy, and around forty-five minutes later, he figured he was as clean as he was going to get. All pruned up and a little less sore from the hot shower, he shut the shower off with his foot, slowly climbed out, and lay down on the bathroom floor. Another dizzy spell came on and wobbled the room before making everything go dim. He finally stood up with great effort and looked down upon the bath mat.

Holy shit, was all that Whistle could think to himself as he looked at all the blood on the bathmat. Very shakily, he got one more drink from the bathroom faucet, walked to the bed, and very gingerly laid down. Whistle immediately fell asleep and dreamed of getting another crack at the hillbillies that messed him up. All he knew was they better hope they don't run into him again...Yeah, sweet dreams, Whistle.

CHAPTER
FORTY-ONE
God Bless Blake Hayes

T he next morning, Whistle was woken up by the shrill ring of the phone
again. Red light as well.

"Hello?" he said.

"Mr. Starr, you owe us for several nights and we require immediate
payment," the stern voice replied.

"Okay, I'll be there in a bit." He groaned as he stretched to hang the
phone up in the cradle and flinched when he turned the wrong way. He stood up
with the help of the bureau next to the bed and slowly made his way to the bathroom. He started the shower, relieved himself in the toilet and noticed more
blood coming out. Brushing it off, he got in the hot shower and pulled himself
together as best he could. The boy had a good cry and thought about his options.
Now cleaned up, all he wanted to do was square up with the front desk and get
on his way. Unfortunately, he was completely out of money so he was down to
one choice: sneak out the back door and hope nobody sees him. Before he left,
he relieved himself one more time and checked himself out in the mirror. He
looked like a horror show, and the lighting in the bathroom made it look even
worse. The red in his eyes was alarming. His lips were split everywhere and his
broken nose gave him raccoon eyes. For the first time, Whistle noticed that his
left earlobe was cleanly split in half. Okay, regroup. Back door, here we come.

Just like that, Whistle walked out the back door and into the woods. He felt horrible about not paying the bill, but he didn't have another choice.

Whistle was still in a lot of pain as he found his way deeper into the woods and settled down for the night in some scraggly brush. He was too tired to look for better so he took what he could get. Sleep came easy as his body continued to heal. Whistle was so tired and knew his body had to rest, so rest he did.

The next day, with great effort, he managed to find a better spot with a rock overhang and a cold brook. After making the best bed he could out of the materials he found lying on the forest floor, he climbed into the brook, clothes and all. More grime flowed downstream from Whistle and his clothes. After a long swim/bath/laundry session, he got out and hung his clothes on some branches and lay down in his makeshift bed, as comfortable as can be.

Thirst quenched but still starving, he drifted off. Solid sleep carried over until the next day, and when he woke up, he was thrilled to find his clothes were more or less dry, save for a few stubborn spots: jean pockets, shirt collars, and sock heels. His body felt better overall and his urine was only slightly pink.

Undressed this time, he climbed into the brook again. Drank more, sent more grime down the brook and cleaned up with a bar of soap he took from the motel. All rinsed off with the soap suds rushing away, he climbed back out. He laid out on a rock in the sun to dry off. The afternoon turned to evening, so he got dressed and went back to sleep in his makeshift bed for the night.

Two days later, hunger drove him to pack up and finally move on. His body wasn't quite ready, but he literally had no choice, as he hadn't eaten in days. Walking out of the woods, he made his way back to the Bounty. As he opened the door, the bartender looked at him with shock on his face.

"Holy shit! I thought you were dead!" he exclaimed under his breath as he looked around to make sure no one else was around.

"So did I," Whistle wearily shot back. "I'm starving, do you think you could hook me up with something to eat?"

"Yeah, sure...uh, what do you want?" the bartender asked.

"Water and whatever's quick," Whistle replied.

"How about a cheeseburger and fries?"

"Yes please! Listen, I don't have any money, I'll wash dishes...Whatever I can..."

"Don't worry about it," the bartender interrupted him.

"Thanks...thank you," Whistle said, almost in tears.

"Don't worry about it, really," the bartender assured him.

The food came out; the kitchen worker gave him a strange look, and promptly walked back into the kitchen. Whistle devoured the cheeseburger, fries, and pickle in seconds flat. He would've taken his time to enjoy his first meal in days, but he was too hungry and there was too much heat around, between the motel bill and guys that beat him up. After he was done, he just sat there with his head in his hands, trying to think.

"You alright?" the bartender asked.

"Yeah, just, please give me a couple of minutes," Whistle said, closing his eyes.

The bartender gave him some time to collect himself, but after a while, he had to speak up.

"Listen, I don't want to bother you, but those boys that busted you up could show up here any minute and I don't think you want to deal with that. You better come with me."

"Where?" Whistle asked.

"I have a small efficiency apartment at the end of the motel with a couch you can crash on."

"Really?" Whistle couldn't believe his luck. "Do you think I could have a shot of Jack first? I could use a little numbing."

"Yeah, I'll have one with you, buddy." The bartender poured them both a shot, which they toasted and quickly knocked back.

"C'mon, grab your stuff," the bartender said as he locked the register, came out from behind the bar, and led Whistle out the door and down the hall to the last door.

Opening up the door, the bartender said to Whistle, "Make yourself at home. There's a couple of beers in the fridge and there's the TV, help yourself. I'll be back around one thirty."

"Thanks again, really," Whistle said to the bartender as he waved over his shoulder and shut the door behind him. The boy was too worn out to bother with the beer or the TV for the time being. He just sprawled out on the couch and drifted in and out of a blissful relaxing sleep. He heard people, presumably a family, on the other side of the wall in the next room, walking around and talking, and it was actually comforting to Whistle.

The boy woke up the next morning to the sun coming in through the window and the bartender sitting in a chair with his coffee, watching Tom and Jerry beating the shit out of each other on TV. He was trying to be quiet, but laughed out loud and looked over, hoping he didn't wake Whistle, but he saw he was already up.

"Good morning."

"Good morning," the boy returned. His body felt better and he made his way to the bathroom. No blood in the toilet today, which was a huge relief to Whistle. Looking in the mirror, he saw that his face was healing nicely and his nose looked relatively straight. His lips were starting to heal up as well. The only thing that bothered him was that his eyes were still really red. He walked out and sat across from the bartender at the table. In front of him was a delicious looking breakfast.

"Dig in, buddy," the bartender said.

"Thanks!" Whistle said, immediately, well, digging in.

"Who are you?" the bartender asked.

"Whistle Evel Fonzarelli Starr, what's your name?" he asked back, taking another bite, followed by a swig of refreshing orange juice.

"I'm Blake Hayes. You know, I gotta tell you, there are a lot of people looking for you right now," the bartender replied, taking a sip of coffee. "The guys that dragged you out of here are afraid you're dead somewhere, the girl you were with is a wreck, hoping you're ok, and that's just the beginning," Blake explained to him.

"What do you mean, just the beginning?" Whistle asked.

"Whistle, your room looked like a murder scene when you left. Word is they had to rip everything up out of there because of all the blood. You didn't pay your bill, and they want their money."

They both sat and finished their breakfast before they spoke again. Whistle was thankful for the food, juice, and coffee. When they were done, the conversation continued.

"You don't have any money, do you?" Blake asked.

"No, I'm completely broke," Whistle responded. Not the slightest bit worried about appearances.

"OK, chill here for a couple of days and we'll figure it out," Blake said.

For the next five days, Whistle stayed at Blake's to heal up and try to figure out a plan. He ate good, slept good, and kept a low profile. By the time he was ready to move on, he was still plenty sore, but he was certainly operating at a full enough capacity to get out of Dodge. His eyes were now only slightly pink, all his clothes were clean, and Blake gave him whatever he could. A few T-shirts, a few pairs of socks, and a used but still intact pair of sneakers.

"Thank you so much, Blake," Whistle said, voice on the verge of getting emotional.

"Listen, follow the back road for two miles and you'll come into town. Take the turn down 17 South and you can probably hit New Bern by nightfall," Blake said, handing the boy a bag.

"What is this?" Whistle asked.

"Just take it," Blake answered.

Whistle finally left and started down the back road. Two miles later he was heading down Route 17. Sure enough, the boy was camping in New Bern by nightfall. A warm, light rain started to fall, but the boy found an overhang along the back of a strip mall that kept him dry. He used his small amount of supplies to make a bed and pillow, then just went to sleep.

A little before first light, he was packed up and headed for the closest woods. After finding the closest spot that was still out of the way, he settled in. It was a small stand of very large pine trees. The floor was made up entirely of soft, dry pine needles that smelled fresh and felt great underneath him. Whistle decided to spend the night and evaluate his situation in the morning.

He set up his small camp and leaned back against a very large pine trunk. He knew his general goal was to keep heading south. Was this just because he wanted to get away from the northeast winter? He wondered if it was just out of habit. Either way, he had time to think about it, at least till the next day.

He decided he would take an inventory of his supplies before nightfall. Opening the bag that Blake had given him, he found sugar packets, bars of soap, small bottles of shampoo, a few bottles of tabasco sauce, and a roll of toilet paper. He knew Blake was not a man of means and Whistle appreciated that the guy helped him out as much as he could.

With the sun setting through the pine trunks to the west, Whistle started to get sleepy, as he fought to keep his eyes open. He wondered why he was getting tired so early and thought it might be due to the beating he had taken about a week prior. In a perfect world, he would go see a doctor and maybe get an x-ray, but given his situation, that wasn't an option.

As he was about to tap out for the night, laying on his side, he noticed a small, white triangle sticking out from the top of the bag. He blinked hard to assure himself that he wasn't seeing things.

"What the…? he said to himself as he sat back up, with some help from a pine trunk. He grabbed the white triangle and pulled out a small envelope with "Whistle" written on it. Astonished, he looked around for a moment. Huge tree trunks and golden skies surrounded him. He looked back down to the envelope again. He was dumbfounded. Taking a second to, for some reason, enjoy the suspense, he sat and looked around at his surroundings. The golden rays of sunshine streaming through the pines above, a robin or two picking through the needles for worms and bugs. Squirrels clamored through the treetops, chasing each other for who knows what. Digging for seeds and nuts maybe? Whistle marveled at the system of nature. These creatures, large and small, moving and still, birds, bugs, furry mammals, trees, seeds, mushrooms and frogs, all somehow knowing their purpose and taking their direction from some benevolent force. Every pine needle accounted for…

Whistle proceeded to open the envelope, confirming that it was from Blake. Here's what it said:

Take care of yourself. I still can't believe you're alive. I've never seen a beating like that in my life, and I've seen more than a few, working at the Bounty all these years. I'm sorry I wasn't there to help you that night, but I am dug in there. I've lived in town all my life and I would pretty much been have been a marked man, and I don't have the means to just pick up and move overnight.

I don't know you that well, but I admire your moxie and best of luck on your journey. Most people never take the first step, let alone take a beating like that and keep going.

May the Road Rise,
Blake Hayes

Whistle folded up the letter and put it back in his pack, tucked into a fold at the bottom to make sure that it wouldn't fall out. He started to get a bit choked up again as he somehow felt bad for Blake, stuck tending bar in a dead end town, dealing with drunk assholes in the middle of nowhere for a living. He hoped maybe someday he'd get out, maybe. Whistle lit a fire under him, at least that's what the boy hoped as he tucked his bag under his head and stared up at the stars. He fixated on the constellations until his eyes got too heavy.

Just as he was about to fall asleep, the boy felt a slight pressure on his right foot. He lifted his head and looked down.

"Hello buddy," Whistle said to the porcupine now sitting on his foot, sniffing his calf. For some reason, the boy wasn't startled at all. He didn't sense a threat and neither did the porcupine, apparently. He climbed on and off Whistle, checking out the boy and his belongings. He started to work his way into Whistle's bag, which was currently being used as a pillow. Whistle laughed as he felt the porcupine tenaciously rooting around under his head.

"Alright buddy, get outta there. I barely have enough for me," he said to the little scavenger.

He closed his eyes again and felt the porcupine's feet on his face. He opened his eyes to find the creature staring right at him, nose to nose. Whistle laughed again as the porcupine scurried off again and the boy was finally able to fall asleep.

CHAPTER
FORTY-TWO
A Huge Kick in the Ass

The next day, Whistle got up, walked, and eventually crossed the Neuse River. He continued south along Route 17. Thumb out, he finally caught a ride from a guy in a red pickup truck. Barely remembering the ride, he was dropped off at Calabash, North Carolina, right at the border.

The boy simply walked into the woods and lived off the land for the next three days. He whittled down his supplies to almost nothing. He knew then that it was time to get a move on, so he headed south. He crossed the border, looking at a sign that read in white and blue, "Welcome to South Carolina." He entered the state hungry and broke, but was lucky to run into a Burger King in Little River that was set in front of some woodland. He figured it was a good place to camp as it might land him some free food. He'd been around long enough to know that fast food places threw out perfectly good food multiple times a day and the people that would take the trash out would just as soon give it to someone as throw it in the garbage.

His belly full, and plenty of water later, he crashed out in the woods for the night. The next morning, he knew he had to get a plan together. He was tired of just wandering generally south at a snail's pace. He went out to the highway and his intention seemed to bring him a lucky break as a long haul trucker pulled to the side.

"You need a ride?" the trucker asked.

"Yeah!" Whistle replied, not even thinking to ask him where he was headed.

"My name's Whistle," the boy said as he climbed up into the cab.

"Marc Brace, nice to meet ya," the driver replied. "Where are you trying to go, my brutha?"

"South, west, or any place in between," Whistle responded.

"Alright buddy, I'll be heading in that general direction for a while. You look beat, if you don't mind me saying so. There's a cab in the back; if you want to, you can climb in back there and grab a snooze," Marc offered.

"Thank you!" Whistle said as he grabbed his bag and climbed in the back. The windows were open and the sound of the road and engine lulled him to sleep almost immediately. Marc was occupied talking on the C.B. and listening to Eddie Rabbit singing about driving his life away on the radio....Gotta keep a-rollin'.

Whistle woke up sixteen hours later from the best sleep he could re-member having in his life. They were past Bluffton and well into Georgia. They stopped and grabbed some food, coffee, and a few waters as well. When they were done, Whistle climbed in back as Marc told him to help himself to the port-able TV in back and more comfortable accommodations as well. As the saying goes, why stand when you can sit and why sit when you can lie down, especially on a nice, comfortable cot?

It didn't take Whistle long to fall right back to sleep to the hum of the open road coming in through the open windows. It did wonders for the boy. Early the next morning, Marc pulled off the highway and into a Chick-Fil-A.

"Wake up, Whistle," Marc called from the front.

"Huh?" Whistle replied, groggily.

"I gotta let you out here, pal."

"Okay, thank you so much!" Whistle said as he climbed out from the back cab.

"Wait. Take this and make sure you stay on Route 17 until you hit 25 in-to Florida, then either keep going or head right on Route 10." Marc shook the boy's hand, slipping him a twenty.

"Thanks Marc, I really appreciate it!" Whistle said as he opened the door and climbed down to the pavement.

Well rested, well supplied, and a crisp twenty in his pocket, Whistle stood and watched Marc drive that black and chrome behemoth up the ramp and back onto the highway. He squared up and decided to head south with the goal of living in Florida, at least for the time being. Living in Key West would be un-believable, he thought to himself. People work in a miserable, crime infested city, just to vacation there two weeks every other year. He could get a job in a hotel or tending bar or whatever and just live in a cheap shanty or trailer. It was within reach and Whistle was ready for a vacation.

That night he camped in Waverly and the next morning he made it to White Oak, Georgia on foot. He decided it was time for another motel stay for a shower, some food, and a real bed. After walking for a few hours, he eventually found the Sanilla River Motel. Again he had plans to really make the most of the luxury he was paying for, but after a long, hot shower, he was so wiped out that he got under the most comfortable sheets he'd ever felt and fell asleep before he even had a chance to turn the light off.

In the morning, he walked to the lobby, checked out, and helped himself to the continental breakfast, which was deliciously made in house. He grabbed some waters for the road and he was on his way, full bellied, well rested and happy. The day was beautiful. Not a cloud in the sky with a cool, dry breeze. He stopped and grabbed a coffee at the donut shop and headed out to the highway.

He walked for a good part of the day and by afternoon he was ready for a quick rest. He found an old, stone wall that ran between the highway and the trees. He walked on the wooded side and sat against a section that served as a comfortable backrest. He learned to take a rest when his feet started to hurt as they were his only one hundred percent reliable source of transportation. After his rest, he figured he'd keep going till night, head west and then hit Route 10, all the way down Florida to the Keys, where he would live the good life that most only dream of.

In late afternoon he decided that a water and sugar fix was in order. He found a gas station, walked in and grabbed a Snickers and went to the counter to pay. Looking at the cashier, he could tell by the young man's eyes that something wasn't right.

"You ok?" Whistle asked.

"Yeah," the cashier replied, eyes darting left and right at something behind Whistle. He turned around to see what it was and there stood three men, the one in the middle pointing a nine millimeter right at Whistle's head.

"Get the fuck down, ya little bitch ass," the man said as one of the other men grabbed him by the back of the neck, shoving him down onto the cold tile of the gas station floor. As he lay there fuming, he realized the gunman's feet were right in front of him and all three thugs were focused on the cashier and his ability to open the safe. Even though it was most likely that this whole episode would end with these guys cleaning out the station and being on their way soon after, Whistle couldn't help himself. Maybe it was leftover rage from the beating he took not too long ago, maybe it was the fact that he had the opportunity to be a hero; either way he launched into action.

Whistle ran at the gunman as fast as he could, fully confident he could mitigate the situation. A few muffled *paps!* later, Whistle twisted the gunman's hand and shot him in the face. He instantly dropped and everyone ran out of the store. Now quiet, he looked down at the blood spreading over the white tile. He put the gun down, put his hands up and waited for the police. When they got there, the shock in their eyes confused him.

"Are you shot?" the officer asked.

"Holy shit! I guess I am!" Whistle replied, feeling around to find two wounds in his shoulder and one in his abdomen. The loss of blood and shock of the moment caused him to go weak in the knees and immediately pass out.

The next three weeks were spent in the hospital and Whistle was deemed a hero without him even being made aware. The gunman was dead, the other two men were caught, and Whistle was cleared of any charges pending. He cut out the article from the paper and folded it neatly in his backpack along with Blake's letter.

A week later, he walked out of the hospital healed, with a nine millimeter lodged in his shoulder. The fact that he was still alive amazed him. He walked less than four miles before his next situation presented itself.

"What the?" was all he could get out before everything went—

CHAPTER FORTY-THREE
Lost in a Tough Deal

The vibration stopped and the engine cut out. The boy exhaled and listened. He heard two car doors open and close, followed by muffled voices. As they got closer to the back of the car, Whistle finally caught a sense of what they were planning and it wasn't pretty.

"This mother fucker killed Rod and got away with it, so we gotta kill him," a male voice said with anger.

"Hell yeah," another male voice said as it got closer, along with footsteps approaching. Putting a couple of things together really quick, Whistle knew he was at huge disadvantage and surely wasn't gonna survive this one. Whistle Evel Fonzarelli Starr instantly knew that these two men were Rod's brothers and they had nothing on their minds but to kill him and dump him in some out of the way ravine or quarry.

He tried to come up with any wisp of an idea or some thread of hope to hang onto. At least he wasn't tied up, that was one point in his favor. Did they have guns or knives? Were they planning to throttle him with their bare hands? Whistle didn't know, but it was fight or flight time, and he was going to have to weigh his options on the fly.

The key turned in the lock with an audible click in his ear.

"You ready?" he heard one of Rod's boys ask.

"Mmm," he heard the other one mutter.

Whistle sensed apprehension in their voices and decided his best bet was to come out swinging, stay low and try to break through and make a run for it, like a quarterback sneak. If he made it past them, it was full speed ahead, no looking back.

"He killed Rod and got away with it, so what do you want to do?" the first one asked.

"Open it up," the other one said, now sounding angry.

The latch clicked open and the trunk went up. Whistle shot up, but was instantly blinded by the scorching midday sun blasting right in his wide open pupils. He fell back into the trunk, completely disoriented. He was certain it was the middle of the night, and between the hours of his eyes being adjusted to the dark and the fight or flight adrenaline screaming through his veins, he was reduced to a blind, flailing ball of directionless energy. The two men grabbed him. One by the hair and collar, the other by one of his arms and one of his legs. They more or less yanked him out of the trunk and dropped him on the ground like a wood pallet. His throat was so dry he could barely even beg for his life. All that would come out were croaks and wheezing. He pointed to his mouth, miming desperately for a drink of water.

The two men looked at each other, not appearing to be a whole lot more in command of the situation than Whistle. This could be his only chance. His left hand found a jagged rock the size of a baseball and instantly launched it at the first face he saw. Miraculously, the rock connected with one brother's forehead and he dropped like a sack of potatoes.

Holy shit! Whistle thought to himself just as the other brother punched him in the nose, which had just healed up from the beating at the Bounty. He fell and blood poured everywhere and he was once again blinded temporarily. He shook it off as best he could and saw the guy he didn't hit tending to the one he did.

Whistle had a clear shot at the shin so he bit it as hard as he could. The guy fell on the ground as well. As he was rolling around in pain, Whistle grabbed a handful of sand and promptly threw it in the man's face, rendering him useless. Whistle would never know it, but he exploded Rod's brother's left eye. His eyeball was literally replaced instantly by a crude, dirty rock.

In the land of the blind, the one-eyed man is king. But in the here and now, the one-eyed man and his momentarily one-legged brother were in the rearview as Whistle just scrambled into the woods as fast and as far as he could go. He could work out the fine points later. He heard the two kidnappers in the distance swearing, yelling, and scrambling to find Whistle. The main thing, only thing really, was to escape the two men who at this point were most certainly not gonna be reasoned with.

Whistle kept running through the brush and thick trees. He saw an opening in the trees as the sun grew brighter ahead of him. The ground was hard to see and one step later, the boy was airborne. Looking underneath him, the ground was more or less vertical and Whistle tumbled a good thirty feet. He bounced and rolled until he got wedged between two large trees covered in moss. He passed out again with no idea where he was, but happy and thankful to be alive.

The next morning was greeted with a steady, warm rain. Whistle woke up and realized he was at this point completely soaked. What he didn't realize was that he was smack dab in the middle of the Okefenokee National Wildlife Refuge. All he knew was that he was alone and alive. That was a good start. The boy slept all day and all night, letting his body rest.

As the sun rose on the second day, Whistle woke up and began to collect himself. Then he utilized one of his greatest assets. Whistle paused, stayed calm and took stock in his situation, surroundings, and available tools and resources. He watched where the sun rose, so he could get his east-west bearings. He was extremely thirsty and hungry as well, so he knew he'd have to catch another lucky break. He wouldn't last long without it and he didn't want any wild animals getting at him either. One direction was deeper into the woods and it right away gave Whistle an uneasy feeling, so right away that option was off the table.

Whistle followed the sun until it dipped below the horizon in the west. As it got dark, Whistle began to slow down against his will. Almost as if his faculties were slowly slipping from his control the darker it got. Whistle was having a tough time in the terrain and just collapsed. In his dizzy mind, he had planned to get back up after a quick rest.

Waking to early sunlight, the boy realized he had slept through the night, and by this point he figured he'd need to find water within hours or else he was a goner. He decided south was again the best option and started on his way. Luckily, it was a relatively cool day and Whistle could have sworn he felt a mist of water in the air. He couldn't tell if it was real or just the heat and dehydration playing tricks on his body and his mind.

Through a thick row of trees was a clearing. He walked through and he couldn't believe his eyes. There before him was a natural spring pond, with water so clear and clean that he could see the rocks, sand, and tadpoles all the way to the bottom as he walked right in and dove headfirst into total rejuvenation. He drank in as much as he could, swam underwater, splashed around and floated on his back, looking up at the sun, now smiling down on him as opposed to draining the life from him just minutes before. Benjamin Franklin said fire is a wonderful servant and a horrible master, and Whistle was learning this firsthand.

After saturating himself until every cell was quenched, he went out to lie in the sand and dry in the midday sun. After taking a nap, he woke up happy, but feeling weak. He would need to find food. There had to be something nearby. After all, where there's soil, water, and sun, things grow. He noticed some brush that looked a little different and it drew him closer. Something in the deep recesses of his mind told him to go check it out....and sure enough...fresh blueberries!

Whistle picked and ate as fast as he could. Blueberries being small, he had to clean out the entire bush before he put a dent in his hunger, but luckily there were more than enough to at least keep him fed for a few days. If he stayed put for a day or two, he could refuel and try and figure out the best route forward. He might even get ambitious and try to light a fire, maybe even catch a fish or some other form of substantial protein.

There was a problem with that plan, however. Besides the elements nipping at his heels, there were two men very interested in his whereabouts, and if they knew the woods and had flashlights, they could cover a lot of ground at night, and a fire would make Whistle easy to find.

CHAPTER
FORTY-FOUR
Roxy Bruins

Whistle woke up the next morning, drank as much water as he could, dunked his head to stay cool, loaded up on blueberries, and got on the move. He jumped and shimmied through the dense oaks and maples, occasionally tripping on a root or stone. It was tough terrain and Whistle was wondering when he might catch a break.

Not five minute later, he stepped out onto a dirt logging road. He just could not believe it.

Thank God! he thought as he looked up and down in both directions for any hint of a clue as to which way to go. He checked the pines for northern moss, found some, and going by that and the sun traversing the sky, he found what he believed to be west, and started on down the road. It felt good walking in the direct sunshine again, not having to dodge obstacles.

He also started to relax a bit as he imagined he'd put a good amount of miles between him and Rod's brothers. The boy was starting to wear out his sneakers, but his spirits were high. He was alive and on a road that led some-where.

Whistle walked hard until darkness, stepped off the road, and bedded down. His bed was simple because he literally had no supplies. The last of the blueberries gone, he started to drift off to complete silence, besides crickets and two owls calling each other from far away. These miles were easy compared to what he'd dealt with the past several days and it lifted Whistle's spirits and calmed his mind as he drifted off to dreamland.

As soon as he was asleep, oranges and black covered his vision and he instantly knew it was because he was in a huge pine forest. Or maybe it was that time of year when the butterflies were passing through on their journey to South America. Whatever it was, the orange and black shuffle steeped to black and gold.

He was now the starting left defenseman for the Boston Bruins in game seven of the Stanley Cup finals against the Montreal Canadians. There were three minutes and eleven seconds left in the game. The Garden was rockin'. The face-off came back to Bobby Orr and was immediately passed up the right to Rick Middleton. They worked into the offensive zone and tried to find Terry O'Reilly at the front of the net. The pass skipped over his stick and hit the left corner boards.

With thirty-four seconds left, Derek Sanderson hit Whistle with a perfect pass back to the left point. He skated to his right and made his way around Montreal's right-winger. Whistle looked around to find a pass to a much better goal scorer than he would ever be. All the passing lanes were closed as he slid a little deeper into the middle slot.

That's when he realized he was completely open and was staring at the great Ken Dryden. He worked in deeper with eleven seconds left and a chance to win the Stanley Cup. He skated in untested and hoped his instinct would carry him through. Everything screamed shoot high corner, but something made the boy go left and carry the puck behind the net on his forehand. He stopped directly behind the net with no Canadians moving in.

Whistle couldn't believe it as Ken worked the net back and forth, looking for him to come out somewhere. All of a sudden a crazy thought came to him. So Whistle flipped the puck up onto the back of the net. He scooped it off the back and cradled it more like a lacrosse stick with the blade.

He just flung it over, hit Ken square in the back and bounced the puck down into the net. So as far as he was concerned, Gretzky's office should be called Whistle's office. After all, it happened four years before the greatest player to play in the NHL even started. Goal scored, the crowd roared, and all the rest, the hoisting of the cup, the interviews, the Duck Boat and ticker tape parade, all the glory swirled into a magnificent crescendo as Whistle's mind's eye was once again filled with the orange and black of the monarchs.

The next morning came and he continued down the road. After a while, he realized he was starting to get dehydrated again. He was starting to cramp up and his hunger was gnawing at his stomach at an accelerating rate. The fact that the sun was already high in the sky and shining down hot didn't help the situation. Throughout the day, Whistle had to take many rests. Dizzy spells got worse and worse as he began to momentarily black out. At one point he dry heaved uncontrollably on the side of the road. His body simply had nothing left to give. He passed out, dropped and didn't wake up for two hours. Heat stroke was starting to get the better of him and he knew he was in real trouble. On top of everything else, he felt a hole wearing through the sole of his right shoe, which could make further travel rate anywhere between mildly annoying and excruciating, and it didn't take long to go from one to the other.

Yesterday's high of finding the road was quickly replaced by the low today due to his current condition. He was actually starting to hallucinate, and the feeling of hopelessness grew stronger with every step, each a little more painful than the last. Blisters were forming on the bottoms of his feet again. If he wasn't completely dehydrated, tears would be flowing.

Finally, the sun set and the temperature cooled a bit, giving Whistle some relief. He literally lay down on the side of the road and fell asleep fast, knowing his chances of waking up weren't exactly one hundred percent.

The next thing he knew, he thankfully regained consciousness and, perhaps even more thankfully, he found himself in the back of the cab of an old truck, rumblin', bumblin', ramblin' and tamblin' down what he assumed was the old dirt road he was lying on the side of last he was aware. The next thing he noticed was the smell of diesel fuel, cigar smoke, and the kind of body odor that comes from an honest day's work.

"Where am I?" Whistle asked the man driving the truck.

"On your way to the hospital. Here, drink this," the man replied as he reached back and handed Whistle an ice cold bottle of water from the cooler on the floor on the passenger side. He guzzled the water, spilling more than he liked, due to the bumpy ride. He once again felt the effects immediately.

"Here, you better take another," the man said as he reached back with another one. Whistle's stomach was adjusting to the onslaught of cold water, almost like it was doing cartwheels of joy. He gave it a minute and drank the next one at a more measured pace.

"Take this too," the driver said as he tossed Whistle an apple and a package of peanut butter crackers. "That's all I got left over from my lunch. Boy, I thought you were all done out there."

"So did I," Whistle responded as he took a giant bite out of the apple. After just a few more, he had made the whole thing disappear, core, seeds, and all.

"Thank you so much, sir," Whistle said over the racket of the truck. "What's your name?"

"John Bunyan," the driver responded.

"John Bunyan? Like Paul Bunyan?" Whistle asked.

"Yep. I'm actually believed to be Paul's great, great grandson."

"Wow! That's cool! My name is Whistle Evel Fonzarelli Starr, no relation to any of them," the boy responded as they both chuckled.

"Listen, I'm going to take you to Lexington Hospital in Bainbridge. They'll check you out and probably run some tests, but I'm gonna have to get back here before morning. Gotta move twenty-two cords of wood tomorrow."

"Well you saved my life, John. I owe you one."

"Don't sweat it. You probably wanna grab some sleep, you're probably gonna be up all night."

"Yeah, you're probably right," Whistle said as he tried to get comfortable across the two seats in the back. He finally managed to get in a position on his side where nothing hurt and it almost felt like a bunk bed.

He slept for a solid four hours as the water and nutrition worked overtime within his body, well enough to keep the hospital from chalking him up as a lost cause. As the steady hum of the truck, "The Blue Ox," as John called it, lulled him to sleep, when they got into town, the herky jerky of the traffic rousted Whistle from his nap. He sat up, only slightly dizzy and bleary eyed and asked, "What state are we in?"

"Georgia...Southwest Georgia to be particular. A town called Thomasville."

As they hit some late traffic, eventually they made it to Bainbridge and into the ER entrance of Lexington Hospital. John got out and helped Whistle out of the back of the cab. As they stood face to face, Whistle was shocked to see John was only about five seven, five eight. Not short, necessarily, but if he were from the Paul Bunyan family tree, he was plucked a little early, Whistle thought to himself. He did, however, have a huge beard with the tiny nub of a cigar popping out of the corner of his mouth. He appeared to be blind in one eye as it was completely clouded over. Whistle wondered if he was legal to drive and if he was taking a chance driving into town to take him to the hospital.

"Hey buddy, I'm not going in. I gotta get back, but just go check in at the desk there and they'll probably have you fill out some papers and bring you in, take a look atcha. I've been in and out of here a time or two, they'll take care of ya."

"Thanks again, John! You saved my life," Whistle said with a firm, sincere handshake.

"A 'ight, den," John responded as he turned on his heel, gave Whistle an informal salute, and hopped back up into his truck, slammed it into gear, and was off to deal with twenty-two cords of wood waiting for him at the other end of his journey.

Walking into the entrance of the ER, right away Whistle noticed every-one looking at him with either concern or disgust, or some combination thereof. The next thing he knew, Whistle was lying in a bed with a large bore IV in both arms. The heart monitor was beeping steady, so he figured that was a good indi-cation. The boy just laid there for a long time before a nurse came in. She looked a bit rattled by Whistle's condition for a split second, but immediately pulled it together and got down to business, asking the usual questions and taking notes on her clipboard.

Shortly after that, he was wheeled into an operating room and asked to count backward from ten to one. He only got to seven before it was lights out. No dreams, no tossing and turning, no nothing but out coldness for six hours before Whistle woke up, this time in a rather comfortable hospital bed, room lights dim and the TV on the wall tuned into the news. The weatherman was saying it was going to be hot and humid for the better part of the week, as if it were ever anything else down this way. The boy watched the news and eventually fell back asleep during the sports wrap up.

The next morning, Whistle woke up to a different nurse checking on him, asking him how he was feeling in general.

"Well, not too bad in the middle, but my face and my feet are sore as all get out. What happened?" Whistle asked.

"We had to lance the blisters on your feet and reset your nose. What's going on Whistle? Because none of this is normal. If you need help, we have re-sources," the nurse responded matter-of-factly.

"I'm fine, thank you. I just need a day or two to heal up and I'll be good as gold."

A day or two turned into a solid week of healing up, eating up, drinking up, and plenty of tests. He also got a haircut, a shave, manicure, and even a nose hair trim...Good for another one thousand miles.

Whistle was lying in bed, dozing in and out while reading a local paper, when he heard a timid little knock at the door and an adorable little southern accent whisper, "Hello?"

"Hello?" Whistle responded.

"Hi, Mr. Starr. My name is Nurse Roxy and I'm here for your sponge bath."

"My what, now?" he shot back, thrown off guard.

"Sponge bath, we're gonna clean you up real good." A slight hint of flir-tatiousness came into her voice; however, it still sat just this side of "profession-al."

Nurse Roxy started with Whistle's neck, chest, and arms. She then worked her way down to his stomach, sides, and thighs. Roxy continued down his legs to his ankles, then started working her way back up. That's when Whistle realized he was fully aroused and his face flushed pink with embarrassment. He pushed his hands down to stop Roxy from continuing back up on him. She pushed his hands away and kept going.

Before Whistle knew it, Nurse Roxy put the sponge down and was using her bare hands. He could barely contain himself, but he tried as best he could.

"You look like you're ready to pop!" she purred.

"This isn't fair!" Whistle responded as naughty Nurse Roxy exposed him.

"Do you think you're ready for this?" she whispered as she got up and slowly walked across the room in her sexy uniform to lock the door. "I'm assigned to you aaaaallllll night," she said as Whistle realized he was in for the time of his life.

"Come here," Whistle commanded. She came over and it was on. Tongues were down throats and every other place they could find. When Nurse Roxy climbed on top of Whistle, they enjoyed long, slow, deep thrusts together. As they both neared climax, they looked into each other's eyes as Whistle cupped her breasts and played a little game of Tune In Tokyo. as she pealed with delight. They kissed deeply as the two finally slowed down. Calmly, they both recovered and Roxy asked, "Are you hungry?"

"Actually, I am," he responded.

Before he knew it, Nurse Roxy put her sexy uniform back on and stepped back out of the room and down the hall. Sleep after sex comes easy for a man, so needless to say, Whistle nodded off before the door fully closed. After a few minutes, Nurse Roxy was back with Salisbury steak, mashed potatoes, corn bread, and jam. Whistle Evel Fonzarelli Starr chowed down hard as Nurse Roxy went back to lock the door after setting the tray down for Whistle. As he set his fork down to take a drink, the insatiable nurse took the tray and set it on the desk by the door. She started undressing again and....well, you can guess the rest.

After the second round of festivities, Nurse Roxy snuggled up to Whistle as they both fell asleep, carefree as can be. After a good long snooze, the sun began to come up and Nurse Roxy awoke with a jolt.

"Oh shit! What time is it?" She looked around frantically, almost on autopilot in that moment where the "you" in you is still pulling out of whatever dream world people go to when they sleep.

"Huh?...uhhh." Whistle mumbled, pretty much still out himself.

"My husband must be freaking out right now! I gotta go!" Nurse Roxy said as she jumped out of bed, gave Whistle a quick peck on the cheek, and hauled ass out the door and down the hall.

Whistle was none too happy about being the unwitting participant in marital infidelity. Like he needed this drama, especially stuck in a hospital with nowhere to go if, let's say, Nurse Roxy were to get in a drunken argument with her husband and said something to the effect of, "Oh yeah? You think I need you? I just fucked some kid at the hospital and he was a WAY better lay than you'll ever be, blah, blah, blah........" Perfect.

Luckily, Whistle spent another week in the hospital and never saw Nurse Roxy for the remainder of his stay. Feeling pretty much good as new, the day came for him to get up, get dressed, and sign out. Whistle couldn't believe he just spent a couple of weeks in the hospital, got laid, and walked out without paying a cent. He was grateful but also knew something was wrong with that. Whistle walked as the sun settled in the west, turning the sky a shade of magenta he had never seen. He weighed his options and wasn't looking forward to sleeping on the ground after two weeks of luxury had softened him up mentally if not physically. Or maybe having the time to reflect made him realize that throwing caution to the wind and relying solely on the kindness of strangers for his own survival was kind of irresponsible and selfish....Yep, it was time to grow up and become self-reliant.

CHAPTER
FORTY-FIVE
Madison or Adventure

A couple of days later, and a few rides west on Route 84, he slid from Georgia to Alabama. Still feeling quite good, he eventually made his way to the small city of Dothan. That was when he decided to slow down a bit. In rather short order, he was employed by McDonald's and rented a tiny place in the basement of a couple that had to be at least ninety years old.

Two years later, he found himself managing the McDonald's, renting his own one-room ranch, driving a beat up Chevy pickup, and living with a girl he could never stay with. That's when he realized that responsibility and the lack thereof was a tradeoff.

"Good morning, babe," Madison Cooke said, snuggling up to Whistle.

"Morning," he replied as he moved away from her, not feeling like snuggling on this hot, muggy morning.

"What do you want to do today?" she asked, trying to move closer again.

"I don't know," he replied, pushing her away a little this time.

"What's wrong?" she asked.

"Nothing. It's just hot," he replied as he threw the covers off. "Why, what do you want to do?"

"I thought maybe we could walk down to Congdon Park and get lunch at Skippy's," she chirped.

"Okay. I'm gonna go take a shower," Whistle replied as he got up out of bed and into the bathroom. As he turned the water on in the tub, Whistle felt bad because Madison was a great girl, but he knew that today was the day he was going to finally break it off with her. It had been settled in his mind for a while now, he was just procrastinating, plain and simple, and the time was right. It was for her own good as well as his.

The two got ready, then made the walk to the park. At Skippy's, they drank a few cheap beers and shared a huge order of nachos that weren't great, but decent nonetheless.

"Whistle, what is wrong? You've been acting weird all day, actually for a while now. What is going on?"

"Madison, you know I care a lot about you. I just don't feel like this is going anywhere and every day is just like the last. You need someone who is 'The One' and I'm not him, and I feel stuck. I didn't grow up here so it'll never feel like home to me. I got to go."

"I know, and I guess I have known for some time. I just never wanted to admit it to myself."

They hugged and kissed each other on the cheek and even got a little teared up. As they sat there, a waitress came up and asked them, "You two okay?"

"Yeah, sorry. Let's go, honey," Whistle said as he laid the money for the beers and nachos, plus a solid tip, on the table. They were both happy to get out of there, but sad because it was just another step towards not being together again. Silently, they left the park and made their way home, content to hold hands and enjoy each other's company. After they got home, they hunkered down on the couch and watched a *Rocky* movie marathon on the classics channel together. They held each other under the blanket and could feel their heartbeats beating in unison. It was truly a magical moment between two young lovers.

Sunlight faded to night toward the end of *Rocky Three*.

"You want to watch the rest of this in bed?" Whistle asked.

"Yes," she replied, kissing him on the neck. Both happy to go to bed but sadly knowing it was the next step toward the end of their time together. In bed, *Rocky Three* worked its way into *Rocky Four*. Ivan Drago had killed Apollo Creed and Rocky was now training in Russia for his next fight. Whistle and Madison made slow, deep, meaningful love, staring into each other's eyes. When they finished, they lay together tired, happy and sadly crushed all at the same time.

"When are you going to leave?" she asked.

"I figure next Monday. I'll work the weekend and get my last check. I want you to keep the place, and I'll give you anything I can. We'll figure out the details tomorrow, but for right now I'm exhausted," he said, eyes closing. They both drifted off and Whistle would never know that a truly awesome, very similar boy to him was conceived that night.

The following Monday came and they awkwardly delayed the inevitable, barely able to look each other in the eye. Whistle's pack was well packed with supplies for days. He handed Madison seventeen hundred dollars and pocketed three hundred dollars for himself. They hugged each other hard and started crying again as they finally let their eyes meet.

"I love you so much Whistle," Madison said, lower lip quivering and eyes starting to tear up.

"I love you too, Madison," Whistle replied, looking twice as sad as her.

"Please don't say goodbye, because maybe we'll be together again someday," Madison said.

"I never would because you can never say never," he replied as a small smile crept across his face. Looking at one another, they both knew it was time. They kissed, then put their foreheads together. Holding each other's faces and looking deep into each other's eyes, not another word was spoken. After a very long pause, Whistle Evel Fonzarelli Starr turned on his heel, again squared up, and walked out the door, trying to control his emotions. Barely able to hold back the tears, he walked down the front steps. At the bottom, he walked the short distance to the street and hung a left onto Cypress Street.

He walked through the neighborhood, through the edge of town, and finally to the highway. In the late afternoon sun, the boy had another decision to make. Should he take 84 West or 52 West? He was familiar with 84 so he decided to stick with it. Plus the late afternoon sun poured over the entrance ramp while 52 was dark and shadowy. He took that as a sign and it confirmed his decision.

Knowing he could have stayed on the ramp and thumbed a ride, probably making good distance west, his desire to spend the night in the woods was too strong. Second thoughts about leaving Madison filled his mind, and maybe he didn't want to go too far in case he changed his mind. He knew that wasn't going to be the case, however. He knew the call of the open road when he felt it, and second guessing himself was just part of the process.

He bedded down comfortably that night, knowing he was well prepared for at least the near future. The boy didn't have any specific dreams that night as far as he could remember. He thought about Madison and reflected on the last two years of his life. He never dreamed he would spend all that time in Alabama, but he did. Then an absolutely crazy thought struck him: *How the fuck old am I?* Awake enough to recognize this as a conscious thought but asleep enough to hear it in his mind as a question posed to him from somewhere else, he dwelled on it. *Am I twenty-four, twenty-eight, thirty by now?* At the moment, Whistle could not figure it out. He knew his birthday was September 11, but that was all he could be sure of. Then solid sleep hit him hard and he didn't wake up until late the next morning.

When he did wake up, he got his first chance to see his surroundings. For the most part, they were similar to all the other little camps in the woods he had made for himself throughout his travels over the years. Dense, close to the highway, and if he was lucky, near a body of water. Well today, he was in luck. Just fifty feet down a hill was one of the clearest, cleanest streams he had ever seen. Of course he went over and drank deeply. He loved that feeling of water instantly working its wonders on his body and soul. He stripped down, jumped in and swam. He felt absolutely incredible. After getting out, he found himself a warm, flat rock to lay down on to dry off in the Alabama sun.

When he was done, he got dressed and happily made his way back to camp. Deciding to spend another night where he was, he built a fire. With a basic camp layout set up, Whistle made sure he had enough firewood. Feeling he had everything taken care of, he opened a can of beef stew and placed it over the fire on a hot rock in the middle of the pit. A short time later, the rock and stew were removed. A plastic spoon and a pack of peanut butter crackers with a bottle of water were in front of him. In a short time, the boy was full and beyond content.

Whistle took a dusk swim in the stream, cleaned himself, and filled his water bottles a little upstream before he eventually hoofed it back up to camp. Crawling into bed as one last sliver of deep red sky dipped behind the horizon, Whistle felt content and happy with his situation. He was learning that the key to freedom in life wasn't in having lots of possessions, but in the ability to do without them and still be satisfied. He was still ruminating over his age, however. Somewhere in his journey, he lost track of time, and he really had no way to figure it out, at least for the time being.

CHAPTER
FORTY-SIX
A Rather Spirited Stretch

Packed up and moving through the woods, heading further west, Whistle worked his way along 84. He was back on the schedule of walking all day and camping all night once the sun set, or if he was feeling ambitious, keep walking until it was completely dark out, which could mean an extra few miles, depending on the terrain. He had relatively easy travels for a few weeks before supplies eventually got low, his feet got sore, and hunger set in hard. Luckily, his stomach had adjusted to drinking any water of reasonable quality, so thirst was one obstacle out of the way.

With the full three hundred dollars still in his pocket, Whistle walked into the tiny town of Babble, Alabama. Walking into Skitter's, a small diner mainly frequented by local farmers, he ordered a breakfast special advertised on the wall. Two eggs, bacon, home fries, toast, and coffee for five dollars. The toast came with some homemade strawberry rhubarb jam that was absolutely delicious. Whistle paid the bill and left two dollars and eighty-nine cents for a tip. He asked the waitress if there was a motel nearby and it turned out there was. The Laughing Gator Inn was just seven blocks away and was given good reviews by the waitress and one of the farmers drinking a coffee at the counter. Good enough for Whistle.

He walked down the road and soon enough, he saw the orange and white sign with a green alligator who was, you guessed it, laughing. Whistle checked in, went to his room, and washed his face and hands in the sink. Out in the main room, he noticed the color scheme was consistent with the sign and the rest of the exterior of the motel. Bright orange bedspread, pure white popcorn textured ceiling with a few watermarks here and there, green chairs around a brown table by the window. He turned on the TV, flopped down on the bed, and before long, was out cold. Full, cool, comfy and happy.

When he came to a couple of hours later, he still felt groggy but wanted to enjoy his stay. He jumped in the shower and turned the water on lukewarm. As he cleaned up, he gradually turned the water colder and colder. Something about cold water somehow made him feel cleaner. Twenty minutes later, he got out, dried off, put on his cleanest set of clothes, combed his hair and brushed his teeth. He realized he would eventually need new socks and shoes as both were getting worn out. Putting himself together the best he could, he locked the door behind him and walked down the hall to the Blue Lagoon Saloon.

He found a seat at the very end of the bar and kept to himself as much as he could. Placing a menu in front of him, the bartender asked, "Would you like a drink?"

"Just a Bud, thanks," Whistle replied as he opened the menu.

After another Bud, he decided on a rib-eye rare with garlic, mashed potatoes, and a side salad. By his fourth Bud, he had cleaned his plate and was full again. He noticed that the bar was filled with smoke and it gave Whistle a nostalgic feeling. Voices echoed, blending all around him. It was starting to get crowded in there and Whistle was figuring it was a good time to get rolling.

"Here, have a drink on me," Whistle heard as someone slid a shot of whiskey in front of him. Whistle took a sip of his beer and looked to his right and there was a gaggle of young people holding shots of their own, having a grand old time.

"Thanks. Uh, what's this for?" he asked as he raised the glass.

"Nothing! We're just having a good time and you seem like a cool guy," one of them said as he turned back to his friends and yelled, "Cheers!"

They all toasted to whatever the occasion was and downed their shots. The whiskey burned Whistle's throat but it was a good burn. Everyone slammed their shot glasses upside down on the bar so Whistle did the same. He took a long draw off his Bud as a chaser and felt everything fall into place.

"What's your name?" he heard to his right. With a comfortable buzz going, he looked over and saw a huge guy in a John Deere hat and a cut off T-shirt, like he could be a defensive lineman for the Crimson Tide.

"Thanks for the drink, pal. What's your name?" Whistle said, finishing his beer.

"I'm Tommy Jaxx. What's yours?"

Whistle took a moment to weigh whether it would be a good idea to give his real name, seeing as there were people looking for him, and he wasn't up for another ride in a truck to the middle of nowhere, but he figured enough time had gone by and enough miles were between him and that whole fiasco.

"My name is Whistle, Whistle Evel Fonzarelli Starr."

"Well I'll be. Now if that ain't the craziest name," Tommy yelled, slapping Whistle on the back hard enough to knock the wind out of him.

Someone ordered another round of shots and the party continued. Whistle and Tommy got to talking.

"So where y'all from?" Tommy asked.

"New Hampshire," Whistle answered.

"Man, you got the craziest accent I've ever heard," Tommy chuckled.

Somebody turned on the jukebox, Allman Brothers' "Jessica" to be specific. The group got more raucous as Tommy and Whistle became fast friends, and thanks to the whiskey and southern hospitality, Tommy's friends became Whistle's as well. The party raged on, the jukebox played Skynyrd, Johnny Cash, Little Feat and Tom Petty, the booze flowed and a good ol' time was had by all.

After a few more drinks and some pool, darts, and laughs, Tommy banged on the bar….Loudly.

"Hot Tub!" Tommy roared, and just like that, the whole posse rumbled out of the bar and out to the pool area, with a bottle of whiskey on the side. Whistle jumped in and found a good spot where a jet was hitting his back, which felt great after sleeping on the ground for a few weeks. He was pretty sloshed at this point, and he just sat back and watched all these young people having fun. It was a gigantic friendly mosh pit. Whistle was getting drowsy and started to drift off, letting everything go….until.

"WHISTLE!" Tommy yelled approximately a half inch from his face, "Wake the fuck up! Haha! Drink this, you sum'bitch!"

"Ok, ok!" Whistle took the bottle of Jim Beam from Tommy and took another swig, even though he was already inevitably going to cap off the evening by passing out. Tommy turned his attention back to the slow motion mosh pit in the hot tub, now spilling over into the pool. He was fading fast as the gulp of whiskey proceeded to slam dunk his ass, putting him out to pasture for the night. He fought to keep his head above water and his eyes open. They'd close for a few seconds involuntarily, only to open again to see a well-endowed college girl jumping on his lap, taking her top off and trying to breastfeed him.

One guy was dancing on the diving board waving a gun around, freaking half the group out and inspiring the other half to cheer him on. This brought Whistle to the last slide of the night, a dizzying stumble back to his hotel room with a couple of near misses along the way, waking up several other guests to the sound of someone trying to clumsily unlock their door in the middle of the night with the wrong key.

He eventually found a door that would open with his key and stumbled to his bed, simultaneously hitting the mattress face first and letting out a huge snore. He slept in that position pretty much till noon the next day, when the phone smacked Whistle upside the head with its screamingly harsh ring....Well who could this be?

"Umph....ughhhh, uh. Hello." Whistle was barely able to keep down the contents of his stomach.

"Mr. Starr, I hate to bother you, but it's past checkout time."

"I'd like to check in for another night, if that's ok," Whistle mumbled.

"Absolutely, Mr. Starr. Enjoy your stay," the clerk replied.

"Thank you," Whistle replied as he fumbled around to hang the phone back up in the cradle. Once that seemingly Herculean chore was accomplished, he fell right back to sleep as the daylight streamed in around the edges of the thick shades pulled down over the windows.

He awoke a while later and noticed his left arm was asleep. He looked over and there right next to him was one of the girls from the hot tub last night. She was sound asleep. *Did I have sex with her?* Whistle thought to himself as he tried to free his arm from under her head. Almost completely out from under, the girl snorted and a pair of eyes popped up from behind her.

"What the fuck!" Whistle actually said out loud as the girl still snored, asleep and oblivious.

"Mornin,'" Tommy Jaxx said from across the bed. His fat face and beady eyes looking at Whistle.

"What happened?" Whistle asked as he got his arm free without waking up the girl.

"Quite a night, huh?" Tommy Jaxx said.

"I'll take your word for it," Whistle replied as he rubbed his face, and noticed that his hand was swollen and all chewed up around the knuckles. All he could think about was how he'd get rid of Tommy and the hot tub girl. He was about to say something when Tommy saved the day.

"Crissy, get the fuck up!" Tommy hugged Whistle and within minutes they were out the door. Whistle would never forget Tommy Jaxx. The boy knew he was a man of good and bad all at once. He definitely liked him and would truly never forget him. Whistle went back to his bed and fell asleep.

When he finally woke up he looked at the clock and saw that it was 8:00 p.m. and he'd slept off a bit of his hangover. He still had that headache and mild nausea that drinking all night and sleeping all day tends to give you, not to mention messing up the old sleep schedule. He got up, brushed his teeth, and drank several glasses of water before jumping in the shower, turning the water on cold to snap out of his midnight shift malaise. Getting out and drying off, he felt good enough and more than hungry enough to order some room service.

Finally, he sat in front of the TV as a pot of coffee brewed on the table in the corner. His dinner of fried chicken, green beans, and roasted potatoes was brought in and he chowed down as he watched *Sanford and Son*. He washed it down with an ice cold Coke and followed that up with a coffee. All the caffeine helped get rid of his headache, but did little to wake him up much so he set his plate, glass, and tray outside in the hall, locked the door, and turned the light out before crawling back under the covers and enjoying a *Happy Days* block on Channel 7.

Whistle smiled as he watched the Fonz smack the jukebox at Arnold's, starting up Fats Domino, Potsie and Ralph looking on in admiration. Ritchie needed advice about a big date up at Inspiration Point. The college banners on the walls made Whistle wonder what he would have studied had he graduated high school and went on to university. Nothing really came to mind as he started to drift off, sleeping straight through till nine the next morning.

Waking up, he recovered nicely and felt like his normal self. Ready to take on the day, he showered, got dressed, and packed his bag. It was a bright, sunny morning, Whistle found, as he opened the blinds. He was even going to make the bed, but thought better of it as he wouldn't be doing anybody any favors if the maid assumed the bed wasn't slept in and didn't change the sheets. Whistle paid his bill at the front desk and walked out the front door and down to Barque Hill Drive, ready for his next adventure.

CHAPTER
FORTY-SEVEN
Chipmunk Guardians

Walking out of Babble, he found the on-ramp for Route 84. An hour later he sat in the passenger seat of a nondescript dark brown sedan moving west. After exchanging small talk and pleasantries, he was thankful for the silence. Not that he didn't want to get to know the man driving him; the cast of characters he'd just met was more than enough for now. Whistle dozed off to the familiar, comfortable hum of car tires on highway asphalt.

The engine cut off and Whistle opened his eyes. Looking around, he realized that they were at a gas pump. After pumping the gas, the man walked into the convenience store at the station. What felt like a long while later, the car door opened and then closed. A Slim Jim and a Coke were set in his lap. As Whistle instantly cracked the soda, the driver told him that he'd have to get out here if he wanted to continue along 84, as he was headed for Mobile.

Whistle thought for a minute and decided to stay for the ride. He'd heard the Bob Dylan song about being stuck inside of Mobile with the Memphis Blues and he figured that alone was a good enough reason, seeing as he really didn't have any specific plans at this point. He finished his Coke and rested his head on his pack and slept the rest of the way.

The next thing he knew, he was woken up in the parking lot of some motel in Mobile. He thanked the driver and got out. He stood in the parking lot of Isabell's Inn, debating on whether he should be spending more money on motel rooms, as long as the weather was tolerable. He walked behind the main office and found a maintenance shed. It was locked, so he went around back and found a relatively comfortable spot surrounded by thick bushes. Settling in, he felt relaxed as he lay there, actually enjoying living outdoors. He thought about how his life was turning out and how being a vagabond suited him just fine. He wouldn't change a thing.

Drifting off, his thoughts turned to dreams. They were detailed if mostly random, and eventually subsided. He woke up with the sunrise and walked into the motel, found the bathroom and used it. When he was done, he walked out and noticed judgmental looks directed at him from behind the lobby desk. He looked back and gave the best smile he could, trying his best to appear like he was a guest and had every right in the world to use their facilities. To survive on the road, confidence is key. If you're going to be somewhere, act like you belong there. Not in a cocky asshole way, but don't walk around with a gigantic "Excuse Me" sign over your head either.

Asking a guest which way was west, he was pointed toward the ramp to Route 10. He made his way to the ramp and up to the highway. About to put his thumb out, for some reason he had the overwhelming urge to walk through the woods along Route 10. It had been a while since he'd hoofed it and he was feeling like he was moving just for the sake of it, and should slow down until he figured out where he was going and why he was going there. The ground was solid, flat, and easy on the feet, and the trees were far apart, making travel swift and relatively effortless. The vegetation was fragrant and the air was sweet. The sound of the cars on the highway gave Whistle a feeling of security and nostalgia.

For five days and five nights, Whistle hiked along and enjoyed it immensely. Whistle saw plants, animals, and trees that he'd never seen before. The weather was absolutely invigorating and his feet and back were in no pain whatsoever. Sleep came easy and was filled with pleasant dreams. For the time being, life was good.

On the sixth day, he woke up, did his typical routine and squared himself again. After a few hours, he stopped and sat for a while on a hollowed out log. A few minutes later, he noticed a quick movement to his right. After a little while he let it go and looked around. There were great colors everywhere and sunlight projected kaleidoscopic patterns on the forest floor. He noticed another movement out of the corner of his eye again. He focused on the general area where the action appeared to be coming from. After a few minutes of seeing nothing, he was about to give up. Just then something shot across his field of vision. Suddenly it stopped, turned around, and ran back about ten feet. Freezing in place, its head turned and stared directly at Whistle. There before him was the cutest little chipmunk, completely still with caution. Whistle didn't move either, knowing that if he did, the little bugger would be gone in a blink.

Fifteen feet apart, they stared at each other, Whistle with his head in his hands and the chipmunk with his cheeks full of nuts and seeds. The dark stripes down its back and slightly twitching little whiskers intrigued him. This went on for a long time when a second chipmunk came out and sat right next to the first one. The stare off continued, but now it was two on one.

It occurred to Whistle that the pair of little guys looked like two small guardians of the forest, doing their job and standing at their post. Almost as if he got up and tried to pass, the chipmunks and whatever might be the second line of defense that Whistle was currently unaware of would take care of the situation in short order. This was not a bad thing because to Whistle, it felt like he knew that somehow nature would always take care of herself.

After about five minutes, his back was getting sore and daylight was starting to get a bit short. *Time to go,* he thought to himself, with a final look at the little guardians. He stood up and they were gone, just like that. So fast that Whistle had to wonder if they were just a figment of his imagination.

A quick pause later, he walked off with a definite spring in his step and a smile on his face. Moving along for a couple more hours, the land sloped down and to the left, leading him toward 10 West. Eventually, the land flattening out with a thin row of trees shielding him from the cars, the walking was easy, so he continued on. He felt so good, almost as if he could walk forever and never stop. Just then, he saw a large sign to his left through the trees that was of a different color scheme than what he had seen in a good long while. Making his way through the trees, he couldn't believe his eyes…."Now Leaving Alabama."

"Wow!" Whistle laughed to himself as he ducked back into the woods to continue on. About a quarter of a mile later, he saw yet another sign, this one red, white, and blue with a flag incorporating the old stars and bars, same as the roof of the Duke boys' General Lee. This one read, "Welcome to Mississippi."

"Yes!" Whistle yelled over the roar of the eighteen-wheeler flying down Route 10 as he punched both fists in the air in victory. A victory over who or what he wasn't sure, but a victory nonetheless.

CHAPTER
FORTY-EIGHT
Tom's Truck Stop

A s he passed by, Whistle couldn't help but run out fast, jump up and slap the sign, then dart back into the trees. Continuing on till dusk, he then bedded down. The stars were incredible that night in the southern sky and the next two nights followed suit. The next day, as Whistle was winding down for the night, he suddenly saw a huge sign light up. It was along the highway, far away and definitely on top of a pole that had to be at least forty feet tall. Looking at the sign, two colors and four letters met his eyes. A bright white background with a bright blue "Tom's" stared back at him.

Lying back, he couldn't help but stare at it. What the hell was Tom's? Instantly he decided he'd been walking a good spell and Tom's was his destination tomorrow. Whatever it was, he was sure enough going to find out.

After sleeping for only a few hours, he was wide awake again. The sun was up and it was another bright and beautiful day. He gathered his few things and made a beeline for Tom's. As he walked down a hill, he slipped on some grass that was wet with morning dew. He got up and realized he had bruised his hip, rolled his ankle, and worst of all, tore the sole off his shoe, exposing his sock covered foot directly to the earth.

Taking uneven steps, he continued on for what felt like hours. Whistle couldn't see the sign anymore but kept the sound of traffic on his left close. Late morning turned to high noon and he began to worry that he wouldn't make

Tom's that day. He didn't know why he was so drawn to this sign off in the distance, sticking up over the tree line, but he was, and he was hoping to reach it today. Sunset was racing around again, and travel was tough at night and in some cases impossible.

When the next hour had about passed, he was looking to his right for a good place to rest. He was now hurting, especially his bare right foot with the rolled ankle to boot. Literally steps away from being done, he crested a small hill and there it was, the still unlit Tom's sign taunting him. This energized him to the degree that some of his pain subsided, so he pressed on. It was a mellow downhill slope all the way to Tom's, which appeared to be a mile or two away now.

He walked closer, the sign got bigger and the sky grew darker. As he got closer, he noticed two things. The noises he heard ranged from idling engines to people yelling loudly, and under the Tom's sign was a smaller sign that read, "Truck Stop."

Now, with full night set in, he got close to the perimeter. The slight smell of diesel floated across the massive complex Whistle was looking at. He noticed several buildings, dozens of eighteen-wheelers, endless blacktop and even more endless activity. Curiosity drew him closer but intimidation made him hesitant.

Whistle decided he'd move up to the edge of the truck stop, camp out, and observe everything while staying as invisible as possible. He spent the entire night barely blinking and taking it all in until the sun started to rise. In that time, endless men, presumably truckers, walked back and pissed near him. He figured the only thing that saved him from getting directly pissed on was that he had picked a spot behind a camper.

He withdrew into the woods of Tom's Truck Stop at the meeting point of Routes 10 and 49 to collect himself. Realizing how tired he was, Whistle crashed out for a couple of hours. Waking when the Tom's light came on again, he sat up and cleared his head. Back at the edge, Whistle watched all the action back at Tom's.

After several days of doing recon from the woods, stabbing in to forage whatever food and water he could, he figured he would have to either enter the world of Tom's Truck Stop or skirt around and move on.

Wondering how to walk in with one shoe and clothes that no one in their right mind would be weaning in public, not to mention smelling bad enough to scare maggots from a rat carcass, he hemmed and hawed until his desperation finally propelled him to go in. Whistle went in through a side entrance with his head hung low in shame. He walked along the back wall, hoping he would come to a bathroom so he could clean himself up enough to not be completely offensive to anyone with eyes and a working nose.

The din of voices filled the building and the fluorescent lighting made Whistle panic with embarrassment. His heart rate quickened and he began to get dizzy and his eyes could only see bright light with no shapes or colors. He could only hear a loud buzzing in his brain until…

"Holy shit!" someone exclaimed as they gently slapped his cheek, with a murmur of concerned hustle and bustle swirling around him from all directions.

"You okay?" the voice said, again accompanied by slightly more vigorous slaps this time.

Cold napkins were placed on his forehead as he started to come back around.

"Ugh, he smells like shit! I wonder where he's been," he heard another voice say in the hushed yet panicked tone of a curious onlooker.

You have no idea, Whistle thought as he tried to pull himself together.

A bottle of water was handed to him, which he promptly took a generous pull from. Almost instantly he felt somewhat better if not exactly ready for the prom.

"Alright buddy, we're starting to attract attention. Can you walk?"

"I…uh, I…" Whistle tried to answer. But before he could say anymore—

"Fuck it." The boy was pulled to his feet in what felt like dreamlike slow motion as he was led down a hallway. He tried to look to his left and see who had their huge right arm around him, leading him to who knows where.

"Where are we going?" he asked, or at least mumbled.

"Stop talkin', keep walkin'," the mystery man said.

Unable to focus, time seemed to go by at glacial speed. Voices and colors continued to pass by in slow motion. *What's going on?* he thought to himself as this rather large, muscular arm led him down the hall.

They took a right around a corner and the noise faded. Moving down, the light quickly dimmed and the voices were completely gone. Shortly down the hall, light became an uncomfortably bright orange with black perimeters, like a sadistic version of the monarch butterflies' home team uniform.

"Come on!" the voice said, urging him on.

"Hey, I think there's been a mistake!" Whistle said, now coming to but panicking all over again.

"No, I don't think so," the voice replied as he pushed them both forward again. They went about fifteen feet and at that point, Whistle found himself pinned against a metal door.

"Please don't hurt me!" Whistle pleaded, too weak and tired to come anywhere close to defending himself.

"Shut up," was the answer to his plea…Not good.

The next thing he heard was a key sliding into a door lock, which brought Whistle back to his wits even more, his mind and body slamming into survival mode. Trying to fight his way out of this would have been futile on a good day as the man was just too big and strong to be overpowered by someone of Whistle's stature.

He heard the key click a quarter turn to the right and felt the man's breath on the back of his neck. The door flung open and Whistle fell forward, hitting his head hard on the floor. A grey wave took him over and he knew he was in big trouble. Turning back and looking up into the dimly lit doorway at a dark, hulking man looking down, all Whistle could say was, "Please don't!"

CHAPTER
FORTY-NINE
A True American Trucker

Instantly pulled up and led to a locker room, Whistle heard, "Take a shower."

"No!" Whistle protested, knowing what would most likely be coming next.

"Shut the fuck up and take a shower!" the man replied, as he pushed Whistle into the stall, throwing his grimy bag in behind him. The man turned and walked out. Alone, Whistle looked around with complete confusion taking over. About to lose control over his desperate situation, he closed his eyes and thought, *Calm down, calm down, just calm down.* A conscious thought of what an incredible tool the "Calm" mantra was occurred to him and it would continue to serve him well the rest of his years.

Opening his eyes, he instantly had a revelation. This trucker wasn't trying to rape him; he was trying to help him. Without any further hesitation, Whistle was stripped down and standing in a blissfully hot shower. Steam shrouded him completely and all his worries were gone. The warmth of the water penetrated through his flesh and deep into the center of his bones.

Looking around the walls of the shower, Whistle noticed random bars of soap and random bottles of shampoo. On the floor in one corner stood three empty bottles of Rolling Rock Beer.

Turning his attention back to the bottles of shampoo, the boy grabbed a bottle of Pert. A huge squirt later, and the bottle set back down, the lathering began. Holy moly, was it some kind of heaven. The smell and feel of pure cleanliness enveloped him. Steam continued to comfort him. Picking up a half used bar of Irish Spring, Whistle washed off the three or four stray hairs and figured, clean enough. He even washed his hair again with the soap. Deciding rinse and repeat was the best way to go, he, well, rinsed and repeated.

When he was done, he stepped out onto the cream colored floor and almost slipped and fell on his ass. Walking over to a drier area, he found a Teenage Mutant Ninja Turtles towel and wrapped himself in it. Whistle felt great, and the sound of the ceiling vent blotted out the rest of the world. He pulled his slightly less grungy bag out of the shower and hung it on a hook to dry.

Turning to the sink, he noticed a brand new toothbrush, a travel size tube of toothpaste, Speedstick, and a blue Bic disposable razor accompanied by a travel size can of Gillette shaving cream.

When he was done grooming himself, he walked out of the bathroom and there on a chair were all his clothes and a brand new pair of no name brand sneakers. Instantly a tear fell down his cheek. Wiping it away, he got dressed. The clothes were still warm from the dryer. Shaved face, clean, warm, and brand new kicks, Whistle felt like a million bucks.

"You hungry?" Whistle heard as he nearly jumped out of his skin.

"Yes sir, I am!"

"Names Kenny." The large man got up, effortlessly crossing the room, and stuck out his gigantic hand. Somewhat hesitant, Whistle reached out and watched his hand get enveloped by a scarred and greasy paw. Dirty fingernails and callouses got his attention immediately, followed by enough pressure on his hand to make him wince. Sensing this, Kenny let up a bit.

Their eyes met, and Whistle noticed a certain kindness in Kenny, shrouded in road hardened years of life.

"Hello Kenny, my name's Whistle and it's great to meet you."

"Good to meet you, Whistle. Let's go eat."

"Okay!" Whistle replied.

And just like that, they were out the door. Before he knew it, a huge plate of bacon, eggs, home fries, pancakes, and white toast with plenty of butter was placed before him. Next to that was a steaming hot cup of coffee with plenty of sugar and cream. A large orange juice completed the setup.

"Thank you, Kenny," Whistle said, digging in ravenously.

"Slow down, buddy," Kenny said with a hearty pull off his Miller Lite.

"I know, I'm sorry," the boy replied, coughing, then taking a sip of his juice.

"It's alright, just take your time, no rush...so, what's your story, anyway?"

"I don't have a story, Kenny."

"Bullshit. Everybody's got a story, and a guy with your accent around these parts, in your condition, no offense, has to have a story. How old are you, anyway?"

"I'm...uhhh, I...don't really know."

"What!?"

"Yeah, I don't know. My birthday is September 11 and I must be somewhere around my late twenties, maybe thirty. I doubt I'm any older than that," Whistle replied, still lost in thought, trying to put together the math and figure out his own age.

"Thanks for breakfast, Kenny. You really helped me out."

"Don't worry about it, you seem like a good kid who was just in a tough spot. Listen, you can crash on the couch till tomorrow morning, then I gotta roll west, so if I see you, I see you. If not, good luck to you."

As they walked down the hallway, their backlit silhouettes looked like David and Goliath, or a sasquatch and a Christmas elf. They turned into the room and Kenny said goodnight as he went into his bedroom for the night.

Whistle immediately climbed under an afghan with a pillow under his head. He snuggled deep into the cheap cushions, getting slight residue of who knows what kind of grime. He was so tired he didn't care. Before he knew it, he was sound asleep. No dreams, no tossing and turning, just a complete lights out reboot for tomorrow. As he drifted off, the last thought he had for the night was simple. It was one word Kenny had said: WEST.

"Hmmm...An awesome guy like Kenny, long haul trucking west could be fun," Whistle whispered to himself as he dozed off.

The next morning came and the boy was awakened by a small sliver of sunlight that found its way through the side of the window shade. He squinted, rolled onto his side, and slowly let his eyes adjust to see his surroundings. The first thing he noticed was his grungy bag laid out on the coffee table completely dry with all its contents next to it.

Whistle sat up, wrapping the afghan around him. Just then, the door opened and Kenny walked in.

"Well...Good morning, Whistle."

"Mornin' Kenny," the boy answered, yawning.

"I have to go soon, but you can sleep in a bit if you like, as long as you're out of here by eleven, you'll be fine."

Whistle paused, stretched his arms out and ran his fingers through his hair, trying to think.

"Kenny?" he called out.

"Yeah?" came the reply from the other room.

"Could I come with you?" Whistle asked, meekly looking up as Kenny came out of the bedroom and went to the kitchenette. He put his hands on the counter and sighed deeply. The pause continued long enough for Whistle to figure the answer was no.

"I'm sorry Kenny. You've already done more than enough for me, forget I asked."

"Jeez, Whistle. My brain tells me I should say no, but my gut tells me yes....Alright, but pack your stuff quick, because I have to get on the road stat," Kenny said as he ducked back into the bedroom to get his things packed.

Whistle got dressed and packed his bag as quick as he could, excited to hit the road, get out of Tom's Truck Stop, and move toward whatever his destination might be. A short time later, Kenny walked out of the bedroom with his own bag slung over his shoulder.

"Ready?" he bellowed, like a friendly drill sergeant.

"Yes sir!" Whistle saluted.

"Alright, let's go."

As they walked out of the room and down the hall, Whistle noticed how swift Kenny was on his feet, especially for a big guy. It was almost as if he danced, or slid through life. Whistle slung his own bag over his shoulder and followed, a bit more spring in his own step than he had yesterday when he met Kenny.

The two men continued on down the hall and grabbed a quick breakfast and coffee. Excitement ran through Whistle's entire body. The possible adventures that lay before him were endless. This revelation, coupled with the caffeine from the coffee, made him quietly giddy and slightly shaky.

"Time to go," Kenny said, taking a swig of coffee. Whistle took his last swig and they were out the door. The cool morning air hit him and it felt great. Early eastern sun lit the massive parking lot in a way that made Whistle feel as if he was bursting with optimism.

"So where are we going, Kenny?" Whistle asked, trying to keep up with the man's massive strides.

"My truck's in Lot C, it's not that far," Kenny answered over his shoulder. About ten minutes later, they took a sharp right, weaved through several trucks, took another right and stopped.

"There she is," Kenny said with a subdued pride in his voice.

"Holy shit!" Whistle responded, genuinely floored by the sight of the truck.

"It's fuckin' awesome, Kenny!"

"She," Kenny replied, matter-of-factly.

"What?"

"It's a she...Her name's Carla."

"Nice to meet you, Carla," Whistle said as he patted the side, right over the wheel well.

The sight of "Carla" was really something to behold in the morning sun. The entire truck was painted as an American flag, all red, white, and blue metal flake with chrome appointments...it was stunning. Sorry—SHE was stunning.

"Climb aboard," Kenny said as he unlocked the truck. The earth shook beneath Whistle's feet as the rumble of the engines of all the trucks in the lot greeted this new morning and a new beginning.

CHAPTER
FIFTY
Good Time, Bad Dream

S itting in the passenger seat of the cab, Whistle was amazed at all the action
happening in the dash. All kinds of lights came alive, gauges performed a
self-test, the fuel needle jumped up to full, and on the radio was a man who
apparently had some important inside information. The devil went down to
Georgia for a bit of a battle of the bands, and the stakes could not be higher. He
didn't remember anything like this going on north of the Mason Dixon, just rock
concerts at the Garden and the Providence Civic Center, usually brought to you
courtesy of Frank J. Russo.

Whistle watched Kenny go through some kind of checklist. The veteran
trucker flipped switches everywhere. Whistle absolutely felt like he was in a space
shuttle about to blast off for space. Kenny's massive hand finally engulfed the
key and gave it a final turn. After a slight pause, the diesel engine came alive. The
whole cab shook and settled down into a slow and steady hum. A slight diesel
smell reached Whistle's nose and it was intoxicating. All of a sudden, a new voice
spoke from somewhere.

"American Bear, you rollin' out?...Over."

All of a sudden, Kenny pulled a microphone off the ceiling, tethered by
a curly Q-cord.

"Yeah Razor...I gotta hit San Diego, but I'll be back here in a few weeks.
I'll hit you up...Over."

"Roger buddy. Keep the wind at your back and stay safe, over and out."

And with that, Kenny hung the C.B. back up on the ceiling. Carla was dropped into gear and she started to roll. The boy literally had goose bumps raise on his arms from excitement.

His seat was so comfortable, it just didn't seem possible. They weaved their way through the parking lot and before he knew it, Tom's Truck Stop was behind them. Next, they took an on-ramp as Carla sped up, heading down Route 10 West.

After being on the road for a couple of hours, Kenny pulled off into a rest stop.

"I'll be right back, I have to go make a phone call," he said as he glided over to a very old set of payphones by an old brown building with restrooms, vending machines, and an information desk, closed of course. Whistle had to empty his bladder and decided on the woods, primarily out of habit at this point. They both met back at the truck at the same time. Kenny looked at Whistle with a huge grin on his face.

"You ready?" Kenny shouted as he hopped back up into the truck in one swift launch, almost as if he were weightless.

"Oh yeah!" Whistle responded happily.

"Hungry?" Kenny asked as he turned out of the lot and back onto 10 West.

"Yeah!" Whistle replied.

"Alright. There's a great place on 10 just north of Biloxi where we can grab a bite."

"Cool," Whistle answered. About an hour later, they pulled off into a dirt parking lot. After finding a spot off to the side to park, Kenny turned the key back and Carla rumbled to a stop. The two got out and did their Sasquatch-Elf walk again towards the Sergeant's Diner.

Entering, the small bell above the door jingled.

"Kenny!" a rather large black woman with a very pleasant smile called out from behind the cash register.

"Dora!" Kenny bellowed back as he and Whistle walked over and sat at the counter.

"How are you?" she asked.

"Fine, just fine! Dora, this is Whistle."

"Nice to meet you, honey...Now, what can I get you boys?"

"Dora, we'll have two cheeseburgers and fries and two beers."

Right away, two Miller Lites were place before them.

"Cheers, you crazy little fucker," Kenny said, raising his beer.

"Cheers, you enormous, somehow smooth moving bastard," Whistle replied with a clink of his glass with Kenny's.

The burgers and fries were ready with an "Order up!" from the kitchen and two heaping plates put in the window between the kitchen and the counter. Dora took them and turned right around and set them in front of the two hungry road warriors.

They chowed down as Kenny caught up with Dora. Whistle watched a baseball game on TV and didn't really mind not being involved in the conversation much. He was enjoying his authentic American greasy spoon roadside diner burger and the sound of two old friends catching up. He thought about how truckers were at home everywhere in the country and they were the lifeblood of this great nation, endlessly flowing through the asphalt arteries east to west, north to south, and he was thrilled to be along for the ride.

Two more beers and it was time to hit the road. Kenny paid the bill, along with a nice tip for Dora. She gave Kenny and Whistle a big hug and after a quick pit stop in the restroom, it was time to, as Willie Nelson said, get "On the Road Again."

Back in Carla's cab, the sun gleamed gloriously off the red, white, and blue of the hood. For some reason, that combination of colors had a certain power that generated happiness and strength. Wherever those colors flew, you were home and you were free. Key turned, the engine fired up and they were rollin'.

"Breaker, breaker, this is American Bear, come in, Ladybug," Kenny said. "Breaker, breaker, America Bear here, you out there, Ladybug?" he repeated after waiting a minute or so.

"Ladybug here. How you doin' big fella?"

"A lot better now that I hear your sexy voice! I just crossed the Pearl and I'm comin' in. Are you around?"

"I sure am, handsome!" she replied, with obvious excitement in her voice.

"Well that is good news! Say, would Cinnamon happen to be around? I've got some company with me," Kenny said, shooting Whistle a curious glance.

"She's right here."

"Great! We'll be there in a while. The Landing Pad still open?"

"You know it! Just roll on in clean, American Bear."

"Roger that, over and out," Kenny said as he let out a small chuckle.

"What?" Whistle asked.

"You'll see," Kenny replied.

About twenty minutes later, they came to a major crossroads. Kenny took a ramp, looped around, and steered Carla back onto the highway. Only now, the highway ran more south than west. Another twenty minutes went by when suddenly they saw a massive bridge ahead. When they got close, he read the sign that announced, "Lake Pontchartrain." The crossing felt like it took about a half hour.

After they cleared the bridge, they followed the shoreline. With the massive lake to their right, the sun was now dipping orange to the west, leaving millions of golden slivers dancing all over the vast body of water. Looking over at Kenny, he noticed the cab was filled with a reddish orange hue that was more perfect than anything anyone could create on a movie set.

A short time later, Whistle read the next sign, "Welcome to New Orleans."

"Holy shit, Kenny! We're in New Orleans!" He was practically bouncing up and down, clapping his hands.

"Yup," Kenny answered with a smile that lit up almost as bright as the sun.

"Where we goin'?" Whistle asked, beaming.

"You'll see, you'll see."

Kenny took an off-ramp and slowed Carla down to a stop at a red light at the bottom. The light turned green and Kenny took a left under the overpass. A few turns later and Kenny pulled the air horn. One long blast followed by one short blast. It actually startled Whistle.

"What was that for?" he asked.

"You'll see," Kenny replied, driving on down a two-lane road. After about a mile, Kenny swung a wide left to make a right down a small alley. Slowly, the truck clattered down to a long cement pad. Carla rumbling idle, the two looked at each other. The lights from the dash instruments lit their faces. Pointing down toward the cement below, Kenny raised his eyebrows and said, "Landing Pad."

Whistle could not help but start laughing. Someone opened the door on Kenny's side; a husky voiced woman said, "Get out here, big boy! Let me take a look at ya!"

"Okay, okay." Looking back at Whistle, he was laughing himself.

"You ready, Whistle?" he asked.

"Sure am!"

Kenny went through a short procedure to shut down the truck. Carla let out a few clicks, ticks, and pings, and she was retired for the night.

"Come on," Kenny said as he shut the door behind him. Whistle could hear a female voice laughing from the driver's side of the truck. He got out, climbed down, closed the door behind him and was now himself standing on the "Landing Pad." Everything was almost dark now and the boy's eyes were having a tough time adjusting to the dim light.

"Whistle, get over here!" Kenny's voice boomed from the other side of the truck.

"Comin'," he replied as he walked around to the other side, wondering what he was in for.

Chapter Forty-One
What an Introduction

Whistle stepped around the front of Carla, took a few more steps, and saw the silhouette of Kenny and a slender woman holding hands. It was too dark to make out any more than that.

"Let's go in," the woman said. He heard the spring as the back screen door opened. They all stepped into a narrow back hallway. It was lit by a single small bulb. After the three were inside, Whistle heard the spring again, followed by the slam of the door closing. Eyes still not adjusted, he looked through the next doorway into a room that was better lit. He had a hard time seeing around Kenny and his lady friend, but the room looked to be a kitchen.

The two walked through the doorway and Whistle followed. Stepping in, he looked around real quick. First impression, it was an average apartment kitchen with the aroma of coffee permeating the room.

"Whistle, this is Ladybug," Kenny said as he waved his hand toward her in a gracious gesture. Whistle noticed that she was indeed a slender woman. A brunette that was definitely a bit older, but still very attractive. Dressed in a fitting red blouse, tight jeans, and black boots, her emerald green eyes met Whistle's.

"Hello," she said to Whistle, pausing for a moment, looking at him intently.

"Hello. My name's Whistle."

She still stared at him, making him slightly uncomfortable. She stepped forward and gave Whistle a big hug and an earnest, "Welcome!"

It had been a good, long while since Whistle had been hugged by a woman and it felt great. He giggled a bit, feeling a bit nervous as Ladybug continued to hold his gaze.

Kenny walked over to a cabinet and set three shot glasses on the counter. He took a bottle out, took the top off, and promptly poured them three shots of Jack.

"Cheers!" said Kenny as they raised their glasses. Surprisingly the shot went down rather smooth. The three set their glasses down and Ladybug welcomed them in as she turned on her heel and opened a door on the other side of the kitchen. A quick glance at each other, Whistle and Kenny followed.

Walking through the door, the first thing Whistle noticed was the faint smell and haze of cigarette smoke hanging in the air. It had a bluish tint to it due to the light from the television. Turning the corner, the next thing he noticed was a woman sitting on the couch, backlit by a lamp. She was watching the television with a cigarette in her hand and a beer and ashtray on the table next to her. Whistle couldn't see much of her, but what he could make out intrigued him right away.

"Whistle, this is my daughter, Cinnamon," Ladybug said.

"Hey," the girl said, looking over her shoulder and giving a small wave before taking a drag from her cigarette and turning her attention back to whatever she was watching.

"Nice to meet you, Cinnamon. My name is Whistle. Whistle Evel Fonzarelli Starr," he said as he stepped a little further into the room. His name alone drummed up some curiosity from the girl. She looked back at him.

"Rrreeaally...like Evel Knievel and the Fonz?"

"Yeah," Whistle responded, feeling a little embarrassed and proud all at once.

"Cool," she said, standing up and walking over to him to shake his hand. Locking eyes, she said, "Well, Whistle Evel Fonzarelli Starr, I have a good feeling I'm gonna find out it was very good to meet you."

He blushed and noticed that Cinnamon's eyes were emerald green and even brighter than her mom's. Her hair was fiery red unlike her mom's black hair. But both had long, luscious locks that cascaded easily down around their shoulders.

Kenny had silently slid back out to the kitchen and retuned with the Jack and four shot glasses.

"Shots!" he loudly announced, passing them around. Once everyone was set, Kenny spoke up again.

"Hold on, hold on! I'd like to make a toast." Looking at each of them, he continued.

"First of all, I'd just like to say I am very happy to be here right now. Ladybug, I missed you like nobody's business and every time I see you, we always have a blast!" he said as he squeezed her hand and gave her a big kiss on the lips.

"Thank you, baby," she responded.

"Hold on, I'm not done." Looking at Cinnamon, he continued.

"You! Yeah you, girl...You're like a daughter to me. You are so much fun and I always enjoy the time we spend together."

Kenny gave her a peck on the cheek and Cinnamon replied, "Thanks, Kenny. We missed you!"

It was clear to Whistle that American Bear was getting a little emotional. He figured this had to be the closest thing he had to a family.

"Now for you, Whistle," declared Kenny, turning and looking at him.

"This guy...Oh hell, this guy. I met him at Tom's Truck Stop and he was not doing good. But, he was a hot shit from the get go. Ladies, you are gonna love him. I have the weekend here and we are gonna have a blast! Whistle, tomorrow night we are going to Bourbon Street and you are gonna be blown away! It's unbelievable. So, cheers guys!" They clanked, they drank, and the glasses were slammed down on the table.

"Shit, I talked so much, we need another shot."

Poured and passed, the shots of Jack went down and the glasses slammed the table again. After some chitchat, the girls went into the kitchen to make dinner. Kenny and Whistle sat down and watched a game on TV. In short order, Cinnamon returned and handed each of them a beer. They both thanked her and Whistle noticed her eyes pause to look at him an extra moment. He noticed her mom did the same thing when she met him. He wondered if it was a genetic trait or if she could be interested. He felt himself blush.

"I think she likes you," Kenny said after she returned to the kitchen.

"C'mon, Kenny. She seems nice, but her mom seems to hold eye contact a little longer than normal too. I think it's just a family trait. Kind of like their emerald eyes."

"Ha! Yeah, come to think of it, you're right. I still say she likes you...We'll see."

"Ok, we'll see," Whistle replied.

"Boys, dinner's on!" came a cheery voice from the kitchen.

"Comin,'" Kenny replied.

The boys were greeted by the sweetest sight two road dogs could hope for, a giant pot of real deal Cajun heat. N'Awlins shrimp gumbo, collard greens, black beans and fresh baked French bread....Fit for a king!

"Kenny, open the wine and I'll say grace," Ladybug said while she went to the stereo to put on some dinner music. A local radio station, which happened to be playing "Such a Night" by Doctor John...Such a Night indeed.

"I heard he's been stopping in at Preservation Hall to sit in with the locals lately. Bob Dylan, too. Word is he rented one of the old mansions downtown and is recording with the Neville Brothers," Cinnamon chimed in.

"You think they'll be there tomorrow night?" Whistle asked.

"Maybe...Bob's usually riding around on his Harley. Word around town is he's a nice enough guy, just likes to keep a low profile."

"Cool. I don't blame him," Whistle replied.

With the cork popped from the Merlot and the wine breathing nicely, everyone sat down, joined hands, and said a prayer to give thanks for the generous bounty, good friends, and new adventures. With grace concluded, they proceeded to dine on what was maybe the finest meal Whistle had enjoyed in his life. He didn't know how much Cinnamon contributed, but even if she just baked the bread, that alone qualified her to be marriage material.

As dinner wound down, Kenny excused himself to run out to his truck to check in with his boss on the C.B. and Whistle helped the Louisiana lasses, as Kenny referred to them, with clearing the table. He carried a good sized pile of plates to the kitchen sink where Ladybug was starting up the hot water and soapy suds.

"Thank you sweety," she said as she gave Whistle a peck on the cheek. "Kenny's very fond of you, I can tell. I'm glad you're out on the road with him. It's good for him to have a copilot out there. For safety and sanity."

"Kenny's a solid guy, really a kind soul and I'm honored to ride along with him on the *SS Carla*."

"Yeah, his mistress...or maybe I'm the mistress, I can't tell. She weighs a lot more than I do, so I got that going for me!" Ladybug wisecracked.

"That's right, plus she's been around a lot more," Whistle added, trying to up the ante on the comedy, but almost wanted to pull the words out of the air and stuff them back in his mouth as they were coming out. It just sounded bad. Ladybug was unfazed, thankfully!

"Don't count on it, honey! Haha," she replied as she tickled his ribs, letting him off the hook for his faux pas.

"Here, take this beer and go relax. This kitchen's not big enough for the two of us...Literally."

So with that, Whistle returned to the living room at the same time Kenny was coming in from his check in with the boss. He looked preoccupied, a little less jovial than at dinner.

"Everything cool?" Whistle asked.

"Huh? Oh yeah, yeah. No problem."

"I'm not getting you in trouble, am I?"

"I've been in and out of trouble since before you were born, Tonto...And no, you're not causing me any trouble whatsoever. Glad to have you along for the ride."

"Well I'm glad to be along, Kenny. Thanks again...for everything. Cheers."

"Cheers, Tonto."

After a few minutes, Ladybug and sweet, lil' Cinnamon bounded into the room with four more beers. Whistle could hold his own but man, he was starting to get seriously buzzed. Ladybug sat down on Kenny's lap and Cinnamon sat on the couch next to Whistle, a little less shy than when they got there earlier. The conversation livened and music continued on WWOZ. Whistle was mesmerized by the music of New Orleans. It sounded exactly the way he was feeling right now. Buzzed, well fed, and in the mood for romance.

As Kenny and Ladybug playfully argued about the best places to hit tomorrow night in the Big Easy, Cinnamon got up and went into her room without a word to anyone. A few minutes went by and Whistle started to feel awkward when she didn't come back out. Kenny and Ladybug were rubbing noses and kissing, making Whistle feel a little bit like a third wheel. What should he do? Sit there like a ninny? Ask where he's sleeping for the night? Was Cinnamon in her room waiting for Whistle to man up, follow her in there, and make a move already? What if he did pull such a bold move, eased open the door and heard, "Hey! Get the fuck out of my room!!! Fucking creep!" He hated how women expect you to be a mind reader.

Luckily, Cinnamon came out, and not a moment too soon, with a bong and a bag of weed that was as fragrant as the jasmine coming in through the windows on this sweet summer night.

"Whistle, do you smoke?" Ladybug asked.

"Sure do!"

"Well, you haven't smoked anything like this," Cinnamon cooed in his ear as she handed him the fully packed ceramic bong.

"Go easy, it's creeper weed," Kenny added.

"I got it," Whistle responded as he lit the bowl and inhaled hard for a good three or four seconds before he eventually choked on it, hacking, wheezing, and instantaneously filling the room with clouds of sweet, thick, rolling, smoke.

"Yeah, you got it...I think it got you first, sonny," Kenny chuckled as the girls giggled.

"Cough to get off," Cinnamon said as she took a hit and finished off the bowl like a pro. To be fair, it was her bong. Home field advantage.

As it got late, Cinnamon was starting to get a tiny bit flirty with Whistle. Nothing major, strict junior high moves. Knees touching, handing him a lighter and making sure to touch his hand in the process. Not enough to let Whistle know she was all in for whatever, just enough to let him know she was, maybe, interested.

After a while, the Lady(bug) of the house spoke up. "We've got a big day tomorrow, what say we call it a night?" Everyone agreed and Kenny went and grabbed Whistle a big cotton comforter and pillow from the closet. Ladybug kissed Whistle on top of the head and went into her room with Kenny soon to follow...

"GoodnIIIIiiight," Cinnamon said in a manner that could have been taken any number of ways as she smiled over her shoulder and started to unbutton the top button on her blouse before she shut the door to her room...MOST of the way.

Whistle lay on the couch in the pitch black living room as Cinnamon turned on a nightlight in her room that was a pinkish orange hue. Every so often, she'd walk by the slightly open door, slightly less clothed each time. Shirt unbuttoned, then no jeans, the next time she walked by in just her bra and panties. The poor boy was going out of his mind out there on that couch.

Again, what was he supposed to do? Was she teasing him? Was she waiting for him to go in there? Was that assumed? Did she even know he could see her? She had to be pretty drunk, maybe she thought she closed the door all the way. GRRRR! "I swear, they do this shit on purpose!" Whistle fumed to himself as he tried in vain to close his eyes and fall asleep.

She seemed to be in bed now as he heard the radio go on low, though the nightlight was still on. Was that nightlight her signal to him to go in? What about the way she said goodnight? What the fuck was that all about? He went back and forth about what to do until eventually she turned the nightlight out and the radio off. Whistle was in the dark, both literally and figuratively. At least he could finally put it out of his mind for the night and try and get some sleep. He was just about to doze off when he heard the sound of muffled giggling, whispering, moaning, and eventually bed springs squeaking coming from Ladybug's room...

Ah well, good for Big Bear at least, Whistle thought to himself as the weed and wine tamped down his hormone induced insomnia and eventually, mercifully punched his ticket to dreamland on his first night in the Big Easy. Not as easy as it looks.

CHAPTER FIFTY-TWO
Just the Beginning of a Crazy Twenty-Four Hours

The next morning, Whistle woke up to the familiar swirling aroma of bacon, eggs, pancakes, and coffee. Everywhere you went in the good ol' USA, lunch and dinner could consist of anything, depending on where you were, but breakfast was always breakfast.

"Come and get it!" Ladybug chirped as she pulled the string on a Salvation Army sized bell which under normal circumstances would be pleasant, but this particular morning it didn't go over so well, judging by the disapproving groans of the rest of the fairly hungover revelers.

Whistle went to use the bathroom, ran his head under an ice cold shower, gave his hair a quick combing, and splashed some of what he assumed was Kenny's aftershave on and made his way to the kitchen, where he was greeted by the sight of a breakfast spread to rival the feast from the previous night, which, by the way, he was still full from.

"Wow!" Whistle exclaimed, "You guys know how to eat down south. You both are so petite, where do you put it?"

"We burn it off," Cinnamon purred seductively.

"ooOOOOOOoooohhhh…" Whistle replied with a slight wink, hoping to let her know that he got the message and was not going to puss out again should the opportunity present itself like last night. Cinnamon had officially been put on notice.

Kenny sat down, said a quick but effective grace, and started passing around the morning grub. Once everyone was served, the chowing down commenced and the coffee and fresh squeezed orange juice flowed and brought everyone back to life, put the hangovers on the run and fueled them up for what was shaping up to be a beautiful day in the Big Easy.

As breakfast was finishing up, and coffees were being topped off, Whistle heard a click. Looking over, he saw Cinnamon lighting a big, fat joint. She got it going with about five tiny puffs and finally one good, long inhale, holding it in until the smoke expanded to the degree that her lungs couldn't contain it, as she blew out a huge plume that hung over the entire kitchen table.

"Wake and bake?" she said as she offered the joint to Whistle.

"Sure. Why not?" Whistle took a small hit as he didn't want to cough all over the rest of everyone's breakfast.

"We should probably try and be out the door by noonish if we want to show Whistle all the cool stuff in one day."

"Shower first! Called it!" Cinnamon said as she shot up out of her chair, playfully pushing off on Whistle.

"You can go next. Age before beauty," Kenny teased Ladybug as she punched him in the stomach playfully, but playfully hard! After everyone took turns showering and getting ready, they headed out on foot for a big day of adventure.

It was only a few blocks before they were eventually entering City Park. Looking around, Whistle was very aware of how beautiful it was. The different gardens they passed were meticulously pruned and cared for, and all the ponds full of fish, frogs, and birds were clean enough to see clearly through. After about an hour of stoned sightseeing, they exited the park and crossed Robert E. Lee Boulevard. Another twenty minutes of walking and they came upon Lakeshore Park and stood at the shore of the immense body of water that Kenny said was Lake Pontchartrain.

"Wow! It's massive!" Whistle said, mostly to himself but loud enough for everyone to hear. They all agreed. Sitting on an ornate iron bench, Ladybug and Kenny got close. Cinnamon sat next to Whistle and moved close to him, and Whistle couldn't deny that it felt great. The four looked out over the lake and took it all in. High early afternoon sun warmed them and the silent company they shared was a comfort that Whistle never felt before. Then, Cinnamon took Whistle's hand in hers and lay her head on his shoulder. She sighed with obvious contentment. Whistle felt great. Another joint was passed around and another forty-five minutes went by.

"Lunch?" Kenny asked as everyone got up and nodded in agreement. Taking a left, they followed the shore for a while before eventually coming to a place called the Mudbug. Luckily enough, the four were seated at a table on the back deck that was literally over the water. The sound of small waves lapping the shore came up from below. A waitress by the name of Becky came up to the table and asked them if they were ready for a drink. Kenny spoke up.

"Becky, we would like the party crawfish boil and two bottles of the house red wine."

"You got it," Becky replied as she tucked her pad and pencil back into her apron before hustling back to the kitchen.

"This is just great!" Whistle said as he felt Cinnamon's leg press against his.

"Not too shabby," Ladybug chimed in.

Cinnamon turned and kissed Whistle on the cheek. Looking up, she said, "Wait till you see this lunch!"

Whistle couldn't imagine how he could possibly deserve to be in this situation right now. The wine showed up and Becky filled their glasses. Of course the Big Bear wanted to make a toast, but Cinnamon shut him down point blank.

"My turn, big boy," she said as Kenny replied with a nod and a wink.

"The floor is yours, m'lady," he added before Cinnamon began.

"Mom, I love you. You truly are my hero. I have always looked up to you and always will. You're so responsible but still know how to enjoy life. I can only hope I will be as great as you someday."

"Baby, you're my hero," Ladybug replied, getting a little teared up.

"Kenny, you're the closest thing I have to a dad and I love you. You take great care of my mom and I, and even though we miss you when you're on the road, it only makes it that much sweeter when you do come home."

"Thanks, honey," Kenny replied, wiping a tear away. Cinnamon then turned to Whistle. He started to feel flush as his cheeks turned red. He could have sworn the whole restaurant stopped and listened in.

"Whistle, I'm so glad I got to meet you and I'm glad you're on the road with Kenny. Here's to good times, cheers."

Almost on cue, the party crawfish boil showed up. A young Latino man came out of nowhere and rolled thick brown paper across the entire table. Ripping it off, he gave a slight nod and a bow before heading back inside. Not more than a few seconds later, the entire party was dumped and spread across the whole table.

"Ooohhhh yeahhhh," Kenny said as Whistle looked at the spread in disbelief. Crawfish, Andouille sausage, pearl onions, red potatoes and quartered corn cobs, spiced perfectly. A large bowl was placed in the middle for shells and cobs. Glasses topped off, Becky walked away again. They dug in for the second time that day and didn't say a word for a while. The shell bowl filled and the glasses were emptied; this process was repeated several times until they were stuffed to the top. With the last big bowl removed and the wine bottles taken away, everyone was too stuffed and tired to speak. Except for Kenny, who had one more word to say as he raised his last glass of wine…"Cheers."

"Cheers," the group answered back. They sat for about another half hour telling stories and cracking jokes before they decided to get on with their walk back to Ladybug's place. Kenny paid the bill and Whistle wished he had something to contribute, but he was flat broke. It felt good, however, to walk off lunch and not feel overly full by the time they got back, but between lunch and the wine, everyone could use a nap when they got back, so that's exactly what they did. Kenny and Ladybug retired to her room and this time, Cinnamon snuggled up to Whistle on the couch.

After a couple of hours, everyone started to stir and get ready for round two, a big night on the town. Cinnamon was still out, however, so Whistle lay still so as not to disturb her until it was absolutely necessary, and seeing as Ladybug and Kenny were taking a shower together—to save hot water of course—he closed his eyes and caught a few more ZZZs.

"Come on kids, time to get ready," Ladybug said, accompanied by a light, rhythmic knock on the wall.

Cinnamon gave Whistle a small kiss on the neck and rub on the belly. "If you want to go first, you can," she said.

"I'm good. You should probably go first since you do your makeup and hair and all that."

"Good point," she replied as she pushed herself up off his shoulders and turned to go into her room and get her clothes ready. She passed by Kenny and gave him a wolf whistle, approving of his attire for the night's festivities.

"Welcome to the real world," Kenny said to Whistle as he handed him a beer. They clinked bottles and both took a swig. The Great American Bear was dressed to live up to his nickname tonight. Polished black boots complete with silver side spurs peeking out from the cuffs of his white leather pants with one blue and one red stripe on the sides. He had on a big black leather belt with an even bigger belt buckle front and center. To Whistle, the buckle seemed to be the size of a license plate. The silver with the detailed etching was beyond impressive. Outlined and in gold were the words "Keep On Truckin'." All this, with a crisp, freshly ironed white cotton button-down shirt with red and blue accents and a white Stetson cowboy hat with an elaborate band that would make Richard Petty jealous, topped off with a badge that had the initials D.I.L.L.I.G.A.F. in the same outlined, gold initials as Kenny's belt buckle. Whistle figured he had them custom made.

"Jeez Kenny, you could give Elvis a run for his money," Whistle said, staring in awe at the Big Bear's get up.

"Gotta go big when you're in the Big Easy." Kenny chuckled.

"What does that stand for? D.I.L.L.I.G.A.F."

With a huge, hearty laugh and a smile to match, the Bear tipped his hat, met Whistle's eye and said, "Does it look like I give a fuck?"

"Haha! Right on, Kenny. You are a man of great confidence."

"You gotta be to pull off an outfit like that! Somewhere in between Uncle Sam and Elton John," Ladybug good-naturedly wisecracked as the Bear lifted her over his shoulder and gave her a spanking and she laughed uncontrollably, yelling, "Put me down! You're gonna mess up my makeup."

"Eeeasy princess," Kenny replied as he set her down on purple suede boots, topped off with a Stevie Nicks inspired dress, hair, and makeup style.

"Wow! You look incredible, Ladybug," Whistle said, genuinely starry eyed.

"Why, aren't you just the sweetest!" she responded, with a kiss on the cheek.

Finishing his beer, Whistle brought the empty bottle to the kitchen, threw it in the trash, and returned to an absolutely stunning sight. Cinnamon was in a tight red dress, looking like a sensuous saxophone solo, but for the eyes. Pouty red lips, cute as a button nose and electrifying emerald eyes were framed perfectly by her, well, cinnamon locks, framing her gaze in a way that made Whistle turn to jelly.

"Wow...just....wow!" he said, unable to find the words to do her justice.

"Thanks," she said shyly, trying to hide her mile wide smile and blushing cheeks.

"Uh oh, Whistle's got a real firecracker on his hands tonight, Ladybug!"

"I'll say!" she replied.

"Hey, let's take a shot for the road before we rock and roll out," Kenny said as he went to go get the Jack. Ladybug followed him into the kitchen and the moment she was around the corner, Cinnamon grabbed a quick kiss, but a real one. Even slipped him a little tongue before Kenny came back with the Jack, followed by Ladybug with the four shot glasses. "Alright, alright. Break it up, break it up," Kenny chuckled as he handed them their shots.

"To Bourbon Street!" Kenny said as he raised his glass.

"To Bourbon!" Cinnamon added as everybody laughed, threw back their shots, and filed out to the courtyard once again to make their way into town for what was shaping up to be a beautiful evening.

Whistle was not feeling his best however. Everyone else was decked out to the nines for a night out in what may be the most decked out city in America, and here he was in a rather shabby pair of jeans, dirty no name sneakers, and a T-shirt that had butter stains on it from the feast at the Mudbug earlier that day. Maybe the weed was making him paranoid, but it all of a sudden became painfully obvious to him that he looked like a scrub compared to the rest of them and he imagined that they might be going to some places with a dress code. He started to panic as he walked along with Kenny, slightly behind the girls.

"Psst, Kenny. Can I talk to you on the down low real quick?" Whistle said in a hushed tone.

"Yeah, what's up?"

"Listen, you guys go ahead and have a good time tonight. If it's ok, I'd like to just go back and stay in tonight. I don't feel great," Whistle said, holding his stomach.

"Come on, Tonto. You were fine just a few minutes ago. Plus, you can't let that fine lady walk around Bourbon Street unescorted, it's just not right."

"Look, I'm gonna level with you, Kenny. You guys all look like a million bucks and I'm wearing the same dirty clothes I've been in for days and quite frankly it's humiliating," Whistle said, looking down.

"I get it buddy, but trust me. Bourbon Street is a big mix of the well to do and never-do-wells, saints and sinners, poets, politicians, priests, princes and paupers. You'll fit right in. You wanna borrow my D.I.L.L.I.G.A.F. hat badge? You could probably wear it as a belt buckle, ya skinny little som'bitch." Big Bear chuckled as he put Whistle in a brotherly headlock. "As a matter of fact, here, take this and buy that beautiful lady in red a drink or two tonight. Consider it an advance," Kenny said as he slipped Whistle a crisp hundred-dollar bill.

"Kenny, I can't take this."

"Yes you can. You're a great copilot and maybe you can help me unload some deliveries or clean Carla. We'll figure it out. Besides, you didn't ask to come here. Just show Cinnamon a good time and have a good time yourself. The place we're going is pretty wild. All kinds go there, you'll fit right in."

"Thanks, Kenny. You're the best!" Whistle said as he gave Big Bear a hearty pat on the back of his massive shoulder.

"Come on guys, keep up, will ya? We're wearing heels and we're about to lap you!" Ladybug shouted back.

"You can't lap someone going in a straight line! Try to keep up, will ya?" Kenny wisecracked, much to everyone's amusement.

The guys caught up to the girls as they waited on the corner of Esplanade Avenue.

"Sorry ladies. Tonto and I had to have a little powwow," Kenny said as he grabbed Ladybug around her waist from behind and kissed her on the cheek.

Passing under Route 10, they continued southeast. Ten minutes later, they crossed Burgundy Street and walked two more blocks. The four of them stopped and looked to their right to see that they were standing at the north end of the French Quarter.

"Buckle your bootstraps, zis is 'ze famous French Quartair," Kenny announced in a jovial accent.

Grabbing hands, they all crossed the street and stepped onto the cobblestone crosswalk. With those few steps, the entire length of Bourbon Street was before them. It was truly a sight to behold.

CHAPTER FIFTY-THREE
Bourbon Street

iggling, they all walked hand in hand for one block. On the corner of Bourbon and Barracks Street was a line about five people deep. Kenny insisted they get in line, so they did. It wasn't long before they were next and asked by a sexy young woman in a tiny white shirt and somehow even whiter teeth whether they wanted a Hurricane or a Grenade. Before Whistle could even ask a question, Ladybug spoke up.

"Two Hurricanes and two Grenades, please."

The drinks were served, Ladybug slid the money, and Whistle couldn't believe what he was looking at. The Hurricanes looked like bongs filled with cold red liquid with a neon green straw sticking out of each. The Grenades were a green liquid poured into large plastic containers that were literally molded into the shape of grenades. Instead of neon green, their straws were neon orange.

The girls took the Hurricanes and the boys took their Grenades. Slowly meandering the streets, Kenny and Whistle lagged once again.

"You love Ladybug?" Whistle asked Kenny.

"Yeah, well...it's complicated," he replied.

"Bullshit, ya big bastard," Whistle chuckled, playfully punching Kenny in the arm.

"I'm on the road so much and she...Look, let's just let it go and have fun tonight. Let love take care of itself."

"Alright buddy, you're the boss," Whistle said with a sip of his Grenade.

The guys caught up again and they all stopped on the corner of Philip Laffite's street to finish their drinks and toss the plastic cups in a nearby trash bin. They all looked over and viewed a very curious sight. It was too intriguing for any of them to resist. An arch of neon purple glowed bright with an arrow pointing down some brick steps to a lower level. The sign read, "The Blacksmith."

"Let's go!" Cinnamon chirped excitedly. They all walked down the stairs and Whistle's comfort level dropped rapidly. It was a dead end that went one story underground with a huge muscular man sitting by a door with a gun visible under his unbuttoned blazer.

"America," Kenny said to the man in a hushed tone. Apparently it was a password. All Whistle could think of was Luke Skywalker saying to the storm troopers, "These are not the droids you're looking for."

The big behemoth of a man opened the massive, black steel door that led into the entrance. Stepping through, the four continued down a flight of stairs. There was an intoxicating aroma coming up from the room they were heading towards. Cigarette smoke, weed, booze, sweat, and ammonia.

"Here we go," Kenny said as they entered through a curtain of amber beads. The Kinks were singing about wishing they could fly like Superman. Whistle imagined this was what Studio 54 must've been like back around a decade earlier, minus the cold New York winters and Andy Warhol.

The four of them pushed forward towards the main bar. It was so loud that Whistle felt lost. Cinnamon grabbed his hand firmly.

"Come on." She smiled as "Superman" segued into "Low Budget." If Kenny were Superman then Whistle figured that made him Low Budget. He laughed ruefully to himself.

Finally stepping to the bar, Ladybug said, "Let's get some drinks." They all wholeheartedly agreed. A few minutes later, with rum and cokes in hand, they turned to the crowd. They all looked around to scope out the vibe, so to speak.

The first thing that struck Whistle was that verbal communication was going to be more or less out of the question as the music was unbelievably loud. It was a good kind of loud, lots of low-end rumble and mid-range punch without the shrill high end. He figured all the flesh in the room soaked up all the offending frequencies. Everything said was going to be a combination of hand gestures, touches, and subtle looks.

Sure enough, saying "Let's dance," was easy when two bodies pressed together a bit in just the right way. On the floor, Whistle was impressed with how naturally Kenny and Ladybug moved together. Getting a little lost in watching them, he felt a hand grab his face and turn it toward Cinnamon.

"I'm right here!" she yelled, still unreadable. Absolutely understanding, his attention shifted immediately to the sexiness that stood before him. Looking down into her face, they kissed, then started to dance. The red dress, gold zippers, emerald green eyes and boots completely intoxicated him. Flowing red hair, moving completely in synch with her body, she was almost a Jessica Rabbit-like animation come to life underneath the flashing, hot lights. It was obvious to him that their bodies moved together just right. Loud music and loud voices swirled with excitement all around the dance floor.

After more dancing and a few more drinks, Whistle found himself in the men's room. Fluorescent light washed over him and the thump of the music rattled the bathroom stalls. Finishing emptying his bladder, he turned around to see Kenny standing there.

"Ready?" he asked with a great big grin on his face.

"Ready for what?"

"This!" Kenny replied, unrolling a baggie of coke out of his hand in one smooth snap.

Before he knew it, Whistle and Kenny were snorting coke off the toilet tanks through a rolled up dollar bill. After Whistle took his turn, a complete stranger joined in. The burn in his nose and the feel of the drug flooding into his system took him over. That's when Whistle's night started to get away from him. One more line, then Kenny and Whistle went back out to join the girls.

About an hour later, Whistle ascended the brick steps and exited through the same massive steel door they entered through. With a wobble in his step, he looked up at the huge bouncer and asked, "Can I shoot your gun?"

With arms crossed and a bored look on his face, the bouncer said, "Just move along, son."

With that, Kenny whisked him up the stairs and out onto the sidewalk.

"I love you guys!" Whistle said, hugging all three of them and kissing Cinnamon on the neck. Just then he thought to himself how delicious she smelled, and how gorgeous she was. At that moment it became crystal clear to Whistle that she was nothing short of perfect. He felt loved and knew he was with some wonderful people in a kick ass city that had everything to offer.

The next thing Whistle remembered, he was in a boiling hot club called the Cat's Meow. On stage and shirtless, Whistle was singing and pointing out at the crowd while on American Bear's shoulders, waving his shirt around his head. The venue was packed and Whistle literally felt like a rock star watching the ebb and flow of the crowd. The best part was looking down into the front row and seeing Ladybug and Cinnamon looking up, enthralled with what Whistle and Kenny were doing. With sweat dripping in his eyes and coke running through his veins, he couldn't imagine a more perfect moment ever to be had.

The rest of the night came in bits and pieces. He was aware that the crowd loved him and the four never paid for another drink the whole time they stayed there. After leaving, the rest of the night was only blips of memory and blackouts. Hawaiian blue shooters, one final bump of coke, and they were on their way. The last thing Whistle remembered about being at the Cat's Meow was saying to Kenny, "Big Bear, I don't know what happened to my shirt!"

"Don't worry about it, Tonto. You don't need a shirt," he slurred as they walked on.

All Whistle remembered about the rest of the night on the town was as follows...Chocolate cupcakes, all four of them inappropriately urinating in a back alley, laughing hysterically. A cat's body scaring the living daylights out of Cinnamon, which added to the laughs. Somehow beef tacos and cheap margaritas found their way into Whistle's memory of the night. Standing on a third-story balcony looking at big breasts with hard nipples and lots of multi-colored beads around a woman's neck became a quick memory flash.

Lots of walking down more cobblestone streets followed. The four staggered and swayed, happy as clams. The next memory Whistle had was walking through the back door of Ladybug's place. The four had one final shot in the kitchen and then Ladybug and Kenny retired to her room for the night once more. That left Cinnamon and Whistle alone in the kitchen, each waiting for the other to make a move.

Finally, evoking Sandy in *Grease*, Cinnamon said to Whistle, "C'mon, Stud," as she took his hand and led him to her room and to quote yet another icon of the seventies, Jacksonville's own Ronnie Van Zant, if you know a little 'bout love, baby you can guess the rest...

CHAPTER
FIFTY-FOUR
A Few Much Needed
Days of Rest

Nothing could be better than the situation Whistle was in. He just had the best night of his life in New Orleans, Louisiana and now was in bed with the beyond beautiful Cinnamon.

Both comfortable and satisfied, they slept deeply. The warm night enveloped them and their mutual strong feelings for each other fit exactly right. Through the night they continued to move closer to one another. Eventually they were as close as two people could be.

Two a.m. quickly slid to three, followed by four. Five welcomed the very beginning of the day's sunrise. After using the bathroom Whistle got back into bed and grabbed Cinnamon warmly with a content sigh.

"Mmmmm…" She snuggled in further. They both fell back asleep genuinely happy and supremely comfortable with each other. Morning was inevitable and they just wanted to enjoy themselves for a bit longer. Nothing was sexual at this point; everything was more emotional. They both knew they could be incredible together, but they also knew that Whistle Evel Fonzarelli Starr would be moving on shortly. That being said, the two slept with little smiles on their faces and light touches to comfort one another.

The sun grew longer, and the time grew shorter. Next thing Whistle knew they were up, and he had one day left with this amazing girl. It was spent quietly, which was good because they could all use some much-needed rest. As the day waned on the two talked on the back porch.

"Whistle, what are you going to do?" Cinnamon asked.

"I'm going west with Bear. I'm going to the Santa Monica pier. Cinnamon, I swear I'll make it, I have to!

"If you say so." She said while rubbing the back of his neck and kissing him softly on the cheek.

"I will miss you greatly Cinnamon, but I have to do this." Sadness washing over him.

"I know you do, but I will miss you like crazy." Cinnamon's sadness matching Whistle's. Their eyes met with sadness and love blended equally.

"Let's please just enjoy today and we'll deal with tomorrow, …tomorrow," Whistle said trying to put the best smile on his face possible. The two paused and kissed. The rest of the day was spent with Ladybug and Bear. Just a little weed and one bottle of red wine led them to a perfect dinner of crawfish, dirty rice, andouille sausage, and buttery kale. The slightly burnt rolls hit the spot, always great for dipping.

After that, the four of them settled into a showing of *The Shining*. It was especially fun because Whistle got to hug Cinnamon a lot on account of her great fear of horror flicks. He also noticed that the Great American Bear was treating Ladybug with the same care. The four sat quietly, watched the movie, and nibbled on delicious popcorn. Next *The Great Gatsby* came on. Robert Redford stole the show as the four drifted off and dreamed about the green signal beacon beckoning from across the bay. What might be over there, everybody wondered.

Eventually everyone made it to bed. Whistle felt like the luckiest, most thankful man in the world. Drifting off, Whistle and Cinnamon held each other until they were finally asleep. It was truly one of the best night's sleep either of them would ever have. Unfortunately, the next morning would not be so pretty. Sure enough, it was not. But, for now he would dream about the excitement of the last few days and the adorable girl Cinnamon that he was blessed enough to be holding at the moment. The biggest smile hit him as he continued to dream.

CHAPTER
FIFTY-FIVE
A Dream Leads West

The next morning, Whistle woke up feeling like a dried up cow patty. His breath could only be described as wretched and he hoped to find a glass of water on the nightstand, but apparently neither he nor Cinnamon had the presence of mind to grab one last night. As Cinnamon slept, curled up in a ball facing away from him, he eased out of bed to go to the bathroom, take a whiz, dunk his head under a cold shower and drink from the faucet...Much better! He went back to Cinnamon's room, snuck back under the covers, and drifted back off to sleep as Cinnamon turned around and put her arm around Whistle's neck as she snored just once. She was adorable.

As Whistle began to dream, he found himself seated at a coffee table in an extremely dingy and cheap motel room filled with cigarette smoke, lit only by a black and white TV set. Across the table was a silhouette that he thought he recognized. He thought for a minute, but he couldn't figure out who it was. Just then, the figure pulled a pack of cigarettes out of his shirt pocket, shook one out, gripped it in his mouth and lit a match, revealing the wrinkled, weathered face of one Shortstop Nipples. He lit the cigarette and continued to let the match burn, eventually lighting a candle in the middle of the table. His face broke into a huge, beautiful grin as his dark almond eyes twinkled in the candle light. This vision grabbed his heart completely. Candles, cigarettes, ashtray and scotch on the rocks spread out on the coffee table before them, Whistle had a feeling this was going to be one heck of a conversation.

"How have you been, son?" Shortstop's deep voice asked. As he swirled his ice and crossed his legs, he raised his left eyebrow in a suspicious manner.

"You know, ups and downs, same as everybody else in the world. How about you?"

"Gettin' by on the fly," Shortstop replied with a deep drag of his Winston.

"Whistle, I'm here to ask you a very important question," he said, leaning forward and folding his hands.

"Oh boy, what would that be?" Whistle chuckled nervously.

"What's your plan?"

It didn't escape Whistle that this question was coming from a homeless man who lived in a literal garbage heap Whistle asked, a bit irritated, "What's your plan, Mr. Nipples?"

"It's too late for me, Whistle, that's why I'm asking you. I don't want to see you fuck your life up like I did. You need a direction. You need a plan!" Shortstop said, almost as if he was a counselor at an inner city YMCA. He stared at Whistle intently as he poured himself another scotch, as well as topping off Whistle's glass.

"I know! I fuckin' know! But what am I supposed to do? My whole life I've only had one thing driving me. Head south and stay one step ahead of the cold and a few steps ahead of anyone that was after me."

"That's called running away, boy. The question is...what are you running to?"

"What do you mean?" Whistle replied.

"You were put here on earth to serve a purpose. You gotta find out what that purpose is. What do you love to do? What's your passion? What interests you?"

"Well..." Whistle thought for a moment. "I like hiking, I love nature and animals, I love meeting new people and seeing new places. Experiencing different cultures and customs throughout this great land. I suppose, if I'm being honest, I always find myself getting into a jam and having to figure a way out. It seems stupid when I say it out loud, and it's no way to live, taking one step forward and a few steps back, but that's been the story of my life if I'm looking at it objectively."

"You said a mouthful, son. Lots of good info there to pick apart and put together again. When I was around your age, I went out west. Was stationed in California when I was in the Navy. I went to the Santa Monica Pier with a cute little girl I met out there that worked in administration. We rode on the Ferris wheel, the one you always see on the postcards. I remember sitting up at the top there and looking out over the Pacific Ocean. Was a good way to get some perspective on things. So continue your journey west and make sure you go to the Santa Monica Pier. But in the meantime, start thinking about what you want to do with your life. Drifting along like a piece of seaweed on the ocean is no way to go through life."

"Do you feel you've had a good life, Shortstop?" Whistle asked, earnestly.

"That all depends on who you talk to. I've done a lot, learned a lot...I've been fortunate enough to hopefully make some people happy and certainly have left my share of people not so pleased." Another sip of scotch and Shortstop continued.

"You know, I left a wife and three kids behind in Hershey, Pennsylvania and that's something I'll never forgive myself for. Easily the biggest regret of my life. To this day, I'm pretty sure I'm actually still married, if you can believe that." Shortstop let out a huge sigh as Whistle remained silent.

"But, on the other hand I saved a three-year-old boy from drowning at the bottom of a hotel pool in Burlington, Vermont. I brought him up to the side and gave him CPR till he threw up a bunch of water and started breathing again. I was so relieved, and that just goes to show you how such extreme good and bad can exist together." Shortstop said, now getting emotional.

"Magical and brutal," Whistle whispered to himself.

"I've saved plenty of homeless friends from freezing to death during the long Boston winters, yet I've mugged a businessman in broad daylight on Boylston Street for thirty-five dollars. I've also snorted so much cocaine, yet also gave money to panhandlers."

Whistle remained silent while Shortstop poured the scotch and lit another cigarette for himself and one for Whistle.

"Thanks," Whistle replied. "Please keep going."

"Okay...So, have I had a good life? I believe so, I hope so."

Next, Shortstop posed a question to Whistle.

"Boy, have you ever got a free meal from the basement of a church?"

Welling up a bit, he responded, "Yes."

"Well, I guarantee you I've gotten hundreds of free meals but still had no problem one day swiping a whole case of hot dogs, and a huge bottle of yellow mustard." They couldn't help but laugh a little bit.

"We ate hot dogs in the courtyard for a week, but I still felt shitty about it. Eventually, I went back and put a five-dollar bill in St. Joseph's collection basket." He pondered to himself for a moment.

"Well, that probably cut the mustard," Whistle joked as he took another sip of scotch.

"Haha, yeah, well, the bottom line is, I've done both good and bad, but in the end I hope I end up in the good column."

"I know you will, buddy. I know you will," Whistle said, smiling back.

Just when they were about to finish their drinks then retire for the night, the bathroom door cracked open, sending a thin beam of light across the carpet and up the wall.

"What the fuck?!" Shortstop asked.

"Dunno!" Whistle answered.

Waiting, they watched as the door creaked open further and further, slowly showing a shadow cast across the floor.

"What's up, motherfuckers?" Vinny, the violinist dwarf asked with violin in hand.

"Oh, hell no!" Shortstop jumped up.

"What the hell is going on!?" Whistle asked as Vinny stood before them in brown cowboy boots, a leopard print speedo, and a bright white cowboy hat, holding a violin in one hand and a machete in the other hand.

"You're about to see, motherfuckers!" Vinny shouted as he clubbed Shortstop square on the head, knocking him down with his violin. The boy ducked right and his instinct took over instantly before Vinny's machete even had a chance to be a problem. Whistle's fist hit Vinny so hard that he heard facial bones breaking and he watched the violinist land flat on his back with a deep thud and exhale.

Very satisfied by that, he didn't like that Shortstop was knocked out as well. The boy stood in the smoky room looking down at the unconscious men on the floor and finished the last sip of his drink. Wanting to hurt Vinny more, he decided it would be wiser if he walked over and lay on the bed. Sleep came immediately. In his dream, he had another dream, trying to figure out what he was going to do with Vinny and Shortstop.

He got Shortstop in the bed to where he appeared comfortable and threw Vinny in the bathtub. Taking the machete and holding it high above his head, he was about to finish off the dwarf to get revenge for Shortstop. Just when he was about to plunge the machete and do the unthinkable, he heard a voice.

"Whistle...Hey....Whistle, wake up. You okay?"

"Yeah, uh, I'm alright," he replied as he kissed Cinnamon on the cheek. Looking at the clock he saw that it was seven thirty in the morning.

"Whistle, get up buddy, we have to go," Kenny said from the hallway as he knocked on the bedroom door.

Bleary eyed, the two young lovebirds met Ladybug and Kenny out in the kitchen for a hearty breakfast before they got on the road. Eggs Benedict, cranberry juice, and mixed fruit was exactly what the doctor ordered. As they all got their cups filled with freshly brewed piping hot coffee, everyone started to snap out of their sleepy haze. With all the bags packed, including plenty of groceries, Whistle stepped onto the Landing Pad and up into Carla.

Girls kissing them and saying final goodbyes for now, a bittersweet feeling swept over Whistle. Knowing that he could very well fall in love with Cinnamon, and that it was fairly unlikely that their paths would cross again, he fought back a tear as American Bear fired up Carla in the early morning Louisiana rain.

CHAPTER
FIFTY-SIX
Jumbled, Are Ya?

W ith New Orleans in the rearview and Route 10 West rolling out before them and holding great promise, Baton Rouge led the boys to
Port Allen, just across the muddy Mississippi River. They stopped at
Chickie's and caught a late lunch. Stomachs full, the two drove on. Lafayette
came and went as the American Bear pressed on. Late that night, they finally
pulled off the highway and grabbed a cheap room in Lacassine. After an une-
ventful night with a huge dinner and a great sleep they moved on.

With the orange red sun just starting to warm the day before them,
Kenny and Whistle crossed the Sabine River into big ass, bad ass Texas. They
both took a moment and smiled at each other.

"This should be fun!" the Bear said.

"Hell yeah!" Whistle agreed as he snapped into a Slim Jim.

Kenny asked for a root beer out of the cooler and as Whistle handed it
to him, Kenny responded by handing Whistle a huge joint.

"Jeez Kenny!" He chuckled as he took the joint and pulled a good, long
toke from it.

As they roared down the highway toking joints, snapping Slim Jims, and
sippin' on root beer, Whistle was about as content as a guy could be. He was
thankful for the time he shared with Cinnamon in the great city of New Orleans,
and the great new friend he found in Kenny. He started to think about the dream

he had about Shortstop and immediately it became clear as day to him that his destination would be the Ferris wheel at the Santa Monica pier. He didn't know how or why, but he knew Shortstop wouldn't steer him wrong. He closed his eyes as Kenny got on the C.B. to catch up with his fellow truckers, Carla rumbled on through the Lone Star State and well, well, what a surprise...here come the monarch butterflies.

Eventually waking up, Whistle noticed that Kenny looked very tired.

"Hey Bear, you wanna pull off for the night?"

"No, I'm good." So Whistle drifted off again. That was all great for about twenty minutes until Carla swerved sharply to the left and the Bear reopened his eyes. Hitting the next exit, Kenny said, "Okay, let's pull off." In a grocery store parking lot, they slept in the truck.

The next morning, with coffee in hand, they pulled out of Flatonia, Texas and continued west on 10. A few hours later, they rolled into San Antonio and it looked super cool to Whistle. He also noticed how clean it looked for such a big city.

"Kenny, are we stopping here?" Whistle asked with a smile.

"I know a place for lunch, but that's about it. Unfortunately I have a tight schedule to keep," he said, looking over at Whistle.

"Understood," answered Whistle, looking back. Following Route 10 to Exit 5-70, they pulled off and were smack dab in the middle of the city. Driving down a side street, Bear pulled into a dirt parking lot behind a large brick building painted bright pink. Letting Carla rest, Kenny said, "Let's go."

And off they went. Walking around the building to the front, Whistle saw a neon sign that read "The Honey Hole." Entering a dark hallway, he heard music coming from somewhere. Continuing on, they walked through another door into an almost empty strip club. The smell of stale smoke and stale booze permeated everything. Sitting at the bar with a stripper dancing on the stage behind, the bartender asked, "What can I do for you boys?"

"Two shots of Jack and two Millers...oh, and two country fried steak specials, please." Turning toward Whistle and winking, the boy couldn't help but smile and shake his head a bit. With the Jacks shot, they sipped their Millers and watched the stripper. It was obvious that the afternoon caliber of stripper was not quite the same caliber as the evening stripper. It was also obvious that Lexi, Raven, Cherry, or whatever her name may be was well aware of this. Her movements were listless and her eyes carried a hundred yard stare. This made Whistle instantly feel extreme sadness and wanted to somehow help the poor girl.

"Here you go, boys," the bartender said, laying the country fried steaks down before them.

"Thanks, honey. Two more shots of Jack and two more beers, please," Kenny said with a quick raise of the eyebrows.

"You got it, handsome," the bartender replied, turning away with a smile.

"Kenny, how the fuck do you do that?" Whistle asked as he finished his first Miller.

"Do what?"

"Charm everyone you meet into either wanting to be your friend, have sex, or fall in love with you?"

"Whistle, just eat your lunch." Kenny chuckled as he took a bite of his steak, obviously embarrassed and wanting to change the subject.

The shots and beers were set before them. Another smile came Bear's way from the bartender. After the shots went down with a "Cheers," the guys truly dug into their lunch. With listless Lexi going through the paces, they devoured the steak, not even noticing her anymore. She was also painfully aware of this. The mashed potatoes with gravy, sweet corn, and steamed carrots were good.

After they were done, they sipped the last of their beers. Looking up, Whistle noticed a different stripper was on stage. This one was even more listless than the last. Sadness hit him again. The American Bear squared up with the bartender and Whistle couldn't help but notice that she passed him her number with a blown kiss and a wink. He raised an eyebrow her way with a smile. Then the two turned and walked back out into the sunlight of San Antonio.

Just as fast as they blew into the city, they blew out, heading northwest on Route 10 again. It was only twenty minutes later before Whistle couldn't hold his tongue any longer.

"So how the fuck do you do it?"

"Stop with yourself. I don't do anything," Kenny said as he looked at the road. Not willing to let it go, Whistle asked again.

"Bullshit, Kenny. How do you do it?"

"Whistle, I just am who I am. I don't DO anything but be myself."

"What do you mean?" Whistle persisted.

"For fuck's sake Whistle, you're starting to piss me off," Kenny shot back, scratching his forehead.

"Answer my question because I truly want to know." The final bite of another Slim Jim was taken.

"You ask again and I'm gonna drop you off."

"You Great American Bear, how the hell do you charm everyone you meet?"

Immediately Carla slowed down and within minutes, Kenny pulled off of Exit 343 and pulled over.

"Get out, good luck, you ain't gonna see shit for over a hundred miles until you get to Sheffield. That is, if you even make it to Sheffield."

"Fine Kenny, I'm not afraid of walking, and I'm certainly not afraid of being alone. In fact, that's what I've done my whole life," Whistle said, grabbing his meager bag and jumping down to the dry earth.

"I only asked one simple question. For fuck, I thought we were friends," he groused, starting to walk west along dusty Route 10.

A pissed off American Bear put the pedal to the metal and covered Whistle with dry dust as he slammed by. Whistle watched Carla disappear fast and truly didn't fully understand what had just happened. He knew he could take care of himself, but he also thought he had finally found a friend that would be a lifelong one. Possibly a family in New Orleans with Ladybug and Cinnamon. He guessed not and once again Whistle Evel Fonzarelli Starr was on his own.

The boy walked and quickly understood that this ball game was hugely different from the East Coast. Already becoming very experienced about life, Whistle knew that water would be the number one objective. He walked another seven miles and felt he was done. He couldn't go any further. His thirst grabbed him fully. Whistle's brain couldn't make sense out of anything. Sitting down, he tried to open his pack, but he had no motor skills working anymore. Thirst was overwhelming. Dark blind spots danced before him in both eyes. Minutes later, everything went black and he simply dropped on the side of Route 10. There was no dream this time. Whistle was completely dehydrated.

At that very moment, Whistle was very comfortable with dying. After all, what was a total fuck up like him still doing alive anyway? He didn't know but the thing that he did know was the blackness of nothing in his mind was comforting.

The middle belly of Texas was a very unforgiving place. The occasional car passed by with him passed out on the side of the road in plain view. Not one car stopped to help him. They just sped up, wanting nothing to do with him or his situation. Whistle was lying there on that barren stretch of highway, completely abandoned. *Perfect*, he thought, *I'm gonna die alone. I would expect nothing less.* Finally total blackness grabbed him tightly.

Whistle died that day, or so he thought. The boy didn't realize that one very guilty feeling Bear circled around and came back, finding him unconscious on the hot pavement. Kenny put Whistle in the passenger seat and continued to drive on. With the air conditioning on full blast, Kenny wet a cloth and put it on the boy's forehead. About two hours later, the two rolled through Fort Stockton and Whistle stirred. Handing a very confused boy a bottle of water, Kenny said, "Welcome back. Drink slow and don't drink too much."

"What?" Looking over at Kenny, he asked "What happened?" Taking a drink that felt great. Greedily, he continued to drink.

"Slow down. You drink too much, you're just going to puke it up."

He stopped, but wanted nothing more than to keep going. Taking one more swig, he held the water in his mouth and closed his eyes. Trying to collect himself and work things through his head, Kenny spoke up.

"Whistle, I'm so friggin' sorry. I never should have left you like that. You did irritate me but I made a huge mistake. I have no excuse and once again all I can say is I'm sorry."

"That's alright, I just don't remember what happened. The last thing I remember I was asking you a question and now here I am." Whistle took another drink.

"Well, you were asking me how I was so charming and for some reason that pissed me off so I kicked you out of the truck and drove on. After a while, I calmed down and started to feel guilty so I came back. I didn't see you for a while so I started to think you had ducked off somewhere, but then there you were lying on the side of the road. I didn't know if you had been hit by a car or what, but I definitely thought you were dead." Kenny scratched his forehead again. After handing Whistle another bottle of water and reminding him to drink slow, the American Bear continued.

"I was panicking because if you were dead, I knew it would be my fault and there was no way I could ever live with that. When I saw you were breathing I was so relieved and I put you in the truck. I cranked the AC all the way up, put a wet towel on your head and now here you are. Here, eat these." Kenny handed Whistle a bag of peanut M&Ms. Feeling the effect of the sugar almost instantly began to perk him up a little, those little colored balls of deliciousness couldn't be chewed fast enough. With the candy gone and the second water finished, he was feeling much better. By now, the sun had dipped to the west and Kenny suggested they pull off for the night.

"We'll find a motel, get a good meal, a few beers and a good night's sleep."

Whistle happily agreed and they pulled off Exit 140-A into a small town called Van Horn, Texas, wedged between the Apache Mountains to the north and the Wylie Mountains to the south. Right off the exit, they pulled into the Oasis Motel and got a room.

After settling into their room, the two walked down the hallway, across the parking lot, and into the Desert Dog. The bar looked like it could be a lot of fun. There was even a table of women that definitely took notice of them, but they were too beat and just wanted to chill out and recuperate a bit.

Whistle enjoyed three southwest pulled pork tacos with a side of guacamole while Kenny tackled the three-quarter pound burger cooked rare with a huge order of Cajun steak fries that came with a small bowl of chipotle dipping sauce. Four Rolling Rock beers later, they were done and returned to the room. Settled in for the night with the lights off, they watched *The Shining*. That ended and the TV slid into a viewing of *Jaws*. They both fell asleep with full bellies, completely content.

The next morning, they checked out and went back to the Desert Dog for breakfast. After a huge meal of waffles, bacon, home fries, and orange juice with two coffees to go, they were back in Carla and on the road again. By noon, they both felt great and were rolling along perfectly. Passing the sign for the town of Sierra Blanca, they continued on.

Around one thirty Kenny asked, "Are you hungry?"

"I could eat," Whistle replied.

"What do we have? Or do you want to stop?" Kenny asked.

"Actually, I kind of have to piss," Whistle replied, looking back over at Kenny.

"Alright. Start looking for a place to stop."

After a while, they found a tiny place that was simply named "The Diner." Inside, they both decided on the BLT with salt and vinegar chips and a half sour pickle spear. An ice cold Coca Cola rounded out the meal perfectly. A piss in the bathroom and they were off again, enjoying the afternoon drive on the longest, straightest stretch of road Whistle had ever seen. That's when the Bear asked, "You wanna drive?"

"What?" Whistle replied, thinking that he must've misheard Kenny.

"Do you want to drive?" Kenny asked again.

"Hell no!"

"You pussy," Kenny chuckled.

Eventually, the Great American Bear convinced Whistle Evel Fonzarelli Starr to take command of Carla. The next thing he knew, he was behind the wheel and Kenny was snoring away in the passenger seat next to him. Knowing it was pretty crazy that he was driving an eighteen-wheeler across Texas while Kenny was sound asleep, somehow he did find himself getting more and more comfortable with the situation.

As dusk started to settle, the sky was completely golden and Whistle was so happy. Looking over at the Bear, he couldn't help but laugh as a big string of drool ran down his chin and soaked into his Lynyrd Skynyrd T-shirt.

All was right with the world, but he couldn't help but think about how his life was such an extreme rollercoaster. The last three days had been the epitome of brutal and magical all rolled into one big ball. For now though, he was charging west, in control of Carla with Kenny trusting him enough to go to sleep for a bit. The only word that truly fit was magical.

That was, until he crested a small hill in the Quitman mountains only about thirty miles north of the Mexican border. Ahead of him in that golden sky, a large black plume of smoke rose up on the horizon.

"Kenny, what is that?" Whistle asked, poking the Bear.

"Kenny!" Another poke.

"What?" Kenny snapped, waking up annoyed.

"What is that?" Pointing to the smoke on the horizon.

"I don't know. Looks like smoke. Probably from a factory or something." He dozed back off.

"Something about it doesn't look right to me," Whistle said as he drove on. About fifteen minutes later, Whistle shouted, "Kenny!" as he sharply pulled off the road. Kenny instantly saw what Whistle was looking at.

"Holy shit!" he whispered.

CHAPTER
FIFTY-SEVEN
Fire, To Hospital, To Dream, To Hope

Thick smoke poured out every window of a two-story house. Jumping out of Carla, a woman was in Whistle's face, screaming that her children were upstairs and she didn't know where her husband was. Looking at each other without a word spoken, the two men ran through the front door. Straight ahead was a staircase and Whistle went for it. His eyes were burning and his breath started to become harder to find. Making the top of the stairs, everything was black and breathing was next to impossible.

He crawled forward blindly until he saw an open door to his right with Oprah Winfrey on TV, telling everyone how great everything would be in the end.

"Fuck off, Oprah!" he actually whispered to himself as he crawled on and choked down more smoke. Crawling down a hot hallway blindly, Whistle felt completely lost. Breath quitting on him rapidly, he was ready to lay on the floor and give up. Blackness filled him up completely. Once again, Whistle Evel Fonzarelli Starr was dying.

Until he heard a faint scream coming from the end of the hallway. Crawling as fast as he could, he stopped at the end. He paused to listen and that small hesitation almost killed him. It was an eternity, but he knew if he took a wrong turn everyone would die and he could never live with that.

At the end of the disgustingly hot, black, unforgiving hallway with no breath left in him, he paused again. Door to the left and door to the right made it a fifty-fifty situation. Whistle actually pointed his finger up and asked, "God, what do I Do?!"

A phrase entered his mind out of nowhere, "Right is Right," so with no time to think any more about it, he crashed through the door on the right. In the room, the smoke wasn't as bad. He closed the door and looked for a window. The glow of the window across the black room beckoned to him. Finding it, Whistle breathed in fresh air. Looking out, he noticed the fire department was now there. All he wanted to do was to get the fuck out of there when suddenly he heard a soft cry.

"Help!" he yelled to a firefighter below as he took a huge breath and went back into the room. Immediately, Whistle found a small girl. Bringing her to the window, a firefighter took her from him. Whistle took a deep breath and went back in. Searching along the wall and under every nook and cranny, Whistle gave up. Making his way to the window, he felt a light tug on his right ankle.

Fuck! he thought to himself as he grabbed a small boy by the right shoulder and pulled as hard as he could. Pulling the boy to safety, Whistle heard the collarbone snap under his hand. The next thing he knew, Whistle poured a screaming boy out the window to the firefighters waiting outside on the ladder.

Going back in, Whistle was beyond spent, but he kept going. To help strangers out is not common, but Whistle was truly an exception to the rule. Fighting his way down the hallway, looking for a third child and a husband, Whistle felt the hair on his head burning away. Suddenly, the whole room flashed over and his clothes were burning. Whistle ran down the hallway and dove through the window. Fortunately, a firefighter grabbed him before he went down. On the ground, he was hosed down with a fog pattern spray.

He was immediately whisked into the back of a rescue where the EMTs went to work. A large bore IV was put into each of his arms. Fifteen liters of oxygen was delivered via a non-rebreather mask. The last thing Whistle remembered was trying to ask where Kenny was. Nothing would come out of his mouth as morphine dripped into his veins to ease the pain. Truthfully, he didn't feel any pain for now as he struggled to keep his eyes open. Within a minute, his eyes closed and he was unconscious

Completely unaware of what was going on, Whistle Evel Fonzarelli Starr was transferred to a life flight helicopter. Forty-five minutes later, the helicopter landed on the roof of the only trauma center hospital in El Paso. Immediately he was brought to the main trauma room in the ER. A small dose of ketamine was given to keep him out.

After that, his clothes were cut off and peeled away. Burnt skin clung to fabric and fabric melted down into muscle. His vital signs showed low blood pressure with an accelerated pulse, indicating that his body was trying to compensate for shock.

Sure enough, shock took him over. His body shivered with cold that wasn't there, and his hands tightened into fists that shot great pain into his arms. Rolled down the hallway, Whistle was placed in a lukewarm water bath. He was left to soak for twenty minutes. After that, four nurses came in and laid him on a dry white table. They dried him off, then Whistle was transferred to another tub of warm water. There he was rinsed off then placed back on the table with new towels. After being wrapped in a gel blanket, sleep took him over for the next three weeks. Time passed and his body slowly recuperated. Still sore, Whistle slept on. Day after day, things finally started to come together. Monarch colors infiltrated all his dreams and made him want to move on. His brain told him to find Kenny, get in Carla, and head west. Santa Monica Pier, here we come.

Finally, the morning came when he opened his eyes and looked up at a doctor looking back down at him.

"Can you hear me?" the doctor asked as he stepped closer. Whistle's eyes fluttered as he tried to clear his head.

"Can you hear me? Hello?" the doctor asked again.

"Illiiryyeah," was as close as Whistle could get to answering. Completely understanding, the doctor told Whistle to go back to sleep and regain his strength. Another three weeks in and out of reality followed until the one day came. It started in a most unusual way.

"I gotta take a shit!" He pushed a nurse away, standing up. She just stood there as Whistle hobbled to the toilet and painfully did his business. It was so painful that tears flowed freely down his face. When he was done, he shamefully accepted the nurse's help to wipe his ass. All cleaned up, he was back in a crisp, clean hospital bed and another dream took him over. Unfortunately....just then, Whistle's eyes fluttered open for a moment. He was all alone in the stark, white room, but ready to move on in the worst way. Another night's sleep, and Whistle awoke as a nurse entered the room.

"Good morning Whistle. How are you feeling today?" she asked.

"I'm good. I'm ready to get outta here." He looked up coyly.

"Well, the doctor will come in and talk to you." Smiling, both understood that he wasn't leaving today.

"Fine," he responded, wearing his disappointment openly. After doing a few more nurse chores around the room, she smiled at Whistle once more before she walked out. A small breakfast and an apple juice hit the spot. He turned on the TV to watch *The Price Is Right* and it reminded him of staying home sick from school. He couldn't believe it was the same music, same set, same cast; it was like a little trip back in time.

He started to feel really comfortable and eventually fell asleep before the "Showcase Showdown" between a housewife from Illinois and a navy man on leave from Hawaii. He was again reminded of the dream in which Shortstop urged Whistle to go to the Santa Monica Pier. He figured while he was out there, maybe he could swing by Burbank and try his luck on *The Price Is Right* as well. Only thing, what would he do with all that stuff if he won? Maybe have it shipped to Cinnamon and Ladybug as a thank you for their hospitality. He fantasized about the delivery truck pulling up onto the Landing Pad and unloading all those goodies as the girls stood there, speechless. Eventually, this fantasy turned into a nondescript dream which turned into a good long nap.

Later that afternoon, a doctor Whistle had never seen before came in. Sitting up a little with a decent amount of pain, he looked at her.

"Hello Whistle, I'm Doctor Elizabeth Lamothe. How are you today?"

"I'm fine, how are you?" he asked back politely.

"I am good, thank you for asking," she replied as she walked over and turned off the television. She turned back and asked him, "Can we talk?"

"Please," he replied immediately. "I've been so lost. How long have I been in here?"

"You've been here for just over four months," she replied.

"Holy shit!" A pause. "I'm sorry, I mean holy cow!" he amended, trying to clean up the sentiment.

"Don't worry about it, Whistle. You've been through a lot," she said as she pulled a chair up to the bed.

"So, what's the story, Doc?"

"Just call me Betsy, or Doctor B.," she said.

"Ok...Doctor B. it is. Am I ready to get out of here?"

"Not yet. You're still on a morphine drip that's keeping the pain at bay, so you feel a lot better than you would without it. Your body is still healing and still trying to regain strength. You're looking at staying another month to six weeks."

"Wait. What? No! I have to get out of here! I've already been here for too long," he said, growing slightly agitated.

"Whistle, calm down. I have a lot more to tell you." Just then the door opened and a nurse stood silhouetted against the hallway light.

"Doctor B.?" the nurse called.

"Not now," she replied, putting her hand up.

"But..."

"Nurse, please. Not now," Doctor B. repeated as she turned to the nurse, her hand still up.

"It's just that…"

"Go!" Doctor B. said sternly, and just like that the door closed and the nurse was gone. That's when Whistle's trust in Doctor B. set in. He could tell she was a straight shooter and would be honest with him.

"Okay, so six weeks tops and I'm out of here?" he asked.

"Not exactly." She moved her chair a little closer.

"Why not?" He was trying to shrug his shoulders with no success.

"Your morphine drip is going to take another month to wean off of."

"What do you mean?"

"Once you don't need the morphine for pain, you need to come off a little at a time, or you'll go through tremendous withdrawals and either wind up right back in here anyway or become a heroin addict. We need to do this right, Whistle."

"Fine, I understand this but something tells me you have more to tell me, Doctor B."

"I do," she answered, lifting his chin up until they made eye contact.

"Oh boy," Whistle said, almost under his breath. Taking his hand very carefully, Doctor B. continued.

"I want you to heal your body, end the use of pain meds, then get some counseling before you leave here. Whistle, you've been through an experience that no person should ever have to go through." Doctor B. actually wiped a few tears away without letting him notice. After all, she was still supposed to remain a professional.

"Well, believe it or not, I somehow understand this without even knowing why. Let me ask you this, though. Why can't I start therapy now to save time?" he asked.

"That is a good question. Here's why. You need to be healthy, stronger, and clean to benefit from therapy. It will be psychological and physical. Whistle, I ask you not to bail on this because it will benefit you immensely. I just want your life to be as good as you deserve, because you truly deserve it." Another tear discreetly wiped away.

"So what are we talking, Doctor B.? About a year all together?" he asked, squeezing her hand.

"I think that sounds about right," she replied, squeezing back.

"Will you be my therapist?"

"No Whistle, I'm an ICU doctor, but I will make sure that when you leave here you'll be transferred to a great group of physical therapists, and I happen to be very good friends with an incredible psychologist named George Zeep. Just call him Z. He likes that."

"I don't know, Doctor B. I kinda want to get out of here as soon as possible," he said, looking down. Lifting his chin, Doctor Elizabeth Lamothe spoke.

"Whistle, you are a more incredible man than you know. You've been through hell and back. All you need is the correct help to get your life moving on in the right direction again." Doctor B. couldn't hold her emotions in any longer and started to cry. He sat up and hugged her with very great pain shooting through him.

"I will check on you from time to time," she said, now weeping out loud. "I just want you to get through the other end of this and be healthy in every way." He held her head up and wiped tears from her eyes with his thumbs.

"I'll be fine, I promise," Whistle said as he braved the pain in his shoulders to give her another hug. "I'll spend another however long it takes to leave here completely healthy, but promise me you'll come visit me from time to time," he added, now welling up himself.

"I promise, Whistle." With that, Doctor B. slowly got up and gave his hand one more soft squeeze before she walked back out of the room and down the hallway.

CHAPTER
FIFTY-EIGHT
Doctor B. and Doctor Z.

Another month passed and Doctor B. kept her promise and checked in on Whistle from time to time. Whistle stayed positive and felt his healing was going quicker than expected. He even had his drip knocked down substantially. The estimated time of healing was shortened to five weeks. After that, his weaning program went quicker than expected as well.

One month later, Whistle had a clear head, a healthy body that just needed a lot of exercise. Throw in some brain work and the boy figured he'd be right as rain. A few days later, he was transferred again to a new wing and therapy began.

After settling into his new room, Whistle was told that dinner was at five and he would meet with Doctor Giorgio Zeep in his office at seven o'clock that evening. He sat by himself in the cafeteria, and enjoyed a rather tasty Salisbury steak with mashed potatoes and green beans. A soft dinner roll with butter and an ice cold root beer complimented the meal just right.

Satisfyingly full, Whistle returned to his room and took a shower, dried off, and put on some nice, clean clothes. No doubt he was feeling a lot better. The pain of his burns was almost gone. The morphine was out of his system. He felt like he was ready to get out of here and on with his life.

"Whistle Starr?" came a voice from the doorway.

"Yes?" Whistle responded, turning and seeing an old, frail doctor standing there.

"I'm ready to see you now, please come with me," the doctor said as he turned back toward the door.

"Alright." Whistle got up, wanting to get on with it. Walking out the door, they turned left and Whistle followed the old doctor slowly down a very pale hallway. A few more turns and a staircase up, they stood before a brown door with a placard that read "Dr. Georgio Zeep."

"Come in son and have a seat."

Cautiously stepping forward, things started to come into perspective. This was a comfortable office with comfortable furniture and a pleasant enough looking doctor. Sitting in one of two brown studded leather chairs, Whistle looked across a rather grand mahogany desk accented with another placard and two old fashioned pens. A green shaded lamp off to each side lit the area perfectly.

He could see plenty of framed certificates in the background along with shelves of endless important looking books. Somehow, he felt surprisingly comfortable. He sat down.

"Welcome, Whistle." Looking across the desk, he saw an olive skinned man with salt and pepper curls of hair down to his collar. The doctor's hands were held before him on his desk blotter, and his dark brown eyes were framed by stylish black glasses frames. Those eyes looked directly at Whistle as the lamp light reflected off the lenses of his glasses.

"Uh, thank you," mumbled Whistle, half asking and half answering as he folded his own hands upon the very front edge of the desk. With a fraction of a second glance down from the doctor, Whistle almost involuntarily removed his hands and sat back immediately.

"Sorry," he whispered.

"No worries, Whistle. My name is Doctor George Zeep."

"Doc, I'm Whistle Evel Fonzarelli Starr and Doctor B. told me I should call you Doctor Z."

"That'll be just fine, Whistle," Doctor Z. responded, smiling.

"Cool," Whistle responded, smiling back. He already liked Doctor Z.

"So let's get right into it. You're going to require a lot of physical therapy, and you and I have to have many conversations together."

"I understand, and I'm more than ready," Whistle responded, holding the doctor's gaze.

Closing his file, Doctor Z. shook Whistle's hand and said, "Tomorrow, you'll go to your first day of physical therapy, then I'll meet you back here at seven again."

"Sounds good," Whistle replied as he got up and thanked the doctor before heading back to his room.

Once he was there, he felt at ease and got into his bed, ready for a good night's sleep. Unfortunately, he stayed awake the entire night. His mind was too preoccupied with what tomorrow might have in store.

The morning sun arrived to find an exhausted Whistle. As it usually goes, he was just about ready to fall asleep when it was time to get up. He went to breakfast, but ate very little. He drank some coffee to try and wake up, but it didn't do much for him.

The next thing he knew, he entered what he would come to know as the torture chamber for the first time. These monsters took him and physically pulled him in what felt like every direction possible. They grabbed him and moved him all around, telling him things like, "Relax," "Go with it," and "You're fine."

Finally back in his room, Whistle broke down and cried all by himself. He was done and just wanted to go to sleep.

"Whistle, you ready?" Doctor Z. asked as he knocked on the door.

"No!" Whistle shot back, closing his eyes.

"I'm ready for you," the doctor replied, waiting patiently, like he probably had a thousand other times with a thousand other patients.

"Fuck it! Fine. Let's go," Whistle said, getting up reluctantly.

Sitting back in Doctor Z.'s office, he waited.

"Are you okay, Whistle?"

"Fuck no, I'm not okay! I've just been physically abused and I'm quite sure you're about to try to fill my head with some kind of bullshit! Are you trying to brainwash me or something?" Whistle raged, sitting forward in his chair, clenching his fist.

"I'm afraid you have it all wrong. We just want you to be all set before you get back into society. Those 'monsters' will get you strong again. So the quicker you believe that, the quicker we can all get this done."

Whistle was too tired to argue as he sighed, "Okay."

The next morning, Whistle woke up and literally couldn't move his body at all. He had never been so sore in all his life. Suddenly he was placed on a hospital bed and rolled into the torture chamber for the second time.

Fuck! was all he could think. He repeated the whole routine of the previous day. It wasn't any easier and the physical pain wrung tears from Whistle's eyes once again. Seven o'clock eventually came and brought with it another meeting with Doctor Z.

Afterwards, back in his room, sleep was not easy on this night either and the process was repeated over and over for a solid month. Finally, the day came where the soreness began to subside and Whistle began to regain his flexibility. There was no more pain from his burns and he could listen to Doctor Z. with a clear head. Weight lifting, flexibility training, and proper diet, the training finally led to the first real therapy meeting with Doctor Z.

"I'm ready to go, Z." Whistle was by now comfortable enough to lose the doctor part.

"I understand that you feel that way. You look great, but it's time we talk."

"Why?" Whistle asked, "I feel great."

"Fine, I'll cut to the chase. You were a national hero for a week without you even knowing about it. It was all talk about how you pulled those two children out of the fire." Memories started to flood back into Whistle's mind as Z continued.

"The rescue report showed that the last few things you said were questions. You asked where the third child was. You asked where your friend Kenny was, and you asked where the father was. Then you went unconscious."

Not wanting to deal with any of this, Whistle stood up and said, "I gotta go."

"Sit down, please."

"The woman was screaming in my face and then I just ran in. I remember seeing a couple of cats run by my right side and seeing Oprah Winfrey on a TV. After that, I woke up in the hospital with a tube down my throat."

"That's enough for today," Z. said, with true concern.

"No! Fuck that! Did their dad make it?" Whistle demanded.

After a long pause, Z. responded.

"I'm afraid not. He was found underneath the window you brought the two children out of.

"I remember stepping on something soft to get a little height to the window for the kids." So without ever knowing it, the father did, in fact, play a role in saving two of his children's lives. Whistle felt horrible, but decided he could live with this.

"What about the third kid? I couldn't find him."

"Your friend, Kenny, got him out and he's fine. The mom and all three kids are doing well," the doctor said with a small smile, knowing what was coming next.

"That's great news! So where's Kenny?"

The doctor paused before breaking the news. "Whistle...I'm sorry."

"No...Fuck no! Don't you say you're sorry!" Whistle said, standing up and taking an aggressive posture at the doctor's desk. "Tell me where the Great American Bear is."

Leaning back calmly in his chair and crossing his hands, the doctor said, "Kenny didn't make it, Whistle."

"Fuck you!" Whistle shouted, slamming his hands down hard on the desk. The doctor waited until he wore himself out yelling at him, until he finally sat back down, then the doctor continued.

"Whistle, Kenny brought the boy down the stairs and out the back door. They were both on fire but Kenny had the boy shielded with his arm and body. In the rescue van, he went into cardiac arrest."

"Shut the fuck up, the Bear has Carla rumbling in the alley right around the corner waiting for me." Whistle smiled and laughed in an inappropriate way. Doctor Z. continued on.

"Between the rescue and the emergency room, Kenny's heart stopped five times. They pushed every drug, and did everything they could, but Kenny didn't make it."

Reality setting in, Whistle completely lost it. His sobs came huge and full. Whistle's mind shot back and forth that he was all alone again.

The two talked for hours and hours over days and days. After two more months, Whistle was ready to go.

"Thank you, Z.," Whistle said, hugging the doctor.

"You're welcome," Z. replied as he hugged Whistle back. A small pause later, he slung his pack up on his back and walked out the front door. After fourteen months with his body completely healed and his mind mostly at peace with his situation, he stood on the sidewalk.

A granite curb looked east and west as the road spread in each direction. Should the boy go east, back to New Orleans and into Cinnamon's arms, or should he head west toward the Santa Monica Pier that Shortstop insisted on? Standing there with the warm afternoon wind blowing across the hot Texas desert, he stopped.

"Okay Whistle, east or west?" he asked himself. After great trepidation, Whistle realized he couldn't go back to what he knew before. So he squared up, and continued west. A far off pier called to him and he knew he had to go.

CHAPTER
FIFTY-NINE
Charlie Chaplin Freedom

Getting walking felt great. Whistle's muscles stretched out and his mind stretched west even further. By the end of the day he had walked clear out of Texas and into New Mexico. With the Rio Grande beside him, he briskly walked the rest of the day away. Route 9 West passed along step by step with the Portillo Mountains to his right and the Mexican border to his left.

With low crimson light left, he stepped off the road to find a place to sleep for the night. Whistle Evel Fonzarelli Starr actually spent the night against the border fence with a blue Winnie the Pooh kiddie pool pulled over him. In and out of sleep, he heard helicopters in the distance and he was surprised at how cold it could get.

The next morning came and the boy woke up sweating like crazy. His lips were dry and crusted with sand. Winnie and Piglet stared at him as the sun beat down relentlessly. Whistle pulled a water out of his pack, and a maple oat granola bar. Both gone, he dozed off for another twenty minutes, letting them do their work.

Before moving on, Whistle decided he should go through his pack and inventory his resources. Six bottles of water, two boxes of granola bars, and surprisingly, a bottle of three hundred multivitamins were in his pack. Four pairs of socks, four pairs of underwear, two pairs of jeans, three T-shirts, and a huge comforting black sweatshirt rounded out his clothing. A small pocket at the top revealed two hundred dollars and three books of matches. Another side pocket held a complete morning kit. In the boy's humble opinion, all this was beyond priceless.

The only thing that could possibly be more priceless than all of that happened to be the incredibly weathered copy of J.D. Salinger's *The Catcher In The Rye*. Over the years, Whistle would read that book dozens of times along with many others he would come across in his travels. Stephen King definitely became his favorite author, but he was also fond of many others.

He enjoyed reading tremendously and felt it opened his mind. Drawn to the classics, he read everything from *Of Mice and Men* to *The Great Gatsby*. Let us please not forget *The Chronicles of Narnia*.

The boy flipped the pool off of him and stood up. He turned and looked at the border fence before him, and there stood a woman and a child. She was too proud to ask for anything, but her eyes said it all. Immediately Whistle tossed a box of granola bars over the fence and slid two bottles of water through. Knowing he needed those things, he knew they needed them more. Their eyes met and he saw tears of deep appreciation fall down her face. Without a word spoken, they both turned and walked away. Where they went, Whistle would never know. All he knew was he walked back to Route 9 West down a box of bars and two bottles of water.

Confident that karma would be his friend, Whistle moved west.

His desire to walk and be in the open was immense. Two pleasant days passed by rather easily. Warm sun followed by incredible stars at night then repeated again. No one bothered him and that was good because there was nowhere to hide. No woods to duck into, just open desert land all around, as far as the eye could see. That was the main reason he decided to switch back to thumbing for a ride.

So the next day, he started hitchhiking again. Not seeing a single car for hours, Whistle continued on. The few cars and trucks he did see didn't stop. Not giving up, late afternoon came when, through a huge Route 9 West mirage, the first real town he'd seen since the hospital appeared before him: Columbus, New Mexico.

At that moment, he decided that nearly a week on the road deserved at least one night of relative comfort. Walking in, he found Main Street and it was about what he expected. The classic signal stoplight at the intersection of 9 West and 11 North.

This was dotted up and down both sides with various shops, restaurants, and bars. A gas station, a bank, and town hall completed the picture. A few blocks west, Whistle found the Charlie Chaplin Motel. Stopping for a moment, he wondered why on earth there would be a Charlie Chaplin Motel along the Mexican border. Escaping the deep orange heat of the late afternoon sun, he stepped through the front door.

His eyes had to adjust to the dimly lit, smoky lobby playing soft Mexican music in the background. Stepping deeper into the room, he saw that it was empty, aside from the woman manning the front desk.

"Can I help you?" she asked as she stood up.

"Hello! Yes, please," Whistle replied.

With plenty of vacancies, Whistle chose the closest room to the lobby, Room Number 2.

Thanking the girl, he grabbed the key and walked out. Twenty dollars down, he slid the key in the lock and turned. Open door, walk in, close door and turn on the light. Whistle was surprised to find the room extremely neat and clean. Everything had all the colors associated with the southwest. He tossed his pack on the only chair in the room and flopped down on the very comfortable bed. Laying there for about ten minutes, he was almost asleep when he made himself get up and go to the bathroom. Everything in there was also very clean. He did his business and turned on the shower. The pressure was great and the steam came fast.

The next hour was spent grooming himself. Clean face, clipped nails, shortened hair and brushed teeth were followed by trimmed nose and ear hair. All this was then followed by a long, very hot, and very cleansing shower. After that, Whistle dressed in some of his clean clothes and washed his dirty ones in the tub. Wrung out and hung on everything possible, they started to dry and he heard his stomach rumble with hunger. Very awake now, he left the room and went to the lobby. He was actually clean and looked presentable.

With eyes now adjusted, he noticed Charlie Chaplin and other silent movie memorabilia spread around. It was curious to him, but at least there was a theme. The front desk girl was gone and now a younger boy sat there looking at him.

"Can I help you?"

"Yes, do you have a place to grab some food and maybe a beer or two?"

"Right down that hallway," the boy replied, pointing to his left.

"Thank you very much," Whistle said as he made his way down a long, dark hallway. Walking up to a set of closed double doors, the sign above read, "Charlie's Spot."

"Of course." He laughed to himself.

Through the double doors, there was more smoke hanging in the air and more soft music in the background. The patrons were sparse and he found a seat by himself at the bar.

Whistle ordered a Budweiser and asked for a menu. Beer in hand, he noticed that everything on the menu had a name that had to do with silent movies. He finally settled on the silent reel slinger which was a half-pound burger with pepper jack cheese, jalapeno peppers, and grilled onions with a chipotle sauce on a brioche bun. The whole dang thing was delicious.

By the time his plate was clean, including the orange slice garnish, peel and all, he ordered his third beer. Very satisfied, he sipped away and got a shot of Jack. Sipping for another half hour, he paid his bill with a very honest, "Thank you," and a more than adequate tip.

Back up the hallway to the lobby, he gave the boy at the desk a wave and a smile. It had been a long time since he'd had any alcohol at all. Not too drunk, but pleasantly buzzed, he continued to his room. Once inside, he moved his pack off the chair and sat. The room was dark with the exception of dim light coming from the bathroom. A thin slice of hallway light came in through the bottom of the main door as well as the streetlight making its way around the edges of the window shade. The only other light came from the red digits of the alarm clock on the nightstand that read 11:32 p.m.

Perfect, he thought to himself, smiling, as he got undressed, laying his clothes over the back of the chair. He went to the bathroom to brush his teeth and grab a glass of water before he got under the covers and drifted off to sleep in a luxurious, comfortable king size bed with soft cotton sheets. The room was silent and Whistle was happy. He felt strong and clean with decent resources available. A full belly and just a perfect buzz in his head. Smiling, he drifted off.

His main dream that night was not very detailed, just perfectly pleasant. It was like his eyes were open, looking at a continuously slow changing painting with a great background soundtrack. The screen laid out before his mind was a soft, deepish purple, but not too deep. All the edges were filled with his favorite monarch butterfly colors. The black, orange, and white swirled and swayed slowly. Pink Floyd flowed on and on, perfectly choreographed to Whistle's dream screen.

In the middle of it all, faces of his past came in and out of focus randomly. One after another, coming into great detail and fading back out again. They all were smiling with loving, twinkling eyes and it was beyond glorious!

The Great American Bear came first with a huge wink and a thumbs-up. This drifted to Jack Peters.

CHAPTER
SIXTY
A Very Interesting Time

The next morning came way faster than the boy wished, but he was anxious to get going. A small time later, he was all packed up and ready to go. Unable to help himself, he paused and looked around. Taking the room in, he appreciated it. Pack on back, he closed the door and headed for the lobby. Whistle checked out with yet another new person at the front desk.

Thanking him, he got a cup of coffee and four oranges for his pack and a banana for his belly.

He filled his front pants pockets with sugar packets and grabbed a copy of the *Columbus Daily News*. A quick trip to the lobby men's room and a handful of mints from the bowl by the front door and he was on his way.

Midmorning brightness hit him and the dry heat was moderate. A quick smile and step to the side, the boy continued his journey west. Walking out of town without knowing anyone's name and no one knowing his was liberating.

Plenty of road ahead, he got to it. Four days later, he walked into the town of Hachita. His idea was to find another motel for the night, get good food, have a restful sleep, and then continue his journey west. Stopping at a gas station on the edge of town, he used the bathroom and washed up in the sink as thoroughly as possible, considering the amenities. Walking out, he noticed a couple of guys looking at him as if they were irritated with how long he was occupying the restroom.

"Sorry," he quietly said, looking down. He went to the counter and bought a ham and cheese sandwich, cool ranch Doritos, and a Coke. He paid and walked outside and sat at a picnic table with peeling red paint on the shady side of the building. After a large, satisfying swig of the Coke, he dug in ravenously.

After a while, he noticed a couple much younger than him sitting at a blue and equally peeling table off to the side. Trying not to listen to their conversation, but unable to avoid hearing enough of it, he surmised that they were just married and on their honeymoon. He stayed quiet in the shadows until finally hearing one of them say, "New Hampshire." He was too lonely and homesick not to say something.

"Excuse me, I'm not trying to listen to your conversation, but did you say you were from New Hampshire?" he asked as he popped a chip into his mouth.

"Yeah, why?" the man replied.

"I'm from New Hampshire," Whistle said with a warm smile that put the couple at ease.

"She's actually from New Hampshire. What part are you from?"

"I'm from Stewart's Hollow. It's around twenty minutes south of the Canadian border. What part are you from?" Whistle asked the girl.

"Jaffrey," she responded shyly.

"You're kidding! Jaffrey? I grew up hiking Mount Monadnock!" He was thrilled to be talking to people from his neck of the woods.

"Me too," she said, a lot less shy now.

"So, what are you guys doing in New Mexico?"

"I'm from Houston, and we just got married there and we're on our honeymoon for the next three weeks." He looked at her, beaming in a way newlyweds tend to do.

"Wow! Awesome. So, how did you guys meet?" Whistle asked, sincerely interested.

"We both went to the University of Rhode Island, met at a sorority party, and the rest is history," the girl explained, now beaming a little herself.

"Very cool. By the way, my name's Whistle," he said as he put his hand out after wiping the chip dust off on his jeans.

"Nice to meet you, Whistle. Orrin and Melissa...excuse me, Mr. and Mrs. Orrin Bambrick," Orrin said in a humorously formal tone, after a nudge in the ribs from Melissa.

"Great to meet you guys," Whistle said as he got up and threw his wrappers and Coke can in the trash.

"Wait, what's your name again?" Melissa asked.

"Whistle...Whistle Evel Fonzarelli Starr."

"That sounds familiar for some reason," she said.

"So, what are you doing all the way down here at the Mexican border?" Orrin asked.

"It's a very long story," Whistle chuckled, mostly to himself.

"Well, we have three weeks and like a good story. Let's hear it," Melissa said as they both leaned in.

Whistle proceeded to give them the condensed, cleaned up version. After about a half hour, the couple sat in the same place, mouths agape with disbelief.

"You've got to be kidding!" Melissa said as she looked at Whistle, then her husband, and back at Whistle again.

"What an insane ride you've had, my friend. Where are you off to now?" Orrin asked, as he and Melissa sat transfixed, waiting for his answer.

"Oh, I'm on my way to California," he said as he looked west, almost lost in his own thoughts for a few moments.

When he came back to earth, he noticed that the couple's eyes were as wide as saucers.

"NOOOO WAYYYY!" they both said in perfect unison.

"What?" Whistle asked, taken aback.

"WE'RE going to California too!"

"Get out!" Whistle said, laughing at the synchronicity of it all.

"You have to come with us!" Orrin said after Melissa nonverbally gave the go ahead to invite him along.

"No way! You guys are on your honeymoon—listen, it was great meeting you guys. I'm gonna get rolling."

"Bullshit! Dude, trust me. We've got three weeks and the rest of our lives to spend time together! We would have a blast. I got a bunch of weed and two cases of Coors. We rented a beach house in Redondo Beach—where were you headed?"

"Santa Monica, the Pier to be specific," Whistle answered, still trying to extract himself from the situation, not wanting to be a third wheel on a couple's honeymoon.

"Well, at least ride through Arizona with us," Orrin said.

"Please! It'll be awesome to have you along," Melissa reassured him.

The thought of cruising through the desert as opposed to hoofing it was just too tempting. Plus, they really seemed like they wanted him along for the ride and weren't just being polite.

"Alright, but I'm telling you guys, if you decide at any point my charm is wearing thin, feel free to kick me to the curb. I won't hold it against you at all."

"It's a deal, you ready?" Orrin asked, as he started feeling around for his keys as Melissa threw out the trash.

"Born ready!" Whistle said as he got up and threw his bag over his shoulder.

The three of them hopped into a rented red jeep and off they drove down the highway. Young, carefree, and taking the world by the balls. They blasted by Hachita almost before they got a chance to light their first joint. Whistle marveled at his good luck as the stereo blasted "Roll Me Away" by Bob Seger. He also marveled at how much more beautiful the desert was cruising through at eighty miles an hour with the cool early evening breeze blowing through his hair and a refreshing beverage in his hand.

At some point, Whistle fell asleep and woke up around sunrise the next day. Orrin pulled into a rest area for a quick bathroom trip, a coffee and Danish from the diner, and a stretch before they all got back in the jeep and crossed the border into the Grand Canyon State.

"Arizona!" Melissa shouted over the rush of the wind and the rumble of the engine.

"Whoooooo!" Orrin shouted as he handed a lit roach over his shoulder to Whistle in the back seat.

The sun coming up behind them from the east lit the highway perfectly. Long shadows stretched before them and soft yellow hues gently lit the peaks of the Rincon Mountains ahead. They drove over the summit and continued into Tucson. Whistle made it a point to pay for the room at the Turn Key Marriott. On the third floor, they found their room. It was a very nice room and he was glad he paid. It was the least he could do.

They all showered and went down to the hotel bar for some dinner and drinks. Down at the Ivory Tusk, the three sidled up to the big, oak bar. Everyone ordered a Rum and Coke with a gigantic plate of grilled chicken nachos. They drank and picked away happily. More drinks ordered, they each got two carne asada tacos with grilled peppers and onions. Nice flour tortillas hugged everything together. Lettuce, white onions, and tomatoes were topped with guacamole and sour cream. Beyond delicious, especially to three hungry travelers with the munchies.

Completely satisfied, the three ordered one more drink. With a "Cheers," Whistle toasted the happy couple.

"Thank you so much! You guys are unbelievable and you deserve all the happiness in the world." They talked for another hour and then they headed back up to the room. The Bambricks took the bed and Whistle took the couch. They all slept very well and woke up around eight. After getting ready, they got in the jeep and left Tucson. Everyone decided that they should spend the night in Phoenix and see what it had to offer. After all, no one was in a rush. They eventually made their way into town and checked into the State Capital Hotel. The room was not the greatest but it was a place to hang your hat for the night.

They cruised around town and eventually found a place with great Angus burgers and a great little country rock band playing steel guitars and singing in four part harmony. After a full night of drinks, music, and dancing, Whistle and the Bambricks went back to the hotel and passed out happily...

"What a great night!" Whistle said as he began to doze off on the couch.

The next morning, they checked out with Whistle grabbing whatever resources he could obtain as discreetly as possible. Two bottles of water, a box of blueberry pop tarts, four small boxes of Raisin Bran and a pack of a hundred and fifty napkins. He smiled as they walked out. Back in the jeep, they drove all day and reached Phoenix by early evening, the sun lighting up the western sky like a neon oil painting. It was like nothing Whistle had ever seen.

They pulled into the Amarillo Inn on Camelback Road. Paying again, Whistle was almost broke. Six dollars and thirty-eight cents in his pocket, they got the room. Simple and not all that clean, it was what it was.

After washing up and changing, they walked out through the lobby and went looking for adventure in Phoenix, turning down a side street to smoke a joint in between some buildings before taking in the sights. After they were done, they went out to the corner of Olive and Mirage Road and saw a bar by the name of The Scorpion on the opposite side of the road. The name on the sign was red neon. Purple neon lit up a picture of a scorpion with a green neon stinger on its tail. A large bucket of buffalo wings and some Coronas with lime started the night. Many games of pool were played with Orrin and Whistle running the table. The energy of the locals grew increasingly hostile as the two outsiders won game after game.

Finally, Melissa whispered into Whistle's ear. "I think we should go."

"I agree." Whistle started tapping Orrin on the shoulder.

"What?" he replied, fairly drunk.

"Why? We're running the table, man!"

"I know, but I think these people wouldn't mind kicking our asses," Whistle said, finishing his Corona.

"Wait a minute," Orrin mumbled, turning to their current opponents, "are we bothering you?" he finished with a big, drunk smile on his face. Both Melissa and Whistle felt this would not go over well.

"A bit," one of the locals said, sinking the three ball in the side pocket.

"Why?" Orrin asked. Whistle tried to move him away from the situation, but the man jumped in.

"Why? Who the fuck are you to come to my bar and be an asshole?"

That's when Whistle's hackles went up. Melissa grabbed him and said, "Please, no! It's my honeymoon."

"I know, don't worry, I'll take care of it," he reassured her.

"Excuse me, what's your problem?" Whistle said, turning to the man.

"What's my problem? Your friend is being an asshole." Feeling that this was very much untrue, Whistle asked Melissa to go to the bar to get five shots of Cuervo and five Coronas with lime.

"Why is my friend being an asshole?" Whistle asked as Orrin sank the eight ball, the very last thing that would de-escalate the situation. His big, stupid, oblivious smile wasn't helping either. The peace offering of tequila and beer showed up and Whistle did his best to diffuse the situation. Orrin took his shot and unfortunately got in the man's face.

Fuck! Whistle thought to himself as the other two guys stood up. The three men surrounded Orrin in a less than pleasant manner.

"Melissa, grab Orrin, grab the Jeep and get back to the Amarillo. I'll meet you back there."

CHAPTER
SIXTY-ONE
Bar Fight

After a quick but earnest protest from Melissa and Orrin, Whistle basically pushed them out the back door and promised he was just going to calm everybody down and would be back to the hotel shortly. Holding off until he saw that they were out of sight.

"Okay fuckboys, it's on!" he said, jumping up on the pool table and spinning his stick around to where the heavy end was facing out.

"Holy shit my friend, you are in the wrong place," one of the locals said as he picked up his own stick.

"I'm well aware of that," Whistle said as he pointed the butt end of the stick at the local's forehead. "I'm also well aware that your two friends here will probably be followed by the bartender and bouncer. If needed, plenty of other friends are sure to be waiting in the wings. So you know what?" Whistle said, smiling.

"What?" the man asked, getting angrier.

"I'm one hundred percent sure I'm about to get my ass kicked, but I'm also a hundred percent sure I'm about to smoke you out."

And just like that, he swung the cue down like a splitting maul. The man instantly dropped like a sack of potatoes. Whistle would never know it, but unfortunately the man would suffer brain damage and would never be the same again.

After the first local went down, the boy went full on Jackie Robinson on at least three or four more guys. A firm stance on the table suited him well, until someone figured out to take the pool balls out of the table.

"Fuck you!" he yelled as he took the eleven ball directly to the chest.

"Oh no, Fuck YOU!" was yelled back as the seven ball smacked him square in the back of the head. This dropped him to his knees, creating a feeding frenzy. His pool stick was stripped away by the time he was thrown to the ground, plenty of his blood saturated the green felt of the table. Beat up some more, he was thrown out the back door like a piece of trash before he slid into unconsciousness. About four hours passed before he woke up. With a busted up body, he got himself up and walked away, spitting a mouthful of blood on the ground.

Very beat up, Whistle thought to himself how it wasn't that bad, he'd been worse off. Plus his new friends were probably OK, so he made his way to the Amarillo. By the time he limped into the lobby, the few people there all stopped and stared at him. Moving on, he finally made it to the room and knocked. He almost passed out again while waiting. After what seemed like an eternity, the door finally opened.

"Holy shit Whistle, get in here!" a familiar voice said. The voice was Melissa, who instantly burst into hysterics at the sight of him. She led him to the shower and turned the water on. As it started to heat up, she undressed him while his eyes swelled up and became discolored.

"Are you insane?" she asked, placing him under the water.

"Probably." He laughed, spitting more blood down the drain.

"Probably? I'm gonna go with yes!" she said as Orrin walked in, still blurry from sleep.

"What the fuck's going on?" One look at Whistle woke him up instantly and the Bambricks spent the next two hours cleaning and caring for him.

"Whistle, I'm so fucking sorry!" Orrin said with tears streaming down his face as well.

"Will you two please stop crying? That's the last thing I need right now," Whistle said as his right eye swelled completely shut.

"What happened?" Orrin asked.

"It doesn't matter," Whistle replied, grabbing a white hotel towel.

Two bloody towels later, Whistle went back out to the room. The Bambricks offered him the bed, but he refused and took the couch as usual. It was plenty comfortable enough and he knew deep down that he could have easily avoided this whole ordeal if he had just left with the Bambricks and hung out in the hotel for the night, having some drinks and laughing about the close call they avoided. But, if you made it this far in the story, you know that's just not how Whistle is wired.

The next morning, Melissa woke Whistle and Orrin up real early.

"Guys, I hate to say it, but we have to check out."

"Alright," Orrin said as he got out of bed. Neither one of Whistle's eyes would open at all, so Orrin led him to the bathroom and helped him so he could shower and get dressed without hurting himself further. After the couple were done showering and getting dressed, they all went down to the desk, checked out, and sat down for a decent continental breakfast. Eggs, sausage, coffee, juice, toast and a fruit cup rounded out the meal and the young threesome were on their way, happy to leave Phoenix behind.

Back on 10 West, they drove straight through the afternoon in complete silence. They didn't even turn the radio on. The hum of the tires and the wind from the cracked window helped keep Whistle in a deep sleep. Around six or seven, they stopped at a McDonald's in Quartzsite. All used the bathroom and Whistle was able to finally see enough to walk unassisted. There was a little blood in his urine and his own face startled him when he looked in the mirror.

"Holy shit!" Whistle said as he checked out his split lip, swollen eyes, and scratched cheeks and neck.

"You said it!" Orrin chuckled in a way that was more rueful than jovial. Whistle felt bad about turning the Bambricks into caregivers on their honeymoon and let Orrin know.

"I'm sorry about all this, I don't know why I didn't just leave the bar with you guys."

"Don't worry about it. It's my fault for being so good at bank shots. Come on, let's go eat."

The three of them found a corner booth and sat down to mow some quarter pounders, fries, and Cokes. Whistle was able to manage even though his jaw was swollen and it really hurt to chew. After they were done, they refilled their Cokes and got back into the jeep, where Whistle lay down across the back seat and fell asleep as the Bambricks drove through the rest of Arizona, over the Colorado River, and, finally, into California.

CHAPTER
SIXTY-TWO
Western Wonder

After dark, they pulled off Exit 173 and found a supermarket in Chiriaco Summit. Pulling up, they parked in a spot far away that provided a fairly dark location. They all went to sleep for the night.

The next morning Orrin and Melissa went into the market. The first thing they did was use the restroom. Meanwhile, Whistle slowly got out of the jeep and made his way to the edge of the parking lot which met the Joshua Tree National Park. Once there and out of view from anyone, he relieved himself. When he was done he went back to the jeep to find the Bambricks unloading their carriage of groceries and essentials.

"Thank you guys so much," Whistle said as he helped with the groceries.

"Thank us? Thank you, Whistle. Without you, I think we all would have been killed. You were right and I was just plain stupid. I was drunk and cocky and I'm sorry you got busted up."

"This?" Whistle asked, pointing to his face with both index fingers and smiling as best he could. "This is nothing. Trust me, I've been through way worse."

"If you've been through way worse, I don't think we want to know about it," Melissa said.

"No, you don't." He laughed and with that, they decided to go sit underneath a tree on a small piece of lawn and have an impromptu picnic. They grabbed a watermelon, a two liter of Mello Yello, saltines and a block of cheese. The cheap, plastic knife couldn't cut fast enough and the three eagerly ate, talked, and connected even deeper.

When the meal was done, there was nothing left but watermelon rind. Whistle felt better and they all got up, cleaned up, and got back in the jeep and continued their adventure. They blasted through Palm Springs and hit Route 60. Forty-five minutes later, they swung onto Route 91 and Whistle was still awake. That was amazing to him because he was feeling tired as hell.

In Anaheim, they got a super cheap motel room. That night, they went across the street to the Glass Eyeball and tried an appetizer of cactus followed by fish tacos that were excellent. A few beers finished with one shot of Canadian Club and they decided to head back to the room.

After a decent night's sleep, they grabbed another free continental breakfast that included nothing more than coffee, cheap orange juice, mini boxes of Cheerios and Fruit Loops with two percent milk. More than a few boxes of cereal went along with the three musketeers as they checked out and left Anaheim. Before long, in just under an hour's time to be precise, they made their way to Redondo Beach. Getting lost for a while, they decided to grab lunch at a BBQ place called "Freak." It was good, but not great. After that, they drove around for another half hour before they eventually found the beach house.

The situation could not have been more perfect. All getting out, they walked up to a sign that read "Western Wonder" and boy, did it ever live up to its name. The front door was glass that looked straight through the great room and showed huge sliding doors that let in the perfect amount of light, which shone on a highly polished Brazilian cherry floor. Golds, yellows, and reds glinted off the tips of the Pacific waves. A quick flash of monarch shot through Whistle's mind as Melissa opened the door. It was beyond awesome for all three.

They walked in and stood before the western sky pouring in. The foyer was huge, with a twenty-five foot-high cathedral ceiling.

"Holy shit!" Melissa said giggling.

"Holy shit is right," Orrin said, stepping forward. The newlyweds couldn't believe how incredible the Western Wonder was. Whistle felt horrible for being there and told them he had to leave.

"Fuck no! You're part of the family now," they said, grabbing him.

"Ow!" Whistle let out involuntarily, still plenty sore from the body shots he took in the bar fight.

"Sorry! Sorry!" they both said, immediately letting go of him. "Let's check this place out."

"I'm just going to sit down for a minute," Whistle said as he made his way to a massive couch that sported a couple of afghans and plenty of pillows. It was set facing a giant gas fireplace backed up by glass, ocean, and western illumination. He burrowed in and just like that, he was asleep again. He slept solidly the whole night as the crazy kids explored the property.

Meeting on the roof deck, they christened Western Wonder. After all, they were on their honeymoon. When they were both satisfied, they made their way to the master bedroom and snuggled in. They held each other and drifted off in brand new marital bliss. Life for them couldn't get better and Whistle was well on his way to being fully healed.

The next day, they went down to their own private beach, swam, and lay out on lounge chairs. Alternating between sleeping, swimming, and talking, the three couldn't be happier. Somehow, Orrin popped out piña coladas and a huge plate of cold water western oysters on the half shell with tabasco sauce, lemon, and sea salt. It was beyond delicious.

Another piña colada and the three took another nap, went for another swim, and eventually headed back to the Western Wonder. Whistle took a shower while the newlyweds took advantage of the alone time and made love on the dining room table with strawberries, whipped cream, and a whole lot of creativity. Eventually, they all went to sleep for the night and didn't wake up until nine thirty in the a.m. the next day.

The sun was already pouring in through the front door when Whistle woke up. He had to use the bathroom and barely made it in time, limping the whole way. Sweating profusely, his stomach was feeling daggers and cramps. After he was done, he took a cold shower and lay out on the terracotta tile and let his body heat be drawn out literally into the floor. It felt so good that he couldn't move and almost fell asleep. Just before he did, he made his way back to the couch to be as out of the way as possible. He was dehydrated, and his blood sugar had plummeted. That's when his saviors swooped in again and gave him a giant glass of ice water, a Kit Kat, and a bag of potato chips. By the time he finished, he felt pretty much normal again.

"Thank you guys," he said.

"No worries," Melissa said.

The next three days, Whistle and the newlyweds swam, sunbathed, ate, drank, smoked and slept, enjoying beach life to its fullest. Whistle was pretty much fully mended and was really starting to feel like a third wheel. He knew it was time to move on and if he tried to say so face to face, they might talk him out of it again, so he decided to leave that night after the newlyweds went to sleep.

That night, he packed his things quietly, cleaned up, and wrote a note to the couple.

> Orrin and Melissa,
> Thank you guys for everything. I had a great time and truly appreciate all you've done. I'd love to stay, but you guys should enjoy your honeymoon the way it's meant to be enjoyed, alone together. I wish you guys the best, Here's to a happy life!
>
> Cheers,
> Whistle

They found the note in the morning when they woke up. They were both happy and sad at the same time. After a quick breakfast, they made their way down to the beach and, truth be told, did enjoy their alone time in a way that they couldn't when Whistle was there. Little did they know he was camped out about a mile down the beach, second guessing his decision to leave. But he'd already written the note, and he didn't want to go back in case they were actually relieved that he'd gotten a move on so they could have some privacy on their honeymoon.

After a long day of sunning and swimming himself, Whistle got up from his camp in the dunes and stepped out, shaking the sand out of his clothes, hair, and belongings and just gazed out at the ocean. The vastness of the Pacific was humbling. That's the moment Whistle realized his journey just changed from west to north. Deep purple sunk west as he crawled back into his spot. There he slept, excited about the promise of the next day.

In the morning, he took a swim, then laid out to warm up before he fueled himself with a small breakfast of warm apple juice and two honey nut granola bars. After that, he began his trek up the shoreline, wondering what was ahead of him.

CHAPTER
SIXTY-THREE
Billy Carter

C old sand and low, eastern sun quickly changed to high, midday sun and the beach quickly filled up with, well, beachgoers of all shapes, sizes, and degrees of suntan along with the Frisbees, umbrellas, beach towels and inflatable rafts they bring along with them for a fun day on the southern California sand. Whistle passed an irate toddler, a sexy twenty-something in a thong bikini, a sandcastle in progress and another that got bigfooted. The waves continued to lap the beach and Whistle continued to weave through the crowd, trying to stay on the hard, wet, part of the sand. Walk a mile or two through soft, deep, and dry sand, your calves will be screaming at you.

Just as dusk settled from its glowing gold and orange to strips of neon red across a purple sky, Whistle ducked into the scraggly brush where he'd made a quick camp. The night was rather simple. He was not particularly inspired to make a fire as he felt a little more on edge camping in such a coveted area of the country. He wanted to stay out of trouble and keep a low profile. Plus, the sound of the waves and the twinkling stars provided plenty of stunning company on their own.

The waves eventually whooshed Whistle to sleep and served as a soothing soundtrack to his watercolor dreams that night. The next morning, he woke up and moved on, finding a neighborhood just off the coast in the town of Manhattan Beach. Walking down Rocky Shore Lane, he decided it was time to stop and collect himself again.

Slinging his pack off, Whistle sat on the curb in front of 19 Rocky Shore Lane. Placing his elbows on his knees, he bowed his head. Closing his eyes, he slowly calmed himself. At peace, his heart rate slowed. The mini meditation session felt great, until the screech of tires ruined everything. Looking up, he saw a small boy cowering before a huge truck less than two feet away.

"Fuck!" Whistle gasped as he jumped up and grabbed the boy.

"Fuck," the driver said at the same time, as he turned the wheel and drove away, just like that. No "Hey, you ok?" no nothing. Whistle tried to catch the license plate number, but it was out of eyesight before he even had a chance to set the kid down.

"You okay, kiddo?" Whistle asked the boy in as jovial and non-panicked a manner as he could muster.

"Yeah...I think," the boy said as he gave his own arms, legs, and torso a quick once over.

"What's your name?"

"Billy Carter."

"How old are you?"

"Nine."

"Dang, son. You nearly topped out before you even hit double digits."

"Huh?" Billy looked up, confused.

"Nothing, I was just saying that you almost...never mind. You live around here?"

"Yeah. Right around the corner and down the road past the surf shop."

"Cool. How's your bike? Here, let me check it out."

Whistle gave the Huffy—not too different than the one he had many, many moons ago—a once-over. *Little kid dirt bikes don't change a whole heck of a lot through the years*, he thought to himself as he fixed the chain and made sure the wheels and handlebars were still tight and the bike was in a rideable state.

"Good for another thousand miles, pal," Whistle said, rolling the bike to the kid.

"Thanks, Mister."

"Whistle."

"Huh?...uh..." The kid looked kind of sideways at Whistle as he tried to, well, whistle.

"Ha ha! No man! My NAME is Whistle, Like Willie Whistle, the clown with the high voice, on the TV show?"

Now the kid really looked confused.

"Never mind. Go home and have your mom check you out, clean out any scrapes, and make sure you didn't break anything or hit your head."

"Ok, Mister Whistle!" the kid said as he rode off down the street.

Whistle realized he had some lollipops from one of the hotels in his pack and wished he'd remembered to give one to the boy. Then he thought about the kid explaining to his mom that he took candy from a guy named Mr. Whistle who was talking about clowns with high voices. Not a good scenario, not even in Flaky California.

CHAPTER
SIXTY-FOUR
Last Clip to Santa Monica

The next day was a dream with Whistle passed out on the beach in El Segundo. Two days later he ended up in Venice Beach and instantly knew it was a disgusting place to be. Unfortunately, he spent two months there till he got enough money together to move on. When he did, he left with a huge smile on his face, tan, well-rested, and financially set, by wandering drifter standards.

Feeling that Santa Monica couldn't be that far north, Whistle took his time walking up the coast to take it all in. After all, life is what you make it and you gotta make time to smell the roses, or the salt air in Whistle's case. Any experience passed up was an experience lost forever. Whenever he got tired, he just plopped down in the sand and rested.

Beach after beach, wave after wave, the days went by in a *Groundhog Day*-like manner. Whistle met plenty of characters along the way, but made it a point to not entangle himself with anyone and mostly kept to himself. He usually stayed between the coast and the PCH, unless he was forced to go more inland because of all the private shorefront property. Those people don't pay that kind of money to have vagabonds camping out in their backyard.

One more night spent under the western stars and it was time for Whistle to rejoin the real world. He didn't know what he was in for, and nothing could have prepared him. The next morning, Whistle woke up and took a brisk swim and ate a small breakfast to get him on his way. He walked the better part of the day until he saw, gleaming in the late afternoon sun, a sign that said, "Welcome to Santa Monica."

"Oh boy! Here we are!" He giggled to himself, knowing that Shortstop would have been very proud. The boy tapped the sign and moved forward. Walking into the city, the sun set over the ocean. It would most likely be another night before he made it to the pier, but he didn't mind. He found a scraggly bank to hide from passersby and went to sleep.

As the sun rose the next morning, Whistle sat up in the brush and stared at the ocean. The beach was mostly empty, save for a few surfers, joggers, bearded wanderers, and the beach patrol gently urging them to move along as the beach would be open in a few hours. Not wanting to draw the attention of the patrol himself, he gathered his things and got moving.

He walked north along the beach with his eyes focused on the place where the coastline and the horizon meet, hoping to spot that famous Santa Monica Ferris wheel. It got to where he wanted to get his mind off it after a while and decided to walk along the inland side of the highway for a change of scenery and easier walking on the pavement.

As dusk approached, Whistle found a wide road off the PCH and decided to head back down to the coast and soak in the sunset as the sky was particularly stunning this evening. He eventually found himself at the top of a steep hill that led down to the ocean and off to the right he noticed a BMX trail with berms, whoops, and tabletop jumps built in. He thought about the pictures he used to look at in all the bike magazines when he was a kid, with Greg Hill, Harry Leary, and Stu Thompson putting their custom rides through their paces and pulling cross-ups a mile high against the SoCal sky. He wished he had his Huffy with him.

He heard some seagulls caw and watched them fly against the glorious sunset, attending to seagull business. He stood taking it all in; the glowing sun barely peeking over the ocean in burnt orange, the stars glimmering against the rich purple sky above. The neighborhoods sprawled all along the coast, thousands of people getting home from work, school, shopping and socializing. Twinkling house, street, and car lights ran along the coast like a diamond divider between the water and the land. The air was a strange mix of sea salt and emissions from the cars meeting and swirling right at the meeting point where Whistle happened to be standing.

A house that caught his eye due to its perilous perch on a nearby cliff lit up all at once as a Porsche 944 pulled up and into the garage. He wondered what that person did for a living. Were they in show business? A lawyer, doctor, or

Indian chief? Businessman or a higher-up in some criminal enterprise? No way to know, but what Whistle did know was the guy had good taste in music and so did the surrounding neighbors as the home stereo was fired up with "In the Air Tonight." Whistle watched as the man stood on his deck, nursing a presumably good stiff drink and looking pensively out over the vast Pacific. Phil Collins gave way to Bob Seger singing about a boy who was too far from home. This boy wondered if he was too far from home...Then again, maybe home was not far off at all.

CHAPTER
SIXTY-FIVE
One More Night

This is when the next five years of his life began. Sun coming up from behind, the mystery of this new world was laid out before him. It was obvious the city had a lot to see and many stories to tell, but the thing that intrigued Whistle the most was the long pier stretching out into the ocean very far away, with its incredibly tall Ferris wheel.

"Oh man! I can't wait to see that," Whistle said, stepping forward. As the day passed, he left the main road and weaved his way deeper into the city. Buying an orange, a bottle of water, and a bag of pretzels, Whistle found a seat on a lovely wooden bench nestled comfortably under a large willow tree. In the cooling shade he enjoyed his lunch and took in the din of activity that surrounded him. Life was definitely not bad for the boy at the moment.

With a huge smile on his face, he actually said hello to two attractive women walking by. They smiled and said hello back as they moved on. He couldn't believe how good he felt and was more than ready to enjoy a slower life for a while.

With that, he threw his trash away and went back to the bench. Laying down, he fell asleep and the nap that found him was delicious. Sounds, smells, and breezes molded his dreams and they were wonderful. Not complicated and dark like so often before, they were light and enjoyable.

Probably without saying, it's obvious that if his dreams were happy they were threaded through with all the colors of the monarchs and plenty of sunshine. Immediately, he was seated in the very top seat of the Santa Monica Pier Ferris Wheel. All alone and stopped in his sparkled red Number Eleven car, he swung it forward and back as happy as could be.

The ocean and the sky were black, except for the massive top half of the deep orange sun that still showed above the water. This sent a channel of red lit water that came all the way to the end of the pier. It was truly magnificent and made him squint a bit. In his dreams, he closed his eyes. When he opened them again, the boy stood in front of a cotton candy machine with an extremely skinny man swirling him up a blue and purple stick. Knowing it would bother his stomach, he also knew that he couldn't resist the treat.

Suddenly, he found himself seated at a kitchen table as a child again. Northern New Hampshire's brisk morning sun poured in through the windows on his mother and him as they both sipped hot cocoa from their ivory mugs.

"When we're done, we'll go out to the garden and harvest what we can," she said, taking a sip of the steaming hot cocoa.

"Oh yeah, I can't wait to check out the radishes!" Whistle said with a final sip before he cleared the table and washed the mugs.

That's when he suddenly found himself back on the American Bear's shoulders singing his brains out. Everything was sweaty and smoky, loud and glorious. A large group of girls right in the middle of the Cat's Meow lifted their shirts to honor Whistle and Kenny as they led the crowd in a spirited, rousing sing-along as the sweat was stinging the boy's eyes.

Unfortunately, Whistle awoke to find what was stinging his eyes was the droppings of a seagull perched directly over his head in the willow tree above. He was in such a great mood, he laughed as he wiped his eyes with the sleeve of his shirt.

"Good shot, you son of a bitch!" Whistle yelled good-naturedly as the seagull flew away.

Waking up more, he looked around as the dusk settled in. Collecting his things, he started walking. Now he was wide awake and very excited. A block away, he came across Walt's Hot Dog Cart. Knowing money was getting low, the decision to splurge anyway was made. A dollar ninety-nine got him an all-beef hot dog in a steamed bun, topped with diced white onion, neon green relish, and yellow mustard with a slight sprinkle of the ol' celery salt. Devoured in four bites, that hot dog didn't stand half a chance.

He was more than happy he'd spent the money as his stomach was full and his taste buds satisfied. He decided to explore as it was early evening and the pavement started to cool, making walking a lot more pleasant. He weaved through the streets taking everything in, not interacting with anyone, just doing some recon and getting a feel for the place well into the early morning hours.

Eventually, he ran across a twenty-four hour diner where he used the bathroom and got a dollar cup of coffee. The heat and caffeine worked its way through him and he got a second wind. Finishing the cup of joe, he walked out, went around the corner, and found an overgrown lot where he laid down and caught a few hours of ZZZs using his pack as a pillow.

The sun came up, waking Whistle up as well. He sat up, got his mental bearings, and gave his pack a quick inventory check and an even quicker cash count of his now dwindling finances. Twenty-eight dollars to be exact.

Ok, let's see, he thought to himself. *I need to find a temporary camp and learn the lay of the land. Find a job and a place to shower, do laundry, and basically stay fed, hydrated, well rested, and reasonably clean.*

Happy with his to do list, he got up and on his way. Walking out to the street, he found two signs that let him know he was standing on the corner of Colorado Avenue and Lincoln, which ran parallel to the coast. Looking straight ahead, Colorado seemed to lead directly to the pier, so he went in that direction.

As he started down the sidewalk, he was very conscious of his surroundings. Taking mental pictures of street names, businesses, alleyways, even the people and the local lingo. Trying to remain invisible like back in Boston, he kept his eyes open, ears open, mind open, and mouth shut.

Walking on, he noted things like a pawn shop and gas station, which was usually a good place to wash up if options were minimal. He passed a convenience store, liquor store, cigar shop, and a swimsuit shop, which would be a great potential employer, he thought to himself. He noticed a barber shop right next to a wig shop. He chuffed to himself at the back alley deals on used hair swept up, bagged up, and shipped next door. He admired the hustle.

He found a dumpster next to Merv's Pastry to relieve himself behind. Just as he was finishing up, he heard a quick *whoop!* which could be none other than a police siren as the blue lights filled his vision in a flash. He turned around to see a police cruiser with a cop looking right at him and pointed down the road as if to say, "Move along before you wind up in jail for public urination and I have to fill out the stupid paperwork, which is almost as bad."

Whistle gave a quick salute of appreciation and jogged down Colorado Ave. until he didn't see the cop anymore. A few blocks from Merv's, at the corner of Fourth Street, was a laundromat, sandwich shop, Indian rug store and tattoo parlor. He was impressed with how eclectic the neighborhoods in Santa Monica were. Further on down Colorado, he came across the famous golden arches of McDonald's. Crossing the street, he entered and immediately was hit with the most comforting, familiar aroma of those cheeseburgers, fries, chicken nuggets, apple pie and coffee. It made him nostalgic, at ease, and oddly enough, homesick for a thousand different places all across the US.

Hungry as well as homesick, Whistle ordered two cheeseburgers, a medium fries, a Coke, and a vanilla shake for desert. Five dollars and eighty cents later, he took his lunch outside and sat at a picnic table to enjoy the sights and summerlike sea breeze. He couldn't believe how many pretty girls were out here, most of which seemed friendly but with their guard up to some degree. Whistle took this as a good reminder to do the same. Be friendly, but keep in mind that LA County is the wheeler dealer capital of the world. A whole different ballgame.

Finishing his meal at the golden arches, he strolled up to Ocean Ave. and found himself staring up at another arch. A brightly lit blue one with white lettering that promised sport fishing, amusements, and plenty of cafes. It was getting dark, and he noticed a park on the inland side of the street, so he decided to go check it out. After digging in just a bit, he decided that he'd wait one more night before going to the pier. The build-up was almost too much to handle, but he could manage a few more hours.

Finding a dark spot under some elaborate stone stairs, he climbed in. After getting comfortable, he settled for one more night. It was obvious to Whistle now why Shortstop led him here. He was the right man at the right place at the right time. To do what? I guess we'll find out soon enough.

CHAPTER SIXTY-SIX
Welcome to the Pier

Waking up the next morning, excitement buzzed through his entire body. After all, today was his big day. He would check out the pier and at least dip his toes in the Pacific Ocean. He packed up and walked out from under the steps as nonchalantly as possible. Out of that, he walked through the park with his head down. Once out, he crossed the street and made his way back to the McDonald's to use the facilities and take a quick sink bath. Too revved up to eat anything, he bought a coffee and walked back out.

Standing alongside Colorado Avenue, something twisted in his stomach, letting him know that once he stepped through that blue arch with its promises, he would enter a major new phase of his life. Both excited and nervous, Whistle Evel Fonzarelli Starr squared up and stepped. Just a short walk later, he slid under the arch of promises and did literally feel like his life just changed. Only a few steps later, he pulled off to the right and grabbed a railing. He needed a minute to gather himself.

Looking over a parking lot, then a beach, then the ocean, he breathed in deeply through his nose and out through his mouth. Oxygen in, carbon dioxide out, settling the boy down. Once he finally felt better, he continued on. That's when all his senses suddenly popped alive all at once. Sight, sound, taste, smell, and touch were all acute. Whistle also knew that there was another sense that he couldn't quite place. Maybe it was just plain instinct or maybe it was intuition. He didn't know, but what he did know was that it definitely gave him a level of confidence that he hadn't known up to this point in his life. It was especially strange in a brand new situation like this.

Details registered in rapid fashion. The Bubba Gump Shrimp Company was in full hustle bustle mode to his right, and a family was laughing and enjoying the day as a young boy held a cherry red balloon, jerking its white string so the balloon bounced up and down as the young boy walked along to Whistle's left. Directly in front of him was Pier Burger with its bright orange neon sign boasting that it was the last place to get a burger on western land. He saw a sign for the Bay Aquarium and figured he would check it out soon enough; right now he had other more pressing matters to attend to.

Walking left, to the middle of a very wide pier was a gorgeously enticing sign lit by blinking carnival bulbs. Gold words were surrounded by reds, greens, and blues. This enticing sign read, "Playland Arcade" and boasted over two hundred games. Whistle smiled, knowing he would get to know the arcade very well. Literally twenty feet later, he entered "Pacific Park Amusements." To his left was the "Looff Hippodrome Carousel." He decided to pass for now.

As he continued on, he saw the famous yellow roller coaster and just beyond that, he admired the red and yellow cars of the Ferris wheel that loomed high above. The walk proved to be eye opening and still somehow nostalgic. Like being in your own house, but in a different country where they speak a different language. Or like your run of the mill dream, either way. He was right where he wanted to be.

"Sorry buddy, wanna go again?" Whistle heard a carney say to a guy trying to win a prize for his girlfriend at a shell game. There were two muscular guys with handlebar mustaches and one piece old style bathing suits in red and blue stripes. Definitely dressing for effect. He was drawn further along the pier by his nose, however. The intoxicating swirl of ocean air, French fries, doughboys, and cotton candy ran trails of sweet and salty that hooked the boy and reeled him in like a cartoon fish.

"You want your hair braided?" asked a small black woman in a tent chock full of jewelry, knickknacks, and paddy whacks from the islands.

Whistle said, "Nah, thanks," with a chuckle and a wave, which she returned with a giant, gap-toothed smile a mile wide that in a way reminded him of Shortstop. He didn't want to stop to ask if she had any relation to the Nipple clan.

Some other notable attractions were women playing accordions in Stevie Nicks style scarves and lace. Within earshot was a man loudly proclaiming the benefits of solar energy and wind turbines to someone who believed they were nothing but a money grab and did more harm than good. All that talk held no interest to Whistle at the moment, so he continued on past to a guy at a cart cooking sausage and peppers. The aroma was heavenly but Whistle resisted as his funds were too low to splurge on such luxuries as a sausage and pepper sandwich from a cart.

Whistle noticed the same grimy underbelly of the pier as he remembered back at the fair in New Hampshire when he rode the Rock and Roll with a pocket full of money and a first taste of freedom. A young couple sat making out on a bench as a disheveled boozer slept off a drunk night on the next bench over. Tiny little side alleyways contained shady figures and the thick, sweet, seductive fog of California grass escaping into the straight world and mixing with the thick, sweet, innocent scent of cinnamon rolls. KLOS was broadcasting from the pier that night and they were playing Talking Heads through the PA system asking the age old question, "How did I get here?" They weren't the only ones wondering.

Maybe it was a little bit of paranoia brought on by the contact high from walking through a few ganja clouds, but he had a feeling that someone was going to give him trouble. No one in particular was on his radar. It was just an overall sense of all the people, as if everyone had their guard up and game face on. Even the ocean seemed like it was part of a movie set, in a weird way. The salt air was light and there was the scent of jasmine in the air as well. *The Atlantic felt more like the real thing*, he thought to himself, *more salty.*

After reaching the thinner pier at the end of Pacific Park, Whistle continued on as it reached even further out into the water. He passed a svelte, long legged woman walking three adult English mastiffs. He figured she could be a professional dog walker with the amount of control she had over these massive hounds. He passed carts and tents full of everything you could imagine that you could want to buy. He moved along toward another structure surrounded by the ocean. A long haired man played "Pinball Wizard," albeit a little out of tune due to the elements as three younger short haired frat boys played hacky sack.

Coming up on the Mariasol, Whistle walked around the revered local restaurant to continue to the end of the pier. There was a large cluster of people standing there, all smiling and taking pictures. He took a seat and waited till the crowd thinned out a bit as he watched and wondered how many people came to this very spot on the map to celebrate, contemplate, excavate and evaluate their lives. The furthest point west of the famous Route 66.

"Am I really here?" he quietly asked no one in particular.

Yes you are, he heard a voice within his heart answer.

With no one to share the experience with, Whistle just stood and grabbed the pole of the sign, realizing he needed to make this journey as a lone wolf. Maybe someday he'd find someone to share his life with, but up to this point, it didn't feel right and wasn't practical. Traveling light was the only way to fly.

Looking back towards land, he gazed at the Ferris wheel and all the people enjoying themselves and then out to the ocean, nothing but the odd boat traveling north or south across the horizon line. Soft, rolling waves gently kissed the pink sand of the beach.

A bachelor party of seemingly well-to-do preppy blond guys stumbled by and gave Whistle a half empty bottle of champagne—"Cheers!"—with their plastic cups full of the other half. Whistle said thanks and nodded back in acknowledgement and went back to staring out into his own world. When they reached the end of the pier, being fairly drunk and rowdy though it was still early evening, these guys couldn't help but start horsing around and climbing up on the railing, nearly falling in a couple of times. Whistle watched, somewhat amused, as he took a few hefty swigs of the bubbly.

"Hey bro!" one of them yelled to Whistle.

"Yeah?" he replied.

"Can you come take our picture over here?"

"Sure, hang on," Whistle said as he got up, a little unsteady on his feet although he didn't think he'd drank that much. He chalked it up to an empty stomach.

When he reached the party, one of them drunkenly tried to show him how to use the camera.

"I got it, I used to have one of these," Whistle lied, figuring he'd figure it out easier on his own.

"Ok, ready?" Whistle asked as one half sat on the railing behind the rest.

"Dare me to jump in?" another chirped.

"Dude you'll get tore up if you land in between the waves, it's all rocks down there," one of the more sensible ones scolded him.

"I'll give you a thousand bucks right now!" another offered.

"Really?"

"Really!"

"Both of you, shut the fuck up!" the sensible one, now getting irritated, shouted as the rest of them laughed.

Whistle laughed too as he walked over and checked out what all the fuss was about. The water was pretty shallow in between waves, but if one were to catch the timing of the wave, it would be deep enough to provide a smooth landing. Though for some reason his depth perception was off. Again, he chalked it up to hunger, though he was feeling buzzed, but different somehow.

"I'll fuckin' do it," he heard himself say.

"What?" one of them asked as the rest immediately stopped and turned like that old E.F. Hutton commercial.

"Thousand bucks? Let me see it," Whistle said as he wobbled a bit.

"Oh SHIT!" they all said pretty much in unison as they frantically dug through their pockets, laughing with glee.

A thousand dollars was nothing to these guys and Whistle was, at this point in his life, a drifter whose life would be dramatically turned around with that kind of money. He noticed that all the lights had been turned on all along the pier and it was beyond glorious!

As he turned back to see how the ponying up was going, the lights had trails…"Uh, what's going on?" he said to himself, but loud enough for the guys standing around him to answer.

"Count it, one thousand," the most obnoxious one said as he slapped the money in Whistle's hand.

Whistle for some reason couldn't focus his eyes enough to count, so he handed it back saying," I believe you."

One of the preppy boys said, "That dude must be tripping balls right now!"

Whistle gave a slight glance around for lifeguards or cops as there were several postings prohibiting diving from the pier. Disregarding the signs, he climbed up onto the end railing and stared out at the vast sea. As he watched the waves, he knew that timing his jump just right was paramount. If he misjudged, well, it wouldn't be the ideal outcome.

He realized he would have to jump while the water was the shallowest as that would time the impact with the next wave coming in. He knew it was a brainless, risky thing to do. I mean, you travel across the country to ride on a Ferris wheel based on a friend telling you to do so in a dream, you make it there overcoming vast obstacles, just to play Russian roulette with the ocean for a grand.

If you're still along for this adventure, you could probably guess that Whistle screamed toward the sand as the saltwater rushed up. A wave grabbed him and saved his life as well as directly sucked him out to the open sea. No breath came to him for well over a minute. Then he hit his head against something hard. This woke the boy up and he swam to the top. Breaking the water, Whistle gasped for air. Figuring out that he smacked his head on a small outcrop of rock, he climbed up.

Hands, body, and face ended up shredded by sharp stone and unforgiving barnacles. Once on top, Whistle laid on his back and paused. His blood flowed freely on the rocks. He looked back to the pier, seemingly miles away, his new white tuxedoed friends long gone along with their thousand dollars. He tried to make sense of what just happened as he made sure not to fall off the rocks as the waves would surely take him out to sea.

CHAPTER
SIXTY-SEVEN
The Rock and the Seagull

The night passed and Whistle woke up to saltwater mist spraying across his face. High tide had substantially shrunk his real estate. Knowing that he had to wait for low tide, Whistle closed his eyes again. Two hours passed when he felt a rather large thump square on his chest.

"What the fuck!" Whistle exclaimed.

"What the fuck is right. Why are we out here on Retardo Rock while everyone else is having sex and doing cocaine!" A huge seagull squawked.

"Get off me! Who are you?" Whistle demanded, not sure of his own mental status. He felt like he was inside a dream bubble within real life; any reality was subject to change at a moment's notice.

"My name is Milo and I'm here to help you."

"Help me with what?"

"Where do I start? Oh I know, Retardo Rock! Which your dumb ass is currently shipwrecked on. We need to get you back to shore."

"I can swim it, I'll be fine," Whistle said with a wave.

"It'll be a lot easier with me helping out, pal. I know the ropes out here."

"Well…can we wait till sunrise?" Whistle asked, stretching his sore back.

"I suppose," Milo said as he sat at Whistle's feet, looking around with those wise old eyes as Whistle fell back asleep, confident in his night watchman's abilities.

The next morning, Whistle felt sharp, painful jabs in his ribs, in rapid succession. He jumped up and almost fell off the rocks.

"What the FUCK!" Whistle screamed.

"Let's GO! I got shit to do," Milo squawked as he picked at some bugs in his feathers.

"Peck me like that again, I'll smash you!" Whistle grunted, now doubled over, holding his ribs.

"Yeah. Careful you don't smash yourself, Gilligan. Get your shit together. You swim, I'll navigate."

"Fuck you," Whistle said as he gingerly lowered himself down some slick, sharp, seaweed covered rocks into the freezing southern California water.

"I'd tell you to go fuck yourself but you've already done a stellar job of that," Milo replied as he hopped on Whistle's shoulder, giving him a few love taps in the skull with his beak.

Whistle dove under the water and Milo was off his back. The salt water felt instantly healing as it stung all the nicks, cuts, and scrapes Whistle suffered through the whole aquatic misadventure. He dove deep and swam as hard as he could for as long as he could and when he finally came up for air, he was immediately bowled over by a ferocious wave. Scrambling to the surface again, he got a mouthful of saltwater and was able to spit it out and keep going. Milo flew down and dug his sharp claws into his shoulder, almost enough to break the skin.

"Easy!" Whistle yelled.

"Wave!" Milo yelled and flew up as Whistle dove under as the wave rolled over him. Swimming to the surface again, Milo landed on Whistle's shoulder again.

"Not bad for a landlubber. Go right," Milo directed.

Whistle was confident that Milo knew how to get him back, had his back, and was still on his back; the claws in his shoulder were all too evident as he swam with all his strength, trying to focus on Milo's directions through the thundering wash all around him.

"Right! Left! Hold! Wave!" the bird squawked over the crashing waves as Whistle kept his head down, arms reaching and pulling while manically kicking his legs.

"Come on! You swim like old people fuck!" Milo cackled as Whistle was slowing down involuntarily. He was spent.

"I didn't know birds watched movies," Whistle gasped as he floated on his back momentarily to regain his breath.

"You never heard of the drive-in? There's one around here that has the best French fries on the West Coast. Good and salty."

"Sounds delicious," Whistle said sarcastically, having been force fed salty waves for hours.

"Come on, it's not too much further," Milo cawed as Whistle flipped over and resumed his freestyle toward the beach. He was just about out of gas again when he let his feet float downward and land with a muted thump against the sand. Finally! He could walk the rest of the way!

"We made it!" Whistle shouted with joy.

"I know! I didn't think you had it in you. You seem kind of soft," the bird wisecracked.

"Fuck you, Milo...and thank you," Whistle said as he climbed up out of the water and collapsed on the hard, wet sand. He'd never been so happy to see dry land.

"Don't mention it. Just do me a favor. Whenever you're down this way, pick up a bag of fries from the burger stand on the pier for me. I'll find you."

And with that, Milo flew off down the beach and hooked a right out over the grand Pacific. Whistle found a spot underneath the pier out of reach of high tide, but well within the reach of mites and pier spiders, which feasted on his exhausted body as he fell asleep despite the mild bites and stings.

CHAPTER
SIXTY-EIGHT
Tongva Park

The next morning came and Whistle couldn't get in the saltwater fast enough. Cuts, bites, scrapes and stings were overwhelming. The cold and the salt were just what the doctor ordered. He shivered with relief as the tide gently pushed and pulled him in and out with the waves. A big one came along and sucked him down and spat him back out almost on the shore.

"You okay?" a woman with the smallest black bikini asked.

"Yes I am," he replied as he was swished back out with the tide. "Thanks for asking."

"You're welcome. You just kind of look horrible," she said, taking off her sunglasses.

"I get that a lot." Whistle laughed as he dunked his head back to slick his hair back.

"Okay...You're weird, even for this place." She smiled as she turned to walk back up to the beach.

"Yes I am," Whistle shouted to her, still sitting in the sand and splashing around.

He thought about the swim from the rocks as he stared at them across the pier. He wondered if any of it was real. He had a feeling he had been dosed by those guys in the white tuxes. The talking seagull would make him lean toward that conclusion. But then, how could he have ended up here? Everything that occurred over the last day or two was a big banged up blur and he was getting a headache trying to make sense of it. He filed it away for now and got back to what was happening in the present.

After soaking for a good long while, he finally got up and started walking along the beach as he dried in the sun. After a few miles, he stood in front of a forest green sign that announced that he was entering Tongva Park. It took a while for Whistle to get his bearings. His main goal right now was to find the stone steps where he had his camp and be reunited with his belongings.

Before he knew it, dusk splayed monarch colors across the park. Just as he was about to give up, at least for the night, he turned a corner and there at the stairs he found himself. It was certainly a stroke of incredible luck that all his belongings were present and intact. As he climbed into his little fort, he devoured a package of peanut butter crackers, two strawberry pop tarts, and a warm bottle of water, which tasted like liquefied diamonds compared to saltwater.

After wiping his face, he drank another water, ate a package of cherry fruit snacks, a Hostess cupcake, an aspirin and a multivitamin. He lay down, full, satisfied, and exhausted. Night fell and he went from deep thoughts to deep sleep.

The next day, an amazing thing happened. Whistle collected his belongings and wandered the park. The amount of nooks and crannies was astounding. He was lost, but knew he would find his spot. Sure enough, Whistle's spot ended up being in the very center of the park. There was a pavilion in the center that had everything from local bands to Alanis Morisette and the Dave Matthews Band.

This particular night, it was A Flock of Seagulls and a good chunk of the crowd were reliving high school as the haunting yet hopeful guitar lines of Paul Reynolds shot shiny lasers of sound across the park and the water. It was the sound of better times. Music now, that Whistle caught on the radio here and there, seemed too whiny and introspective. Almost made you feel like you were drinking hot tea by a misty window on a rainy day...in a flannel. Songs like "I Ran" and "Space Age Love Song" sounded like the sunniest summer Saturday at the beach. Skateboards, BMXing in the skate park in checkerboard Vans and Op jams. Tons of wholesome cute girls watching excitedly as you defied gravity, launching your chrome and blue Mongoose Supergoose into the equally chrome and blue early summer sky full of youthful optimism. ...*Times change indeed*, Whistle thought as he looked around at the crowd. All in earth tones, goatees, and Doc Martens. He wondered how many of them still had their bikes.

One ray of hope that shone through on this day was Whistle finding a nice little nook for himself in the park. As the strains of "Wishing" echoed through the hills, he stumbled across an abandoned utility hut that had long since been forgotten about, with brush, weeds, and poison ivy basically concealing it from view. Not to mention it sat at the highest point in the park.

It was perfect. Whistle smashed the old, rusty padlock with a jagged rock and opened the door to air it out and give any bugs and critters a chance to make themselves a getaway as he banged around and made as much noise as possible to scare them off.

Bands played below night after night and Whistle turned his hideout into a home as the days passed. He even gave it a name, "High Camp." Plates, glasses, silverware, paper towels, pasta and beef broth were brought in. On a particular night, Reo Speedwagon sang about rolling with the changes, a subject Whistle knew as well as anyone, as he stirred up a pan of fiddleheads, onions, white potatoes, carrots, and ginger. He felt at home for the first time in a long time. No one had any idea he even existed, yet he felt like a king, sitting up in "High Camp" listening to Bob Seger, Pat Benatar, and a whole host of other artists throughout the season.

Whistle knew that stumbling on a home base like this was a tremendous stroke of luck and he couldn't think of any better place to be than where he was. He stayed there the entire year, then the next and the next as well. During that time, he worked a few odd jobs on and around the pier. He counted prize tickets at the Playland Arcade until he was caught in a compromising position in the storage room with the manager's girlfriend. He also worked as a mime for an afternoon, but after making three dollars and fourteen cents, he decided it wasn't his niche.

Working at a carwash was followed by a stint at a record store, where he had a hard time learning the system. The constant frustration was wearing on him as he spent his free time at Tongva Park and the pier. The park was quiet and safe where the pier was noisy and dangerous. Whistle loved both. He not only wanted, but needed to feel everything. All that life had to offer right now in SoCal. All the contradictions and schizophrenia that it's famous for.

Jobs came and went. He sold cheap coins that said "Last Stop Route 66." His stint as the official Looff Carousel operator went well for a good spell. That was until he landed the most coveted job at the pier, first mate on the most prestigious fishing boat in the area, the *Alexandra*.

Three trips in, Whistle and Captain Dave were getting along great. A week at sea and a week on land worked out well for Whistle. Fish hard, get paid really well, and spend it all before it was time to set sail again. The cycle continued for Whistle. His hair was long and his beard was full. Tanned and enjoying the West Coast life, he had it made. He knew everyone in the park and knew how to get what he needed to get by, including where to get water, food, and anything else.

When he wanted to experience life on the wild side, he hung out under the pier. Tourists walked above and the dregs of SoCal society slid around under the boardwalk, and that's where Whistle spent a lot of his free time and hard earned money.

"Here we go," Whistle said to himself as he boarded the *Alexandra* early one morning. Captain Dave was loading ice and smiled at Whistle.

"Get ready for a good haul, word is Catalina's been a gold mine the past few days."

"That's just what I was hoping to hear, Captain Dave."

Two days passed and the fish were on! After a massive catch, the boys went back and sold their bounty. That night Whistle had a fat wallet and a hollow leg, drinking hard and feeling his oats. Wandering around Big Dean's in a whiskey blur, he found himself face to face with Captain Dave's wife in the back hallway. She was pretty, flirty, and at least as drunk as Whistle and before he knew it, she pulled him by the lapels of his jean jacket and pushed him through the back exit doors and that's when things got instantly complicated. He was too drunk, too horny and, truth be told, too selfish to resist. Had she caught him three or four shots or four or five beers earlier, things might have turned out differently. But as it stood now, Whistle had committed adultery with his boss's wife and there was no way he was going to be able to undo the damage he just did.

Guilt ridden, drunk, scared and confused, Whistle suggested she go in first and he'd go in a different door in a few minutes. Captain Dave's wife walked in the back door and Whistle went around front and waited a good ten minutes before going back in.

Out on the water with Captain Dave, whenever the subject of girl-friends, wives, or families came up, Dave seemed to bristle and want to change the subject and Whistle noticed her acting really friendly around the bar whenever she had a few drinks, but some women are just that way and, to be honest, Whistle usually had his mind on other things, like partying.

Whistle collected himself and tried his best to go back in and not betray the guilt he was feeling, pay his tab, and get out quick. He could reassess the situation in the morning. He walked in and as he rounded the bar, he could plainly see that Captain Dave was upset and his wife was nowhere to be found. Did she tell him? She sure liked to push his buttons when she was drunk. Did he know somehow? Did someone see them? Whistle wasn't sure but when he caught Dave's eye, the captain shot him a look that said, "If you value your life, get the fuck out of here and never let me see you again, you ungrateful piece of shit."

Some looks cut straight through the fog of a whiskey drunk and this was one of them. He hurriedly paid his tab at the other side of the bar and scurried out of there like the little rat he felt like.

Stumbling back to High Camp that night, he couldn't believe he had been living there for five years. He realized it was fortunate to find a rent free hideaway in a beautiful park with free concerts in the summer—Jackson Browne tonight—and it was within walking distance to his personal Mecca, the world famous Santa Monica Pier. It was the perfect situation that he couldn't help but sabotage. Maybe he was just born to lose. Or maybe he was born to run, a permanent case of the travelin' jones, and he knew he wouldn't leave this situation unless he had no choice. He lit the roach of a joint he had in his cigarette pack and sat on his favorite rock as one of SoCal's favorite sons serenaded the crowd and his crew with "The Load Out."

CHAPTER SIXTY-NINE
One Final Night Under the Pier

"Hey! What's up, buddy?" Whistle asked Forward Jim, a friend of his who was a skinny, socially awkward fellow who got his nickname due to a habit of being a close talker, and he liked to talk.

"Hey, did you fuck Captain Dave's wife?" he asked, nose to nose as usual.

"Yeah," Whistle answered, figuring the cat was out of the bag.

Moving away from Forward Jim, he moved deeper under the pier where he ran into Mary, a sweet old bag lady who collected cans like Shortstop.

"Whistle!" she said as she shuffled her bottles and cans out of the way to give him a hug.

"Mary, here," Whistle said as he slipped her a tenner.

"Thanks, honey bunch!" She replied as she stuffed it in a coin purse she kept on her belt.

Deeper underneath the pier was where the serious business took place. Most people from the straight world never made it past the one-two punch of a manic close talker and a bag lady with her heaps of cans, bottles, and general disarray. A black man named Axel Proper slunk around the pylons and acted as the resident salesman to the desperate.

"Yo Playboy, what's good?" he asked Whistle as he ducked around Mary's wares.

"Not much. I'm gonna be getting out of town for a while, just wanted to swing down and see you derelicts before I skipped out."

"You need some fishing gear?" Axel asked in code. Fishing gear meant guns and ammo.

"Nah, I'm good."

"You ain't gonna be good if the captain runs up on yo' ass."

"Good news travels fast," Whistle muttered, nodding towards Forward Jim.

"Got us our own Walter Cronkite up in this piece," Axel drawled as he took a drag of his cigarette.

"No kiddin'," Whistle said as he turned towards the Pearson twins, who came over to harass him.

"Hey Fuckface," they said in unison.

"Hey, it's the Ginger Twins. Circus let out early?" Whistle wisecracked.

"Fuck Off," they replied...in unison again.

"Nice language. You blow each other with those mouths?"

Not up for the linguistic jousting, the Pearson twins moved on to bother Mary, who promptly cracked one in the ribs with her cane.

Whistle walked deeper under the pier. He had never ventured past Axel and he was always curious what was going on in there. He never asked and he had to know before he left town.

Surrounded by rocks was a heavy oak door with huge black hinges and an old heavy knocker. Unable to comprehend what this door was doing here, Whistle thought it could only lead to a hideout dug in between the rocks. He knocked and nervously waited.

After a considerable pause, the door cracked open and a small sliver of light lit the sand and the timbers of the pier above. The next thing Whistle noticed was the familiar yet still exotic scent of high quality herb.

"Get in here, boy," a voice said as a strong arm grabbed him and pulled him in. Before he knew it, the door was closed and he had a rum and Coke in his hand.

"This is fucked up," Whistle said as a purple-haired naked woman placed a huge joint in his mouth.

"This is really...oh, thanks," he said as the girl passed him a joint of that high quality herb.

"Someone is very interested in meeting you."

"Me?" Whistle asked as he threw back his drink and took another hit from the joint.

"Yes, Mr. Starr," That's when everyone left the room and the lights dimmed down only to reveal one more door clicking open.

"Holy shit!" Whistle said, stepping cautiously.

"Go on in," the sexy, purple-haired woman said as she handed him another drink.

"Okay," the boy said as he stepped into one more room. This room had every luxury possible and before he even had a chance to decline, a tab of acid was placed on his tongue and a bump of coke was up each nostril.

"Sit down," a curvy blonde said, then disappeared. A fresh rum and Coke in hand, Whistle took one more hit of the joint and snuffed it in his palm.

"Who are you?" Whistle said to the figure he could barely make out in the dim light.

"I'm about to become your best friend," a short, gray-haired man said, moving forward.

"What do you want with me?" The coke was starting to tingle.

"My name is Darringer Phillips and I want to talk to you."

"Okay," Whistle said as his vision got blurry. He looked around and noticed that everything was well kept and looked expensive.

"So what do you want from me?" Whistle slurred.

"I want to know if you had an affair with Captain Dave's wife."

"It lasted all of five minutes, but yes, I suppose I did."

"You are in a heck of a situation, my friend."

"I'm well aware that my charm has worn thin around here, I'll be leaving tomorrow."

"Heh heh! Boy if you wait till tomorrow, you might not be able to leave. Everybody in town wants your head on a stick," Derringer said with a muted chuckle.

"I know. Let me just land for a minute, I got a little buzzed but I'll be fine in a minute. Man, it's nice in here! I think sultry would be the right word."

"Yes, sultry would describe it. Have a seat, tell me a little about yourself."

For the next several hours, Whistle sat and told his life story to Derringer as he sat there and listened like a priest hearing confession.

"Quite an adventure, my friend," Derringer said when Whistle got to the present day in his recounting. "But it's late, I'm tired, and you need to be a ways up the coast by sunrise."

"Yeah, I'm out. Thanks for listening." Whistle said as he got up, stretched, and grabbed his ever trusty duffel bag that's been his one constant companion all these miles and all these years.

"Stay out of trouble, but if you do get in trouble, make sure it's for the right reasons."

"I, uh....huh?" Whistle replied, confused. Derringer just waved him off, leaned back, and closed his eyes, letting Whistle know this conversation was over.

"Alright, then," Whistle said as he let himself out.

A quick, "See ya round," to the stragglers still hanging out under the pier at this late hour, and Whistle was headed north. By sunrise, he had about five miles behind him. The coke and acid were wearing off and Whistle climbed behind a small shed to crash out for a bit. Crash he definitely did and when he woke up, he found himself in the company of two of Santa Monica's finest. Turns out he was on private property and had a few illegal items on him. The fact that he was still riding out the acid didn't help matters, so the cops had no choice but to haul him in.

Whistle spent five days in the slammer and was finally let go as the cops were sick of listening to him make loud yet futile attempts at legally representing himself. Five days of "Why am I in here!?" will wear on anybody.

"Alright, get out." A guard came and unlocked his cell.

"Well THANK you!" Whistle said, exasperated.

"Get out of town and stay gone. We haul you in again, it's a trip downtown to County and you can yip yap to the boys in gen pop. They'll love you, sweet tits."

Whistle didn't appreciate the less than dignified way in which he was spoken to, but instead of making an issue of it, he signed out his bag and got out of Dodge.

Feeling like his stint in jail was actually a much needed reset, he felt eager to put as much distance between Santa Monica and himself. He eventually ended up in Anchor Bay, where he grabbed a cheap motel room for a couple of nights. He remained a ghost till he finally moved on.

The next stop Whistle reached was the border of the Sinkyone Wilderness area. There he got a job collecting campsite trash for minimum wage and free lodging in Cabin Four. It was out of the way and everything Whistle needed. A roof over his head, a decent little general store on the campsite, keeping him in essentials for the duration of his stay, and a steady stream of company as plenty of campers kept the site filled year round. After about a year, he ran into an old "friend" that he spent some time with when he first got there. When she greeted him with "You're still here?" he remembered telling her he was just passing through, and he didn't want to be a semi-permanent fixture like he had become down by the pier. The grass was growing beneath his feet and he didn't like the feeling. A week later, Whistle got his last check, cashed it at the general store, and bid adieu to Sinkyone Wilderness Campground.

CHAPTER SEVENTY
Strickford and Paul Lead to Eureka

The next stop on Whistle's adventurous trek up the wild West Coast brought him to the town of Leggett. There he spent the next year learning everything he could about living off the land. Whistle hunted, fished, and helped a farmer with his garden. At Old Man Grayson's Farm, he also dispatched Cornish game hens, milked cows, shoveled manure, and plucked root vegetables. He had a short but enjoyable time dating the farmer's daughter, but when she started hinting around about marriage, he could see where things were heading, so he headed out to the open road once more.

Saying his goodbyes and making his way north once more, he covered what seemed like ten million miles before he decided to duck into Humboldt Redwood State Park. There he wandered for a few days marveling at the natural wonders. In the middle of nowhere, Whistle found the tallest tree he'd ever seen. It had to be at least two hundred and fifty feet tall with enough girth to carve out a condo tree house if one had the tools and inclination.

Whistle had neither, but he named the tree "Paul Bunyan" and began to climb. The higher he got, the less sure he felt about his decision. One hundred feet became one hundred and fifty, then two hundred. Almost to the top, Whistle found a perfect sized nook in the crook of a massive limb. It was around the size of an extra wide wheelbarrow and just deep enough for Whistle to nestle in and not roll out if he fell asleep, which he eventually did.

He slept till sundown as a sweeping wind and a startling caw made him almost jump out of his makeshift bunk, a long way from the forest floor.

"What the—?!" he said as he sat up and frantically looked around to see what all the commotion was. At the end of the branch he spotted a bald eagle's nest, complete with a bald eagle feeding its young. The eagle was eyeballing him and Whistle's instinct told him to stand, no easy feat on a limb way up in the air, but the edges of his nook provided good footing. The eagle stood up as well and the two stared at each other for what was probably around ten minutes. Whistle then decided to take a step forward. The eagle matched him with a step of its own and puffed its feathers. They both stood frozen, waiting for the other to make a move. After a long enough showdown, both decided to back off and give each other their space and mind their own beeswax. They both fell asleep with one eye open, as they both got used to their new domestic situation.

The next morning, they both woke up and couldn't help but continue their staring contest. After about an hour or so, the eagle got up and walked over to Whistle.

"What's your problem?" the eagle asked Whistle. Was it asked in English? Birdspeak? Telepathy? Kind of hard to distinguish when you don't communicate with other humans much, barely eat enough to stave off starvation, and have taken enough acid in your life to be thrown a flashback here and there. Regardless, he answered.

"I don't have a problem. Did you just talk to me or am I tripping?"

"Yes," the eagle answered, more smartass than cryptic.

"Well that clears that up. I'm Whistle, by the way."

"I'm Strickford...and my wife is Mary. We have two chicks named Thunder and Willow."

Just like that, the rest of the clan stood up in the nest and ruffled their feathers in a semi-friendly manner. Sort of, "We're here, we were here first, and if you fuck with us, it's a long way down."

"Duly noted," Whistle said as he nodded and sat down in his bunk and Strickford flew off to grab some breakfast for the rest of the clan, who sat back down in the nest and stared at Whistle until he fell asleep. He woke up to Strickford pecking him on the shoulder and dropping a beak full of worms, insects, and mucus drenched vegetation.

"Time for breakfast," the eagle said as he swooped out of the nest to feed the rest of the family.

"You guys really eat this stuff?" Whistle asked, more shocked at how gross a mess it was than ungrateful for the gesture.

"I don't see any five star restaurants around here," Strickford said dryly as Mary and the chicks cackled.

"I appreciate it you guys, but I'm good. I have a few Slim Jims and Fruit Roll-Ups. You ever try one of these?" Whistle broke off a piece of his Fruit Roll-Up and set it on the branch with the "breakfast" Strickford gave him.

"Is this plastic?" the majestic bird asked as he took a bite.

"No, it's fruit...strawberry," Whistle said, checking the wrapper.

"This ain't fruit, I'm sure of that. Fruit doesn't stick to the side of my beak like this."

"Well....fruit flavored."

"If you say so," Strickford said as he spit out the remnants of the gummy snack.

A few days later, Whistle was out of Fruit Roll Ups, almost out of Slim Jims, and down to one bottle of water. It was time to go back to life on the flat earth, where he belonged. He waved to the eagles, thanked them for letting him crash on their branch and wished them the best. Not very talkative today, Strickford just seemed to nod, but that was about all. Whistle started shimmying down the tree, wondering if any if not all of his interaction with the eagle family was real or not. Two hundred and fifty feet later, he sat on the mossy ground among the enormous roots of the Paul Bunyan redwood, too thrilled and relieved to question his own sanity; that could wait till morning. It was getting dark and Whistle decided to stay right where he was, and got some much needed shut eye.

Whistle once again woke to a windy thud and a startling caw, but he knew who it was by now.

"Strickford! What are you doing, slumming around down here with all us landlocked cretins?"

The eagle cocked his head as if he was trying to make heads or tails of the strange noises this ragged creature was making in his direction.

"Do you understand me? Didn't we have a good time being roomies up there? I gotta know, am I losing my mind? Give me a signal or acknowledge that you know what I'm trying to say."

The eagle just stood and stared, and just when Whistle was about to chalk it all up to illusion, the eagle lifted his left foot and dropped a dead squirrel in Whistle lap, which made him jump and the eagle fly away and hook around to his nest at the top of the tree.

"Thanks, Strickford. I'll take that as an affirmative."

Whistle was too spent to make a fire to cook the squirrel, so he tied it to his pack and went back to sleep to rest up till sunrise. When it started getting light, the cacophony of birds was too much for anyone to sleep through, so he got up and put on a wool sweater he had in his bag that he'd gotten from the lost and found at the campsite. After a year, if nobody comes for it, first dibs go to employees. He did a quick inventory of supplies, which were running thin, and got a move on. A few days later, a pristine creek, the ability to build a fire, and that now ripening squirrel met up in a most advantageous way as Whistle made a campfire and cooked that squirrel to a crisp. Neither the look or smell of it were particularly mouthwatering, so he kept that thing on the fire till it was a charred chunk of black meat and he realized that it did, in fact, taste like chicken. Burnt chicken, but hey, protein's protein.

Whistle happened to have a map that he also got from the campsite's office. As far he could tell, he wasn't too far from Eureka, so he traveled onward in what he thought was the right direction, if his map reading and amateur astronomy were fairly on point. Turns out they were, and along with a little blind faith and gut instinct, just as he was about to run out of food and water...Eureka!

CHAPTER
SEVENTY-ONE
Hello, Charlie

Walking into town, he noticed an intercoastal waterway to his left. A sliver of land was backed up by the Pacific, which Whistle was well familiar with by now. A few blocks later, he took a right and walked inland several more blocks. If nothing else, he learned that rooms got cheaper the further you got from the ocean. The beer got cheaper and the people got more interesting, all of which suited Whistle just fine. He walked until he came to Bingham Road, took a left and continued north.

A long time passed and Whistle was about to turn back toward the water when he finally came to the corner of Bingham and Cottage Road. In his mind, Bingham represented the seedier side of life while Cottage led toward the ocean, a better life, and more opportunities to be successful and rich.

Regardless, he looked across the way at a rather rundown looking brick building that stood four stories high. Nothing stood out about it except for a large grey sandstone lintel that read "Bingham Auxiliary, Est. 1887." Whistle almost walked right by it until he finally noticed a small sign tucked into the corner of a darkened window reading "Rooms for Rent." It was five large stone steps from the street to the door. Cast iron railings framed each side while an old man sat and smoked a large cigar all by himself.

Whistle Evel Fonzarelli Starr smiled, squared up, and stepped up those five steps into the Bingham Auxiliary. He opened the heavy door, walked in, and heard it close behind him with a click. Instantly, cigarette smoke, a stale beer smell, and the sound of Prince singing about doves filled the funky air. He walked through a plain foyer, then through a smaller door to a main lobby. Instead of having a front desk like a regular hotel, there was a simple bar. Instead of tables and couches, there were pool and foosball tables. He wondered if Jake and Elwood Blues ever stayed here.

Whistle sat at the bar and listened to Prince segue into Neil Diamond. He waited for a while and no one came out. Not wanting to be rude and not seeing a bell anywhere, he drummed along with "Cracklin' Rose" and whistled (how apropos) hoping someone might hear him, and eventually someone did.

This "someone" had a lean build and small, squinty eyes, and in the dim light, an androgynous appearance. The next song up, ironically, was "Lola." *That had to be queued up*, Whistle thought to himself.

"Can I help you?" This person's voice was not clearing up any mysteries. Not knowing what to say, Whistle asked for a Bud. A bottle of Bud and an eight ounce glass were placed in front of him.

"Thank you," Whistle said as he slid a dollar twenty-five across the bar. He sipped his beer and watched as people came and went. After some time, he started to chat with the bartender. He tried in vain to figure out if the bartender was a guy or a gal, sort of like "Pat" from *SNL*, but from an alternate dimension.

"What's your name?" the bartender asked.

"Whistle...Whistle Evel Fonzarelli Starr. What's yours?"

"Charlie Quinn."

"Of course." Whistle chuckled to himself.

"What's that?" Charlie replied with a fresh beer slid in front of Whistle.

"Nothing. Pleased to meet you."

"So where are you from?" Charlie asked.

"Here, there, and everywhere."

"Uh huh...Sooo, do you need a room?"

"Actually, I do. How much?"

"Five dollars a night and you can run a tab as long as I think you're cool," Charlie said, sliding him a key to Room 304. Whistle pulled two crumpled twenties from his pocket.

"Charlie, please give me two nights up front, pay my tab, and buy us each a Jack and Coke." He smiled. Just like that, they were friends. Whistle's intention was to grease the wheels for his stay here, but he naturally got along with Charlie, so it was easy. They sat and talked over a few drinks until closing time. Whistle said goodnight and stumbled up three flights of stairs and eventually found his room. The doorknob was old and a little rusty, so it took a bit of finagling to finally unlock the door and let himself in. After a quick detour to the bathroom, he immediately flopped onto the mattress and passed out.

The next morning, he woke up tangled in the dingy bedspread and the smell of stale urine almost knocked him right back out again.

"Ugh...FUCK!" he said, disgustedly throwing the sheets off of him and hauling ass to the bathroom in time to vomit. His head was pounding as he looked around at the south of modest accommodations. This place was definitely in the running for the Half Star Hotel of the Year award. The bedding had stains of unknown origin, the olive green carpet had the same, plus its fair share of cigarette burns. The ceiling was nicotine stained as well. The one window was dirty and covered with a half of a curtain, held together with a piece of duct tape.

After gathering his faculties, he got up and started the shower. It sputtered to life and thankfully was able to hold a steady stream. Whistle stepped into the shower and got as clean as he could, then proceeded with his normal routine. Fill the tub and let his clothes soak with some shampoo serving as detergent. After a while, he hung everything on the curtain rod to dry, but nothing came out as clean as usual due to the slightly rusty water.

Assessing his current situation, he realized his room sucked, his supplies were running low as well as his cash, and he couldn't even get his clothes clean. Feeling alone and in a rut, he cried into his dingy pillow, frustrated and feeling like he was running in circles. He fell back asleep until noon, then he woke up and took another shower before going out for the day, just to get out of his shithole of a room.

Combing his greasy hair back into a ponytail and putting on his mostly dry and fairly dingy clothes, Whistle made his way downstairs. His beard was getting big and wily and he wanted to shave it, but all he had was a disposable razor and that wasn't going to cut it, so to speak. Walking down the hall, he was greeted when he got to the bar.

"Hello Whistle," Charlie said, putting a Bud and a glass on the bar for him. Whistle sat down and chugged it down in a matter of seconds.

"Ahhhhhhh...Hey Charlie, how goes it?" Whistle said, with a follow-up ripper of a burp. "Woah! Excuse me." He almost apologized for belching in front of a lady, but remembered that he wasn't sure if Charlie was a lady. He didn't care either way, Charlie was cool and that was that.

Charlie placed two shots of Jameson on the bar and they toasted and knocked them back. This was followed by a large order of buffalo wings. The day passed and Whistle didn't want to go back to his crappy room.

"Can I ask you a question?" Whistle piped up.

"What's up?" Charlie asked while tending to another customer.

"No offense, but how do you work here? I mean, it's such a depressing shithole. Why not see what else is out there?"

"I know what else is out there. Down by the marina is nothing but new money snobs and I'll scrub toilets before I wait on those people. There used to be a mine up in the mountains, but that was closed down over ten years ago and all the restaurants and watering holes went with it. So I'm stuck here...in the middle with you."

"I guess so," Whistle replied.

"Cheers," Charlie said as they both raised their glasses and knocked back round two.

"Well unfortunately, I have the room for one more night so I guess I'll go down to the beach and maybe I'll see you again before I leave. I have to be honest with you, I've never seen a nastier room in all my travels."

"I bet," Charlie laughed.

"Alright, I'll catch you later," Whistle said as he made his way down to the beach, his mood lifting and his head clearing, thanks to the rejuvenating salt air. He spent the afternoon taking in the sights and walking up and down the shore. When the sun started to set, he headed back to the Auxiliary. He saw Charlie was still working behind the bar.

"Hey!" Charlie said.

"Hey," Whistle replied. "I'm pretty wiped. I'll see you tomorrow."

"Wait... Uh, how was your afternoon?" Charlie asked, pouring a shot for Whistle.

"Thanks...Pretty good, just trying to get some fresh air and fresh perspective. If the ocean can't do that for you, nothing will."

Whistle downed his shot and headed back up to his room. All his gear was still wet and was starting to smell like a combination of wet dog and dried up dreams. He lay down and sobbed himself to sleep again. He was looking within for answers and coming up empty. He dozed off for the night and the next morning, as soon as he could, checked out of California's very own Heartbreak Hotel. He was on his way out the door when he heard Charlie call him.

"Whistle."

"Oh man," he said under his breath. "Uhhh, yeah?" Out loud.

"Come here."

The boy turned around and walked back. When he reached Charlie, he was grabbed firmly and the two kissed deeply. They were pressed together and after an appropriate amount of time, pulled away.

"Listen, if you want to stay with me, you can," Charlie said.

"Okay," Whistle said, not wanting to stay on the street if he could help it. He was getting too old to enjoy it on any level.

"Go to the beach and I'll come get you when my shift is done later on," Charlie said.

"Right," was all he could answer. So the beach it was. Whistle soaked all his things the best he could but it didn't seem to be working for him. He didn't want to be a house guest and look and smell this dirty, so he decided he was going to skip town before he ran into Charlie. He was just about to leave when he heard Charlie call him...

"Fuck," he muttered to himself.

"Get up here, you awesome bastard," Charlie said. This freaked him out more than the kiss for some strange reason. Whistle walked up the beach and followed Charlie to a beachfront palace that could be on the cover of a real estate magazine.

"This is the spot," Charlie said.

"Yeah, ok," Whistle replied with a smirk. "Listen Charlie, thanks for everything, but I—"

"My friend, this is mine. Come on," Charlie said, opening the door.

Reluctantly, Whistle walked into a massive entry made of marble. He looked up to see Charlie standing at the top of the balcony. With a wink, Charlie was gone. Whistle made his way up the stairs and followed. Walking through an elaborate archway, Charlie smiled and pointed to the right. There, another door stood and waited. Whistle looked at Charlie and Charlie looked at Whistle. He tried to ask Charlie a question but was shushed with a point to the door. So he opened the door to something he would never forget.

CHAPTER SEVENTY-TWO
The Bathroom and the Ferrari

The bathroom he walked into was unbelievable. Pink Floyd softly played in the background and a huge tub was already drawn. There was a platter of fresh fruit and a pitcher of ice cold, top shelf vodka and cran on the side of the tub. Whistle looked around cautiously for a few minutes. Eventually he relaxed and didn't feel threatened in any way, so he got undressed and slid into the tub. He closed his eyes and started to drift off to the sound of "Breathe." The pure white suds started turning grey and the grime on Whistle leeched off of him into the water. He was happy and eventually dozed off. Sometime later, he woke up and ate a bunch of fruit from the platter. Cantaloupe, blueberries, watermelon and pineapples hit the spot just right, along with two shots of ice cold vodka.

Whistle got out and emptied his bladder and looked into the mirror to make sure he looked halfway healthy with all the grime gone. He decided he did and got back into the tub. Almost dozing off again, he heard the door open and close. So close to sleep, he didn't resist the hand that started rubbing his chest. He took another shot of vodka and laid back. The room was hot and the water was even hotter. The hand went up and grabbed his hair, then came down and tugged his beard.

"Oh man," he whispered to himself. The hand slid down to his stomach and Whistle opened his eyes.

"Are you alright, sexy?" Charlie asked, looking down with caring eyes.

"I think so," Whistle replied, nervously.

"Good." Charlie's hand was slowly working its way down Whistle's body. Charlie's left hand found its way to his neck, pressing gently. The right finally found its way down to his manhood. It didn't take long before his back was arched and he was getting ready to release. The water sloshed everywhere. Whistle grabbed Charlie by the neck and they locked eyes.

"Oh shit!" Whistle said with his eyes closed.

"Yeah!" Charlie said, picking up the pace. Just like that, Whistle released. They both cleaned up and Charlie led Whistle to a most fabulous bed.

Whistle slept great that night, feeling safe in Charlie's arms. His dreams were colorful and vivid. When he woke up, Charlie was staring directly into his eyes, face to face.

"You want eggs?"

"Yeah, sure."

After they had breakfast, Charlie finally went to work. Whistle snooped around a bit to find out what he could. Charlie wasn't poor—in fact, he was pretty well off—so Whistle figured he would hang around for a while just because it beat life on the street. Sure enough, Charlie pampered Whistle at every turn. Money was thrown at him and all his supplies were thrown out and replaced with more than he would ever need. But, after a few weeks, Whistle was starting to feel like Charlie's plaything and knew it was time to leave if he wanted to retain any self-respect. Plus, no matter how much snooping he did, he couldn't figure out if Charlie was male or female and whenever they got intimate, it was always Charlie servicing Whistle, swatting his hands away whenever they went wandering below the belt.

"Hey Charlie, I love you but I gotta go," Whistle said, expecting a bit of pushback.

"Cool, let's go," Charlie replied with a smile a mile wide.

Before Whistle knew it, he was sitting in a '78 Ferrari Testarossa doing a buck twenty-five up PCH. The night ripped by and Whistle white-knuckled the dash and almost put his feet through the floorboards.

"Slow down, Charlie!" Whistle said.

"Okay," Charlie said as he stomped the pedal to the floor as the Ferrari screamed.

"Fuck man, slow down!" Whistle screamed.

"Okay...here, take this," Charlie said as he slowed down and gave Whistle a hit of acid on a white square of paper. As if things weren't weird enough. After flying up the coast for another hour, they pulled over and got a blueberry muffin and coffee. Losing all grasp of reality, Whistle was tossed the keys and got behind the wheel. Once on PCH South, heading back, Whistle was determined to get that machine to two hundred miles per hour. Ten minutes later, his hair was pinned back and the light flew by like stars in hyperspace. That's when he felt his fly unzip and Charlie went to town on him, not the least bit concerned with the speed they were traveling at, nor the lack of experience Whistle had behind the wheel of a machine of this caliber. When he climaxed, he nearly lost control of the car and fishtailed just as they were getting off the freeway.

They pulled into the garage, hit the remote and went in the house, and had two shots of whiskey before they went to bed. It was too late and too weird to bring up leaving for real...Another day would be another day.

CHAPTER SEVENTY-THREE
Tonka Trucks and Sandy Towns

A week later Whistle left with all new supplies and twelve hundred dollars in his pocket. He was so thankful to Charlie that they hugged deeply.

"I love you, Charlie," Whistle said, earnestly.

"I love you, too."

One final hug and a small kiss, and the boy started north up Bingham Road. Walking away, Whistle decided that Charlie was both male and female. He knew that he would never know for sure, so he decided to square up and continue north. Leaving Eureka, he walked until deep dusk had settled in.

Whistle chose to bed down on Arcata Beach. He slept while huge waves crashed on the shore, some thirty feet away.

The next morning, he made his way north to a delightful deli in the town of McKinleyville. There, he enjoyed a Salisbury steak, mashed potatoes, gravy, and a huge heap of buttery spinach that might as well be home cooked. Whistle cleaned his plate better than a Maytag, chasing it down with a root beer float from the antique soda fountain. This was the kind of meal you're glad to eat alone, so there's no one to distract you from how delicious it is.

"Thank you! That meal was an experience...like a trip back in time, just wonderful!"

"Well THANK you, sugar!" The nice older woman laughed as he tipped her a ten on the ten dollar meal. "Ya hear that, Will? This nice young fella LOVES my cookin'!" she yelled to her husband working the grill in the kitchen.

"Yes, ma'am! If I'm ever back this way, I know where I'll be for lunch."

"Well we got a heck of a breakfast too."

"I bet you do...y'all have a nice day!" Whistle chimed as he walked out and continued north. He made his way back to the shore again and walked until dark that night and, once again, slept on the beach. He was starting to toughen up a bit, he knew if he could get used to sleeping outdoors mentally, as long as the nights weren't too cold nor the ground too rough, he could save a lot of money.

One thing he learned was that exhaustion made it a whole lot easier to choose the outdoors as opposed to continuing on late into the night to try and find a room. It was a little trick he played on his mind to make the outdoors an easier option to take. He had a lot of miles under his belt by now and all that time was spent thinking. Thinking about all kinds of things really, but mainly, thinking about thinking.

One day, not too long into his journey, a phrase seemed to be running around his brain, almost like a commercial jingle or limerick: "The world is what you make it." He didn't consciously think of it, it just kind of presented itself as he was walking, in time with his footsteps. Sort of like an invisible Drill Sergeant shouting a cadence only he could hear. It seemed to mean everything and nothing all at once. He closed his eyes and fell asleep as he pondered what it really meant, where it really came from and what he should do with it.

About ten the next morning, Whistle was awoken by a direct poke to his forehead.

"Fuck!" he yelped.

"Fuck!" was repeated by a very young voice.

"Don't say that," Whistle said to a little blond boy standing over him, wearing red swim trunks and a toothy, goofy smile.

"You alright mister?" the boy asked, good-naturedly.

"Yeah, as long as you don't poke me," Whistle said as he shielded his eyes from the sun.

"What's your name?" the boy asked.

"Whistle."

"NOOOoooOOOOoooo!" The boy groaned in an animated way as he shook his head in a figure eight type pattern.

"Yeah...Whistle. Whistle Evel Fonzarelli Starr."

"WHHAAAAAT!?" the boy screeched in a sing-songy manner. Yep, he was one of those kids that aren't the most fun to deal with before your first cup of coffee. Much less on a public beach with a small, scattered audience of beach-goers pretending to mind their own business.

"What's your name?" Whistle asked as he looked in his bag for a comb.

"Well, my name happens to be Henry Kramer," the boy said, sitting down and grabbing a big fistful of sand.

"How can I help you, Henry?" Whistle asked, polite, but wanting to get this interaction wrapped up.

"Well, I was wondering if you wanted to play Tonka trucks with me?"

Whistle didn't really want to play Tonka trucks within minutes of waking up on a public beach, but he felt bad for the kid because he didn't have anyone to play with. He seemed a little awkward socially but nice enough, so Whistle obliged.

"Sure, pal," he said as he scooted next to the boy and his big box full of toy cars and trucks.

Henry opened the box and dumped the contents out onto the sand. There was a toy version of almost every vehicle imaginable. Trans Ams, Cobras, Corvettes, Ford Pickups, Dodges and Chargers. There were Back Hoes, Bulldozers, Road Graders and Long Freighters.

"Heck of a collection you got there, Henry."

"Wait! Look at these! the young boy said as he unlocked a section of the box off to the side.

The little nook held a Ferrari, Lamborghini, DeLorean, Saab, and an Audi.

"The foreign section?" Whistle asked.

"Yeah," Henry replied as he set those cars out more carefully.

"We'll pick which ones we want. You first," he said as Whistle looked them over.

"I'll take the Trans Am," Whistle said, picking up the black Smokey and the Bandit hot rod.

"I get the Corvette, HAHAAA!"

Before long, they had a whole race track meets city meets freeway dug out in the sand. Nothing fancy, just functional. The larger Tonkas drove the main roads while the smaller sports cars ripped around the side streets. Two Star Wars storm troopers guarded the prison while Chewbacca got his shoes shined at Denny's Shine Shop. Shoes done, he paid up and walked across the street. The Wookie climbed into a purple Porsche and floored it. Just like that, he tore out of Whistle and Henry's Race Track City (Henry's name).

One really cool thing about their town was Town Hall, where the mayor sat in a grand throne surrounded by columns and mountains. Fitting for the mayor, who just happened to be the Honorable Hulk Hogan. Muscles, golden locks, and a red and yellow uniform.

The afternoon sun started casting longer rays and Henry's mom and dad came by.

"Henry, time to go, buddy," they said as they walked over, schlepping their chairs, coolers, and towels back to the car.

"Okay. Mom, Dad, this is my friend Whistle!"

"Hi. Nice to meet you."

"Nice to meet you. Henry wasn't bothering you, was he?" they asked.

"Not at all," Whistle replied as he helped Henry pack up his toys.

"See ya, Whistle!"

"See ya, Henry!"

Whistle spent the next two weeks on the beach, but he managed to find a more out of the way spot to sleep, further back in the dunes where he stayed out of sight, save for the odd lifeguard who left him alone either out of compassion or laziness. Either way, as long as they left him alone, he was happy.

He ran into Henry a few more times and played Tonka trucks with him, but other than that, this particular beach town had nothing to offer Whistle. So eventually on a foggy Tuesday morning, he moved on.

As he navigated his way north, he continued through numerous towns like Trinidad, Orick, Klamath, and Crescent City. He mostly kept to himself, working odd jobs and staying in different motel rooms, guest houses, outdoor hideaways in the woods and the good old beach, when the weather cooperated. Days turned into weeks, into months, into almost two years. Around this time he arrived at a small town called Smith River.

The first day he spent in town, he found a place to live. A job wasn't hard to find either. He was in the mood to make friends after a long stretch of solitude and self-reflection, but reluctant to make any big moves or get too deeply involved with anyone unless he knew it was going to be a solid move in the right direction. If he wasn't certain it was the right move, he steered clear of it. So he spent a lot of time steering clear and heading north.

Smith River felt like a good place to stay put for a while. He got to know all the locals and had a perfect apartment above a garage with dark wood paneled walls and bright, tacky eighties furniture. It was odd decor but for some reason he always felt comfortable there and it seemed to lift his mood whenever he was there. It even had a makeshift deck off the front, above the garage doors, where he would hang, grill burgers, smoke a joint now and then and chat with neighbors when they'd stroll by walking their dogs and jogging.

Life was simple and Whistle was as content as he could ever remember being. He really got into trapping and fishing. He also saw the first snowfall he'd seen in over thirty years. On the western shore, Whistle looked out at the sunset as heavy, wet flakes fell and instantly brought him back to the beginning of his journey in his mind. It jostled something in him and just like that, he decided to end his stay in Smith River and move on. He cleaned his apartment, packed up whatever he could carry with him, left an envelope with one month's rent and a note thanking his landlord, and left the key under the mat as he said so long to the garage owner's dog and was on his way. After a quick stop at an Exxon for a ham and cheese sandwich, he walked through the night and as morning light rose up from the east, Whistle Evel Fonzarelli Starr crossed the border from California into the great state of Oregon.

CHAPTER
SEVENTY-FOUR
The Miles Roll On

Along the shore, he ducked into Harris Beach for the night. The next day, he made it up to Nesika Beach. There, he spent a few weeks before moving on. Walking comfortably for a few weeks, Whistle finally ended up in Astoria. Winter was starting to settle and he found a small cottage along the Blueberry River. He got a job slinging steaks and serving order after order of delicious garlic fries. The next spring, Whistle packed up and moved on while the weather was ideal. Before long, he crossed a long bridge named Tun. He crossed into Washington State and spent the night in the woods of Chinook.

After that, he made his way into the town of Ilwaco. Then Seaview, then Long Beach. Miles and miles of hard wet sand to walk on and no one to talk to, which suited him just fine. Finally, he ended up at a campground named Ledbetter Point. He paid for a site and settled in. Many weeks passed and he traveled to the northernmost tip of the land, making it there well after nightfall. The weather was relatively warm so he decided to plunge in and take a swim. No one was around and it was dark out, so he stripped down and jumped in for a good long swim. Swimming back to shore, he realized he had drifted a bit and had to walk a good distance to retrieve his clothes. A peculiar blue light left on at a utility building served as a landmark once he got to shore, otherwise he might have found himself strolling the beach naked in broad daylight with no clue where his clothes were. Not a great scenario.

Finding his clothes with plenty of time left before sunrise, Whistle got dressed and went back to a secluded spot between the dunes and took a nap for a few hours. Waking up to the sound of a sand grader early the next morning, Whistle got up, collected his things, and started up the coast to the Makah Indian Reservation. It was there that he took another swim; this one would be the most challenging swim of his life.

He plunged into the water with a forty-pound pack on his back and started across the Strait of Juan De Fuca. It was twelve miles and separated America from Canada. Somehow, Whistle Evel Fonzarelli Starr swam the twelve miles and ended up on the shore of the Pacific Nitinat Lake Reserve.

That was fine with Whistle because he was getting older and decided Alaska was going to be his new destination. He was well across the border into Canada now, as he passed Vancouver Island. British Columbia took forever. Another big swim later, Whistle ended up in the town of Prince Rupert.

He felt comfortable here. Got along with the locals as he'd had enough experience with this particular social dynamic. Being able to blend into the scenery when arriving in a new town was crucial to his survival on the road. Being able to read people was another. At this point, he could spot a bullshitter, troublemaker, goodfella, gold digger, game rigger, or pickpocket a mile away.

He also had a keen ear for the knock of opportunity. Sometimes so faint, he could barely hear it, but there nonetheless. Prince Rupert presented its fair share pretty much from the get-go. He landed a job working on a log line. Grueling manual labor was free exercise as far as Whistle was concerned. He figured you were getting paid for your time; if you were getting into good shape while on the clock, that's a win-win right there.

He entertained a few Canadian ladies while in town, but nothing too serious. Whistle felt deep down that he was a born drifter and unless he met someone that he absolutely fell head over heels in love with, he was going to keep it short and sweet, making it clear up front that he was just passing through. The truth, the whole truth, and nothing but the truth, your honor.

While in town, one girlfriend was nice enough to take him on as a roommate. Rent was next to nothing and he was able to save up enough money to buy a 1982 deep blue Dodge with 1970s shaggin wagon art airbrushed on the hood. He figured he got it cheap because of the knight with the light saber riding a stallion as he did battle with a space alien from the middle ages on the hood. He considered it a bonus. Heck, that was right up there with a custom sound system as far as he was concerned.

"I'm so glad I'm livin' in the USA," Whistle sang to himself as he was closing in on Alaska. He chuckled as he took in the landscape and as he gunned it down the freeway. He was sure that Chuck Berry wasn't picturing any of this.

Regardless, it felt good to be back home, or at least on his way. When he finally crossed the border late that night, he pulled into a rest area, eased his seat back, and fell asleep in an instant. Sleeping in a car felt like the Ritz Carlton to Whistle.

Over the next several days, Whistle drove all day and slept all night in his car, getting out and spending an hour walking around just to keep the blood flowing every morning and once in the afternoon after lunch. He had decided that the route he was taking contained too many inlets, swamps, and impassable woods. Though he loved driving this far out and taking in the fresh, cleansing air, he needed more to look at. One day stopping for lunch at the Midnight Special BBQ in Ketchikan, he asked a bartender if they had a map he could take a look at.

"I'll do ya one better," the bartender responded, reaching behind him to grab a map off a stack that just happened to be next to the cash register.

"Thanks. A lot of people pass through, huh?"

"Mmmmm," the bartender replied, not looking up from his paper.

"Cool." Whistle got the hint and focused on his own reading as he ate his BBQ burger and scanned the map for another route. After loading up on his burger and fries, plus a few beers, it was decided that Anchorage was as good a destination as any.

"How's Anchorage?" Whistle asked the bartender, still reading the paper.

"Mmmmm." This from the bartender as he took a drag of his cigarette.

With a glowing endorsement like that, Whistle was clear in his mission—on to Anchorage!

"You ain't drivin' are ya?" the bartender asked, face in the sports section.

"Yeah, why?" Whistle asked, attentively.

"Mmmm. You want to fly." This didn't really answer Whistle's question, but he was gonna have to take what he could get from this chatterbox.

"Ok, thanks," Whistle said as he settled up and got directions to the airport.

About a block away from the restaurant, there was a gas station already closed for the night with a good number of trees and a used car lot, so he pulled into an inconspicuous spot in the lot to lie down in the back and catch a quick nap before going to the airport. He ended up sleeping through the night and waking up just as the sun was coming up. It seemed that his circadian rhythm was in sync with the earth's after spending so many years sleeping outside. This was Alaska, so the sun and moon were dancing to a different song. It was a long, slow song at certain times of the year and it made a man think differently, feel different, could slow you down...maybe that was a good thing. This was what was on Whistle's mind as he parked his car in the airport lot, not expecting to come back to reclaim it.

After buying a ticket, Whistle had no luggage to check, so he went to his gate to wait to board. He bought a coffee and a paper to read on the plane. He figured it would be a good strategy for keeping his mind off of flying thirty-five thousand feet in the air at five hundred miles per hour in a vehicle that weighs tons. Not able to wrap his mind around this, he started to feel a panic attack coming on. His instinct told him to just try and return his ticket, get in the car, and figure out a plan over a nice breakfast on solid earth.

He started feeling dizzy and his palms were sweating enough that the paper was starting to wrinkle up along the edge where he was holding it.

"Get it together...quit being such a pussy," he said to himself in the re-stroom mirror as he splashed cold water in his face and tried to regulate his breathing.

"You alright there, buddy?" a voice boomed out of nowhere, echoing throughout the tile of the otherwise empty men's room.

"Huh!? Oh sorry, I thought I was in here alone," Whistle said to the businessman coming out of one of the stalls.

"Shoulda given you a courtesy flush, heh heh...Don't like flyin', huh?"

"I wouldn't know, this is my first time."

"Nothing to it...Hang on, I got something for ya," the businessman said as he sat his briefcase on the baby changing station in the corner and pulled out a few small bottles of whiskey, tequila, and vodka.

"Courtesy of the good ol' mini bar. Any two or three of these, you'll be good to go."

"Thanks. I'll take your word for it, cheers!" Whistle said as he immediately popped a mini Jose' and a Jack and he immediately felt his nerves settle. Plus, this guy was getting on the same plane, and he was relaxed as can be.

The announcement came over the loudspeakers that it was time to board and Whistle got another twinge of panic, a little muted and boozy, but a twinge regardless.

"That's us, bud," the businessman said as he straightened his tie in the mirror and flung open the men's room door.

"Yep," Whistle said, following the man out to the gate.

He handed in his ticket and boarded the plane. He tried to focus on the fact that no one else appeared concerned about flying as the liquid breakfast was kicking in. He found his seat and sat down with his stomach flip-flopping be-tween nervous nausea and ralph-inducing rotgut. He had a middle seat but asked to switch with the person in the aisle seat because being in the way of a guy who has to get to the bathroom pronto tonto isn't where you want to be. The man agreed and a deal was struck.

The stewardess did the usual routine, complete with plastered smiles and canned jokes. Whistle buckled his belt and white-knuckled the armrests as he didn't know whether he was more scared of flying or throwing up all over the place. The stewardess noticed him digging into the leather with his nails, swallowing hard and stealing nervous glances out the window as the plane slowly pulled up to the runway.

"Excuse me, Miss? Does that sound right? Sounds like something rattling," he asked the stewardess as she caught his eye, walking down the aisle.

"This plane passes a very thorough inspection before every flight," she responded in a perfectly pleasant and professional manner.

"Thanks," he said. *Bullshit!* he thought.

The plane was squared up at the starting end of the runway, the captain said his peace and they were off...

"OoOoOoOohhhh FuUuUuUuuuck!" Whistle muttered through gritted teeth as the plane began to gradually pick up speed...faster....faster... fasterfasterFASTERFASTER!!!!...

...And nothing. *What!?* **Whoah!!!** Whistle thought to himself as the plane introduced Whistle to the miracle of flight firsthand as it ascended into the clear, blue Alaskan sky. He looked out the window to see the skyline was diagonal...then completely gone as the plane veered left. He looked out the other window to see nothing but land.

"Awesome!" he said to himself as the plane evened out and other people in the cabin started opening drinks, pulling out newspapers, and making themselves at home. The social cues and general vibe made Whistle calm down and enjoy the experience.

Aside from a quick bit of turbulence and slightly bumpy landing, Whistle handled flying like a champ. He thanked his stewardess for calming him down and his neighbor for switching seats, then grabbed his pack from under the seat in front of him. He got off the plane, walked into the terminal, when it suddenly occurred to him, he was in Anchorage, Alaska!

CHAPTER
SEVENTY-FIVE
Welcome to Anchorage

Stepping out the door of the Ted Stevens International Airport, Whistle was as lost as he could be. Not having the slightest idea which direction he should go or why he should go there, Whistle relied on the tried and true coin flip and headed right down the street, along with traffic. *Just go with the flow,* a voice in his head repeated in a sing-song mantra as he walked along on the narrow sidewalk.

"Where are you going, buddy?" two guards asked as they pulled up alongside him in an airport security pickup truck.

"Um, well...I just landed and I'm trying to get to the city," Whistle said.

"Of course you are. Get in and we'll give you a lift," the driver said as he shot the other one a quick glance.

"Cool, thanks!" Whistle said as he got in the back of the cab.

"You don't want to be walking there, not a lot of room between the street and the barrier, plus people don't always watch where they're driving."

"Good point," Whistle said.

They drove for about five minutes before they let Whistle out, once they were off airport property and down the street where the hotels were located.

"You can get a room anywhere up around here, five star to budget. Watch yourself around here, Anchorage ain't a place to be unless you got a good reason to be here. Have a nice day," the driver said sternly with nary a hint of warmth as he shot another knowing glance at his partner before he hit the gas and cut into the busy traffic, leaving Whistle standing in front of a Holiday Inn, slightly frazzled by the word of advice the security guard gave him.

"What was that all about?" he asked himself as he took in his surroundings. He noticed that he was at an intersection where International Airport Road continued on while Jewel Lake Road bended right, moving inland. Meanwhile, Wisconsin Street stretched left towards the water. A big decision lay before him. Being naturally inclined to head towards the shore, Wisconsin was picked.

He followed the road with the airport fence for about a half mile before the fence curved away, sharply. Two miles further along, Whistle came to a stop sign at Northern Lights Boulevard. As the sun started to set, Whistle chose another left and continued on. Another mile on, he crossed Hood Creek and entered Earthquake Park. With it now dark save for a few vivid stripes across the horizon, he started scoping out a place to sleep for the night. He eventually found a relatively secluded path with a park bench, just off of the main road. Once again his pack was his pillow and it was mere minutes before Whistle dozed off from sheer exhaustion at the sound of waves lapping the shore somewhere in the distance.

In the morning, Whistle woke up and immediately jumped to attention and looked around to see if he was alone, surrounded by onlookers, or somewhere in between. In all his years of sleeping outdoors, waking up to who knows what and being vulnerable to all of society and nature was something he never got used to. Luckily today, his only company was a cardinal, which he took as a good sign.

He heard those waves off in the distance and it was almost like the voice of an old friend, much like the highway was in his earlier years. He gave his hair a quick comb through and pat down, having no mirror to see what he looked like. He was pretty good at guessing by this point.

He grabbed his pack and took advantage of the good weather to get off the beaten path for a bit of a nature hike to see if he could find a good place to camp out.

He negotiated the overgrown terrain, ducking and slashing through brush, tall grass and low hanging branches. No low hanging fruit, unfortunately. However, he did eventually come upon a clearing to open up his pack, lay out his things, take an inventory and let everything air out in the sun. It wasn't a washing but it would have to do. He nibbled on a small bag of stale pretzels, drank a bottle of water, and counted his meager funds, just over three hundred and thirty dollars, including the change that was jingling around the bottom of the bag.

His clothes weren't going to land him in *GQ Magazine*, but at least they were clean, albeit a little musty and wrinkled from being stuffed in his pack for a few days now. He was going to have to really hustle to improve his situation. He was too old and too worn out to keep roughing it outside without adequate shelter, food, and water. The thrill was gone, as the saying goes.

Figuring the clothes on his back were the best he owned and not quite ripe, he decided he'd keep them on for another day and pack the rest back into the backpack and head back out to the path, and followed it down to the water. After a while, he walked across an open air field that led to the shore. There, he gazed upon Cook Inlet. And what a beautiful inlet it happened to be. The water rolled golden waves while White Mount Gerdine stood tall in the background. People walked by behind him as he studied a huge, black and rust colored vessel out a long way away, with "Outsiders T 182" painted on its side in dirty white lettering. He took that as a potential sign from the universe as he is, was, and most likely would always be an outsider. He would keep his eyes open for Ts and 182s.

Walking along the narrow shore, with the water to his right and airport fencing to his left, Whistle was stuck walking in deep, dry, but heavy sand. He trudged on for about another quarter of a mile before his legs started cramping and he was physically out of gas. He collapsed on the sand and caught his breath, not to mention his calves were letting him know they needed a break.

Knowing that this was certainly not a great location for much more than a quick rest, Whistle tried to talk himself into getting up and getting to the other end of this long narrow beach running right up along the airport fence, topped with barbed wire and signs forbidding entrance. To give himself a jolt of motivation, he stripped naked and dove into the water. It took his breath away and completely made him forget all about his cramps. They were still there, but at the moment he was dealing with a lightning bolt of cold, shot blasting through his consciousness.

Splashing around and whoopin' n' hollerin' involuntarily for a few minutes, Whistle adjusted to the cold and felt like a new man. He jumped back out to grab some clothes to wash in the water. He didn't have any soap, but he figured the water was cold enough to make any bacteria living in his clothes consider new accommodations.

After getting his clothes as clean as he could, he climbed out and laid everything out on a rock to dry. He lay down himself and took a little nap, feeling better about his situation than he did just hours ago. It's a wonder how a cold swim can completely change your outlook.

He woke back up right around dusk. The sky had that magical golden quality about it with just a few high clouds already headed towards deep purple. He gathered his things and headed down the beach, hoping to find a good place to camp for the night. He eventually came upon some dunes and tall reeds, so he decided the dry sand would be suitable to sleep on and the reeds provided adequate privacy, as this didn't seem like a place that saw a lot of traffic.

Once deep in the reeds, he lay back and looked up into the sky, trying to pick out constellations that he remembered the names of. It was one of the few things that stuck with him from school. He began playing a game that he used to pass the hours from time to time, which was trying to remember his age. He thought about particular events that he could put a year to and try and do the math from there, but there was really no use. His childhood years were easier to keep track of because of school and living in New Hampshire, where the change of seasons was as pronounced as could be. Cold snowy winters melted into the freshest, greenest springs, followed by hot, muggy summers and eventually the fall harvest. Crisp, colorful and glorious, maybe the most breathtaking foliage in the world.

A wave of childhood nostalgia took over and he wondered why he ever left. Could there really be a better place than New Hampshire? Sure, everyplace else he'd traveled through had its charms, but he never found a place he wanted to call home for the rest of his life. As he lay there, in the reeds, in the dunes on a beach somewhere in Anchorage, Alaska, he realized he could be anywhere. Alaska, Atlanta, Santa Monica, South Carolina, didn't really matter. Home was home and he was about as far away as someone could be just deciding to take off on foot one day and only stepping on a plane for the first time just the other day, to bring him here. He laughed at the irony of the situation and felt a sense of pride as he reflected on what a long, strange trip it had been....thus far.

CHAPTER
SEVENTY-SIX
The Dream

The next morning came faster than he had hoped. He would have liked to have grabbed a few more hours of sleep, but the sun was shining too bright for that to happen.

"Shit," Whistle said to himself as he sat up against the fence while a jet took off overhead. He got a packet of oatmeal out of the pack and alternately poured some into his mouth followed by a swig of warm, bottled water. "Better than nothing," he said to himself as he geared up to check out Anchorage.

He walked along for a few miles before coming to Westchester Lagoon. He crossed the bridge and eventually reached town. It wasn't the most glamorous part of town, but he'd seen worse, so he decided to get a cheap room at the King Crab Loft. He was disappointed in himself for splurging on a luxury like a motel room, but he figured he could pick up some kind of job or hustle tomorrow.

Unlocking the door to his motel room, Whistle thought about going back to the main desk and getting a refund. This place was nasty in every possible way while still being somehow cool with the Board of Health. The carpet was dark brown with light colored crumbs of who knows what origin and the ceiling was nicotine yellow, which tied in perfectly with the odor. The decor consisted of framed paintings of high plains cowboys rustling cattle, another branding a bull, and one lone pokey down the line mending a fence. The room was topped off with a lamp with a tan shade and some sorry looking curtains, one being held together by duct tape, from the other side of course. *What is it with these places and the duct tape on the curtains?* Whistle thought to himself.

The bathroom offered no escape from the skeevy dreariness. If anything, it was worse as the light colors showed the grime even more, plus the water pressure was weak and inconsistent. Dribble, dribble, then a blast of hot. Dribble, dribble, blast of cold. With some rust thrown in just in case you weren't all that bothered by the pressure itself.

Muttering under his breath about the half ass accommodations, Whistle flopped down on the bed and sure enough, within seconds, the smell of sweat wafted into his nostrils from the bedding.

"Ugh! What the FUCK!" he growled as he punched the headboard, putting a nice little fist-sized dent in the wood panel, cardboard, cheapest shit possible rectangle screwed to the front of it. He pulled the sheets off as they seemed to be the main offenders, but then he was confronted with a brownish yellow stain about halfway down the mattress. Knowing full well that it wasn't spilled coffee, he flipped the mattress over to thankfully find no stains and a good deal less odor.

"That's what I get for spending money I don't have on a room. I'd have been better off outdoors," he muttered to himself as he stuffed his trusty pack under his head, afraid to catch lice or crabs or who knows what from the pillows. He turned on the TV and watched a rerun of *Growing Pains*. "These pampered sons o' bitches wouldn't know a growing pain if it bit 'em on the ass," Whistle slurred to himself as he drifted off for the night.

As he lay in the dark, his eyes provided trails of pinks, purples, orange and gold. Then, just as he was dozing off, his sleep was disturbed by sharp, piercing needles in his face. Whistle was awakened by an Alaskan king crab clawing into his face. He opened his eyes and met long, tentacle eyeballs staring back at him. He tried to push it off of him but it just dug in deeper. Whistle screamed and the crab just stared back at him.

"Will you stop?" the crab said, tapping the boy on the forehead with his claw.

"Get off me!" Whistle yelled. The crab released and rattled down to stand on Whistle's chest. There was a long silence and he felt tiny rivulets of blood slowly trickling down his face. The blood came from puncture wounds where the crab pierced his skin.

"What do you want?" Whistle asked.

"Listen up, Numbnuts. My name's Larry, and I have something important to tell you."

"Okay, what?" Whistle asked, getting irritated.

"You've come a long way and traveled a rough road. However, you've got a ways to go."

"What do you mean?" Whistle asked.

Larry the Alaskan king crab said no more, blinked his eyes randomly one at a time, and vaporized into thin air. The boy got out of bed and stood up in the complete darkness. After a while, all his favorite colors swirled around him in trail form until they surrounded him like a cocoon. The smell of cigarettes filled his nostrils as he reached out and felt a steel doorknob and twisted it to let himself into the cockpit of a 747 plummeting to earth, the middle of the Indian Ocean to be specific.

Everyone in the cockpit was gone and when Whistle turned around to try and leave as well, the door had been replaced with a solid white wall. No choice but to take the pilot's seat and try to save himself. Looking out the windshield, all he saw was the ocean. The G-force pressed him back against his seat, defying gravity. There were so many gauges, levers, buttons, lights, and switches that Whistle had no time to make any well thought out moves, so he just started pushing, pulling, clicking and twisting everything he could get his hands on. Nothing worked as he braced for impact.

Suddenly, just as he was about to hit the water, he closed his eyes and waited...and waited...and...nothing. He opened his eyes to find himself all alone in a hot air balloon ten thousand feet above the North Pole.

What the...? was all Whistle could muster for a thought. It was night and there was a huge moon above. The stars were crisp and the Aurora Borealis shot around everywhere. Surprisingly, he wasn't cold at all. After a while, he noticed that he was sinking and there was an endless mountain range ahead. Simple enough, he figured. He would just pull the dangling chain in front of him and add more heat to the balloon. He tugged on the chain and absolutely nothing happened.

"Oh shit!" he said to himself as he began looking around the wicker basket he was standing in. There was nothing there to help him, so he just waited as he approached the mountain range ahead. The air was eerily quiet and the mountains were coming clearly into view, jagged and sharp. Rocks, snow, and ice awaited him as he tried to figure out a way to avoid crashing, but it was out of his hands at this point. He once again closed his eyes and braced for impact...

And once again he was transported to an entirely different reality. This time he found himself in a bowling alley at the end of a lane with a ball in his hands, and a 7-10 split down at the other end. His rented shoes were too tight and hurt his feet, but at least he was standing on the ground and not hurtling towards a mountain or the Indian Ocean.

He took a swig of his Budweiser and stepped to the line. This was it. All or nothing. Make it and win or miss it and lose to Troy's Towing, making them the champs again this year. He eyeballed the slick lane ahead with two evil pins at the end laughing at him. Whistle calculated his shot and let 'er rip. The ball rolled as he held his breath. After what seemed like forever, the ball drifted favorably and struck the seven pin, bounced, and hit the ten as well. Just as the pins were about to fall, Whistle woke up with a start. Cold sweat covered him and he was instantly back in his cruddy little room. *What a familiar dream*, Whistle thought to himself as he got up to use the bathroom.

CHAPTER
SEVENTY-SEVEN
A New Old Friend

A quick, functional yet unenjoyable shower, complete with sporadic water pressure and a weird rusty smell, started the day and capped a stay at the King Crab Loft. Whistle checked out and bid adieu and walked out the front door, feeling like he was just let out of the slammer. He walked down the sunny side of the street and stopped for breakfast at the Polar Bear Diner.

He sat at the corner of the counter and took a menu. A haze of cigarette smoke hung in the air and mixed with the smell of bacon coming from the kitchen.

"Two unhealthy things that go so well together," Whistle said to himself. The napkin holders were fully stocked and the salt and pepper shakers were full and at the ready on the olive green countertop.

"Coffee?" an amazingly friendly looking woman asked from behind the counter.

"Yes please," Whistle answered.

As she poured the coffee, he noticed little details about her. Although her hair was black, there were small traces of silver right at the roots. A dragonfly pin was placed where you would usually find a nametag. The wrinkles around her eyes were almost completely symmetrical, perfectly framing her warm, kind, dark eyes.

"What are we havin'?" she asked, pencil in hand, ready to take the order.

"What's your name?" Whistle asked, almost involuntarily.

"Ummm...Denise...why?"

"You just look familiar, that's all," he said, to cover for his random curiosity. "Denise...I'll have two eggs over easy, sausage, hash browns, white toast, and a cranberry juice, if you have it. If not, orange juice will do the job."

"We got cran...annnd what kind of jelly for the toast?"

"Grape or whatever."

"Youuuu got it," she said as she finished scribbling the order in her pad. She shot him a wink, followed by a warm smile.

Whistle sat and enjoyed a coffee, the paper, and before long, a perfectly adequate diner breakfast. After he was done, he paid up and was getting ready to leave. Just as he was on his way out the door he heard, "Excuse me. What's your name?"

Almost slipping and taking out a rack of *Auto Trader* magazines, he caught himself and answered.

"My name? Uh, Whistle...Whistle Evel Fonzarelli Starr."

"Well Whistle, my shift is just about done. Would you like to sit and have a cup of coffee?"

"Great," he responded earnestly.

"Have a seat, I'll be right back," she said as she walked into the kitchen. She was back out in an instant, with two piping hot cups of coffee.

"Theeere we go," Denise said as she gingerly set the coffees down on the table and took a seat across from Whistle.

"So...what's the story?" she asked as she stirred some cream in her coffee.

"Pardon?"

"Look, I don't mean to get too personal. But I know you're not from around here, and you seem a tiny bit down on your luck."

"I'm fine. What makes you say that?" he said, not particularly offended.

"Don't put me on the spot," she said, raising one eyebrow.

"I gotcha. Well, I've been what you would call 'urban camping' for a while now; just caught a flight to Anchorage because over the course of my life, I have managed to make it down the whole East Coast, across the south, and up the West Coast, with various pit stops along the way. Some just a night or a couple of days and some lasted years; I just kind of rode the river where it took me."

"So you just ended up here?" she asked, dumbfounded that anyone could just wander into Anchorage with no real reason to be there.

"Yeah. Stupid as it sounds...I figured I'd check out the city, hopefully find some work..." Whistle trailed off, staring out the window.

"Do you have a place to stay?"

"Well, I'm looking for a new room. Place I stayed last night wasn't exactly the height of luxury."

"Why don't you stay at my place? My kids are away at school and I've got two empty rooms."

"I appreciate the offer, Denise. But honestly, why would you offer someone you just met, that looked like me especially, a bed for the night in your home? Kind of dangerous, no?"

"I've got a gift for reading people, and I know you're a good guy. I've lived here awhile and it wouldn't hurt you to get a little insight on Anchorage before you get out there and start mixing it up. Otherwise, you'll get chewed up. Plus, I'm also a hair stylist, and I wouldn't mind cleaning up that mane of yours, no charge. A haircut and a shave'll make you look a little more employable."

"You got yourself a deal! I was going to buy some clippers and shave it all off anyway."

Back at Denise's house, Whistle was given a quick tour and rundown of all the amenities.

"These your kids?" Whistle asked as he looked at the framed pictures on the wall.

"Yes. This is Blake and this one's Lil' Suzi. Like the song."

"Lil' Suzi's on the up?" Whistle half asked, half sang.

"That's the one. She was conceived to that song, in the back of a Volkswagen Jetta parked down by Brickyard Pond....Boy we used to party down there," Denise said softly as she stared off, laughing to herself at a presumably crazy high school memory, filled with girl-crazy boys and boy-crazy girls, bonfires, and first loves.

"I'm sorry, I time traveled there for a second," she said. "Let me show you your room."

Up the stairs and around the corner was a teenage boy's room, complete with the faintest smell of weed still hanging in there months after Blake had gone off to school.

"Sorry about the weed smell. Blake thinks I don't know because he blows it out the window, but the stuff the kids smoke these days, you can smell it still wrapped up in the baggie in someone's pocket from across the room. He might have left some behind, check in his clothes drawers. Actually, you're about his size. Feel free to grab anything you want to wear; this was all stuff he was supposed to bring to the Goodwill before he left for school. I haven't done it, because he's supposed to go through it when he comes back for vacation. At least he'd better."

"Thanks, I appreciate it," Whistle said, smiling, but with a sadness in his eyes.

"What's the matter hon? Did I insult you by offering you the clothes? I ju—"

Whistle interrupted her. "No, no. I just remember a long time ago, I'd just left home and I was much less smart than I am now, I was just a kid. But a nice couple put me up for the night because their kids were away at school. Even gave me clothes too, if I remember correctly. Anyway, it just made me realize I've been wearing other people's clothes, living under other peoples' roofs, and sleeping in strange beds my whole life. I'm just wondering what I've missed out on."

"Everybody lives their own life, gets their own blessings, misses out on some things. Some gather riches on the outside, others gather experiences that they carry around on the inside. As long as you're thankful and hopeful for a better tomorrow, that's about as good as it gets."

"Can't argue with that logic," Whistle said, feeling better.

"I'm gonna go downstairs and watch my news. Pick out whatever you like and take a shower. There are fresh towels right there in that closet," she said, gesturing to the bathroom.

"Thanks, Denise...Really."

"No problem, kid. When you get done, come on down and I'll give you a trim...Bring a towel down with you."

"Will do," he responded, and he grabbed an IZOD rugby shirt and a pair of cargo pants out of the drawer.

Feeling like a new man after his shower and a fresh set of clothes (even found an unopened package of boxers...Score!) he went downstairs and sat in the kitchen chair pulled out to the middle of the room, facing the TV.

"Alright, so what are we doing?" Denise said as she set down her large and small scissors, comb, electric clippers and straight razor, with shaving cream, of course.

"I was just going to buzz it all off, so whatever you think would look good is fine with me. Don't be afraid to get creative."

"You don't wanna tell me that." Denise laughed.

"Within reason." Whistle chuckled.

Denise cut Whistle's hair and shaved his beard as the two talked and laughed, drank coffee, smoked cigarettes and watched *Dukes of Hazzard* reruns just like old friends. Some people you meet, and it just seems like you've always known them. Like picking up right where you left off in some other dimension somewhere.

"How's that?" she asked, giving Whistle a mirror to hold and look into while she walked around behind him with another so he could check out the back and the sides.

"Maybe one of the best I've ever had," he responded matter-of-factly as he studied his new look with a critical eye.

"You look like a teenager again," Denise said. "You can see that baby face now."

"Yeah, well...I've come a long way, baby," Whistle joked, taking advantage of the play on words.

"You ain't the only one, kid...Well look, I'm working breakfast tomorrow, so I gotta hit the sack, but watch TV if you like, help yourself to anything in the fridge, and set your alarm for five if you want a ride anywhere, or you're welcome to stay a few days to get sorted out...Either way is fine with me."

"Would that really be okay?" Whistle asked. Normally he wouldn't wear out his welcome like this, but Denise honestly felt like an old friend, the kind you felt comfortable asking to crash at their house for a few days...You know you'd do the same for them and they know it too.

"Absolutely, doll! If you want to take off during the day tomorrow, there's a key under the mat on the back porch, and if you're around tomorrow at dinner, I'll make something."

"Thanks again, Denise! You're the best."

"Alright. G'night, kid."

Whistle stayed the next several days at Denise's house, eating well, sleeping well, and getting a heads up on the city of Anchorage. In return, Whistle took care of some maintenance around the house and yard so he didn't feel like a freeloader. The morning he moved on, Denise hooked him up with as many pairs of jeans, shirts, and socks as he could fit in his duffel bag, and one last piece of advice.

"Whistle, be careful. I know you've been around, but Alaska plays by a whole different set of rules. Don't fall asleep on your feet and keep your head on a swivel."

"I'll be fine, Denise. Thanks for everything and thank your son for the clothes when he comes back during the school break. I'll stay in touch."

"All right, kid. Take care of yourself," Denise said as she gave Whistle a big hug and kiss on the cheek...

Okay, Whistle thought, *let's see what all the fuss is about. Come on, Anchorage. Let's see what you've got.*

CHAPTER
SEVENTY-EIGHT
Six Months of Hell

Anchorage wasted no time showing Whistle who was boss. Within six months, he met every sketchy character under the sun. A local "critter" named Walter Frick put the first needle in Whistle's arm. In no time, they became partners in petty theft and heroin addiction. The lost boy met a stripper named Jessica Twist and took her to the top of the town water tower for a roll in the proverbial hay, snorting cocaine off of each other's more interesting body parts. Climbing down the ladder proved to be the most hazardous activity of the evening, with Jessica slipping right around ten steps up from the ground, landing on Whistle who had already made it down, giving him a neck injury that he used as an excuse to keep shooting smack, for the pain, you see.

His neck got better over the next month or two, as it was mainly just a pulled muscle, but the addiction only grew. He partied in town, crashing on couches when he could and sleeping in the woods when the weather was mild. He chased a wild turkey through the woods with no success but drank Wild Turkey like a champ. He felt as if he was circling the drain of life and seeing as his journey was nearing its geographical end, his survival instinct was dimming.

Another guy Whistle befriended was a local roughhouser named Donald Union, a one-man donnybrook. His drug of choice was hard liquor, and Whistle was more than happy to partake when the two hung out together. Walter Frick had been set up in a sting and was now in jail, leaving Whistle no choice but to turn to booze to help him ride out the inevitable cold turkey withdrawals when there was no dope in town, at least for the time being.

Lucky for Whistle, his neck was feeling pretty good, save for the odd night when he slept wrong, but he had made the transition to a legal drug that was always available at any bar, restaurant, or liquor store. One night after drinking tequila at a local watering hole, Donald suggested they take a walk down to the quarry with some girls they met for a late night swim.

"Come on you pussy, it's only a mile down the road," Donald said when Whistle protested.

"I don't want to swim, I want to drink! You guys go ahead."

"You can drink down there, haaaHAAA!" Donald said as he discreetly opened his jacket to show Whistle a bottle of Southern Comfort that he snagged from the bar when the bartender was down at the other end gossiping with her friends, not paying attention to Donald, or any of the customers waiting for a drink, for that matter.

"Come on, let's GO!" Donny Donnybrook persisted, punching Whistle in the arm for emphasis.

"Alright...Fuck it," Whistle slurred as the four stumbled out the door and down the wooded back road to the quarry.

When they arrived, there was another small group of guys already there, drinking beers, swimming, and basically taking advantage of the small window of warm weather they were enjoying.

"Fuck....Oh! Wait a minute, I know that guy...Hey! Quirk!" Donny bellowed across the quarry, his voice echoing throughout, scaring off a bunch of birds and other woodland creatures.

"Donny! Come on over here!" came an equally raucous response.

"You sure these guys are cool?" Whistle asked, more annoyed than nervous.

"Totally cool! I go way back with Quirky."

"Well, any friend of Donnybrook...is bound to be an asshole," Whistle muttered as the girls giggled.

"Just keep walking," Donny said as they navigated the rocks, briars, and maple tree roots by the light of one small flashlight.

The two groups met on the ledge of the quarry and commenced drinking and smoking several large joints while shuffling metal, country, and southern rock CDs on the portable player. Things were relatively mellow, save for the boisterous hootin', hollering, and horsing around, courtesy of Quirky and Donny. Whistle mainly talked to the girls as the guys from Quirky's crew sat quietly and calmly drank their beers. As the night wore on, the attention the girls were paying to Whistle was starting to annoy Quirky. He started letting it be known in the usual way, making wisecracks, shooting looks, and basically engaging in high school posturing.

Whistle just laughed it off as he was used to this kind of thing and knew how to diffuse the situation. This worked for a while, until Whistle was overheard telling the girls about how he used to jump into the quarry back in New Hampshire with his friends. Not bragging, just quietly making conversation. Unfortunately, Quirky overheard him as he was wrestling with Donny in the sand.

"Hold up, hold up! Hey homey, you say you've jumped into a quarry before?" Quirky slurred, as he caught his breath from trying to break out of Donny's headlock.

"Yeah, back home. I was just a kid," Whistle responded dismissively.

"I dare you to jump into this one here," chimed in Donny.

"Nah, I'm good," Whistle said, as he took a sip of his beer, hoping that would be the final word on the matter. No such luck.

"Come on, pussy," Donny said, good-naturedly.

"Yeah...Pussy!" Quirky added...not so good-naturedly. Welp, here we go.

"Give me fifty bucks," Whistle countered.

"Hang on," Quirky said, checking his pockets. "Donny, how much money do you have on you?"

"Twenty-eight dollars and change," Donny replied as he counted the change in his palm.

"I've got fourteen," Quirky said.

"Close enough," Whistle said as he ran toward the ledge while stripping his clothes off, springing himself as far out as he could once he reached the edge.

"YEEEEeeaaahhh...." *Splash!...*

"He did it!" Donny yelled as the group ran to the edge to look down.

"Where is he?" asked one of the girls, concerned that he hadn't come up yet.

"Whoooo!" Whistle hollered as he shot up through the water, spun, and splashed around like Shamu. The heavy duty mix of booze and adrenaline kept the pain of the impact at bay until he swam back to shore, dragging himself out to be greeted by the rest of the crew with a fresh cold one and a T-shirt to dry off with.

"Pretty good, homey. I didn't think you had it in you. Here you go," Quirky said as he handed Whistle the wad of bills and coins with begrudging respect.

"Yeah, me neither," Whistle said as he pulled his T-shirt on and stuffed the wet clump of bills into the pocket of his jeans.

The rest of the night went smooth enough. Whistle even caught a few kisses from one of the girls. The next few months would not, however. He met another heroin connection and was caught up in the throes of addiction once more. He woke up one morning on top of a dumpster behind the local supermarket with a syringe hanging out of his arm. A local pimp named Mister Twister fed him so much coke that he had to be put in a tub full of ice in a motel "get together" on the seedy edge of town. Whiskey was poured, coke was snorted, acid was dropped, and heroin was dug into everyday life. Wake up, try to find enough money to score by hook or by crook, call his guy and buy a bundle, shoot it, and get right back to finding the money for his next fix. He started out chasing the dragon but now the dragon was chasing him.

Whistle also engaged in his fair share of fighting as well. He just seemed to meet every asshole imaginable in Anchorage. He came out on top of a scrum with two guys named Gus and Willy in a back alley. He also got his ass kicked by a Vietnamese five foot five, 120 pound amateur karate teacher named Quest. The man actually tried to warn him, but Whistle was drunk and belligerent and received a perfectly executed roundhouse kick to the side of the head, putting him to bed early that night.

The next day he woke up none the wiser, still letting his mouth write checks that would inevitably send his ass to the collection agency. Broken teeth, broken nose, and broke in general, he punched and got punched and was finally tired of it all.

The booze and drugs beat him up as well, making his insides match his outside, but it took a bit longer for the allure to wear off. One morning after a two day bender, Whistle woke up in his dingy room, under a dingy ceiling, and wrapped in dingy bedding. He greeted the day with an "Ugh" as he could hear the click-clack of his dry tongue and mouth sticking to each other as his head pounded with every step to the bathroom to vomit. He grabbed his water bottle, filled it from the sink, and after expelling a good amount of the toxins still residing in his system from the night before, walked outside to lay in the sun, letting it do its work to bring him back to the land of the living once more.

A few hours of sun, a few bottles of water, three or four Advils and some food, and Whistle felt like a new man. Completely rejuvenated, ready to conquer the world...and bored to tears. So, he proceeded to drop a hit of acid, snorted a few bumps, went down to the packy and picked up a bottle of Crown Royale, along with a pair of twins that worked at the local strip club, Heather and Rebecca, respectively.

Things proceeded as one might expect for the next several hours, with the twins eventually leaving Whistle alone to wallow in the emptiness of what was left of his life. Feeding his base desires and nothing else on a daily basis left him physically, mentally, and for the most part, spiritually depleted. He had no one and he was no one, just an empty, torn up trash bag whirling and twirling any which way the wind happened to be blowing.

He could not stand to be in his depressing, gross, pay by the week motel room any longer, so he checked out and figured he'd head down to the river. Being surrounded by nature by the rushing river was a better situation all around. The energy a river provides was something that stuck with Whistle ever since he was a young boy up in the mountains. It was cold and brutal year-round, but fresh and righteous, clean and honest, always on the move. Whistle knew whenever he stopped moving, that's when things started to go sideways. Problem was, he was in Anchorage, Alaska. Where was there left to go? He laughed to himself as he pictured hoofing it all the way to the North Pole to see if he could help Ol' Saint Nick on the Christmas toy assembly line.

This thought also brought on a bit of a mild hallucination, which made him dizzy, which made him nauseous, which reminded him he was about due for his next fix. He was starting to get up, pissed at himself that he was going to spend the rest of the day chasing down some dope dealer and paying him for the privilege of feeling normal. Sick of it all, through and through, he decided, "Fuck this, I'm done," and decided to kick dope once and for all by that river.

The next three days were beyond excruciating as several times Whistle wished he had checked himself into a facility to do this. He knew you could die from alcohol detox and was pretty sure one could from heroin as well. He, unfortunately, had both monsters to contend with, with a few others for good measure.

He shook, sweated, puked, cried, howled, whimpered, gnashed his teeth and soiled his underwear. He felt like he was living in a loop of taking an accidental step off a cliff. That feeling when your heart goes up in your throat, over and over again...for days...never even entertaining the thought of letting up. If you've never done heroin or became an alcoholic, don't.

Once he made it through the worst of it, after sleeping through his first night not chock full of alternating nightmares and insomnia, he woke up one morning bathed in the sunshine and cold mist of the rushing river. It felt great and refreshing. Whistle felt wrung out and sore, but free of the poison that occupied his being for the past six months and he was ready to move on, to wherever his river was going to lead him. He just had one stop to make first.

Whistle walked up the stairs to Denise's house right before dinnertime. He was starving but not confident in his ability to keep food down just yet, though the grilled chicken and pasta she was cooking in the kitchen with a strong garlic odor wafting through the screen of the porch door was heavenly. He knocked.

"Just a minute!" she yelled good-naturedly from the kitchen as she hurriedly flipped the chicken breast and added a bit of olive oil before jaunting to the front door. Her expectant smile quickly dropped to a genuine look of concern.

"Ooohh, come here kid!" she said as she hugged Whistle tight, instantly he burst into tears, hugging her back...tightly.

"Alllright, alllright, kid...Aaahhht's alllright," she said as she stroked the back of his head, almost as if she'd seen this movie before. Maybe one of her kids or her ex-husbands got themselves caught up the same way Whistle had. Why else would she have warned him so fervently about Anchorage? Either way, she sure knew how to make a guy feel better.

"You come in here. You're gonna eat something," she ordered Whistle, grabbing his hand and pulling him in the house with a surprisingly strong grip...All that waitressing.

"I appreciate it, Denise. It looks delicious, but I'm in no shape for food tonight. I just want to sit down and look at a friendly face."

"You sit down, I'll fix you a drink," she said with a knowing wink and a smile.

"OOOhhhh NOoooo....I'm done, I just spent three days getting clean, I—" Denise interrupted him.

"This is a special drink. No booze...something better."

"You're not gonna dose me, are you?" Whistle said as Denise looked over her shoulder with a dismissive grin.

"This is aaallllll good stuff," she said as she mixed a bunch of different juices and powders in the blender, along with some crushed ice.

"Here, try this," she said as she handed Whistle a big yellow plastic cup, filled with the frosty, blended concoction.

"Well?" she asked as Whistle guzzled it down.

"Wow! Pretty good. Kind of life a fruit smoothie with a fresh cut grass aftertaste. A little bit of a kick on the back end."

"Yeah...Listen, I'm gonna give you a kick on the back end if you don't get upstairs and take a shower. You're stinkin' up my kitchen worse than the garlic. Grab a fresh set of clothes out of Blake's room and take the drink with you. Finish it up."

"Yes ma'am," Whistle wisecracked as he headed up the stairs.

After taking a hot shower and a cold rinse, plus finishing Denise's elixir, Whistle felt like a million bucks. Better than he could ever remember feeling...NOW he was in the mood to eat.

"What WAS that stuff?" Whistle asked, obviously in much better form and spirits.

"Ancient Chinese secret," Denise quipped. "Just all natural good stuff. I'll write it down for you and give you a few hard to find herbs to keep you going for a while. You hungry yet? I just put the leftovers in the fridge. Still warm."

"How did you know?" Whistle laughed.

The two sat and talked for hours over leftovers and coffee and Whistle ended up staying in the spare room for two weeks while he got his strength back, taking care of some handyman work around the house to earn his keep. The morning he left, Denise gave him a few herbs and some more clothes to lighten the load for Blake when he finally got around to the Goodwill.

"Thanks Denise. I can't tell you how much you've helped me out. I love you and I'll stay in touch!"

"Awwwwwww, love you too, kid, c'meah 'n gimme a kiss, MMMMUAH!" she said as she gave Whistle a great big hug and an even bigger, greater kiss on the cheek.

"I don't gotta tell ya to be careful no more, but I will tell ya, you ever need anything, you call me, you understand?" Denise said sternly as she vigorously rubbed the lipstick from his cheek. This made him laugh and feel better inside than all the thrills, spills, frills, strippers, all night rippers and acid trippers rolled into one. All that bullshit laid to rubble by an older middle-aged waitress rubbing her lipstick from his cheek.

He hugged Denise goodbye one more time and he was on his way. The plan was to head north, stay out of trouble, and keep his eyes open for a destination to present itself, wherever that may be.

CHAPTER
SEVENTY-NINE
An Incredible Fishing Trip

Whistle stuck to his plan and his plan served him well. Within a month he'd made his way all the way up to Tanana. There, he hung his hat at the Carriage Inn for two weeks and rested. He ate well at the Inn's homey little tavern. He filled his belly with succulent steak, fried chicken, roast pork, and even some moose. Plenty of root vegetables came with every meal and the homemade bread made store bought taste like styrofoam by comparison. As impossibly delicious as the bread was, the garlic butter spread that it was served along with was enough to make Whistle want to live out the rest of his days there at the Inn. Reading the paper, watching a ballgame, and eating bread.

However, man cannot live on bread alone. So Whistle developed a taste for the local beer with a peculiar citrus and honey aftertaste. That and the company of a cute waitress made moving on harder by the day. One day while watching football on the TV at the bar, Whistle struck up a conversation with a fellow named Digger Davis, who happened to be a fishing guide.

He invited Whistle to go fishing for salmon on the Tanana River with him.

"Digger, I appreciate the offer, but I can't afford that right now. Besides that, I don't have a pole or anything as far as gear goes."

"I got all the gear we need and I won't charge you! C'mon!" Digger said in his always excitable manner.

"Why would you do that? That's how you make your living?" Whistle asked as he kept an eye on the game. He had a friendly twenty bucks on the Pats, his home team.

"I could use the company, to be honest. This month has been slow. Plus you can help me fill my freezer."

"Makes sense to me," Whistle said as they shook on it and enjoyed the rest of the game. Pats won, of course.

After the game, Whistle went to his room to grab his bag and a few extra items to bring to Digger's rustic log cabin, where he spent the night to get an early start the next morning. There, Whistle and Digger enjoyed a hearty dinner of perfectly seasoned, juicy caribou steaks, al dente green beans with balsamic, and mashed red potatoes, buttered along with some of that fresh baked bread from the tavern. "Dinner don't get better than this!" Whistle said, raising his glass of beer. Digger raised his glass and agreed as the crackling fire roared well into the evening.

After the plates were cleared, they had a few shots of bourbon, got the rods and tackle prepared, and packed up for the morning. A few more shots and then it was off to bed. Whistle got the couch right in front of the fire and a heavy, handmade Eskimo blanket to keep warm. He immediately fell asleep with visions of big salmon swimming down the river of dreams.

Four in the morning came quick as Digger woke Whistle up and handed him a welcome mug of black coffee with a picture of Yosemite Sam on it saying "Now Quit Stallin' and Start Roastin'!" One cup went down in several gulps and the second accompanied a "stick to your ribs" breakfast of eggs, sausage, oatmeal, and rhubarb, along with a glass of orange juice.

"Ahhhhh...Welp, I'm good," Whistle said as he got up and washed the dishes and set them in the rack to dry.

"Cool, I'm going to start up the Bronc, just lock the door on your way out," Digger said as he grabbed the supplies and headed outside. Whistle didn't want to be a lolligag or a slob, so he hurriedly washed the rest of the dishes, accidentally chipping his mug.

"Ahhhh shit!" he said as he turned off the water and hauled ass out the door, locking it on the way out. He jumped up into Digger's '78, blue and white Ford Bronco. Nothing better to take you for a big day of fishing.

Whistle and Digger drank their third coffees of the morning from their travel thermoses and listened to an 8-track of Lynyrd Skynyrd on the old Pioneer stereo.

"They say CDs sound better, but I disagree...This sounds right...this sounds PHAT!" Digger said as he turned up "The Ballad of Curtis Loew."

"Yeah, records too. It just hits the spot with the right band playing." Whistle yawned as he leaned his head back and closed his eyes, taking in the music, which lulled him to sleep as Digger thoughtfully turned it down before "Swamp Music" kicked up.

After about an hour, Digger turned off the freeway onto a dirt road, waking Whistle from his snooze. "How you doin' sunshine?" Digger asked with an easy smile.

"Oh man, I'm good," Whistle replied with another yawn, stretching and craning his neck.

"We goin' off roadin'!" Digger hooted as they drove down the bumpy dirt road, then going even deeper into the woods down a trail narrow enough to hear the brush on each side scraping as they drove through. The two laughed at the job they must be doing on the paint job, which was fairly scuffed from who knows how many previous fishing trips.

Another right turn into some even deeper brush that almost threatened to swallow the truck completely before it opened up to a small clearing, right on the bank of the river.

"This must be the spot," Digger said as they got out and immediately relieved themselves.

"I gotta try a few practice casts," Whistle said, taking the fishing gear out of the Bronco.

"Well, go on then. Give it a whirl," Digger said as he came out of the bushes, zipping up.

Whistle cast into the rushing river and almost immediately shouted.

"Woah! Something hit it!"

"Really? Hey, maybe we ain't goin' nowhere," Digger said as he grabbed his tackle box, two beers and his pole, casting in one fluid motion, with the kind of gracefulness one can only attain through years of experience. Cast after cast, the two never fished more than three pools all day, as they had all they could handle right around camp.

By afternoon the feeding frenzy inevitably slowed down so the boys decided to set up camp. Tents up, bedding laid out, gear stowed away and firewood cut and stacked. After a quick snack of Slim Jims and Coke, it was back to the water and lo and behold, the fish were biting again! The cooling, early evening and nymph hatch brought the fish to the surface.

Once the sun was gone and dusk was setting, they stored their salmon, five in all, on a stringer in the water. They took the sixth and made it back to camp. Whistle set up and started a flint and steel fire while Digger expertly gutted and cleaned the salmon. After a while, Whistle lay green branches across the coals so the two could cook huge salmon filets and corn on the cob with pearl onions in the tinfoil pouches. The food came out perfect, with just a twitch of bourbon to land the plane.

"Diggerman, I can't thank you enough for this. It's just what I needed!" Whistle said, laid back in his folding chair as he looked up at the stars.

"Hey, my pleasure. Listen, I love being out here alone but you can go stir crazy after a while. Plus at this rate, my freezer's gonna be full for the first time this year. Actually, about a year and a half it's been since I was fully stocked. So, here's to ya!" Digger toasted Whistle with his flask.

"Besides that, I was getting pretty dang sick of bear meat. Haha!" Digger laughed as Whistle pulled a joint out of his front jacket pocket. They proceeded to burn one down, roasted some marshmallows, made some cowboy coffee, complete with a shot of Southern Comfort, talked about everything and nothing and after a few hours retired to their tents to get a good night of rest in for an early day tomorrow.

Dawn came and they were both ready to go. Breakfast was a granola bar and some more of that cowboy coffee, this time no SoCo. The best fishing was usually earlier than most people like to get up, so there wasn't much leisure time. The morning was quiet and still as the two worked the river. They cast the pools, adjusted techniques and caught plenty of fish. By the time they took lunch, they had four huge salmon on the stringer. With nine fish waiting in the cold river, Digger got two absolutely righteous Italian grinders from Schroder's Deli out of the cooler along with two dill pickles, two bags of chips, and two ice cold Cokes.

"Why do grinders taste so good when you're out fishing?" Whistle pondered.

"What's a grinder?" Digger asked.

"Sub sandwich...Grinder! You never heard that?" Whistle asked, forgetting he was on the West Coast. Way up in Alaska, no less. It felt a whole lot like New Hampshire out here, however. It almost felt like he was transported and was starting over.

After they finished lunch, they packed everything up and loaded the Bronco. A shot of bourbon down the hatch and it was back to the river to see if they could pull a few more fish out of the river for Digger's freezer.

The afternoon passed and dusk dropped its incredible colors everywhere. Once again, all his favorite colors surrounded Whistle. With five more salmon on the stringer, the two packed the cooler with fourteen salmon all told. Digger would be able to take a break from bear for a good, long while. Fishing rods packed, they drove out with over one hundred and fifty pounds of Alaskan King Salmon...BOOM!

After they harvested the haul, Digger would wind up with sixty pounds of salmon steaks for his freezer. They made the long trek back to the cabin and basically collapsed once they finally got there. Sleeping straight through till eight thirty in the morning, they woke up with a quick couple of coffees and got right to work. The Bronco was unpacked in short order. The cooler of fish was placed on the ground next to a large, weathered picnic table with a cheap, vinyl tablecloth covering it. A large cutting board placed down and a sharp fillet knife later, the cleaning began.

Whistle gutted and Digger filleted. Blood slowly washed over the vinyl, dripping down their pants and boots. The fillets got stacked and all the waste was collected in a large, galvanized metal tub. This would end up feeding Digger's friends' sled dogs for a good spell.

When this mighty task was finally conquered, the two were covered in fish guts and blood. They proceeded to pack all the fish in Digger's GE freezer. Sure enough, it ended up weighing in at just over sixty-eight pounds. After cleaning everything up in the yard, they both took showers and put all the laundry directly into the washing machine.

"Man that was hard work, but wow, what a blast!" Whistle sighed.

"You're not kidding! I don't know anyone who pulled that many fish on a trip like that in a long time, probably years. My arms are like spaghetti," Digger concurred.

With that, they gutted and cleaned the salmon they were saving for dinner. It was quartered and seasoned with salt, pepper, and yellow mustard. Rosemary sprigs waited to be placed on top of the fish in the pan.

"Would you like white radishes, baby carrots, celery, with seared goose cubes on the side?"

"If anyone would know what goes good with salmon, that'd be you, my man."

"You got that right," Digger replied with a knowing wink and a nod.

Dinner ready, they sat down to a feast fit for a king. Whistle was blown away by the white radishes. "I always assumed radishes sucked, boy was I off the mark."

The conquering fishermen spent an hour at least just trying to polish off the main course. Leaving just enough room for a few shots of bourbon for dessert. They sat down before the crackling, roaring fire, fat and happy to belch a lot, say little, watch the fire and drift in and out of sleep.

"I tell ya, if you wanna hang around these parts for a while, I'd be happy to hire you when things start picking up. You're a heck of a worker, and apparently a good luck charm," Digger said after a roaring belch, almost long enough to recite the alphabet.

"Man...I would love to, but I've got something I gotta do," Whistle responded with appreciation.

"What would that be, if you don't mind me asking ?"

"Ahhhh, I'm heading north," Whistle said as he got up to use the bathroom.

"Whereabouts?" Digger asked, now genuinely curious.

"I'm not sure exactly, but it can't be that far, can't get a whole lot further north than this."

"Eh, you'd be surprised," Digger responded with a tone of caution in his voice.

When Whistle came out of the bathroom, Digger was stoking the fire and throwing a few more logs on, making it snap, crackle, and pop furiously, spitting glowing embers and sparks as the logs caught aflame.

"Hang tight for a sec. I'll be right back," Digger said as Whistle sat and leaned towards the fire, letting the heat dance around his face until he couldn't take it and leaned back again to feel the cool night air fill his lungs. He played this game a while longer and recalled doing the same thing as a young boy in the White Mountains of New Hampshire. Would he ever get back there? Was there a reason to go? Would anyone be waiting for him there? Whistle pondered these questions as the fire danced and swirled in glowing monarch flames of orange and gold, juxtaposed against the pitch black night and dull, grey smoke. He was just about to get up and fix another drink when Digger came out of the kitchen with two fresh ones and a platter of sliced buffalo sausage and Monterey Jack cheese on Ritz crackers.

"Woah! You read my mind," Whistle said as he took his drink and a cracker sandwich off the platter. The two ate and drank until the first light of morning, at which point they decided they'd better wrap it up and get some sleep. They had no plans that day or the next so there was no need to set an alarm, allowing both to sleep till afternoon. Whistle woke up with a pounding headache and Digger followed soon after. They spent the couple of days eating, drinking, splitting wood, and generally just chilling at the cabin. Eventually Whistle felt the urge to get moving again.

Splitting a particularly stubborn log for the fire, Digger looked at Whistle as he was almost done stacking and decided the woodpile could do without this knotted monstrosity, so straight into the campfire this one would have to go.

"Anything else you need me to do?" Whistle asked.

"No we're good. Let's just clean up and grab some lunch."

Whistle stayed the rest of the day and night in much the same fashion as the previous. Eating, drinking, talking and laughing, capped off with a perfectly restful night's sleep by a low fire of barely glowing logs providing just the right amount of warmth. In the morning he'd have a few cups of coffee, a light breakfast with Digger, take a few frozen salmon steaks for the road and say, "See ya around" to yet another friend along the way to find his true north.

CHAPTER EIGHTY
More Traveling and Save Waldo

Working his way further into the woods up Route 3, Whistle was happy as a clam. He camped out along a trail and feasted on nothing but salmon, trying to avoid having any of it spoil. He kept his fires low so as not to draw attention to himself. Two weeks later, he found himself in Fairbanks. It took less than a week for Whistle to realize that Fairbanks and Anchorage weren't all that different, so he moved on. He chose to leave Route 3 and start up onto Route 2. After two nights of camping, he walked along the side of Route 11. This turned out to be a great experience for Whistle. He walked all his resources out save for the $232 in his pocket.

His shoes were worn, his pack was close to empty, and all his clothes stunk beyond belief. Just as the boy was travel weary, he came upon the People's Public Truck Stop. Straight away he secured a room for twenty dollars a night. In his room, he stripped down and jumped into the shower. The water was hot and felt great. He spent over an hour just standing in there. After that, he washed up, dried off, and simply went to bed.

The next morning, Whistle had a decent breakfast in the truck stop's diner. Then, he took the short walk into town. There, he got a haircut and his beard shaved off. After that, he meandered the streets all day long until night started to fall. That night, he did his laundry in the truck stop laundromat. The dryers were kind of weak so he had to hang his clothes all over his room to hopefully dry everything by the next day, when he was planning to pack up and head north. You don't want damp clothes for trips like this.

He woke up the next morning, grabbed a quick coffee and breakfast, and got on the road. Mostly walking along the road, but off in the woods as much as possible. At this point it almost felt second nature. He hit a little bad weather, but considering where he was, it was more a nuisance than a real issue.

On the road that fairly decent day, a faint hint of smoke hit his nostrils and alerted his primal senses. He looked and listened carefully for any clue of where it might be coming from. It was in his nature to run into the face of danger when it was in service of someone in need. He followed his nose to a hill and in the valley on the other side was a small farm, complete with a little house, a couple of chicken coops, and a barn, which happened to be on fire.

As he ran down the hill, a woman in a flannel shirt and blue jeans was running from the house toward the barn as well.

"Is there anyone in there?" Whistle asked as he grabbed her wrist, afraid she might try to run in.

"Only Waldo, but I can't lose him!" she said, getting hysterical.

Just like that, Whistle pulled the barn door open and ran in. It was hot and black, smoke instantly started to choke him out.

"Waldo!" he yelled, hoping for some kind of response...no luck.

"Waldo!" he yelled again, choking on the air he drew in to yell. He dropped to his knees where the air was a little more tolerable.

"Hello! Anybody in here!" Whistle was about to give up and belly crawl out to safety when he heard a loud thud to his side in one of the stalls...He found Waldo, or at least knew who he was looking for and which general direction to crawl.

"Where are you, buddy?" Whistle called out in the black smoke, trying to follow the sound. Another kick got Whistle to the correct stall where he took in a deep breath of somewhat useful air and held it as he stood up and unlatched the stall gate, which thankfully was not locked. He pulled it open and without resistance, led Waldo out before he dropped to his knees, losing his breath and quickly losing a battle with the carbon monoxide.

One more deep breath of air from floor level, and Whistle got up and led the frightened animal toward the door as the hay lit up like a torch and the barn crumbled around them. Flames, smoke, and flying, glowing embers spooked the horse and made Whistle's mission seem impossible in the moment; it wasn't looking too good.

No time to formulate a plan, Whistle just grabbed Waldo and pulled him along as he made a run for it toward the faint square of daylight he could see through the chaos. They plowed through with all their might and made it outside.

Whistle stumbled out the front door and in the clear daylight, realized he was holding onto the horn of a huge bull steer. They managed to get far enough away from the barn before it collapsed in on itself. The woman apparently called for help as fire trucks began to pull up to try and mitigate the situation. It would definitely be too little too late as all that was left was in a burning pile.

As the fire team dealt with the fire, Whistle brought Waldo over to the pasture, far away from the action to give him a chance to calm down. The last thing a fireman needs is a freaked out bull steer in the mix. Whistle wiped some of the ashes from the steer's rust colored coat, then gave him a soothing pat on his white striped snout. The steer looked at him with what Whistle took to be gratitude, or at least trust.

The barn was pretty much completely gone; all that old wood went up in no time, leaving not much more than a smoldering black spot where the barn used to be. With plenty of people around now, first responders, other members of the family, and even a local news team, Whistle saw an opportunity to duck out and just be on his way.

Eventually, the commotion at the barn settled down and everyone was looking for the boy who saved Waldo, who happened to be the number one ranked bull in the state. But that boy had things to do and more importantly, places to go. No thank yous were needed, he was just happy he could help.

For the remainder of the year, Whistle would continue north in a fairly familiar fashion. There were hotels, dinners, women, drugs, roughing it on easy street and taking it easy in the wild. He got a job as a pottery glazer that carried him through. He built up some savings to make his final push north. After all, he wasn't getting any younger. If he were to continue on, he would have to do it now.

Giving his two weeks' notice at the pottery shop, Whistle eventually packed up and started hiking again. After about a week, he walked into the tiny town of Coldfoot.

CHAPTER
EIGHTY-ONE
Welcome to Coldfoot

I t all started with a waitress named Emily Shue at the Kodiak Diner.

"What'll it be?" she asked, not even looking up from her pad, pencil at the ready.

"Coffee and the number three, please," Whistle said, settling in.

"Coming right up," she said as she turned on her heel and walked through the swinging kitchen doors. Looking around, Whistle noticed a few details about the diner. First off, it only had five customers, Whistle and two couples. Second, there was an incredible jukebox at his disposal. Unable to resist, Whistle put some money in and queued up Meat Loaf "Bat Out of Hell" and AC/DC "Back In Black." Realizing he was the only one in the mood to rock, he immediately turned it down to a reasonable mid-afternoon volume.

He got his BLT and fries, along with a Coke, and proceeded to make himself at home, reading the local paper, listening to the jukebox and trying to chat up Elizabeth. She was not in a particularly chatty mood this afternoon, but Whistle was nothing if not persistent and after three days of returning for lunch and a fourth for dinner, Whistle finally convinced her to go on a date with him, which worked out beautifully. He eventually was able to rent a place on the edge of town from a guy named Willy Thompson. Spending the rest of the year there in Coldfoot, he stayed at Willy's place, dated Elizabeth on and off, worked odd jobs here and there and eventually saved up twelve thousand dollars, which he hid in a metal box under his shack.

Remembering how much he enjoyed staying at Digger's cabin, he decided he would like to buy one for himself, if he could find one for a decent price, which he was able to. Right on the eastern edge of the Arctic National Park. He figured at the very least he could sell it if and when he decided to move and get his money back, maybe even a little extra if he found the right buyer. Working the log lines and guiding hunting excursions added to his ever growing nest egg.

He eventually saved twenty-five thousand dollars, which this time he kept under his bed, along with a Smith and Wesson. He had quite an ordeal with a gopher pulling the stash out from under the shack he rented from Willy.

Alone in the woods, Whistle had plenty of time to get his life organized. His cabin was sparsely furnished and his possessions were few, so he decided to turn his attention to the land and make an attempt at starting a vegetable garden. There weren't many neighbors this far out, but he did manage to make a few friends as the people out this way tended to be solid, no bullshit people.

The first was a woman named Linda Dahryl, whom he met within a week of moving to the area. She was a fiery redhead that took an immediate shine to him. Her ice blue eyes caught him and he already knew that he was as close to being in love as he would ever be. Their relationship flourished and a routine was established. This included Linda showing up every last Saturday of the month with whatever groceries Whistle might need.

She would stock his cabinets and they would drive down to the lake. If the weather was warm, they would go skinny dipping and make love in the glow of the sunset. Then, it was back to the cabin for a late dinner and a bottle of red wine by the fireside where they would usually fall asleep.

Sunday morning, they would make brunch, enjoy the afternoon doing whatever came natural, before Linda would eventually head back to town in the early evening. Whistle, realizing that he was content to be a lone wolf, made peace with the idea long ago. This was nice, though. He and Linda were happy to give each other their space, and live their own lives. She worked in town during the week and Whistle worked on his homestead. It was such a perfect situation he, for the first time in his life, didn't feel the pull of the open road.

Goats were raised and deer were shot. Fortunately, he was able to buy a Springfield 1911 World War I rifle that had been reworked for hunting. It went from killing men to putting food on the table. It was beautiful and Whistle loved it. "This is my rifle. There are many like it but this one is mine," he would recite to himself humorously while hiking out into the wilderness to hunt.

He spent his considerable downtime at night writing down the recollections of his life on the road. It started out when Linda gave him a few notebooks and a package of No. 2 pencils and an antique pencil sharpener. Whistle would tell her stories about his adventures and she would badger him good-naturedly to write a book or at least write a column for the local paper. Plenty of time and plenty of material kept his momentum up as he filled the box marked "stories" that he kept next to his writing desk, a big, rough-edged piece of tiger maple that was the perfect size and shape for writing.

When Linda came out for one of her visits, she would always ask to read and maybe submit one of his stories. He would always answer back with a curt, "They're not done yet," or, "You've already heard them." Each visit she would try, and each visit her request would be gently batted down, as the paper stacked up.

Outside of those thoroughly enjoyable visits from his lovely Linda, Whistle was on his own. If your daily rations consist of squirrel, chipmunk, and mouse, you know you're on your own. Whistle's cabin was small but well built. It held in the heat in the winter and stayed cool in the summer, thanks to a window air conditioner that was just enough to keep the whole place at a perfect seventy-three degrees.

He decided that this was as good a place as any to grow some roots for once. He didn't imagine that he would find a better situation and he took pride in his homestead. The more work he put in, the more pride he felt. He was always happy to show off his latest project whenever Linda would come out on one of her weekend visits.

A few years rolled by easy with everything needed to be happy. The beautiful woman that would be his only companion was growing older along with Whistle. Both their hair began to turn white as well, Linda's developing a shocking white streak along her bangs, where it was parted on the side. Whistle's was more of a gradual salt and pepper that was more prevalent in his beard.

Whistle celebrated his fiftieth birthday without even knowing it. It fell on a weekend and Linda was up at the cabin. They threw axes at a makeshift target in a throwing lane they marked off. After she beat him, they soaked in the jacuzzi Whistle built all on his own over the summer. She stayed over and headed back Sunday evening, like always. Whistle was in a reflective mood as he sat down to do some writing.

He sat there, staring at the paper, just daydreaming and taking stock of his life. He loved Linda, she loved him, but he couldn't help but wonder if she wanted more from him. She wasn't the type to complain and neither was Whistle, which was probably why they got along so well. But if it was starting to feel like *Groundhog Day* to him, he had to imagine she felt it as well.

His finances were dwindling as well. He figured he was spending an average of two hundred dollars a month. Going by his admittedly rough math, he had enough to get through the next nine years. He made a point to ask Linda to bring out extra supplies each month. He stocked up on aspirin, water, canned goods and ammo. Plenty of seeds and grain stored in his cupboards, Whistle decided it was time for a caribou hunt. After a few days of prepping the homestead and getting his supplies in order, he headed out into the wild.

After hiking for two days and sleeping only a few hours each night, he eventually came upon Wiseman's Ridge. The view was awe inspiring, so Whistle decided it was as good a spot as any to set up camp. He spent hours glassing Red Fern Hollow below. He ate cold baked beans and beef jerky as he shivered in the dark. This lasted another two days until a curious thing happened. Whistle had been glassing a large bull across the valley and getting ready to make his move when a bright glint came through his scope from atop the ridge across the way.

"What the?" he whispered to himself as he continued to watch. After another night of camping under the stars, he figured the glint that he saw was from another hunter glassing the same caribou. The two slowly made their way down to the valley. By the time they got there, the caribou was long gone. They cautiously stayed away from each other for a while until finally Whistle spoke up.

"Lower your gun, I'm coming out." The two left their rifles and stepped out into a small clearing. Looking at each other, Whistle noticed the man standing before him was olive skinned, with long, jet black, straight hair and a full beard. After a bit of a pause, the man spoke up.

"That was one big son of a bitch, wasn't it?" he said, immediately putting Whistle at ease.

"You are not kidding, my friend." Whistle chuckled, more from relief than anything. Somebody could shoot you way out here and nobody would ever know. Whistle stepped up and put his hand out.

"Pleasure to meet you. The name's Whistle. Whistle Evel Fonzarelli Starr. What's yours?"

CHAPTER
EIGHTY-TWO
Johnny Appleseed

"I'm Johnny Appleseed," the man said with an easy smile.

"Excuse me?" Whistle asked, thinking he misheard him.

"I'm Johnny Appleseed. Actually, my name was Johnny Clipclop. I'm originally from Wolfeboro, New Hampshire. I'd gotten into some trouble down in Concord and had to leave. So I changed my name to Johnny Appleseed and I moved out here." He shrugged with a small chuckle of his own.

"You're not gonna believe this, but I'm from Gorham, New Hampshire originally. I've been on the road my whole life!" And just like that, the two became friends. They decided to team up and set up camp in a great little spot that night, building a great big fire, and got to know each other. It turned out that Johnny had a cabin about seven miles from Whistle's. They both grew up playing hockey and they shared the same love of the great outdoors.

At dawn the next morning, they woke up and had a minimal breakfast before heading up to Wiseman's Ridge for one more look before they headed out. Sure enough, there that one large bull caribou stood. By four thirty that afternoon, the two finally got within one hundred yards of their target. At exactly five-o-nine, Whistle took the shot from a bedrock outcrop. It was perfect and the great animal dropped instantly. The two ran down and congratulated each other with great enthusiasm. That's when the herculean task of harvesting began. It was an incredible bonding experience, but just as importantly, they both knew their freezers would be full for the upcoming winter.

By nightfall, the caribou was gutted, skinned, and dressed into quarters. They ate the heart, liver, and brains that night and went to bed with full bellies. The rest hung in a tree, high enough to be out of a bear's reach.

The next morning, they packed everything up, and hiked out together. Their packs were so heavy, it took two full days to make it back to Johnny's cabin. Finally arriving, they froze all the meat and both enjoyed some bison burgers with buns, lettuce, tomatoes, and onions. Mmmm mmmmm good!

After stuffing themselves silly, Johnny cracked a bottle of Johnnie Walker Black and the two sat and toasted their hunting skills and strong backs. They stayed up drinking and swapping stories all night until the first eastern light rose over the mountains. They fell asleep and woke up the next afternoon, then Whistle headed out with his belongings and caribou meat. The two said goodbye knowing they had just had their first adventure with a new, lifelong friend.

Once home, Whistle stowed his caribou and spent the next several months cutting wood, canning vegetables, and locking everything down for the winter ahead. Linda came out one final time at the end of October before winter set in like she always did. With extra supplies, she stayed an entire week. He always appreciated her as they put the sugar, spices, coffee, and tea in the cupboards before spending romantic evenings by the fire, in the jacuzzi or in the king size bed Whistle built by hand.

This routine continued season after season, making it easy to lose track of the years rolling by. When Whistle was a boy, marking the years was easier due to school and cultural shifts in music, with easy listening mellow gold giving way to rock, then to disco, punk, new wave, etcetera. Bell bottoms gave way to parachute pants and striped Bobby Brady shirts gave way to Ocean Pacific and Vans checkerboard slip-ons. Once he hit the road, however, these became frivolous matters and clothing was for protection, warmth, and functionality.

The years he spent on the road were a little easier to lose track of as he was living by his own timeline. If it felt right to stay in a certain place for a while, he did. When moving on was his only option, he moved on, and when you're in survival mode, recollection can get fuzzy. Nevertheless, spending the majority of his life on the road, making his way down the East Coast, across the south, and eventually up the West Coast at least gave him some sense of traceable time and motion.

Up here, away from society in the still of the wilderness, three winters can turn into five, five years can turn into a decade, and the older you get, the more it happens. "Is this necessarily a bad thing?" Whistle pondered one evening as he sat by the fire with Johnny, who came up to help Whistle with an outbuilding he was trying to finish as winter was slowly but surely approaching.

Finishing the project with time to spare, Johnny hung out for a few ex-tra days to do a little hunting. Running down a trail one day, Whistle tripped on a tree root and broke his trigger finger, which Johnny was able to splint quite nice-ly. Luckily, there was plenty of meat in the freezer so hunting was more for sport at this point in the year than survival.

Whistle and Johnny's friendship carried on for years and years. One night, Whistle jokingly asked Johnny what he wanted to do when he grew up as they say by the fire, knocking a few back.

"Actually, I always wanted to be a picture framer," Johnny replied, ear-nestly.

"A picture framer?" Whistle asked, perplexed.

"Yes, there's a lot of creativity involved. Figuring out sizes, colors, and formats. Does someone want single matte or double matte? Do they want high gloss or a satin finish? Should the glass be ultraviolet protected? A lot of options to choose from and all art needs a frame. A movie needs a silver screen, a musi-cian needs a stage, a story needs a frame of reference...All art needs a frame," Johnny said as he shot Whistle a knowing wink as he took a sip of his Crown Royale.

"You never cease to amaze me, you crazy bastard." Whistle laughed as he toasted Johnny.

"What did you want to do when you grew up?" Johnny asked Whistle.

"I'm not sure. I know I always wanted to travel and I've certainly done my share. I wanted to experience as much as I could along the way and I've done that as well. As far as me wanting to 'be' a specific thing, the only thing that ever hung around in the back of my mind was that I'd one day like to maybe be a hunting and fishing guide, or maybe a park ranger. I don't know, just as long as I spent most of my time in the wild, that was good enough for me."

"Well, it don't get much wilder than living in a cabin in the wilderness of Alaska, so I'd like to propose another toast...Mission Accomplished."

"Yeah...Thanks buddy. I can't believe I met another Granite Stater way out here, in a valley hunting caribou, but I'm sure glad I did. It's almost like meeting a long lost brother you never knew you had."

"Likewise my friend...Likewise," Johnny said as he got up to throw an-other couple of logs on the fire.

CHAPTER
EIGHTY-THREE
Linda's Last Visit

Linda came up to the cabin a little later than usual this time of year, but fortunately brought extra supplies. She looked sickly but Whistle held his tongue. He made her a nice dinner of turkey leg with spinach, onions, and garlic on the side. Wild rice rounded out the hearty meal with a hefty supply of carbs. After dinner, they sat on the couch and watched *Back to the Future* on Whistle's VCR while munching on kettle corn.

Whistle noticed that Linda was not enjoying herself and was spending more time in the bathroom than usual. After a while, Whistle couldn't take the suspense any longer and stood outside the bathroom, listening as Linda was clearly ill and vomiting painfully. Giving her time to finish, flush, and clean up, Whistle made his way in and grabbed her tight.

"I'm so sorry to tell you this, Whistle...but, I have stomach cancer." She sobbed into his shoulder.

"It's okay....it's okay," Whistle whispered, trying to be strong. "There's lot's they can do these days with medicine and chemo—"

Linda stopped him. "They tried everything. I have two months at the most," she burst out with a good long cry as Whistle shed plenty of tears of his own, taking her to bed and gently stroking her hair as she eventually fell asleep. It made Whistle happy that she was comfortable enough to do so.

In the morning, they got up and Whistle made her a mild breakfast of toast, cereal, fruit, and Coke as it helped settle her stomach.

"I just want you to know, you are the love of my life and I always wanted to make it official, but I always assumed you wouldn't want to be stuck out here with me. I'm not exactly Prince Charming and this isn't a palace by anyone's standards," Whistle said as he welled up a little, trying his best to hide behind his cup of coffee.

"I love you, Whistle. I know you love me too. Not all little girls dream of the same things."

"Marry me, Linda. Please...marry me right now!" Whistle said as he got up and swiftly pushed his chair out of the way to get down on one knee before her. It happened so fast, she hardly had time to chew her toast before she could say yes.

After breakfast, Whistle called Johnny to tell him the good news. Johnny offered to come up that afternoon to perform the ceremony down by Whistle's creek. Afterwards, the three sat down for a feast of caribou, baked potatoes, corn on the cob, and a fresh raw veggie salad. Linda tried her best to keep up appearances as she and Whistle decided to hold off on the news regarding her health. They wanted to keep this a happy occasion and Whistle could tell Johnny later on.

As it started to get dark, Whistle started working on a campfire while Johnny and Linda cleared the table. Once everything was cleaned up, Johnny announced, "Well guys, it's been a blast, but I'm not hanging around to be a third wheel on honeymoon night."

"Come on, Johnny. It's going to be dark soon. You can leave in the morning," Linda offered.

"Yeah Johnny, don't be ridiculous," Whistle chimed in.

"No, I'm going to get going. I have a flashlight and a rifle. Don't give it another thought. Congratulations you crazy kids," Johnny said as he gave Linda a hug and a peck on the cheek.

"Alright big guy, be careful...and thanks for everything!" Whistle replied as he gave Johnny a big bear hug.

Seeing Johnny off with some leftovers to take home with him, the newlyweds wasted no time consummating the marriage. As a matter of fact, once Whistle carried Linda over the threshold, they stayed right there on the front porch all night, enjoying life as man and wife.

Linda stayed another three days, as Whistle cared for her, fed her, and did his best to make her feel as comfortable and content as he possibly could. On the day she headed back to town, they hugged, kissed, and held each other, never wanting to let go.

"Linda, you are the love of my life and I can never put into words what you mean to me. Thank you, I love you so much!" Whistle sobbed as he grabbed her as tight as he could.

"I love you too, Whistle. This isn't goodbye. I'll see you again. Someday, some way, we'll be together again."

With that, Linda got into her car and drove away, leaving Whistle standing there watching her make that drive back into town one more time. He spent the rest of the night crying, drinking, and regretting not making Linda his wife sooner. It was a tough night, but he got through it. Exactly two months from the day he married her, Linda passed and Whistle, with the help of his best friend Johnny, prepared her resting place on top of a hill where they used to go to watch sunsets. Whistle would go up there by himself and talk to Linda. Sometimes he would get little signs that she was listening. He'd always plant flowers every spring and within a few years, Linda's hilltop became a gorgeous garden which Whistle meticulously tended to with love.

As life went on for Whistle, he eventually came to the realization that he would most likely never be with another woman again, so he focused on his homestead and his friendship with Johnny. The two got together at least once every couple of weeks to check up on each other. But as the years passed, the hike to Whistle's cabin got tougher on Johnny's legs. The visits got less frequent and Whistle was feeling more alone than ever.

CHAPTER
EIGHTY-FOUR
The Beginning of the End

Whistle was experiencing a pretty tough stretch of cabin fever one winter. With not much to do besides hunting, shoveling snow, and throwing wood on the fire, and no one to talk to, he could feel his mind starting to slip. He began hearing voices, seeing ghosts and losing touch with reality. He needed something to do to keep his mind sharp. It was then that he decided to write a book.

On a rare trip to Coldfoot, Whistle walked into the grocery store and along with his normal supplies, he picked up four thick notebooks, ten black BIC pens, and a pair of reading glasses. With his supplies collected, he made his way back to the cabin knowing that the cans of Spam, Dinty Moore Beef Stew, and coffee would most likely be enough to see him through the winter.

So Whistle Evel Fonzarelli Starr sat at his writing desk in front of the fireplace and began to write. A clear, glass oil lamp lit the page and his thoughts poured out endlessly and effortlessly.

The next year was spent writing, fishing, hunting, and gardening. The firewood was stacked tight and plentiful as was his freezer. His hygiene and health were starting to slip, however. Eventually, just the simple chore of bringing in firewood became difficult. Nevertheless, he continued writing and doing the best he could to maintain his homestead which his very survival depended on.

He bathed in the shallows twice a week and tried to maintain a routine. It wasn't easy as his appetite and weight both slowly diminished. He spent summers trying to stay cool by laying in the creek and sitting in the shade. His little window air conditioner stopped working years ago and he never bothered to replace it. He sure wished he had now.

The winters were even tougher as he spent the long nights curled up on his couch under mismatched quilts while trying to keep the fire stoked. His writing continued and his dreams became more and more vivid. All of which revolved around the people in his life that were no longer around, but meant everything to him.

All day, in between the chores that he could still manage to do, Whistle sat and wrote about his adventures, of which there were many. He grew more tired by the day and he spent more hours sleeping than anything else. Not out of laziness. Whistle was never what you would call lazy, he was just exhausted trying to survive in the wilderness alone, which some would say is a young man's game.

But survival was not a game, and neither was finishing what he started, at least to Whistle. He struggled to stay up and write even when his body and mind were begging him to pack it in for the night. His back hurt badly if he sat in his chair for too long, but he persisted and one day, finally finished his book. He placed the four notebooks neatly on his desk with his last pen set on top, never to be touched again.

Life continued on as Whistle's health continued to decline. He was down to one meal a day and his normal bodily functions were becoming more erratic and problematic. The fire was lit less often and the woodpile was perilously low. Sunrises and sunsets were missed as sleep continued to eat up most of his days and nights. Hunting was now out of the question as just preparing a meal and eating it were enough to thoroughly wipe him out. Depression set in as he cried himself to sleep every night on his dingy couch, deep in the wild of Coldfoot, Alaska.

Whistle knew that things were bleak and his time was growing shorter. He spent the next several days on the couch with no fire going, just waiting for an end to the suffering.

"Is this how it's supposed to end?" he asked himself on more than one occasion as he drifted off to sleep, wondering if it would be the last time.

CHAPTER
EIGHTY-FIVE
One Final Incredible Dream

Of course Whistle's final dream opened up with his favorite colors. The orange, black, and white of the monarch butterflies. This led to the most beautiful sunrise he had ever experienced. He sat on the very top of a mountain overlooking some unknown, beautiful land. He was completely content and detached from his body. No pain, no hunger, no thirst, no problems at all. Two hawks flew together in the distance. The sun continued to rise and light up the sky.

As he sat atop this mountain, he was detached from time and space. Almost out of nowhere, he heard a familiar voice from his early life, his stepfather, Jack.

"You have to skate harder into the corners and hit them hard." With that, he winked and vanished, being replaced by Whistle's mom, who kissed his cheek and told him she loved him. The warmth of the golden sun grew as his mom was replaced by a succession of childhood friends, teachers, and random strangers who were kind, again sequential to Whistle's life but existing outside time and space.

"I almost shot you in the face, but you turned out to be a good guy," said one Hellcat Wilson, laid back with his legs crossed, hands intertwined and a piece of straw sticking out between his teeth. He drifted away and there sat the one and only Shortstop Nipples, Indian style, like he used to in his little fort next to the Mass Pike.

"Heh, heh...Son, you've had quite a trip since I last saw you."

"Shortstop! I made it to the Santa Monica Pier just like you told me to!" Whistle said, thrilled beyond belief to see this old man again and break this great news to him.

"Yes you did, and thensome, by the looks of things," Shortstop replied, surveying the glorious valley.

"Where are we anyway?" Whistle asked, genuinely perplexed.

Shortstop just smiled as he faded away. Whistle called for him a few times, as he had more that he wanted to ask him. Just then, he felt a delicate set of hands gently rubbing his shoulders. He turned around to see Silvia Rose Delvecchio as the sun surrounded her like an aura of blinding light. Not a word was spoken, not a word needed to be said.

Silvia eventually morphed into Nurse Roxy, who morphed into Madison Cooke and eventually Cinnamon, almost as if they were all made of the same loving energy, sisters of the same aura.

As Whistle laid on the mountain top with Cinnamon, he felt a cowboy boot gently tap the top of his head.

"Get up, you lazy sumbitch, time to hit the road." Whistle would know that voice anywhere.

"Big Bear!" Whistle yelled as he turned to see the Great American Bear and his Ladybug standing there in all their splendid, star-spangled glory. They all hugged, sat down as Carla gleamed in the sun just down the mountainside. They laughed about the great times down on Bourbon Street, singing at the Cat's Meow and keeping Whistle out of trouble with armed bouncers.

They spent the rest of the afternoon laughing, crying, drinking whiskey from the bottle and talking about the old times. Whistle sat back and rested his eyes for a second and when he opened them again, Big Bear, Ladybug, and Cinnamon gone. He heard Carla fire up with a hiss and a rumble as he exclaimed, "Wait! I wanna go with you guys!"

"Soon enough, Tonto! Soon enough!" came Bear's voice over the loudspeaker mounted on the roof of the big rig as it rounded the mountainside and disappeared.

The roar of the eighteen-wheeler began to resemble the roar of the ocean as the unmistakable smell of salt air hit Whistle's nostrils, and seagulls began to traverse the sky. The valley below turned to the ocean in the blink of an eye as one seagull made a beeline for Whistle's face, forcing him to duck and cover his head.

"What the!?" Whistle said, shook up from his daze.

"Got something for you, landlubber," the seagull said as he dropped a Matchbox Corvette in his lap. Whistle recognized the voice immediately.

"Milo! What are you doing here?"

"Your buddy here forgot this on the beach one day a long time ago."

"What buddy?" Whistle asked.

"That buddy," Milo replied, motioning with his head to Whistle's side before flying away.

Whistle looked to his side to see little Billy Lee Carter, with his shovel, pail, lollipop, and Matchbox cars. "I've been looking for that one! Can I have it, please?"

"Uh...sure," Whistle said as he handed the car to the boy, already consumed with building a city in the sand with his shovel.

"Hey Billy, uh...where are we, exactly?"

"Do you have a Jaguar over there?" Billy asked, ignoring Whistle's question.

"Um...I don't think so," Whistle replied, as he looked around him in the sand and checked his pockets, reflexively. "No, I don't....Hey, where did you go?" he said as Billy vanished into thin air, giggling mischievously.

Familiar faces and sweet memories continued to propel this otherworldly dream as Whistle was visited by Denise, Digger Davis, and finally, good ol' Johnny Appleseed just as the sun began to set. He sat down, popped a bottle of bourbon, and asked, "Are you ready for your journey, old buddy?"

"Ready as I'm ever gonna be, Kemosabe," Whistle replied.

"You'll be alright, a heck of a lot better than you have been in a while, I promise you that."

They sat on the mountainside as the sun disappeared behind the mountain range on the opposite side of the valley below, now resembling the place where Whistle met Johnny on the hunt for that majestic caribou. They talked well into the night, pouring bourbon into thick, glass tumblers, which they knocked back in short order.

"Well partner, I'll see you on the other side," Johnny said as he hugged Whistle, vanishing in his arms. It was dark now and Whistle was alone and at peace. The stars were bright and dazzling as the Northern Lights shot across in every direction imaginable. Green, purple, reds, oranges and yellows were painted across the sky like a grand light show set to music too sweet for human ears to hear.

He sat hugging his knees, rocking to and fro, now feeling his human frailties creeping back into his consciousness. He could feel his body shutting down. His respiratory system and pulse slowed as he laid on his side, hugging himself tightly. He was about to leave this world with no one to see him off. He would be a lone wolf to the very end. He was about to stop breathing when he heard, "What are you doing, my sexy man?"

"Linda!" Whistle cried as he saw his beautiful bride appear just as she had on the day that he met her. Young, with beaming blue eyes and flowing red hair. Almost too beautiful to be real. Whistle grabbed her and held on as tight as his weak and sickly arms could manage. They hugged, kissed, made love, and talked over a bottle of red wine like they had so many times over the years. Whistle didn't want this moment to end, but he knew it would.

"Stay with me, Linda. Don't leave me," he cried.

"I have to, but I'll see you again. Love is forever," she whispered as she kissed him one last time and walked out the door. Whistle was too weak, even in his dream, to chase after her. Alone once again, he felt his muscles cramp from dehydration as he tried to find a comfortable position on the couch, waiting for his number to be called.

Everything happened at a steady even pace. The stars faded from the sky, leaving nothing but blackness as his breathing slowed and became shallow while his heart followed. He fell into one final, dreamless sleep and before the sun came up, Whistle Evel Fonzarelli Starr completed his earthly journey.

His body lay there on the couch for over three weeks before he was found by the Coldfoot Police doing a well-being check as he hadn't been seen in town for longer than usual. Whistle's body was removed and his cabin was aired out. Over the next few months, everything was removed and the cabin was eventually sold off. A young couple with two dogs moved in and did a thorough job bringing the property back up to par. That would have certainly made Whistle happy as he always took great pride in his homestead. He was gone, but his spirit would always be present in many places across this great country, but most of all here, in Coldfoot, Alaska, a place he could truly call home.

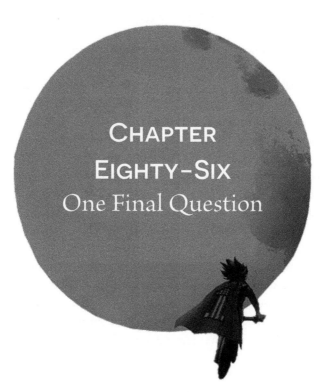

CHAPTER EIGHTY-SIX
One Final Question

A woman named Vicki Cressy bought all of Whistle's belongings for the cheap and stored it deep in the back of her antique store along Main Street. There they sat for years and years until Vicki got older and passed away. Her daughter ended up taking over the shop and took an interest in cleaning the place up. Her name was Crispen Cressy and she was vigilant. All the items were either given to Goodwill, thrown in the trash, or cleaned up and put out for sale.

Over ninety percent of Whistle's stuff got chucked, including one final can of Spam. A few items remained, including a clear glass oil lamp, a small, beat up pine desk, and an odd stack of four notebooks. The lamp went quick, but the desk and notebooks hung around for a few more years.

Eventually, a dealer walked in, on vacation from New York City. The desk caught his eye because of its simple, aged character. The wear and tear was unmistakable. He bought it for thirty-five dollars and had it shipped to his store back in the city. Six weeks later, a crate showed up at the store and for some reason, it intrigued him.

With a small hammer and crowbar, the crate was opened, spilling packing peanuts everywhere. He chuckled as he pulled the desk out because he loved it. In fact, he had already decided to keep it for himself. After that, he put the crate up by his front desk in his study. It was perfect for a side desk for paperwork and the odd bottle of scotch with a couple of glasses to celebrate a deal struck with a client.

Eventually, he upgraded his study with new furniture and decided to throw out the crate. He dragged the crate to the sidewalk and it fell over when he tried to place it next to his trash. About to walk back in, he noticed a notebook laying halfway out of the crate. Exploring, he pulled out three more notebooks and brought them back inside.

The man spent the next few weeks reading every word written in these pages. He devoured and loved it all, only wishing he could have met the man who wrote it all. Upon finishing, he decided to sell the notebooks to an old woman who ran a small publishing company by the name of Whistle Penn Publishing, located in West Virginia.

The dealer walked into Whistle Penn, located at the corner of a busy intersection in the center of a quaint little town full of antique shops, restaurants, coffee bars, and bookshops, with a beautiful view of a majestic river directly across the street. He sold the notebooks to the woman, made some small talk, browsed a bit, and left to go have dinner at one of the bistros along the water.

The old woman closed the shop and took the notebooks with her to the upstairs office to thumb through before going home. Almost immediately, certain things she read got her attention. She was instantly taken back to her hazy, not particularly proud days in northern New Hampshire many years ago. Painful days of addiction, abuse, and abandonment, running away from the only family she had with whatever that loser's name was.

Dropping her glasses on the maple desk and running her hands through her striking gray hair, she exhaled loudly. The tears began to flow silently down her still delicate face. It slowly dawned on her what she was reading and what a miracle it was that it found its way to her.

She spent the next several months immersing herself in the story, getting to know the man and what became of his life. Plenty of nights were spent burning the midnight oil, tending to every fine detail so his story could be told. These four notebooks that were part diary, part travelogue, part memoir, and all in all, one amazing journey, eventually became a novel that sold so well that it provided the old woman a level of wealth and security that she would have never thought to dream of. Inspired to see the world for herself, she spent the rest of her life traveling and writing with a grateful heart and free spirit.

So the final question is this: Is it possible that you yourself just read the actual book that was written by the absolutely astounding Whistle Evel Fonzarelli Starr?

About the Author

Photo by Ben Drumm.

Shane Joseph Hopkins is a twenty-three year veteran on the Newport, Rhode Island Fire Department. He has been an Emergency Medical Technician for the last twenty-eight years. Before that, Shane served his time in the military during "not so friendly times." After his tour of duty, he was honorably discharged from the United States Navy.

He now lives with his wife Lisa in their log cabin surrounded by plenty of woods and wildlife. They have two grown children, Kelcey Read, and Dryden Peter. They also enjoy five crazy grandkids, Catalina May, Dryden Shane, Nadia Read, Delilah Rayne, and last but not least, Mabel Lily.

This is Shane's first novel to be published, but definitely not his last....